THE
BLOOD
IS STILL

Also by Douglas Skelton

Thunder Bay

THE BLOOD IS STILL

A REBECCA CONNOLLY THRILLER

DOUGLAS SKELTON

ARCADE
CrimeWise

An Arcade CrimeWise Book

First North American Edition 2021

This is a work of fiction. Names, places, characters, and incidents are either the products of the author's imagination or are used fictitiously.

Arcade Publishing books may be purchased in bulk at special discounts for sales promotion, corporate gifts, fund-raising, or educational purposes. Special editions can also be created to specifications. For details, contact the Special Sales Department, Arcade Publishing, 307 West 36th Street, 11th Floor, New York, NY 10018 or arcade@skyhorsepublishing.com.

Arcade Publishing® and CrimeWise® are registered trademarks of Skyhorse Publishing, Inc.®, a Delaware corporation.

Visit our website at www.arcadepub.com.
Visit the author's website at douglasskelton.com.

10 9 8 7 6 5 4 3 2 1

Library of Congress Cataloging-in-Publication Data is available on file.
Library of Congress Control Number: 2020943451

Cover design by Erin Seaward-Hiatt
Cover art: © Dennis Barnes/Getty Images (Culloden Moor); © Miemo Penttinen/Getty Images (sky); © Nico_blue/Getty Images (blood)

ISBN: 978-1-951627-31-7
Ebook ISBN: 978-1-951627-62-1

Printed in the United States of America

'There are open wounds, shrunk sometimes to the size of a pin-prick but wounds still.'

—F. Scott Fitzgerald, *Tender Is the Night*

1

He lies on his back, arms outstretched, his legs apart, his eyes open, watching the soft snow float towards him. He knows he is dying but he can do nothing about it – not pinned down the way he is. There is no pain, merely a numbness that he knows is not wholly caused by the damp heather beneath him. It is as if he has been given a local anaesthetic that has desensitised his body but left his mind active. It creeps through him, stealing all feeling, all mobility, all life.

His blood, though, he can still feel. Or at least he thinks he senses it bubbling from the wound. If he could move his head, he might be able to look down and see it oozing freely around the cold steel, soaking through his clothes . . .

No, not his clothes, these are not his clothes.

. . . and seeping through to the earth below. This earth is no stranger to blood. It is steeped in it. It may have been spilled 275 years before but the blood remains, mixing with the roots of the heather, settling between the rocks and the pebbles and the grit to rest in the muck below; sinking, perhaps, to the very centre of the earth.

A faint mist drifts through the darkness but he does not feel its icy caress. He thinks he sees shapes in the swirl: nebulous, without form or flesh, but there all the same. Men, long dead, yet still tied to the blood-saturated ground they no longer feel beneath their feet. He senses them clustering around him like pallbearers, studying him, studying the clothes . . .

No, not his clothes.

They are at once so familiar and yet so very alien. On some level he understands their confusion, for he is dressed as they but he is not of them. His garb is of more recent manufacture, carefully contrived to look homespun. And yet, despite this, he knows these ethereal figures are ready to welcome him to whatever world of vapour and shadow they now call their own.

He hears – thinks he hears – sounds.

Muffled. Faint. Flat.

The clank of metal on metal. A stutter of gunfire.

Groans. Harsh cries of anger and agony. Screams as iron rips flesh.

Tears.

Men weeping as they die or as their brothers die. Highland voices keening as their comrades' lives slip into the dank air. Tough men, for whom life had been hard, now reduced to sobs over the futility of it all. He wants to weep with them and for them but he has no tears. He has no time. He has nothing.

He has not been a good man. He had not known it then – it had never occurred to him – but he knows it now, as he lies on the cold earth waiting for a death he can do nothing to prevent. He has accepted it and has made his peace. He might as well try to stop every snowflake from hitting the ground. But no, he has not been a good man. He has not been evil, though he has known evil men, but he has not lived his life well. He wonders if somehow he deserves this.

The numbness has stolen just about everything from him. The shapes tighten around him, waiting, for they also know his time of flesh and bone is nearing its end. He too must become a creature of mist and memory. They will help him, he knows that. They are strangers, separated by time and mortality, but they are brothers in death. The sounds of battle fade. He watches the snowflakes as they drift gracefully from the dark skies to settle on his upturned face, a slight breeze catching them and sending them into a soft spin – slow-motion ballerinas swirling to music no one can hear. Finally, inevitably, he lets the cold take him until he becomes one with it.

His blood is still.

2

As demonstrations went, it was unlikely to rival *les gilets jaunes*. In fact, there was only one hi-vis yellow jacket in view, perhaps worn by someone who had been watching CNN and been inspired by the Paris movement. Or perhaps it was merely a workie who had stopped by to find out what the fuss was all about.

The supporters bulged around the small woman as she stood beneath the sign that detailed parking restrictions outside the red-brick building. *Too many for a knot of people, not enough for a throng*, Rebecca Connolly thought. Some of them leaned on the half-dozen blue bollards that surrounded a 'no parking' area marked by yellow crosses on the tarmac. She saw a handful of hand-made signs – cardboard stapled or glued to sticks or broom handles, words scribbled in marker pen expressing their reason for gathering here on this nippy, dull March morning. There had been a light fall of snow overnight but it had not rested on the city streets. A few people stood on the opposite side of the narrow road, watching and listening, but they were merely passers-by, lingering to find out what was going on. Rebecca saw a man in the upper window of the guest house behind them, a saucer in one hand, cup to his lips, the events outside the council headquarters proving more interesting than *Homes Under the Hammer*.

Rebecca watched Mo Burke work the crowd and could not help but be impressed. In another life, another world, she could have been a politician, or at least a community leader. The people listening to her knew what she really was, but still they paid attention, they applauded, they nodded their heads in assent. Perhaps they did so only because they had been urged to come along by Mo and her sons, for when a Burke urges, it is best to fall in line. Perhaps it was merely because she was telling them what they wanted to hear, giving voice to their own thoughts, strengthening the words with a powerful delivery only partly aided by the microphone and megaphone. The thing was, she didn't really need it – her voice was strong enough to carry her words. She was not a large woman, but she had a presence. Star quality. If star quality was packaged in bleached blonde hair and a smoke-roughened Glasgow accent. Many years of living in the Highlands had done little to soften its edges.

Chaz Wymark was down at the front, grabbing shots of Mo as she spoke. She had given him a few suspicious looks; she did not generally welcome press interest, but she had opened this particular door, for some reason, and had to accept it. Rebecca had snatched some shots of the crowd with her phone for the *Chronicle*, her newspaper budget no longer stretching to the hire of freelance photographers such as Chaz. She was no snapper so they would have to take what they got, not that they cared much any more. But she did make sure Mo was in the frame.

Mo Burke, given name Maureen, sometimes known as Ma, was a drug dealer, if only by repute, for the truth was she had never seen the inside of a court room on charges relating to supply, at least not from the point of view of the dock. Rebecca had done her homework before heading out to cover the demo, so she knew the woman's husband, Tony, was a different matter. He was currently doing time for assault to severe injury after having a close encounter of the hurt kind with an Edinburgh-based thug called Sammy Lang, who was trying to horn in on the Inverness market. Sammy was known as the Slug because he left a trail as he walked. He also, Rebecca was told, had a liking for underage sex.

Given the Slug's sexual predilections, Rebecca wondered if it was a coincidence that Mo Burke had chosen to champion this particular cause. A rumour had gathered strength in the city's Inchferry area that the council planned to rehome a convicted sex offender there in a vacant flat. Predictably, officials refused to either confirm or deny the story and, just as predictably, that was instantly taken as confirmation. It was Mo Burke who had taken it upon herself to organise the demo outside the Highland Council's complex in Inverness's Glenurquhart Road. Rebecca saw Mo's two sons among the crowd that had rallied round her flag, which was actually a sign behind her that said 'WE ARE NOT A DUMPING GROUND'. That was a far more preferable war cry to the crude placard being held aloft that read 'NO PERVURTS HEAR'.

Some of the supporters had wandered away from the main body to linger on the vehicle entranceway, where they were advised to return to the pavement by one of the three police officers on duty. Rebecca was surprised there were so few, the Burke family reputation being what it was. She kept her distance on the opposite side of the entranceway, where she leaned on the sign embedded in the grass that carried the council logo and stated that this was the *Prìomh Oifis* – the headquarters. She wondered how many of those attending had the Gaelic, or cared that nearly every official sign was bilingual. Not many, she suspected.

'They think we are stupid.' Mo was talking into the microphone, her free hand jerking the hand-held loudspeaker in the general direction of the building. 'They think we don't know what they're up to. But we know. WE KNOW!'

This was met with more nodding heads and a few grumbled 'ayes' and 'naws' and a 'You're right, Mo.' She seemed satisfied with the response but she still hammered her point home.

'WE ARE NOT A DUMPING GROUND,' she shouted, the shriek of protest from the speaker forcing her to modulate her tone. 'We're here to let them know that we're not some sort of dustbin for all the perverts in the Highlands. We're no having it. We're no having them rehousing even *one* of them in our streets. Right?'

The supporters responded with 'No way', 'Bloody right', 'You tell 'em, Mo', along with an assortment of grunts and more nodding heads.

'We elect they folk in there, and not just to plunk their backsides behind a conference table and claim all kind of expenses. They're there to represent us, to do what *we* want. Right?'

More agreement from the crowd.

'And what do we want?'

'Perverts out!' someone shouted. Rebecca thought it was Nolan Burke, Mo's eldest son. She spotted him in the middle of the protesters, handsome in a 'Ben Affleck in his prime' way, his black hair perfectly groomed, his skin tanned, whether from a recent visit to sunnier shores or a sunbed she couldn't say. She had seen him before, although not face to face. He was a regular attendee at the sheriff court on what were generally minor charges – breaches, small acts of violence – although there were whispers he was capable of more serious offences. Appearances by both him and his younger brother Scott were numerous enough for one of her colleagues to resurrect and amend an old joke: *What do you call a Burke boy in a suit? The accused.*

Nolan wasn't wearing a suit today, though. He was encased in a heavy sheepskin flight jacket, which made her wonder where he'd parked his Sopwith Camel. He caught her staring at him and she looked away again sharply, searching for his brother's familiar head of blond hair. Scott would be around somewhere, she knew. He was a tall lad, though took after the mother in terms of colouring; Nolan was more like the father.

She spotted Scott wandering the fringes of the crowd, a strange little smile on his face, his hands thrust in the pockets of his lightweight camouflage jacket – what was it with the Burke brothers and their military clothing? The cold obviously did not trouble him. He was Scott Burke, after all, a tough guy. He was slightly slimmer than his older brother but there was muscle there. His features were weaker and not as attractive, while that smile twitching on his lips just came across as nasty.

7

Rebecca had the sensation of being watched and, despite her best efforts, flicked her gaze in Nolan's direction again. Yes, he was still looking at her, eyes narrowed slightly, as if trying to place her, even though he would have seen her in court. When he caught her look returning to him, he nodded and smiled. It wasn't a discomforting smile, not like his brother's, but he was still Nolan Burke.

She returned her attention to his mother just as Mo nodded in her son's general direction. 'Aye – that's right. Perverts out. Keep our streets safe. Keep our kids safe. No pervs in our scheme. Perverts out! Perverts out! PERVERTS OUT!'

The crowd's response was far from ecstatic. A few stalwarts picked up the chant and, like Mo, began to pump their fists in the air. Scott Burke gave one recalcitrant youth a nudge and a nod to urge him to join in. The young man did as he was told, it being less harmful to his health.

What chanting there was began to stutter and still as people turned to look at a tall man emerging from a taxi. His tanned face was younger than his thick white hair might suggest, and he was wearing a pinstripe blue suit, a blue shirt, with pale yellow tie and matching handkerchief carefully composed at his breast pocket. Another two men joined him on the street – large men, thick-set men, who bore the frozen-faced expressions of large, thick-set men who could do, would do and quite possibly had done damage to those who were less large and thick-set than they, and who had the temerity to approach and even molest their employer. They could not have been more obvious if they had worn T-shirts saying 'We're his bodyguards, so don't mess'. The crowd parted to allow the three men to pass among them. Rebecca didn't need to hear the whispers to know who the smartly dressed man was. She had seen him talk on TV, had even been present at a press conference held to announce his candidacy to stand as an MSP.

Finbar Dalgliesh. Well, well. He was the lawyer who had spearheaded Spioraid nan Gàidheal – Spirit of the Gael – or Spioraid for short, a new ultra-right-wing political movement that believed Scotland would be better on its own. Where it radically diverged from the mainstream nationalist cause was its message that Scotland would be even better with only white, home-grown Scots. No foreigners, no gays, even women were suspect. They were so far right they made Attila the Hun look like Mother Theresa. Finbar Dalgliesh affected a 'man of the people' persona – all pints and fags and jolly banter – but he was as oily as the sea around the *Exxon Valdez*. And if he was here, he smelled votes.

Mo had fallen silent, as had the crowd, and Rebecca saw her shoot a glance like a slap towards Scott. It was plain Dalgliesh's presence was a surprise to her, if not to her son, who shrugged. Whether he was denying any part in this or dismissing the rebuke, Rebecca couldn't tell.

Dalgliesh reached Mo's side and gave the crowd a wave before placing a hand lightly on her shoulder to turn her away in order to exchange a few hushed words. Rebecca was a good few yards away but Mo's rising anger was apparent as she listened. However, the woman nodded and stepped aside, her eyes finding Scott again and burning a promise in his direction. Chaz focused his lens on Dalgliesh as he stepped forward to face the crowd; he studiously ignored the camera, yet made sure it caught his good side. The two bruisers positioned themselves close enough to intervene should anyone prove too boisterous yet far enough away so as not to draw attention.

Dalgliesh stretched out his arms like he was appealing for a group hug. Some of the crowd seemed willing to share the love but others looked like they would rather cuddle a rabid grizzly.

'Friends,' he said, 'I'm Finbar Dalgliesh.'

Rebecca rolled her eyes. She'd seen him do this before. They knew who he was. He knew they knew who he was. This idea that he might be unknown to them, that he had to introduce himself, was a pose. If there was a media lens uncovered in Inverness, Finbar Dalgliesh would turn up eventually, flashing the best dental work money could buy and turning whatever issue was on offer to his advantage.

The 'Tan in the Suit' was his nickname among the press pack, which at once deplored and cultivated him. He was a walking story. Wherever he went, quotes and sound bites followed. And here he was, doing the Dalgliesh Hustle at Mo Burke's demo. Mo was clearly unhappy about the situation – she might be the rock on which he would perish.

Even so, Rebecca's pen was poised to take notes.

'I'd like to thank Mrs Burke for allowing me to say a few words.' His voice was strong and firm, sand-blasted by years of cigarettes and expensive whisky. Rebecca had to admit it was a good voice. Cultivated, yes, but still recognisably Scottish. 'I won't keep you long in the cold, I promise.'

There was a smattering of laughs and he smiled benevolently at his audience. Finbar was their pal. He was one of the lads. He smoked. He drank. He said what he thought. The fact that his suit probably cost more than many of them would earn in a month didn't seem to occur to anyone who supported him.

The smile died. It was as if someone had turned off the sun. 'I'm grateful for the opportunity to talk to you today about this very serious issue. When I was informed about the plan to rehouse a—' He paused to find the right word, the struggle plain on his face. It was another pose, of course. He knew exactly what he was going to say. If there was one thing Finbar Dalgliesh didn't struggle with, it was expressing himself. He gave out a theatrical sigh. 'Friends, let's be perfectly frank about this. Let's be honest about what we're dealing with here. We're talking about a deviant. A sexual predator. And there are people in there' – he turned in a graceful movement to point at the council building, like an actor on a stage, giving a performance – 'who want to place this evil individual in *your* midst. To make him *your* neighbour. To allow him free access to *your* children.'

There were murmurs from the crowd. Even those who didn't like the man agreed with him on this occasion.

'Now, let me tell you this, my friends. I don't live in Inchferry, it's true, but I know you all to be wonderful people. Kind, warm-hearted, loving. And it pains me to think that your community could become' – he indicated the banner behind Mo Burke – 'yes, a dumping ground for such monsters. They have a word for these people in prison. Beasts, they call them. And that's what they are. Beasts. Sick, depraved creatures who prey on the vulnerable and the defenceless, who slake their evil lusts on the young, the impressionable.'

He paused to let the drama sink in. He eyed the crowd, waiting for the right moment to speak again, gauging the temperature. In politics, like comedy, timing is everything and he knew it. And when he did speak again, after a few moments, it was to unleash the full stentorian force of that smoke-blackened voice.

'Well, I say NO!'

A cheer, then. Rebecca couldn't tell if it was started by Scott, but there was no doubt Finbar was winning them over. Yes, he was playing to their confirmation bias, he was telling them what they wanted to hear – and it was working.

'NO, I say,' he repeated. 'He's had a few years in prison, perhaps not many. I ask you, is that punishment?'

There were a few desultory negative responses. They weren't sufficiently enthusiastic for Finbar.

'I ask you again – is that punishment?'

The cries of 'NO' were louder this time. Behind Dalgliesh, even Mo nodded her assent. She might not have invited him, but he was underlining her point.

'No, it's not punishment,' said Finbar, happier now with the crowd. 'And yet this deviant can come out of prison and expect to be molly-coddled by the system. Is that right? Is that the way it should be?'

The outraged cries of 'NO' were stronger still. He had won them over.

'We must send them a message, right here, right now. We must tell the councillors and the officials and the social workers that we are not standing for this. If they feel this individual, this pederast . . .'

Oh, good word, Rebecca thought. It never hurts to remind the masses that you've read a book or two, while still retaining that common touch. This was Dalgliesh at his best.

'If they feel this pederast deserves a second chance, then why doesn't one of them take him in?'

More nods from the crowd, more murmured 'ayes' and 'rights'.

'Why don't they find him a place in *their* area, in *their* streets?'

He had them eating out of his hands now.

'But no, they won't do that, will they? They'll inflict this deviant on you. Just as they and their masters in Holyrood and Westminster inflict everything on you. They don't feel the pain you feel. They don't understand the pressures you experience every minute of every day of every week. They don't know what real life is like. None of them. They are locked in their own little bubble of self-interest. Of party and personal gain. Not public gain. They don't do anything that is solely for the good of the voters. Only what is good for themselves and their friends.'

He stopped to let this sink in. 'Well, friends. Let's send them that message. Let's make sure that *this time* they DO think of you! Lift your voices, make them loud and clear, and tell them. No perverts here! NO PERVERTS HERE!'

The chant was picked up, louder than when Mo had used the same words. More fists raised towards the grey skies like exclamation marks, while the makeshift signs were waved with considerably more vigour. Finbar Dalgliesh had done what he always did: attack the establishment and work the crowd into a frenzy. The police guard looked edgy.

Chaz Wymark limped towards her, his camera around his neck, his bag in one hand while in his other he gripped a smart-looking cane of dark polished wood. He really didn't need it to aid his movement – she'd seen him hobbling about without it often enough in order to snatch the best pictures. His partner Alan was fond of saying that he just liked to pose with it. 'It makes him feel like a boulevardier,' he said. 'He can pretend he's on the streets of Paris at the turn of the century. I'm thinking of getting him a top hat.'

Rebecca stared at Chaz, visualising him with a top hat instead of the black woollen cap he had pulled over his blond hair. She thought he'd suit one. But then Chaz was handsome enough to suit anything. Certainly the limp and the cane gave him an air of mystery.

'Suddenly got exciting, didn't it?' He jerked his head towards Mo and Finbar, who had turned to face the council building, both now leading the war chant. 'What do you think? Something going to happen?'

There was heat, certainly, most of it coming from Dalgliesh's mouth. It looked more likely they would start some kind of haka than anything more serious, though. Rebecca shook her head. 'No, I think it's all noise.'

Chaz studied the crowd, making his own assessment. 'I think you're right. Well, hope you are anyway. I'd hate to miss anything.'

'You've got to be somewhere?'

'Got a call from the office.' Chaz worked for a Glasgow-based news agency on a freelance basis. He didn't make a fortune – little in the modern media world paid well these days – but it helped keep him in walking sticks. He was also doing what he loved. 'When's your meeting?' he asked.

'Half-eleven,' she said, her heart sinking at the thought. Someone new was being sent by the accountants in London to ensure things ran smoothly on their empire's northern frontier. And by 'running smoothly' they usually meant 'see where costs could be cut'. A project manager, this person was called. The industry didn't seem to have editors or sub-editors any more. They had been replaced by project managers, line managers, content managers and team leaders. It was only a matter of time before reporters became content originators. Dear God, she thought, Lords Rothermere and Beaverbrook would be birling in their graves. To the right, of course.

The glint in Chaz's eye grew into a beaming smile and she knew he was going to try to lure her over to the dark side. 'Fancy a wee trip to Culloden?'

Chaz no longer liked to drive. Never at night. Or in the rain. His courage would not carry him that far. Since the accident on Stoirm he avoided

13

getting behind a wheel, though he could do it when he needed to. He simply made sure he didn't need to.

'The battlefield?' she asked. 'What is it, another demo about the housing development? A bit late, isn't it?'

Plans approved by the Highland Council and the Scottish government for housing to be built overlooking the historic site had excited a great deal of passion. Rebecca couldn't blame those who opposed it, for the whole idea did seem ill-advised.

'No, there's been a body found over there.'

Rebecca frowned. 'By body, you mean a new one? Not one from seventeen whenever it was . . .'

'Seventeen forty-six,' said Chaz. 'Jesus, I'm not even Scottish and I know more about your history than you do.'

'Ach, history is a thing of the past.' Rebecca grimaced. 'So this body – they think it's not a natural death?'

'Aye,' said Chaz, coarsening his accent, which despite his English birth was already pure Scots. 'There's been a *murrd-err.*'

Rebecca winced. 'Please don't do that again.'

'You got time to come with me? We should get there and back for your meeting. Has to be a line in it for you.'

Culloden was only about six miles away, off a B road to Nairn. They could get there very quickly at this time of the morning. She looked towards Mo and Dalgliesh and bit her bottom lip. She wanted to get a quote from one or both and should really hang around and get a face to face with the woman, and now something from Dalgliesh. And then there was her editor. She was still in trouble over her visit against his explicit instructions to the island of Stoirm the year before. Sure, it had generated a few stories – exclusives, too – but she would never be able to report on what had actually occurred. She had told Barry everything – well, nearly everything – but he still kept her pretty much on a tight rein.

Rebecca shot another look at Mo as she continued to harangue the unseen representatives of local government. She wasn't showing any signs of running out of steam and seemed to have come to terms with the Spioraid leader's involvement. It would be some time before Rebecca could pin her down, if she'd even speak to the press.

Rebecca sighed, her breath misting up the air between them. 'Shit, you know I can't say no.'

He smiled again. 'That's what it says on the toilet walls . . .'

She gave him a mock glower. 'Yeah, right beside your name.'

As they moved away from the demonstration, she risked another glance at Nolan Burke, but his gaze was fixed once again on his mother.

3

Rebecca thought Culloden Moor a bleak place when the sun was shining, but on a cold Monday morning with sleet pockmarking the grey sky and the air a chilly wet kiss, it was even less hospitable.

The battlefield itself was visually unremarkable, little more than a field of rutted heather sliced by pathways to allow tourists to wander over ground that looked as if it was still stained by the blood spilled almost three centuries before. What always amazed Rebecca was the silence; she could feel it that day, even with the activity that surrounded the murder investigation. She had been a child when she visited the battlefield for the first time. That was on a bright summer day and the site had been dotted with visitors staring at the memorials on the Avenue of the Clans and wandering among the blue or red flags fluttering against a cobalt sky. Her father had told her the history of the site, but she didn't take much in. She was eight and stories of rebellion and royal succession carried little interest. Then he told her to stand still and listen and she did as she was told. She heard birds singing, somewhere far off, and the soft breeze moaning in the long grass and heather as if yearning for a long-dead lover. But there was nothing else. The tourists' voices were muted. Even the cries of two younger children chasing each other along the pathways were strangely stifled. A car sliding past on the roadway made barely a ripple in the atmosphere.

It always gets me, said her father, *that silence.*

She recalled him standing beside her, his eyes narrowed as he looked around, as if he could see the aftermath of the battle: the men, dead and dying, the victors moving among them and finishing them off. And the blood, always the blood.

Maybe I imagine it, he said, a laugh forcing itself into his throat. *Maybe my Celtic upbringing makes me fanciful. But this place always gets to me. That silence. Here and Glencoe, both the same. The quiet places. Do you feel it, Becks?*

She had nodded and that seemed to please him. She always wanted to please John Connolly, at least at that age. Of course, when she hit her teenage years and the hormones kicked in it was a different matter. She hadn't exactly been wild but she had been awkward and had given both him and her mother more trouble than she should have. But they came through it, as families do more often than not.

But then he had died. Too young. Too soon. Cancer, the disease that is spoken of in whispers, as if the very mention of it will bring the utterer its unwanted attention. It would feel at home here, in this place of death, where voices are hushed and the sounds of nature muffled.

The quiet places, her father had called them, but Rebecca had heard them described another way by a crime writer she'd interviewed when he was in Inverness to promote his new book.

Thin places.

Sites where the veil between this world and the next is fragile, almost sheer, where the past lives on beside the present. Thin places, where some of us can sense more than what can be seen, touched or tasted. On Stoirm, these people were called the *fey*. Rebecca wasn't sure if she believed in it, but she did feel something otherwordly whenever she visited Culloden and Glencoe, just as her father had. Or perhaps, as he had said himself, she was merely imagining it. Perhaps, because of the bloody history and stark tragedy, she wanted these sites to feel different.

The police had cordoned off the entrance to the battleground and half of the narrow road, where a uniformed constable directed traffic in a contraflow system. Rebecca had brought her car to a halt as close as she could to allow them to walk along the verge to where two officers were holding back a small band of onlookers, most of whom had their phones up and were snapping away. Cars drifted by slowly, some of the occupants turning their faces towards the moorland, where a tent had been erected beyond a cluster of gorse bushes already flowering yellow. A bright light beamed through the fabric and dark shapes moved back and forth. Forensic specialists and police officers entered and exited, their bodies clad in disposable overalls, their heads, feet and hands encased in protective gear, designed not to keep the weather out but any contaminant in. The moorland inclined slightly up and away from them, but she could just about make out the very top of the visitors' centre. On the verge, she spotted one or two professional photographers and a BBC TV crew, the pretty, dark-haired but diminutive reporter doing a piece to camera with the tent, glimpsed through a gap in the gorse cover, behind her. The cameraman, a balding veteran with a long white beard, was telling her to move slightly to her right so he could get more of the police activity in shot. She did as she was told. The visual was as important as the aural on the screen.

Chaz had selected a long lens and was snapping away at a line of officers in waterproof gear stretched out across the moor, searching the heather for any evidence. They moved slowly, etched against the dull skyline, the ground between them a patchwork of white and brown thanks to a fall of snow in the night. Their eyes cast downwards, long sticks in hand, they sought to probe and clear the undergrowth. Rebecca knew instantly that would be the image on many front pages in the morning.

'That's whatshername, from the Beeb,' Chaz said as he fingered the shutter.

'Lola McLeod,' replied Rebecca.

'Lola? Think that's made up?'

Rebecca had no idea. 'She used to be a showgirl at the Copacabana.' She waited for him to laugh but he merely gave her a puzzled look. 'Don't tell me you don't know the Barry Manilow song.'

'What, you think cos I'm gay I know Barry Manilow songs?'

'No.'

'Should I know showtunes off by heart, that what you're saying?'

'No, I—'

'And I should idolise Judy Garland, right?'

She realised then he was winding her up. 'Bastard,' she said, and he laughed.

She recognised one of the officers on duty, a young cop she had seen at court and at other incidents, and knew him to be reasonably approachable. He was watching the news crew with some interest, seemingly entranced by the magic of TV. The reporter had fluffed a line and was laughing at her own mistake. Rebecca heard her apologise, but the cameraman nodded and said he was still rolling, so she suddenly became serious, as if a switch had been thrown.

'Cold work, this,' Rebecca said, letting her gaze follow his.

'Aye,' said the officer.

She kept one ear open for what the BBC reporter was saying. No details yet forthcoming. Police tight-lipped. Body found just before nine that morning, when mist lifted.

Rebecca said, 'Don't suppose you're going to tell me anything about this?'

His eyes moved away from Lola and her Mediterranean looks. Rebecca saw recognition in his eyes as he looked at her. 'You suppose right.'

She nodded. She hadn't expected anything less, but God loves a trier, as they say. 'Do you know if there's a press conference organised?'

'Not a clue. You'd need to ask the media people. Or the boss.'

'Who's the SIO?'

SIO. She felt like she was in *Line of Duty* when she used abbreviations, but 'senior investigating officer' was such a mouthful.

'DCI Valerie Roach,' said the officer.

The name meant nothing to Rebecca. 'She new?'

His head inclined slightly. 'Up from Perth. Knows her stuff, they say, but not met her myself.'

Rebecca took a long look at the scene on the moor. She wouldn't get anywhere near it today and she wouldn't want to. Her father had investigated enough murders in his day and had told her that the press can be both a help and hindrance. He'd once personally arrested a young reporter who thought he was Woodward and Bernstein all rolled into one and had managed to sneak onto a locus without anyone noticing.

Don't ever be like that, he'd told her. *Get to the truth, if you can, but don't get in the way.*

Get to the truth – *if you can*. She had learned how difficult that was. The truth can be a slippery creature with many faces. For a lawyer, the truth is what they can prove in court. For a police officer, it is whatever brings a conviction. For the journalist, it is whatever sells the story. And back-up, if need be. For politicians it is something to be avoided at all costs. She thought back to Finbar Dalgliesh addressing the crowd.

She glanced at her watch and realised time was running out if she was to make her meeting back in Inverness. Although she'd gathered some colour – the tent, the activity, the line of searchers – it was clear she wouldn't glean much more, so she stepped away from the officer, glanced at Chaz as he crossed the road to find another angle and pulled out her mobile. She thumbed through the news feeds, looking for any mention of a body found on Culloden. The main headlines were about New Dawn, a group so shadowy they made MI5 look like gossips, sending suspicious packages to political leaders in Holyrood and Westminster. At this stage no one knew if they contained bombs or dangerous substances. That made her think about Dalgliesh again, for the rumour was that New Dawn were effectively the paramilitary arm of Spioraid, rumours which he managed to deny without actually condemning their actions.

So far only the BBC had anything on the murder, which came as no surprise. But the rest wouldn't be far behind, New Dawn or no New Dawn.

If she wanted to stay ahead of this story in some way, she'd need a line that was hers and hers alone. She scrolled through her contacts, found the number. It was answered on the third ring.

'Bill, need a favour,' she said.

There was a grunt on the other end. 'No surprise there. But not even a hello or how are you? I thought *I* was supposed to be the gruff bastard.'

She smiled. She hadn't liked former Detective Sergeant Bill Sawyer much when she'd first met him. She'd thought him not just a misogynist but also corrupt. He did have an attitude towards women, but he also had one towards men, which made him an equal opportunities offender. She had grown used to his chauvinistic tendencies, even come to accept to them. After all, it takes all sorts. They had been on opposite sides on Stoirm, but since then had come to like each other. It's amazing how both of them being viewed with some suspicion by some very unpleasant people had acted as a bonding agent.

'Hello, how are you?' she said, with a smile to herself.

'Leg hurts, thanks for asking. This bloody weather doesn't agree with it.'

Bill Sawyer had broken his leg after being thrown from a speeding vehicle, and it had curtailed his hillwalking considerably. It had happened the same day as Chaz had had his accident. The island's little hospital had been very busy for a short time.

'You do know a lot of it's in your mind, don't you?'

'No – I know that a lot of it's in my leg, smart arse,' he said. 'And that's no way to butter me up for a favour, by the way.'

'Ach, Bill, I thought we were past the buttering-up stage, you and me.'

She heard him give a short laugh. 'I don't think we ever reached the buttering-up stage, darling. What's on your mind?'

'There's been a body found up on Culloden.'

'The battlefield?'

'No, the children's soft play area. Of course it's the battlefield.'

'Well, there's a village too. And a luxury hotel. Not to mention the moor itself. I just needed you to be specific, that's all. I thought it was a reporter's job to be accurate . . .'

'Yeah, yeah. I need a line on it.'

'So, what do you want me to do?'

They had danced this particular jig before. She needed his help and he played hard to get. She kept her voice steady but her teeth had gritted. He could be so bloody annoying.

'See if any of your old pals can feed you something, anything that the big boys don't have.'

She wanted to have something that was exclusive to her – just a detail – that she could drop online right away and hopefully draw people to buy the paper at the end of the week. The TV, radio and dailies used to have the advantage over the local weeklies in that they were more immediate, but the internet was a great leveller. Now she could break a story before or at the same time as them. She just needed something unique.

'Is it a murder, Becca?' he asked.

'That's what I want to know. They've said nothing so far, but there's a lot of activity. The SIO is a DCI Roach. She's new to Inverness.'

Sawyer fell silent, trying to place the name. 'Val Roach? A DCI, out of Perth? Tall and slim, with short, dark hair?'

Rebecca couldn't confirm her build or hairstyle, but other details matched up. 'You know her?'

'Never heard of her,' he said, and laughed.

Everyone's a comedian, she thought. 'So you think you can get me a line?'

'Aye, but the question is, why should I?'

This was part of the dance. 'Old times' sake?'

'Our "old times" only go back to last autumn, darling. Hardly makes us BFFs.'

'Bill, you know you're going to do it.'

'I do, do I? And what makes you so sure?'

22

'Because you like me. Because the stories I did about the Stoirm business helped your reputation . . .'

As a cop, years before, Sawyer had been suspected of falsifying a confession and the doubt the defence cast over it had helped a man get off a murder charge on a Not Proven, the 'Bastard Verdict' they called it, occupying a shadowy middle ground between guilty and not guilty. Some said that it was a jury's way of telling the accused that they thought he did the crime but the evidence just wasn't there. Others point out that it was a hold over from the old system of justice in Scotland, when a charge was found either proven or not proven, for guilt or innocence didn't enter into it back then. Rebecca's story about what happened on Stoirm suggested that the man had been responsible after all. However, she hadn't been able to print the whole truth behind the events the previous autumn; she and Bill Sawyer both knew that. Guilty men certainly walked free. Some of the island's secrets had to remain closed.

'I don't give a toss about my reputation and you know it. I've got my pension and a wee bit of work on the side, so the Job can stuff themselves.'

She knew this was bluster. The bit of work on the side was often investigative – he picked up a few quid from Elspeth on occasion – and Rebecca knew the stories had helped him. 'But you'll still get me something, right?'

He sighed. 'I'll ask a couple of questions, best I can do. But you don't get anything that could impede the investigation, right?'

'Right. Absolutely.'

'And you don't get anything that could only have come from one source. I've only got a few pals left in the Job and I don't want them put in any compromising positions. Clear?'

'Of course.'

There was a pause as he considered his own conditions. 'Okay, fine. Leave it with me. But you owe me a drink. A big one. Maybe even a meal.'

'Without a doubt. One slurpy and a Happy Meal coming up,' she said and heard him grunt. 'What do you think I am? *The Sun*?'

4

Chaz pinged his shots from his laptop to the Agency in Glasgow as they headed back to Inverness, technology being a wonderful thing. She was aware of his regular looks in the passenger side mirror, even if they were fleeting, but didn't pass comment. He didn't know he was doing it but she knew some part of him was looking for a vehicle he would never see again. She dropped him off at the flat he and Alan rented near her own, then drove to the *Chronicle* office as quickly as speed limits and traffic allowed. For decades the paper had operated out of a two-storey brown sandstone building overlooking the River Ness. However, with the closure of the onsite press in favour of outsourcing the printing – and the company printers going the way of the typesetter and the compositor and the dodo – those premises were deemed to be financially unsustainable, so they had moved the reporters and office staff to a business and retail park. A rival title also had offices nearby, but that really did not matter these days, as not many readers – or 'end users', as one visiting expert had called them – visited the office. Rebecca had never worked in the old premises, so she didn't know how busy it might have been back then, had never known the excitement created when the presses were rolling or the thrill of holding that first printed copy. Elspeth had once told her there used to be a steady stream of people through the door to talk about stories or to book small ads, however the number-crunchers down south had decreed that the footfall wasn't high enough to merit the overheads of the by-then virtually deserted town-centre premises. Elspeth said she'd fought the move but she'd always known she was on a loser. At least the *Chronicle* was still in Inverness – the same move had seen their sister papers in Elgin and Grantown uprooted from their communities to share the new space.

She climbed the stairs to the large open-plan office. She was relieved the meeting had not already begun, so there would be no wrist-slapping from Barry in her immediate future. The reporting teams and the two 'content managers', as sub editors were now known, were already clustered at the far end of the room, where she could see a large flat-screen TV had been positioned. The door to Barry's office was closed, so she assumed he was in there with the new miracle maker. Behind her she could hear the advertising staff beginning to follow her up the stairs. She took off her coat, hung it on the rack behind the door and joined the other staff members.

'What's the story so far?' she asked Hugh Jamieson, the oldest reporter on the team. He was tall and cadaverous and had been with the Grantown paper since the 1980s.

'Barry has been ensconced in his office with the bloke for half an hour,' he said. 'There's no blood trickling under the door, so we're taking that as a good sign.'

'We're getting a project manager. That's never a good sign.'

'True dat,' said Hugh.

Rebecca stared at the blank TV screen facing them. 'We going to watch a movie?'

Hugh's lips thinned into a grim smile. 'I suspect a message from Big Brother. And I don't mean the one with Davina McCall.'

'So what's he like, this new guy?'

Hugh shrugged. 'Didn't see him. I was out the back having a fag when he arrived.' The no smoking rules meant that any staff addicted to the weed had to go outside. 'I came back to see this telly in place and the office door closed.'

The office door opened and Barry appeared, clad in his customary denim shirt and trousers, ahead of a fresh-faced young man in a smart suit carrying a laptop. His skin was delicately tanned, but it failed to hide the ghost of teenage acne. His hair was expertly cut and if Rebecca had been able to look closely enough she was certain his fingernails would have been just as expertly manicured. It all made him appear very business-like, but he still looked about fifteen years of age.

'Jesus,' Hugh whispered. 'Has he got a note from his mammy to let him out of school?'

Barry gave them all a glance, nodded at Rebecca to show he was gratified to see her there, then took a seat on the edge of the desk furthest away from them all. So the new guy was going to lead the meeting. Something told her that Barry – the editor of all the titles in the north of Scotland – being side-lined was not a good sign.

The young man attached a cable running from the rear of the TV to his laptop and placed it on the nearest desktop, the screen facing him.

He's got a PowerPoint presentation, Rebecca realised. *God help us.*

He looked around at them for a brief moment, then spoke. His accent was from London, with just enough of a hint of *EastEnders* to show he was one of the boys. 'Hello, and thank you all for coming along today.'

Not that we had a choice, Rebecca thought.

'My name is Les Morgan and I have been sent by head office in London to give you all a helping hand. You might not think you need it, but circulation, as you well know, is struggling. The newspaper industry is facing its most challenging period ever. In fact, I've never seen a time like this in all my years in the press.'

Rebecca heard Hugh snort softly.

'Sales are down, revenues are down, and we need to find a way to at least bolster them, if not ensure they rally. Your jobs, all our jobs, depend on it. We have to work together to make sure that these grand old titles continue to bring the news to the people of the north of Scotland and the Highlands, both in print and online, for many years to come.'

He paused – his speech was beginning to sound like a press release – and glanced at Barry. The editor's face was impassive but he ran his fingers through his hair, which was his tell that he was on shaky ground. That was also not a good sign. Rebecca noted for the first time that Barry had visited the barber. The day before he'd been sporting his customary mullet, but now it was somewhat shorter, if still not fashionable. He had made an effort to smarten himself up. Something was most definitely in the wind.

'Here it comes,' Hugh whispered, as Les Morgan took a deep breath.

5

DCI Valerie Roach stared down at the body on the heather and wished she had a coffee in her hand. It was her habit to brew up the good stuff before she left home every morning and carry it with her in a thermos to consume at work, it being her experience that the muck they served in police stations was not something she wanted polluting her system, thank you very much. She was gasping for a hit, but there was no way she would bring the thermos onto a crime scene. She recalled as a child watching Columbo wander round a locus smoking his cigar and dropping ash everywhere. Or egg shells, if it was an early morning call-out. But that was fiction, this was reality. Science had taken over murder investigations. She'd been told by one retired CID officer that at one notorious murder in the sixties they'd brought recruits in to show them the body *in situ*, everyone – detectives, uniforms, even police cadets – traipsing across the crime scene in their size tens, contaminating evidence and leaving bootprints and who knew what else. DNA changed it all, she knew. Contact traces – the idea that everyone either left something of themselves at, or took something away from, a scene – had been around for decades, but once people realised that genetics left their fingerprints everywhere, the boffins really took over. DNA can fly from a person to a radius of five metres, apparently, hence the need for the full-body suits, lest a random follicle or skin cell drift from the investigators and screw everything up.

She *really* needed a caffeine fix.

She wondered if she had a problem. Did she have a caffeine monkey on her back? Should she consider kicking it cold turkey? Or – worse – drinking something green that tasted like the water brussel sprouts are boiled in?

She thrust the thoughts from her mind. She knew what her subconscious was doing: it was compensating for where she was and what she was looking at. She had been a cop for twenty years and she had seen death in many forms: peaceful, violent, young, old, premature, overdue. She'd seen blood and brains and bodily fluids and faecal matter smeared, spattered and spurted. As a uniform she'd found the body of a drug addict in a public toilet cubicle, dead from an overdose as she defecated, the syringe still jammed into her arm. She had once retrieved a head from a drainage ditch after a motorcyclist had skidded into a lorry. She had prised an infant boy from the arms of a woman who was still talking to him, still rocking him, even though the child had been dead for over a week.

Those incidents were sad. They were horrific.

But this?

This was both but it was also downright weird.

The flap to the protective tent was unzipped and DS Paul Bremner ducked inside. He was similarly dressed to her in disposable overalls, his mouth masked and his head encased in the elasticated cap, even though he was unlikely to cast any hair because he was as bald as a coot, earning him the nickname 'Yul' Bremner from officers old or savvy enough to have seen *The Magnificent Seven*. She thought about that film now. It was one of her husband's favourites. Or rather, had been. She felt the familiar stab in her chest as she thought of Joe, but she forced it away. *Concentrate on the job in hand, Roach.*

'Anything new?' Bremner asked, his eyes on the body. He had left her forty-five minutes earlier to help co-ordinate the search teams combing the heather.

'Confirmation just in,' said Roach, hoping he didn't hear the catch in her voice. *Damn it, Joe has been gone a year now.* 'Just as we thought – guy's dead.'

Bremner nodded. 'Aye, well. I'm not surprised.'

They remained silent for a moment as they each studied the body for perhaps the dozenth time since they'd arrived two hours before.

Roach stared at the weapon and asked, 'You've never seen anything like this before, I suppose?'

'Hell, no. You?'

She shook her head. Yup, this was just plain weird.

'You think it's real?' Bremner wondered.

'Real enough, I'd say.'

'No, I mean, you think it's an antique or a replica?'

Roach leaned closer. 'Looks old, but what the hell do I know? I'm not on the *Antiques Roadshow*. Forensics will probably have a metallurgist give it a look-see.'

'A metallurgist?'

'Yes, an expert in metals and their alloys.'

'I know what a metallurgist is, boss. I just didn't think there'd be one on call.'

'You can find an expert on anything these days. The internet is a wonderful thing.'

Knives, guns, hammers, baseball bats, cricket bats, car jacks, even a golf club once – a nine iron, if memory served. She'd seen them all used to take a life. But this? This was unique in her experience. Not many killers carried a full-sized claymore around with them.

But the weapon wasn't the only thing that was weird about this case.

Bremner knelt beside the body, still careful not to touch anything until the scientific carrion had picked it clean. 'What about the togs? You think they're period?'

'No idea. That's something else for the experts to tell us.'

The man was wearing a traditional belted plaid, its colours muted and soft. Underneath was a rough shirt. And on his head was a cap with a sprig of holly pinned to the peak. It looked to Roach as if the corpse had been transported forward in time from the battle in 1746.

Bremner straightened. 'It's the anniversary in a couple of weeks. The battle.' After a pause he added, just in case she didn't know what he was talking about, 'Culloden.'

'Significant, you think?'

He made a plosive sound with his cheek. 'Beats the hell out of me. I mean, all this is a new one on me. Jesus. It's just so bloody . . .'

'Weird?' she offered.

'And then some.' He fell silent again, his teeth working at his lip. 'You know they're making a movie about the battle, don't you? Filming up at Glen Nevis.'

She had already thought of that. There hadn't been so much excitement about a Hollywood roadshow since Mel Gibson had clipped on his hair extensions for *Braveheart*. The production company had been shooting *Conquering Hero* all over Scotland, for interiors utilising the studios near Cumbernauld normally reserved for the *Outlander* TV show. The film wasn't so much about the battle as Bonnie Prince Charlie and his opposite number, the Duke of Cumberland. The news had reported that the whole thing had proved controversial because the script was less than flattering to the Highlanders, or at least that's what was being claimed by Spioraid nan Gàidheal.

'You think maybe all this' – Bremner waved a hand over the body like a magician's assistant at the big reveal – 'came from there?'

'At this stage I don't know what to think. But a chat with the film people is definitely on the cards.'

Bremner nodded and they watched the technicians snapping, snipping, dusting and probing. One eased the man's hands into plastic so that any residue under the fingernails or on the skin was protected. Another unrolled a larger section of plastic sheeting to wrap around the weapon as it was carefully removed.

31

Roach stared at the dead man's face, the skin pallid, the eyes open as if staring at the tent covering him. He needed a shave, she realised. His hair, what she could see under the bonnet, was long and lank. She tried to guess his age. Late thirties, maybe? Early forties? Death had smoothed his features and the lack of colouring didn't help. The dead don't boogie, she was once told. They also don't age.

Her mind asked him questions.

Who are you?

What was your life like?

Were you married? In love? Do you have kids? Is there someone waiting at home, wondering where you are, even now frantically dialling everyone she or he knows, looking for you?

How did you get here?

What the hell happened?

Naturally, she didn't hear any replies. The dead don't talk much either.

She sighed. 'I hate a mystery.'

6

The child still lives within. The years pass, geography changes, yet the child lives and breathes. And remembers.

The memories are living, breathing things too. They have a will of their own. They can be forced down, they can be locked away, but they always find a way to resurface and to break out. It can be the tiniest inducement that awakens them. A smell. The way light strikes water. A form of speech. A musical phrase.

Something, anything, from a past that is best forgotten. That is best dismissed as having never actually happened. That it was someone else's memory, someone's else's history, someone else's pain.

But then comes that nanosecond of stimuli, that's all it takes, and it comes flooding back.

For the past is present, the present is past.

The house.

The stairway.

The sounds from below.

The room.

Always that room. And the child is back there.

That tiny, square room with the white walls and the worn carpet and the single bed and the wooden dresser and the window that lets in light but little of the outside world. The glass is artificially frosted, sticky plastic sheeting clinging to the surface to prevent glimpses of the world beyond or, more importantly, the hell within. A corner of the plastic has come loose and the child is able to *pick at it and peer out, but the view is limited: the corner of a roof, the branches of a tree, a patch of sky. To pull the cover back further would result in punishment and the child is punished enough. All that can be seen through the opaque glass are smudges and the suggestion of movement in the street below, people and dogs and cars, of lives being lived. That is the world beyond that room and that staircase and that house. An ill-defined world of shadows, vague silhouettes oblivious to what is happening just a few feet away from them and of the child who yearns to be free.*

That's all it takes. Just a second. The merest glimpse of a face among many. Older certainly, yet still the same. A sentence overheard and a voice still recognisable. And once seen and heard, everything collapses into rubble. A life carefully constructed, a fiction society has assisted in maintaining, cracks and splinters. And is revealed.

It cannot happen. The child cannot allow it to happen.

7

Elspeth McTaggart was squat. There was really no other way to describe her. Rebecca had seen photographs of her old boss in younger days – she might have been called dainty back then. But her enjoyment of life had left her torso larger while her stature remained diminutive. Her face was lined and leathery, her hair, dyed a curious shade of red unknown in the natural world, always cut short and tight to her skull. Her eyes were forever lively, bright, ready to signal a sharp question or a cutting remark. She sat behind the desk in her small first-floor office above a coffee house on Union Street. They called the patchwork of streets and lanes where Elspeth had her base the Old Town and it was a part of Inverness Rebecca enjoyed being in. She had snagged a parking space in the square outside the railway station and walked towards the news agency Elspeth owned and ran as a one-woman concern. It was early in the year but the tourists were already in evidence, walking the narrow streets and alleyways and peering into the shopfronts amidst a babble of languages and the clicking of shutters. Inverness was an all-year tourist city and although not as sprawling as Glasgow or Edinburgh it was still cosmopolitan. And it was growing fast.

Elspeth was hunched behind her desk like Yoda, if you could imagine Yoda smoking three packs of cigarettes a day and drinking tea like it was the elixir of life. The year before she had taken a tumble and damaged her hip, so she now used a cane to help her get around. *You and Chaz should form a club*, Rebecca thought, seeing it propped up against the desk to Elspeth's right-hand side. Luckily her vast network of contacts meant she could sit in the office much of the time and still keep her finger on various pulses around the Highlands.

'So, they're still trying to reinvent the wheel, eh?' Elspeth's voice was like packed earth during a long, dry spell – hard, cracked, unyielding. In her journalistic career she had taken on local councillors and MPs, high-ranking police officers and low-life crooks. She had shown no fear or favour to any political party or special interest group. She'd stood up to her own management while other editors had held their acquiescence before them like a shield.

Her nickname during her latter years editing the *Chronicle* had been satnav because she would happily tell anyone where to go.

Rebecca had taken a very rare lunchbreak to visit Elspeth to tell her about Les Morgan and what he had said in the staff meeting, then later in Barry's office with the door closed. It had all been very brief, to the point. The industry was in crisis. Drastic measures were needed. Changes had to be made. More emphasis on digital content. Post stories there first.

'Yeah, yeah, yeah,' said Elspeth, firing up another cigarette with a gold lighter given to her by her ex-husband, a man who owned five hotels across the Highlands. They had divorced after ten years of marriage because they had different needs. As Elspeth put it, he needed a wife who would stay at home, cook his dinner and clean his boxers. She, however, needed her career and a succession of one-night stands with younger women. She had come to terms with what she had suspected about her sexuality, on some level at least, only after she had married. It had come as something of a surprise to her husband, though. Despite that, twenty years after the divorce, they remained on friendly, if not intimate, terms. Elspeth had played the field for a few years but had recently settled down into what she called a close approximation of wedded bliss with a woman called Julie, ten years her junior, who owned a small café-cum-bookstore in Drumnadrochit on the shores of Loch Ness. In the eighteen months that Rebecca had worked for Elspeth at the *Chronicle*, she had never once made a pass at her. She didn't know whether to be relieved or insulted.

Elspeth blew a long line of smoke into the air. This was a place of work but, as she was the only one who worked here, the law against workplace smoking could go take a flying jump to itself. Satnav had spoken.

'They never bloody learn, do they?'

Rebecca shook her head. 'They're amalgamating all the editorial staff so we'll all work on whatever title needs it. A moratorium on new hires.'

'Did he use that word? Moratorium?'

'Yes.'

Elspeth snorted. 'Get it up the pretentious wee sod.'

Rebecca couldn't help but smile. 'There will be no more freelance help, so no holiday cover; the extra work will be shouldered by the remaining staff. Each reporter should be able to create at least fifty stories a week, he says.'

'Christ, it's a production line,' said Elspeth.

'He wants more comment in the paper and online to help engagements.'

'Click-bait. The danger with that is they ignore serious stories in order to draw traffic.'

'Sport is being cut, he doesn't think it sells papers now.'

A ball of smoke erupted from Elspeth's mouth as she considered this and shrugged. 'Maybe he's right. Time was, it did, but the junior football clubs all have their own websites now. Fans can go there and read a report, see videos. And Inverness Cally has heard the siren sound of the nationals and telly.'

'We're losing one content manager,' Rebecca said, and Elspeth wrinkled her nose at the term. She still called them subs, but the industry liked to change job designations. It helped when paying people off. Make a sub redundant, create the post of content manager. Same job, different title, less money.

'And what's Barry saying about all this?' Elspeth asked.

'Nothing much he can say,' said Rebecca. 'He's out, too.'

He had dropped that bombshell in the stairwell after she'd met with Les Morgan. Rebecca had asked him if he was going to fight what was going on and he'd only shaken his head. She had told him that he couldn't let this happen. He was the editor: he had to stand up for the titles, he had to stand up for the staff. He had to fight. He'd said there was nothing he could do.

'I'm out too, Becks,' he said, the words so heavy that he'd had to force them into the world.

She had stared at him, shocked into silence. She'd had her run-ins with Barry, but more often than not she had been at fault. 'But . . .' It was all she could manage.

He'd glanced back at the door to the editorial room, then stepped down a few stairs to take them further away. 'Don't tell anyone, okay? It'll be announced soon.'

'But who will be editor?'

His lips thinned into what might have been a smile if it hadn't been so sad. 'They don't need an editor.'

'They don't . . .' Rebecca couldn't quite grasp what she was hearing. 'They . . . what? I mean . . .'

'There will be a content supervisor,' he said.

In her Old Town office, Elspeth laughed. 'A content supervisor? Oh dear God, they really have taken over the asylum. Any idea who?'

Rebecca shook her head. 'Apparently Les Morgan will take over for a while. The "transition period" they're calling it.'

'Aye, transitioning from one mess into another.'

'Then they'll appoint someone, I suppose.'

'One of the staff?'

'Doubtful. London will want someone of their own in there. Anyway, none of us are experienced enough, apart from Hugh, and I can't see them giving him the keys to the kingdom.'

'True. Hugh was never one to let a shit idea get in the way of making his opinions known.'

'I wonder who he learned that from?'

Elspeth tucked her cigarette into the corner of her mouth and squinted across the desk. 'I've no idea what you mean, young lady. I was a company man all the way.'

'Then why did they sack you?'

'They didn't sack me, I was invited to leave.'

Rebecca laughed.

Elspeth plucked the cigarette from her mouth and laid it in an ashtray that had passed the need to be emptied about ten smokes ago. She leaned forward. 'So how do you feel about all this?'

Rebecca sighed. She hadn't yet fully processed the news. She knew the job would not be what it had been when Elspeth was in charge, when, despite pressure from above, getting the story as close to the truth as possible was paramount. It wouldn't even be what it had been under Barry, when standards fell along with staff numbers. It would be something new; in her opinion, something less than journalism. A process line of copy, covering an even wider area than at present, with little or no time to get out and do what she did best, which was actually talking to people face to face. She had come to an agreement with Barry that, if she could convince him it was necessary, she could get out and do so. He was an old-fashioned hack at heart so generally he didn't take that much convincing, although he was capable of putting up a good fight. It often meant she had to do extra hours to make up for it, but she didn't mind. Her mother lived in Glasgow and her only real friends in Inverness were Chaz and Alan, so lack of personal time wasn't much of an issue. There had been Simon, a solicitor from Nairn, but that relationship had foundered on the rocks of a miscarriage, something no one else knew about, not even Chaz or Elspeth. Or her mother, for that matter. The relationship had been in trouble prior to that, at least on her side. Simon had tried to keep it afloat, but when she'd come back from Stoirm the previous autumn she had finally scuppered it. She had invited him out for a drink – if that hadn't tipped him off something was wrong, nothing would, because up until that point she had never made first contact. They went to a quiet lounge in a hotel across the Ness and had a long talk – well, she had a long talk, he merely sat and listened, occasionally asking a question in a quiet, strained voice. She told him there was no future for them together, that it was not anyone's fault, that it wasn't because of the baby. There just wasn't anything there. She fell short of saying it wasn't him it was her, but it was implicit.

He had sat very still for a long time, staring through a large window towards the castle on the hill opposite, the reflections of its floodlights shimmering on the shifting waters of the river. When he finally looked up at her, she saw the pain and the questions in his eyes and she felt her heart break. She didn't want to hurt him, she'd never wanted to hurt him, but she couldn't go on like this.

He stood up and left without a further word and she felt something like relief mixed with what might have been a little bit of self-loathing. If she was honest with herself, it was loss too. She recognised that, all right. She knew about loss. The baby. Her father.

Her phone, which had been sitting in front of her on Elspeth's desk, vibrated and brought her out of her thoughts. As she reached for it, she realised she'd kept Elspeth waiting for an answer. 'I don't know, I really don't. I'll just have to wait and see.'

Elspeth settled back in her chair, her right hand unconsciously reaching out for the cigarette. 'That's all any of us can do, Becks.'

Rebecca glanced at the caller ID, saw it was Bill Sawyer's number. 'Bill?'

'Spoke to my pal over at Inshes.' Police Scotland's Inverness headquarters was situated in this eastern area of the city, part of a business and retail park near Raigmore Hospital. 'He says they're playing this all very coy.'

'Don't they always?'

'That's all he'd say, though. That DCI Roach, she's tough, and they're all shit-scared about pissing her off. Sorry, love – looks like I'll need to earn that Happy Meal another day.'

Disappointing but not surprising. She knew the police liked to keep as much to themselves as possible.

Specialist knowledge. Her father's voice, as usual, echoed in her mind. *We can't put everything out there. We need to keep much of it back, for evidential reasons, for investigative reasons, for legal reasons. And then there's the wee bits and pieces that we'll maybe use to trip up a suspect, something only the real culprit knows about a crime.* She remembered him pausing then and giving her the smile that always telegraphed something cheeky was on its way. *Of course, sometimes we do it just to piss off reporters.*

'My mate did say one thing, though.' Sawyer's voice interrupted the playback in her mind. She saw Elspeth watching her expression with interest but patience. She must have sensed this was a story-related call but she knew Rebecca would tell her everything. That was the kind relationship they had.

Rebecca asked, 'What?'

'This murder? He said word was that it was weird.'

8

'Weird? In what way?'

Val Roach pushed a tablet across the desktop towards Superintendent Harry McIntyre and watched as he swiped through images with his forefinger. He was a big man, well over six foot tall, and the bulk of what she saw filling his crisp uniform was muscle. He had been an athlete in his younger days and had never lost the need to keep his body trim.

McIntyre blanched as he studied the photographs. Despite attempts by crime writers to convince the world differently, murder was still uncommon in the Highlands and so, by extension, any unlawful killing would be deemed unusual, to an extent. However, this was exceptional, as McIntyre now saw.

He didn't look up at her. 'Well,' he said. She waited. 'Well,' he said again.

'Yes, sir,' she said.

McIntyre sat back in his chair, his eyes riveted on the images. 'I've seen many a thing but that's . . .'

'Downright weird?' she offered when his voice tailed off.

'To say the least.'

Roach smiled but there was little humour in it. She knew her boss was struggling to cope with this, just as she had. Still was, if she was being honest with herself. A body clad in traditional Highland dress – plaid, shirt, bonnet with a sprig of holly – was one thing. But the period claymore pinning him to the ground, shown in the pictures as straight and high as a standing stone, was something else again.

McIntyre finally tore his eyes from the tablet. 'So, nothing on the victim to assist with identification?'

'Nothing, sir. The clothes don't quite fit, so we don't think they were his.'

'And the weapon?'

'It's in good condition, from what I could see. It's bloody heavy, so whoever wielded it has a bit of muscle.'

'So a man, then?'

Typical, she thought, *thinking only his gender could have muscle.* 'Not necessarily, sir.'

'Any other wounds or contusions on the victim?'

'Not that I could see but the post-mortem will tell us more.'

His gaze dropped to the photographs again, distaste pursing his lips. He was too experienced an officer to feel revulsion at the sight of blood and death. No, Roach knew he was a typical cop who, like her, did not like a mystery. Straightforward violence was preferable and understandable – a man kills during a fight, a woman murders an abusive husband. But something like this, something premeditated, something both weird and unusual, was not welcome. It led to expense and paperwork and manpower.

'Nothing obvious, in other words,' he said, a meld of weariness and irritation crisping his voice. 'So what the hell happened? He didn't just lie there and let someone plunge that thing into his body, I'm sure.'

'No, sir.'

'No other signs of a struggle at the locus?'

'We're still searching but there's no blood apart from what was around and under the victim. He may have gone there willingly and then been attacked. But no obvious evidence. It's also possible he was incapacitated in some way, drugged maybe, and taken there to be left like that.' She flicked a finger at the photographs. 'My guess is he was taken there in a vehicle, then carried or dragged across the heather and laid down, then the sword business.'

'Toxicology will confirm if he was drugged?'

'Yes, sir.'

'Access?'

'Have you been to Culloden, sir?'

'I have, but remind me.'

'There's a drive leading to the visitor centre. There are areas where you can pull in and not be seen from the main road, especially at night. The battlefield itself is not fenced off so it would be easy to move the body from a car to where it was deposited.'

'But no physical evidence of that? Marks or disturbed earth?'

'Lots of tyre tracks but that means nothing. It's a popular spot. Nothing in the heather, no drag marks.'

McIntyre's forefinger tapped rhythmically on screen as he studied it. Roach followed his stare and saw a close-up of the body, the sword prominent, the man's eyes open, staring, always staring. For as long as the records exist.

'The bloody media will be all over this,' said McIntyre. 'I hate it when they are all over cases.'

'I'll have to keep as much detail out of the public eye as I can, sir.'

He grunted. 'Bloody reporters are a menace. You know, if it wasn't impossible, I'd advocate that only three or four people know about murder inquiries. That way we could keep everything nailed down tight until we are ready to release it.'

'I know what you mean, sir, but – as you say – impossible.'

'You'll have to give the media something. The fact that the body was found on a National Heritage site will have them wetting themselves – the Highland dress and the bloody sword will make it even worse.'

'The clothes and the sword are two of the points I'd like to keep to ourselves for now, sir.'

He sighed. 'Good luck with that, Val. Some idiot out there will be talking when he should be thinking, I guarantee it.'

She knew what he meant. A murder inquiry was a massive undertaking with a vast array of personnel involved at some point or other. In addition to the police officers, there were medical experts, forensics, civilians and lawyers. And when the interviews began the net would widen.

Facing the press was part of the job she hated. She knew in many ways they could be of assistance but in just as many, if not more, they could be a hindrance. Her job was to catch a killer. Their job was to get a story and outdo each other. They cited the public right to know, but really, during an investigation, the public only needed to know what the police needed – or wanted – them to know. After a trial and conviction, as far as she was concerned, they could print what they liked. Preferably accurately, but then there was never any guarantee of that.

9

Rebecca had almost made it to the office when she thought about Mo Burke. She still didn't have her quote. She could simply phone the woman when she got back, which was always the preferred option of the company, but Rebecca felt the story was more important than that. Just as she had wanted to witness the demo for herself, she wanted to see the woman's face when she asked her why she had taken such a high-profile stance given her family's alleged criminal activities. It would be a difficult question to ask but that was the job: asking difficult questions.

She had reached the Raigmore Interchange, with the traffic speeding above it on the A9. As she headed towards the Longman Roundabout, surface spray from the wet road coated her windscreen and lorries roared past her towards the Kessock Bridge and the north. It occurred to her that she had been out of the office longer than she had intended and that Les Morgan would not be happy. *Still,* she thought, *into everyone's life a little rain must fall.*

They called the area where the Burkes lived the Ferry – not to be confused with neighbouring South Kessock and Merkinch, which were also known by the nickname. Those who were born in Inchferry and who lived there most of their lives often viewed the nearby areas with disdain. 'This is the REAL Ferry, ye know?' was a phrase that had been uttered more than once to Rebecca. If you weren't Ferry born and bred then you were likely to look on its residents with, if not contempt, then certainly suspicion. If you admitted to coming from the Ferry, you had to be a crook or an addict or an unmarried mother. Or all three. It was seen as a hell-hole, as a hotbed of crime, riddled with teen pregnancies and home only to the dregs of society. That was if you were in the habit of holding dinner parties, ate avocadoes and preferred your TV shows to be subtitled. The reality was that many of the residents worked hard for their money, had strong family units and the only drug they took with any regularity came in a tea bag. There were some, though, who gave their neighbours the bad name. Of the latter, the Burkes were the most well known.

There had been an actual ferry here, long ago, carrying passengers and goods across the Beauly Firth, but that, and others, had become surplus to requirements thanks to the Kessock Bridge. The housing estate had sprung up in the years following the Second World War, just as other council schemes had in cities all over the country. It became a gridwork of meandering streets that curved and criss-crossed each other with no apparent design. The housing was a mix of terraces and flats, some tenements four or five storeys high. Others were what they would call duplexes now, with the ground-floor flat accessed from the front and the upper apartment through a door at the side. In the 1970s many of the properties had fallen victim to a mixture of tenant and council neglect, as well as poor construction, but in the '80s and '90s, as the government's right-to-buy scheme took effect and grant money was thrown around like confetti, a few were transformed. Damp courses were squirted into walls, roofing was repaired, rendering was fixed and windows were replaced. The uniformity of the post-war era was made more individual by painting over the drab grey roughcast that had been so prevalent. Walls were now white or cream or, in one that she spotted as she drove, a bilious shade of pink. Even though some gardens had been paved over and transformed into driveways, there was still a sufficient number of cars parked on either side of the street, forcing Rebecca to manoeuvre as if through a chicane, the narrow passage wide enough only for one car. She had to stop two or three times to let a vehicle coming in the opposite direction pass.

The Burke house was a two-storey end terrace which had been recently painted brilliant white. Rebecca found a space a little way down the road and walked back, taking in the expensive black four-wheel drive parked in the roadway and then the house itself, with its sparkling windows, with what looked new uPVC frames, and matching door. Neat concrete slabs, with no grass or weeds growing through the cracks, led from the pavement across a small patch of grass which looked as if it had been trimmed with nail clippers. Her surprise at how fresh and clean the house looked was replaced with guilt. Why should she be expecting some hovel? She was obviously just as prejudiced as the middle-class trendies she had earlier mocked in her thoughts.

As she walked up the path, she felt the familiar nervous tingle and tensing of her stomach. Cold calling was not easy, but it was something she steeled herself to do.

The white-panelled door with two frosted glass panes swung open before she even reached it and Scott Burke was there to face her. At the demo that morning he'd been wearing a cheap-looking military jacket, but she noted underneath he'd obviously been sporting some expensive gear. None of your Primark for him. Unlike Rebecca. His blond hair was smartly cut, his face clean-shaven and now she was close enough she could see he was good-looking enough to front a boy band. Crooks R Us, maybe, or Nedzone. But there was that same smile she'd seen at the demonstration. The same smile she had actually seen him flash around in court. As if he was listening to some sick, perverted little joke that no one else could hear. She wondered briefly whether he'd opened the door by coincidence or if he'd seen her coming. Then she spied the black orb sitting on the wall above the door like a demonic wasps' nest. Security camera. The windows were probably toughened glass, too. Maybe they had laser beams as a deterrent as well.

'Hi,' she said, giving him her best smile. 'I'm looking for Mrs Burke?'

She had no idea why she made it sound like a question, as if she wasn't certain Mo Burke lived here. Too many Australian soaps in her teenage years had affected her speech patterns and she resolved to cut that shit out.

He leaned against the door jamb, folded his arms. 'Oh, aye?'

He looked her up and down. He wasn't too subtle about it, either. There was an element of appraisal in his scrutiny, but she didn't know whether he was assessing her level of threat, her reason for being there or the possibility of a sexual encounter. Rebecca didn't have the kind of looks that made it onto magazine covers but she certainly didn't frighten children, so had experienced men looking at her as if they were imagining her naked. It still didn't make it right. Scott's gaze both pissed her off and alarmed her in equal measure, but she was determined not to let it rattle her. The idea of staring pointedly at his crotch crossed her mind, just to see how he liked it. The thought was very quickly dismissed because he would probably see it as a come-on.

'My name's Rebecca Connolly, from the *Chronicle*?'

Again, that bloody rise in inflection, as if she wasn't sure herself what paper she worked for.

'Oh, aye?' he said again, that smile still ghosting his lips. She waited for him to say something more, but all he did was idle in the doorway and stare at her with spectral amusement haunting his face.

Rebecca held onto her patience as if it was an umbrella in a high wind. 'Is she in?'

He pushed himself upright and yelled over his shoulder. 'Maw – you in?'

The answer came from somewhere within the house. 'You know I'm bloody in. Stupid question. Who is it?'

'Lassie from the *Chronicle* wants to talk to you.'

Mo Burke appeared. She was wearing a shapeless blue cardigan, jeans and a pair of woolly slippers that were somehow incongruous, given what Rebecca had heard about her. The rumours. Now that she and her youngest son stood side by side, Rebecca saw the family resemblance did not end with the colour of their hair. Except the mother looked at her with suspicion while the son smiled and smiled and smiled.

'Mrs Burke, I wonder if you've got a minute to talk about the demonstration this morning?'

Mo's eyes narrowed slightly. 'I saw you there, right?'

Rebecca was unsurprised. Mo Burke was the type who would notice everything. That was the only way she could survive. 'That's right. I had to dash off on another story, but I hoped I'd be able to get a few words from you about your campaign.'

This time the woman smiled. 'My campaign?'

'Yes, isn't that what you'd call it? You don't want the council to rehouse—'

'It's no my campaign. It's the Ferry's. Nobody here wants kiddie fiddlers living beside their weans.'

'I understand that, but you're the spokesperson, right?'

'Only because no other bugger would speak up. They wanted something done, but nobody else would raise even as much as a finger to do it. I had to step up. Me and my boys.'

She reached out and touched Scott's arm, and he took it as his cue to step up again. He nodded to Rebecca. 'Aye, they others out there pissed and moaned about it, sure, but when it came down to it they were too feart to do nothin'. So we did it. We organised the demo this morning, the petition, the objections to councillors and that.'

'How did you do that?'

He smirked. 'We spoke to the folks around here, a wee word in their ears, you know what I'm sayin'?'

Rebecca took a wild guess at how threatening some of those words in ears had been. But then perhaps they hadn't needed to be. Perhaps she was judging the Burke family by their reputation. Perhaps they did genuinely have concerns and no heavy leaning on neighbours was required. Perhaps all those neighbours wanted was someone to take the lead and they would follow.

'And Finbar Dalgliesh? How did he become involved?'

Mo's eyes clouded and a darting glance at Scott seemed to stiffen the air between mother and son. Rebecca had seen Mo's anger earlier that morning, when Finbar had taken over. She had seen that same glance in Scott's direction. Obviously, he was the one who'd got the Spioraid leader on board.

When Mo spoke, her voice was casual, without rancour. She was not going to discuss Dalgliesh. 'I'm no keen on you lot, you know?' she said.

'My lot?'

'The press. The media . . .' She pronounced it *meedja*. 'You lot haven't been particularly supportive of my family over the years. My man. My boys. Like wee flies, you lot, buzzin' all around us and our business. Why the hell should I speak to you?'

'I'm not here about your husband, Mrs Burke. Or your boys. Or your, eh, business. I'm not even here to talk about Finbar Dalgliesh, he's well able to speak for himself.' Rebecca was pleased to see a little light in Mo's eyes. She was willing to put up with Dalgliesh muscling in but that didn't mean she had to like it. 'I'm here to talk about an issue that you've highlighted,' Rebecca continued. 'You've sent letters and you've raised the petition and you organised the demo. But if you want the authorities to take notice then you need us, Mrs Burke. We can bring your campaign to a wider audience. We can focus the attention of the whole of Inverness, of the Highlands – maybe even the whole of the country – on this.'

'Aye. Just so you can judge us and sneer at us, maybe? The way you parade my boys' names across the front page when they're up in court?'

Rebecca took a gamble, believing the woman would like straight talk. 'Then maybe your boys shouldn't get themselves charged quite so often, Mrs Burke. We're only doing our job – justice not only being done but being seen to be done. That's what the local press does, Mrs Burke. The same with your campaign. We don't judge, we merely report. You want what you've done so far to mean something? Then let me report it. Don't let Finbar Dalgliesh and Spioraid hijack the work you've done up to now. Tell me about it and I'll report it fairly and accurately.'

Scott sneered, obviously unhappy with her dismissal of Dalgliesh. 'Do you people know what fair and accurate is?'

She held his gaze. 'We could be the difference between your message being ignored and heard, Mr Burke. Or twisted into something else.'

Mo Burke studied her for a minute, her face blank but her eyes flinty. Rebecca couldn't tell if she'd missed her mark or if she had hit home. Finally, those eyes seemed to soften and the woman took a deep breath. 'Mister Burke,' she said. 'I like that. Polite, so it is. Respectful. You'd be surprised how many folk think they can call my boy by his first name without asking him.' She gave her son a nudge with the back of her hand and turned away. 'Bring the lassie into the living room, Scott. Don't have her standing on the doorstep like a bloody milk bottle.'

Scott's little smile returned and he stepped aside, giving Rebecca a flamboyant wave as an invitation. 'You heard her, step into her parlour.'

Rebecca eased past him.

As she did so, she heard him say, 'Buzz, buzz, buzz . . .'

10

If she had been surprised by the pristine exterior, Rebecca was stunned by the interior. Again, she really did not know what she had expected. Drug paraphernalia lying around, perhaps. Enough mobile phones to open a branch of O2. Dodgy-looking dudes wearing baseball caps and covered in bling. A big dog, maybe. Instead she was shown into a spacious living room that looked out onto the street and the neat square of garden. The room was bright and airy, the walls delicate pastel shades, and dominated by a settee of soft brown leather that looked large enough to sub-let. There was a recliner armchair in similar soft leather, a square coffee table made of heavy wood and on the wall above a high wooden fireplace of dark wood was fixed a large flatscreen TV currently tuned to CNN. Rebecca saw the US president making a speech, his right hand gesturing, as Alan had once remarked, like a children's entertainer who had forgotten his glove puppet.

There was a dog, but it was no mastiff or Rottweiler. It was a West Highland terrier with hair so white it gleamed and it scuttled towards Rebecca from a basket beside the radiator under the window as soon as she entered. The stubby little tail wagged like a royal wave in hyper drive and the dog snuffled round Rebecca's feet, then raised itself on its hind legs to meet her hand.

'Midge,' said Mo, 'back in your bed.'

The words were commanding but kindly and the little dog obediently trotted back to his basket, the tail still wagging. He whirled on the cushion and lay down, but his head remained erect as he watched Rebecca for any sign of a pat going spare.

Mo gave him a stage glare. 'He's all about the attention, that wee dog. Typical man.'

'He's lovely,' said Rebecca.

'Aye, he's a good boy. Sometimes he's the only male I can depend on around here.'

Rebecca caught Scott pulling a face, as if he was used to hearing such sentiments from his mother. There was warmth in Mo's voice, though.

'Take your coat off, hen, sit yourself down,' said Mo. 'You want something to drink? Tea, coffee? Scotty, go put the kettle on.'

As she peeled her coat off, Rebecca's first instinct was to decline but she welcomed the chance to speak to Mo Burke alone. She didn't like the way Scott continued to look at her, as if he was wondering how much she cost and whether he had enough in his pocket.

'Coffee would be lovely,' she said as she sank onto and into the settee. Getting up again was going to be undignified, she realised.

Without a word, Scott headed to a door in the far corner, which Rebecca presumed led to the kitchen. If being treated like a butler bothered him, he didn't show it. He was probably used to it and Mo did not strike Rebecca as the kind of woman to whom you said no.

'And put out the good cups,' Mo shouted as her son vanished through the doorway. 'Don't use they bloody mugs. They're boggin'.'

She listened for a moment as her son opened cupboard doors until she was satisfied her instructions were being carried out. Only then did she settle back in the recliner. She didn't flick the lever to raise the foot rest – this was business and she obviously needed to be alert. She watched closely while Rebecca took out her notebook and then a digital recorder.

'No recordings,' said Mo. Her voice was flat, and it told Rebecca that there was no room for argument here. 'You people can edit they things to make us say whatever you want.'

Rebecca didn't protest and returned the recorder to her coat pocket. Her father's words, as usual, sprang to her mind. *There's nobody more paranoid than a crook*, he'd said, *except maybe a cop*.

'Are you happy with me taking notes?' she asked.

'Aye, as long as you report what I say exactly.'

Rebecca fought the need to point out that the recording would ensure that. Mo Burke had survived by being strong-willed and careful to the point of obsession.

They think differently from us, Becks. Her father's voice, back in her mind, where he lived. *Suspicion is a way of life for the dealers and those in the life. That's how they live. That's how they stay living. We call it paranoia, they call it self-preservation.*

Rebecca heard footsteps on the stairs and Nolan Burke appeared from the hallway, a copy of *The Guardian* in his hand. The day was full of surprises, Rebecca thought. *The Guardian*, no less. If she had thought the Burke boys could read at all, she might've expected a red top. But *The Guardian*? Who knew Nolan Burke was a liberal. She wondered if he drank green tea and ate quorn nuggets.

Then she caught herself. Maybe she was being just a tiny bit judgemental once again. The same as those who thought the Ferry was a hotbed of crime and sin.

Rebecca saw Nolan flash his mother an enquiring look.

'This is the lassie from the *Chronicle*,' Mo explained. 'She wants to talk about this morning.'

Nolan said nothing as he settled himself in the armchair, the newspaper resting on his lap. His gaze was not quite so disconcerting as his brother's and he did not sport Scott's unpleasant little smile but, when Rebecca turned to face Mo again, she still felt his eyes on her, just as she had earlier in the day, outside the council building.

Mo turned her attention back to Rebecca. 'So, what's your name again?'

'Rebecca Connolly.'

Mo nodded once. 'So, Rebecca Connolly, what do you want to know?'

Flipping open her notebook with pen in hand, Rebecca said, 'What made you want to start this campaign, Mrs Burke?'

A flicker of a smile. 'That's what you want to know? Jesus, hen, I'd think that's bloody obvious, wouldn't you? We can't have convicted paedos in our streets, simple as that. There's kiddies around here and putting one of they guys in here would be like giving the keys of the henhouse door to the fox. Know what I mean?'

'But isn't it the case that a council spokesman insisted they had no plan to—'

'They only lie when they speak, that lot.' Mo's face crinkled as she showed her contempt. 'I know they plan to lodge a perv in the scheme. I know it for a fact.'

'How can you be so sure?'

Mo paused, tilted her head. 'Believe me, Rebecca Connolly, I know. You reporters is no the only ones who have sources. I've got my people, is all I need to say.'

Rebecca was desperate to learn more. Council sources? Police? Social services? The inference was someone, somewhere, was talking and she could well believe Mo had an informant in the system, perhaps more than one. Along with a well-developed sense of paranoia, families like the Burkes survived on their well-structured support systems. But she had learned enough about the woman to know that she wouldn't tell her who it was.

Rebecca glanced at her notes. 'So you've raised the petition, you've confronted councillors at their surgeries, you've had the demo this morning. Did you expect Finbar Dalgliesh to attend, by the way?'

Again that flash of irritation. If Scott had been present, Rebecca had no doubt he would be receiving another glare. 'No, that was a surprise.'

'A welcome one?'

Mo considered her answer, then said, 'He helped get the point across. I'm grateful for that.'

'And will he be part of the campaign from now on?'

'He's promised to take our concerns to them in the council and the Scottish government.'

'Do you think he can help?'

'He can get to places we can't, speak to folk who're off limits to the likes of us.'

'So you're happy to have him and Spioraid involved?'

'If it can stop them moving some deviant bastard into our streets, then aye, I'm happy.'

'How did he become involved?'

Rebecca did not expect Mo to lay it on her son, but she asked the question anyway.

'We've no exactly been quiet, hen,' Mo replied, with barely a pause. 'He just heard about it, wanted to show his support, that's all.'

Rebecca noted her words, then asked, 'So, what next?'

'We keep going, that's what's next. We're not letting this go. They try to move just one perv in here and we let them get away with it, then they'll move more in here. Thin end of the wedge, isn't it? And we're not having it.'

'Do you rule out any further demonstrations? Perhaps alongside Spioraid activists?'

That smile flickered once more. 'I don't rule nothing out, Rebecca Connolly.'

'And if the council go ahead anyway?'

Scott came back in carrying a tray with delicate floral cups and saucers and a packet of chocolate digestives. 'We stop them,' he said, laying the tray on the coffee table.

Mo's gaze flicked over the tray. 'You couldn't put the biscuits on a plate?' Those eyes rolled in Rebecca's direction. 'Men.'

Rebecca couldn't hide a grin. Mothers are the same wherever they are. Whether it was her mum back in Milngavie or Mo Burke here in Inverness, putting the biscuits out in the packet is fine for family but company must always have them arranged on a plate.

She thought she detected another edge to Mo's voice and the look she gave her son confirmed it. Scott had spoken out of turn when he had answered her question. Rebecca, though, had to press the point. It was her job.

'Stop them how?'

Scott gave his mother a look that said he wasn't in her thrall. Mo had genuine affection for her youngest, Rebecca had picked up on that, but he had a mind of his own. She may rule the roost but he could still crow. 'They'll learn that we won't stand for it, is all. They try to move a paedo in here, we'll put a stop to it, simple as.'

'Do you rule out violence?'

There was a silence. Rebecca already knew the answer. The Burke family reputation spoke for itself.

But Scott answered anyway. 'We'll do whatever it takes.'

Whatever it takes. From any other family that could simply mean perseverance, but from the Burkes it meant something else. The story was they were once again in the throes of fending off a new territorial challenge, this time from a Glasgow crew. They hadn't reached the length of exchanging bullets but there had been unpleasantness. One of the Burkes' people – not a family member – had been found badly beaten on a country road near Nairn. That led to a Glasgow visitor discovering that power drills have other functions in the hands of a well-motivated user. Kneecaps are painfully susceptible to such attention. According to word on the street, the DIY enthusiast was none other than Scott Burke, who was at that moment pouring tea like an old family retainer. Whether he had fired up the drill personally, and whether he did so on the orders of his mother, was open to conjecture. The family had shown that they were willing and extremely able to do whatever it took to protect their interests. When Scott said they were prepared to do the same to prevent any attempt to move a convicted paedophile into their area, did that include heading out to the tool shed again?

58

Rebecca felt a tingle of excitement, the kind she felt when she knew she was on to a real story, not just the routine fare of a weekly newspaper. The Burkes' involvement was one thing, but Spioraid made this political. Add its alleged association with New Dawn, and there was a terrorism angle.

She took the proffered cup and saucer from Scott's hand, then waited until he had handed his mother a cup. He didn't pour anything for himself or his brother but merely stepped over to the ornamental fireplace and leaned against the mantel. Rebecca took a sip of the tea and considered her next question.

'Mrs Burke,' she said, 'why are you doing this?'

Mo seemed sincerely puzzled by the question. 'I've already told you . . .'

'No, that's not what I mean. Why you? Why your family?' Rebecca waved a free hand, first towards Scott, who was doing his Cheshire cat act by the fireplace, and then vaguely in Nolan's direction. He was still studying her with that cool gaze of his. She took a deep breath. 'Basically, what I'm asking is this – you know what people think of you and your family. What you do.'

'What we do?'

Rebecca hesitated, then thought, *Bugger it – I've opened that box, let's see what comes out.* 'Mrs Burke, let's not be coy here. I know your family reputation. You know your family reputation.' She waited for a response but nothing came. 'So why do this? Why put your head above the parapet? You must know this will attract attention.'

Mo sucked in a long breath, then leaned forward and placed her saucer on the edge of the coffee table. She sat back again, tucked one leg under the other, gave Rebecca a long, unblinking stare. Rebecca wondered if she had overplayed her hand. She had gambled that Mo appreciated straight talking but perhaps she had gone too far in mentioning the family reputation.

Finally, Mo spoke. 'You know why my man's in the jail?'

Rebecca nodded.

'You know why he took that bloke, that Sammy Lang, in such a dislike?'

Rebecca cleared her throat. *Well*, she thought, *I opened the box, might as well give it a shake.* 'I heard he was, eh, interfering in your business.'

'He was. But that's not why it happened. Well, not completely. My man did it because of what that fella was. A kiddie fiddlin' bastard.' She paused and Rebecca thought she saw something creep into her eyes. Something unwanted. Something painful. A memory. 'He did it for me, you understand?'

Rebecca understood. For Mo Burke, this campaign was a personal crusade.

11

Barry must have seen her pull up outside the *Chronicle* office building because he was waiting for her in reception as she pushed through the doors. He gave her a look she had come to know all too well. She had crossed yet another line, something she had done so often she wondered if there was a union she could join.

'Where have you been?'

'I went to see Mo Burke. I needed a line for the story.'

His irritation was evident. 'Was it necessary?'

She didn't need to give him a look. She didn't mean to give him a look. But she gave him a look that said that they'd been over this before. Barry had come to terms with her wilfulness and knew she put in extra hours to make up for it, so there had to be something else behind his annoyance. She suspected she knew what that was.

'Les has been looking for you, wondering where you were.'

'I was on a story, Barry. I was doing my job. At least what my job should be.'

Barry puffed out his cheeks and shook his head. 'I've been too soft with you, Becks. You won't get away with this shit when I'm gone. You've got to understand that.'

'Barry, they're running these titles into the ground and you know it. Look at the circulation for every one of the papers. They've sunk so far cruise ships could use them as an anchor.'

He sighed. 'Digital is the future, you know that.'

'Yes, once one of the bean counters works out how to make real money out of it.'

'We're in difficult times, Becks.'

'You know something? I've only been doing this a few years, but one thing I've learned is that newspaper owners are always in difficult times. Even when they're making money hand over fist and their profit margins are higher than supermarkets, for God's sake.'

'Christ, Becks!' Barry lost it, and although he kept his voice low she could hear the anger catching his throat. 'You've hardly been in the bloody job two minutes and you think you have all the answers? You don't. You adopt your holier-than-thou stance and judge anyone who doesn't meet your high standards. The bean counters you despise so much? They keep you in a job. They make sure you have the money to pay your rent and buy clothes and spend it on whatever the hell you spend it on. So they make tough decisions. Someone has to. Do they get it right all the time? No, nobody does. Nobody ever did. Are there people in power who really don't know what they're talking about? Yes, but that's the same in every industry. But here's the thing. Nothing has changed, not really. The glorious world of the press you seem to hark back to never really existed. It was over-staffed and over-paid and under-worked.'

'Well, that pendulum sure has swung the other way, hasn't it?'

He opened his mouth to say something further, then closed it again. Barry didn't have the heart to argue with her, and she instantly regretted her sharp tone. The guy had lost his job and here she was being Little Miss Maverick. He was right, she was barely in the door and there were things she didn't fully understand. And life in the glory days probably wasn't as glorious as she imagined. But all she wanted to do was a decent job. To report the news fairly and impartially. To comfort the afflicted and afflict the comfortable. To hold power to account. To uphold local democracy. All that jazz.

'Tell you what, Becks.' Barry sounded weary when he spoke again. 'You go ahead, you carry on the way you have been. You know best. Everyone else is wrong. Don't give Les the chance to make things work. Don't wait and see if he actually does know what he's doing. You carry on the way you always do, snipe, snark, sneer without actually coming up with any real-life solutions. I'm out of it. I'll be here the rest of the week, then I'm gone. You're someone else's problem now.'

He turned and pushed his way through the glass doors and walked into the grey afternoon sunlight. Rebecca had never seen him leave the office during the day. She had only worked with him for a couple of years but seeing him walk away in that manner seemed like the end of an era.

Her phone rang as she climbed the stairs to the editorial floor. She paused on the landing, glanced at the screen, saw it was a familiar name and felt a stab of something she had come to know well. As she slid her thumb across the screen to accept the call, she knew it was guilt.

'Simon,' she said.

The familiar voice was crisp and business-like. That made her feel even more guilty. She had hurt him, badly. That hurt was still raw. 'I understand you've been talking to clients of mine.'

Her encounter with Barry had disorientated her slightly, so it took a moment to realise who Simon was talking about. Then it came to her. 'You mean the Burkes?'

'Yes, Mrs Burke and her sons. I represent the whole family.'

He hadn't been involved in Tony Burke's defence, so he must have taken them on as clients fairly recently. 'I didn't know that.'

'Well, now you do. Mrs Burke has just phoned me to say that her son might have been somewhat, eh, indiscreet.'

Indiscreet. A lawyer's word. Her mind flew through the conversation and landed on Scott's suggestion that the family would do whatever it took to prevent any relocation of a convicted sex offender. Simon knew she would make the connection.

'I'd like to stress that he was in no way implying any form of violence would occur,' he said.

63

She leaned on the railing and laughed. He was talking to her as if she was in court. 'Simon, this is Scott Burke we're talking about. Of course he was implying some form of violence would occur.'

'We know nothing of the sort. Their campaign has so far been peaceful and there is no reason why it shouldn't continue that way.'

'If you say so, Simon. But when Scott Burke says he'll do whatever it takes, it does make me wonder.'

She heard Simon take a breath on the other end of the line and pause for a moment. 'Are you going to print what he said?'

'I haven't decided.'

'It could mean anything.'

'That's my point.'

He tried another tack. 'It was off the record.'

'No, it wasn't.'

'Can you prove that?'

It was her turn to pause. She couldn't prove anything. She had been on her own with the Burkes in the house and Mo had refused to be recorded. 'What are they going to do, deny they said it? Sure, that'll work because everyone will believe Scott Burke. He is such a paragon of virtue, after all.'

'There was something else said,' Simon began. 'By Mrs Burke. She'd rather you didn't print it.'

'About her abuse, you mean? Now, that really was more of an inference than a statement.'

'Whatever the case, her position is that it's a private matter and she doesn't want it spread across the pages of a newspaper.'

She had already decided not to use it, but something about Simon's tone, his coldness, was annoying her, even though deep down she knew she deserved it. 'What happened to her, Simon?'

'I'm not going into detail. It was a long time ago, but these things have a habit of staying with a person. It's their business, Becks. It's their lives.'

'It has a bearing on what she's doing now, Simon. Goes to motivation.'

It was his turn to give her a small laugh. 'You've been watching too many American courtroom dramas. At any rate, the *Chronicle* is not a court of law. That's private, Becks. I'm asking you to leave it out of whatever you write.'

'Are you asking as a lawyer or as a friend?'

'Which would you rather?'

'You know the answer to that, Simon.'

There was a brief silence before he spoke again, his voice soft. 'You know, I really don't.'

She understood that. 'We can be friends, Simon.'

'I'm not sure we can, Becks. Life isn't like that. So let's just term this as a favour, for old times' sake. You don't need to mention anything about what may or may not have occurred in the past. It doesn't affect your story.'

Rebecca felt the guilt stab her again. She could still hear the pain in his voice. She really had hurt him. 'Okay,' she said. 'I won't mention it.'

'And Mr Burke's statement?'

'I won't go into that either. All I'll say is that they won't let this matter rest. How's that?'

'Thank you.'

'But I'm doing it as a friend, Simon. It's not a favour. As a friend. I'll always look on you as a special friend.'

She thought she heard his breath catch, but it could have simply been a glitch on the line.

'It's too late for that, Becks.'

And then he was gone.

12

'Who the absolute hell are these people?'

Alan and Chaz were in Rebecca's flat. They had brought in some take-away: curries for them, chicken and chips for her – she had never developed a taste for spicy food. They were half-watching a TV programme which purported to show celebrities doing something or other that Rebecca had no interest in. Alan loved these so-called reality shows, even though he was well aware there was very little reality to them, and had been staring at the screen while Rebecca told them about the changes at the paper.

Chaz squinted at the television set. He was always complaining that Rebecca's TV was too small and he could barely see anything, but she countered that her flat wasn't large enough to house anything bigger – and then followed up with the suggestion that he needed glasses. His vanity thus outraged, he usually dropped the subject.

'I think she was on a reality show,' Chaz said, nodding to a blonde who was so plastic Rebecca wouldn't be surprised if she had a recycling symbol stamped on her backside. The image then cut to a remarkably handsome man in his thirties with a grin like a flashbulb going off. 'And he was a model, I think. Or maybe he was on a reality show, too.'

Alan grunted, obviously unconvinced by the participants' celebrity status. Chaz grinned at Rebecca. 'So, what do you think will happen?'

'I think that model-stroke-reality-show-guy could have me, if he played his cards right,' said Alan.

Chaz sighed. 'I wasn't talking to you.'

Alan kept his eyes on the screen. 'I know. I just wanted you to know that my head could be turned if he walked in right now.'

Chaz squinted momentarily back at the screen. Raising one eyebrow, he tilted his head to one side. 'Yeah, okay. But you'd have to fight me for him.'

Alan snorted. 'No contest there, big boy.' He jerked a finger towards the cane propped up against Chaz's leg. 'You're physically compromised.'

The corners of Chaz's mouth tightened and he adopted a weary look. Alan feigned concern. 'Oh, love. Are our feelings hurt? Do we need counselling?'

A dramatic sigh from Chaz. 'As Oscar Wilde said . . .' He raised the middle finger of his left hand.

Alan erupted in laughter. 'Always had a way with words, that Oscar Wilde.'

Rebecca smiled as she listened to the two of them bicker. This was their speciality, like a double act. The Amazing Chaz and Alan. Despite their banter, she knew they cared deeply for each other and she hoped that would never change.

Simon popped into her head. There was a time, when they had first begun to go out with each other, that she thought he might be something special. She was wrong. It wasn't his fault – he was a decent, caring man – but even before she found out she was pregnant she had begun to wonder if there was a future for them. Then she lost the baby and any vestige of feeling she had for him vanished. She didn't blame him in any way – the miscarriage was merely the result of faulty chromosomes – but whatever feelings she thought she might have had for him died then too.

'So, what is going to happen *at the paper*.' Chaz laid heavy emphasis on the last three words for Alan's benefit.

Rebecca thought for a minute. 'Well, it won't be the same, that's for sure. Barry was at least an old hack at heart. But this guy? Not so sure. Sometimes he says the right things, but I don't believe he means them, you know? It's as if he's trying to punt something, like a salesman.' She sipped at her glass of wine. 'I don't know, maybe it will all settle down and work out. Maybe Barry's right. Maybe I am just an awkward bitch who thinks she knows best!'

'Or maybe you're right,' said Alan. She knew he'd been listening while watching the screen. He said it was his super power – the ability to appear to be disengaged while in reality taking everything in. It was the primary skill needed to be a first-class gossip and he had perfected it at an early age. Growing up in a house with all brothers, he had needed some kind of edge and discovered the skilful use of eavesdropping gave him knowledge. And knowledge is indeed power. His brothers were dedicated to the pursuit of manliness. They played rugby – football was a girls' game to them – and they hunted and fished and womanised. Listening in on their secrets gave him a measure of protection and, as he had admitted himself, 'It also made me a detestable little shit.'

'I don't think it matters whether I'm right or wrong,' she said. 'The changes will happen anyway.'

'You can't fight progress,' said Chaz.

Alan looked away from the TV set and gave his lover a smile. As usual, Rebecca saw the affection in his eyes. 'Sage words from someone so young. You should put that on a T-shirt.'

Chaz raised his middle finger again. 'Put that on a T-shirt.'

Alan let out a dramatic sigh. 'That's why I love you – your scintillating wit is an inspiration.'

Chaz laughed and looked back at Rebecca. 'So, hear anything more about the murder?'

Alan gave up feigning disinterest and was suddenly all ears. 'Murder? What murder? You didn't tell me about any murder.'

Chaz jerked his head towards his partner. 'It's like living with Miss Marple. You'd think after Stoirm he would of had enough of it. But no.'

Stoirm. The fierce winds that lashed the island still blew in their memories. Chaz and Alan had almost died there. Others had met a worse fate.

Alan waved the words away. 'Yes, yes, yes – I'm a ghoul, I need help, blah-blah-blah – now tell me more.'

'There was a body found this morning,' said Rebecca. 'On Culloden.'

'The battlefield?'

'Why does everyone ask that?' Chaz rolled his eyes.

'I thought you'd have heard about it,' said Rebecca.

'Not a word. I have spent the day in the rarified atmosphere of academe, where the very air, replete with the pursuit of knowledge and wisdom, acts as a buffer against the everyday horrors of real life.'

'You work in the office,' Chaz pointed out.

'Yes, but the air drifts in from the corridors.' Alan flicked him away as if he were a troublesome fly. 'So, what do we know?'

'That's it,' said Rebecca. 'Police aren't giving out any details until tomorrow at a press conference. But I spoke to Bill Sawyer.' She saw Alan's face crinkle with distaste. He and Bill Sawyer didn't get on well. Rebecca suspected the ex-police officer was a touch homophobic and that didn't sit well with Alan, who liked to poke such people for fun. 'He said there was something weird about it.'

'Weird how?'

'That's all, just weird.'

Alan thought about this. 'So, you have a body on Culloden Moor. And it's weird. Were you there? On the moor?'

Rebecca nodded.

'Was it found near the road?'

'No, it was a fair bit onto the battlefield.'

'A fair bit onto the battlefield.' Alan took in the details. 'So not merely dumped at the side of the road.'

Chaz grinned. 'See what I mean? Miss Marple.'

Alan ignored him. 'Why would someone leave a body on the site of an old battle? And what makes it so unusual?'

'I'll learn more tomorrow,' said Rebecca. 'And who's to say the body was dumped? The murderer and the victim could have been walking on the moor when it happened.'

Alan wasn't buying it. 'Who walks over an old battlefield at night?'

'What makes you think it happened at night?' Chaz asked.

'Because the *corpus delicti* would have been spotted in the daylight.' Alan rolled his eyes towards Rebecca. 'It's just as well he's good-looking.'

'Aye, well, Brainiac, *corpus delicti* doesn't mean the actual body. It means body *of evidence*.'

Alan was momentarily stunned into silence. 'You've been reading again, haven't you? I've warned you about that before.'

Rebecca laughed. 'Anyway, as I said, I'm sure I'll find out more tomorrow.'

'You should talk to Anna Fowler,' said Alan.

'Who is Anna Fowler?'

'Professor Anna Fowler, up at the university. She's on the staff in the history department. She knows all there is to know about Culloden. In fact, she's the historical advisor on that film they're making over there in Glen Nevis.'

'What do you think she can tell me about a murder?'

Alan looked at her as if she was a child who just wasn't getting it. 'Because this really doesn't sound like this was a mere deposition site. I don't see someone carrying a body onto the battleground and risking being spotted for no reason.'

'It was pretty misty last night,' Chaz said.

'Yes, but they'd still need to leave their vehicle at the side of the road, or at least park it nearby. That could attract attention. No, someone took a big chance disposing of their handiwork on a well-known historical landmark site. I'd say that was done for a purpose.' He paused and stared at them. Alan liked a bit of drama. Then he said, 'Someone was making a point . . .'

13

In his dream, Chaz was buffeted by winds. They tugged him from side to side, elemental creatures picking at him, as if searching for a way to penetrate. They shrieked around him, a cacophony howling into the night.

The banshee.

The wailing women who herald death. Chaz was born in England, but he knew his folklore. And in his dream they were there that night. On Stoirm. Floating in the winds that threw themselves at the Land Rover he had been driving, each gust a talon clawing at the bodywork.

He could still hear them when he woke. Beside him Alan snored, softly but snoring all the same. Chaz sat up, being careful not wake him, the shrieks still undulating in the darkness of their bedroom. He wanted to click on the bedside lamp but he knew that would disturb his partner so he let the screeching swirl and echo around him.

He thought he was over the accident. He thought he had got past it. But obviously he hadn't. It was still there, in his mind, waiting to be relived. The winds. The twisting road. The headlights blazing in the rear-view. The scream of the engine as he was forced off the road and into the rocks on the shore, Alan's own cries merging with it and ultimately becoming subsumed by it.

And the laughter of the young men in the other vehicle, rising and falling with the keening squall, eddying around him as the sound of metal crumpling against the harsh stone became one with the sharp agony of something thrusting itself deep into his body.

No, he hadn't got past it. He still didn't like driving, especially at night and certainly not when it rained. Alan understood. If Chaz had to go out on a job in such conditions, he always came with him. Alan was not a natural driver, but he did it. For Chaz.

The dream, though, he hadn't had for months and, as the banshee continued to moan in the dark corners, he wondered why it had come back.

Rebecca was still in that netherworld between sleep and wakefulness as she sat up with a start, clicked on the bedside lamp, stared around the room. Her surroundings seemed unfamiliar to her. She recognised them but, at the same time, didn't. Then, realisation edging its way through her dreamlike state, she understood she was in her own bedroom. Those were her curtains drawn over the window. That was her wardrobe, her dresser, her chair with Teddy Edward surrounded by the array of cuddy toys from her childhood. Her clothes tossed on the floor.

But no child.

That was what had pulled her from sleep. The sound of a child crying. But now, as the electric light chased away the darkness, she knew there had been no child. Not one that lived.

The child had not visited her for some time. There had been a time when it was a regular caller. Sometimes she would awake to find her father sitting with her and that would soothe her. But not tonight. There was no vision of John Connolly to ease her mind, only the sound of her own breathing, the furniture and the memories of her childhood staring at her from the chair. A happy childhood. A loving one. Something the infant in her dreams, which lived only in some dark recesses of her mind, would never have.

She got up and eased Teddy Edward from his friends. He was old, much older than Rebecca, and had been her mother's favourite toy before she had passed it on. Some of his fur was on the threadbare side and an eye had gone missing years before, so her mother had fashioned a black eye patch. That and his floppy ear gave him a slightly rakish look.

She clicked off the light, sank under the duvet and lay on her back with her eyes open, Teddy Edward resting in the crook of her arm. Light filtering through the curtains from the street outside left a soft glow on the ceiling. She would not hear the cry in the night again. Not that night anyway. She wondered if that cry would ever fully still, if the child would ever find peace.

She rolled over, clutched Teddy Edward tightly to her body and tried to remember the time before she had learned that life was loss.

14

The past is present, the present is past. What went before lives on.

Footsteps.

The child still hears the footsteps. Like heartbeats. Slow. Steady. Inexorable. Growing louder as they reach the door to the room, where they pause. Always that pause, as if he is debating with himself whether to come in, whether to do what he came up the stairs to do. But always the pause ends and the lock clicks and the door swings and there he is, framed in the light from the hallway outside.

Breathing.

The child remembers his breathing. Harsh after the climb up to the room. He is not a fit man, after all. He stands there, the rasp in his throat reaching across the small room like a calloused caress. Always the same routine, like a ritual. The pause outside before the door is unlocked, a similar pause before he enters the room. The child wonders if it is hesitation. The child wonders if it is conscience. The child wonders these things now but dismisses them. It is just another part of the torment, another way of inflicting pain. Another show of power. He has it all, those pauses tell the child. He can stand there and look or he can come in and touch. It is his choice. What the child wants is not a factor to be considered.

Decisions.

Sometimes he looms there, occupying a curious netherworld, neither in nor out of the room, his coarse breath the only sound. Sometimes he steps back and locks the door once more and the child listens as his footsteps recede again.

Another show of power. He can do what he wants and there is nothing on earth that can stop him.

Tears.

No matter what he does, the tears come. Tears of relief when he leaves, tears of pain when he doesn't. The latter are more common. When he comes into the room and closes the door and steps over to the bed. Agonised tears, angry tears, shameful tears ripped from the child during and after.

The child has not shed a tear since the night he died.

15

The room was fairly large but it looked much smaller thanks to the number of people crammed into it. The table at the far end was set with two chairs and two microphones but was conspicuously absent of the guests of honour. The rows of seats facing that table were filled with representatives of Her Majesty's Press. Rebecca spotted Lola McLeod, the BBC reporter from the day before, and Stan, her cameraman, but there was also a well-groomed man from STV and a crew from Channel 4, plus a scribble of reporters and a click of photographers from dailies and rival weeklies, as well as radio and agencies. Elspeth was there and she waved her pencil at Rebecca as she entered.

News of the murder was out, thanks to the BBC and Rebecca's own story, and it was big news. New Dawn's mail order terror had turned out to be a damp squib – what was feared to be anthrax was an innocuous powder – although an arson attack overnight on a mosque near Glasgow had shown that they were capable of real harm. One man suffered severe burns while others were injured. They had commited similar acts before, including in the north, and Rebecca thought it was time the authorities started taking them seriously.

A body found on the site of an historic battlefield was certainly high profile enough that Rebecca didn't have to fight to get out of the office. Les didn't even look at Barry to gauge his views before he told her to cover the Police Scotland press conference at their Inshes HQ. The fact that there was something unusual about it piqued his interest even more, so perhaps there was a newsman under that designer suit and corporate arse-kissing. It appeared the adage 'If it bleeds, it leads' was not lost on him.

The rumble of voices stilled when a door at the far end of the room opened and Terry Hayes, the tall, blonde head of the Police Scotland communications department at Inverness, ushered in Superintendent Harry McIntyre, a powerful figure in his blue uniform. Behind him was another tall, slender figure, a dark-complexioned woman with cropped black hair. That would be DCI Val Roach, Rebecca surmised. She wore a stylish blue suit over a crisp white shirt and she looked as if she really did not want to be there. Rebecca's father had hated press conferences, too. *No working cop likes them, even though they have their uses,* he once told her. *The only ones who relish them see the Job as a means of climbing the ladder rather than putting away the bad guys.*

Roach's face had an elfin quality. It put Rebecca very much in mind of Audrey Hepburn – her mother's habit of watching old movies paying off once again. Her eyes carried a mixture of sadness and toughness, though, that perhaps came from years of seeing things that people should not be in the habit of seeing. Rebecca knew that look from her father's eyes. He was a kind man, a fair man, but as a police officer he had dealt with many things that reasonable people should never really deal with. He had never spoken of them to her, but she had the feeling that look had begun even before he had joined the force. On Stoirm. Her time on the island the year before had led her to discover why John Connolly had fled the island as a teenager and never returned. The revelation had hit her hard. It was decades old but it still resonated. On the island of Stiorm the past never dies. It merely lingers in the air and rests in the stone. And in the secret recesses of her own mind, she knew, that baby crying in the dark of night was not merely an echo of her own past. It was a darkness she shared with her dead father, a family shame that followed her like a shadow.

Rebecca forced her attention on the two police officers as they took their seats. Superintendent McIntyre was ramrod straight in his chair as he stared straight ahead at a fixed point above the heads of the assembled reporters, while DCI Roach leaned forward to rest both arms on the table before her, a thermos mug cradled in both hands. Her sharp, no-nonsense eyes roamed over the faces before her, as if she was searching for someone, but Rebecca could tell she was studying them, filing the faces away. DCI Roach was a sharp cookie, as her mother would say.

Terry Hayes remained standing and cleared her throat. 'Ladies and gentlemen,' she addressed the room, 'thank you for coming. As you're all aware, there has been a very tragic incident at Culloden, but Superintendent McIntyre, Divisional Commander, and Detective Chief Inspector Valerie Roach, who is heading up the inquiry, will bring you up to date.'

She stepped back. Shutters chattered as Superintendent McIntyre leaned into the microphone.

'Ladies and gentlemen, we'll make this as brief as possible. As you'll understand, time is of the essence. At around 7.45 yesterday morning the body of an unidentified white male was found on the moorland at Culloden, part of the National Trust battlefield site. We are treating the death as one of murder. Inquiries are ongoing in the immediate area but we would appeal for anyone who may have been driving along the B9006 during the hours of 9 p.m. on Sunday and 7.45 a.m. on Monday and who may have seen anything – lights on the moorland, a parked vehicle, a vehicle driving slowly or perhaps leaving the driveway that leads to the visitor centre – to please get in touch.'

A pause, taken as an invitation for questions by a young woman with black hair streaked with green sitting at the front. Rebecca had met her before and knew she was fresh out of university and worked for a free newspaper that had sprung up. It was a glorified advertising sheet and as likely as not would vanish as quickly as it appeared, but she was young and keen to make a name for herself. 'Have you got a name for the victim?'

Something that might have been amusement flashed in McIntyre's eyes as he let the stupidity of the question sink in.

'Maybe you should google the word *unidentified*, pet,' said Elspeth.

The young reporter looked suitably ashamed as laughter rippled round the room, but Roach did not join in. 'Inquiries are ongoing as to the victim's identity,' she said, speaking for the first time.

Even though the first question had been ridiculous, Elspeth took it to mean the door had been opened. 'What was the cause of death?' she asked.

Roach glanced at McIntyre, who indicated she had the floor with a small sweep of his hand.

Roach bent towards her microphone once more. 'He had been stabbed.'

'A knife, then?'

Roach paused and studied Rebecca's former boss. Rebecca felt something in that pause, as if the detective was wondering if Elspeth knew something. That made Rebecca wonder if Elspeth actually *did* know something. She had an army of contacts and people trusted her.

'It was an edged weapon,' said Roach, carefully.

'So not a knife, then?'

Superintendent McIntyre leaned forward again. 'We'd rather not expand on the weapon used, Elspeth. You know the score.'

Elspeth nodded her acceptance. She did know the score, as did Rebecca, mostly thanks to her father. But she still sensed something behind Elspeth's question and the fleeting evasion she'd spotted in Roach's eyes. There was something about the weapon. Was that what was unusual? Had one of Elspeth's myriad contacts tipped her off?

Elspeth, however, wasn't finished. 'What about his clothes?'

Roach's face remained impassive, but her eyes bored into the woman facing her. The room was quiet, everyone seemingly sensing something in the air. His clothes, Rebecca wondered. What about his clothes? And why had the very mention of them caused McIntyre's face to contract as if his sphincter had suddenly clenched?

Roach had still not answered when her boss filled the void. 'Yes, Elspeth, he was wearing clothes . . .'

That sent laughter scattering around the rows of seats again. The air cleared. Rebecca saw some of the reporters give each other looks and one or two heads darted in Elspeth's direction. The old dear's lost it, those looks said, but Elspeth had lost nothing. She knew something.

Elspeth wasn't completely satisfied. 'So, nothing to tell us about the clothes the man was wearing when he was found?'

McIntyre's face remained tight. First the suggestion about the weapon and now this. Rebecca would bet all £210.47 she had in her current account that he was wondering who the hell had been talking.

It was Roach who bit the bullet. She glanced once at her superior, then looked directly at Elspeth again. 'As I said, inquiries are ongoing and we're not in a position to release many details at present.'

'And there was nothing on the clothes to help identify the victim?'

A pause. 'No.'

'No tags, no labels, nothing in the pockets?'

Another pause, another long look from both police officers. 'Nothing that assists us.'

Elspeth nodded as if she was finally satisfied and jotted down the answer in her notebook. Rebecca almost smiled. Whatever Elspeth knew, they had somehow confirmed it.

Rebecca decided it was time she made her presence felt. Recalling the conversation with Alan the previous evening, she asked, 'Are you able to tell us if the victim was murdered at the scene?'

Roach's scrutiny left Elspeth and switched to her. 'We believe he was murdered at the scene.'

Lola McLeod piped up. 'How close are you to making an ID?'

'As I said, inquiries are ongoing but the media can assist us.'

Terry Hayes saw this as a cue. 'An image of the victim's face will be issued directly to newsdesks as soon as we have it and will also be made available on the Police Scotland website and Facebook page, and we would appreciate it if it could be circulated as broadly as possible via traditional media and social media. If you have any trouble accessing it, get in touch with my office. It is vital that we identify this man, if only so relatives can be informed as soon as possible.'

There was a brief lull before Roach felt she had something more to say. 'Can I emphasise that this is not simply a story. This man was real. He had a life and it is likely he had a family, friends, relationships. They have all been taken away from him. It is our job to find whoever did that. It is your job to help us do it, as much as you can, and not engage in any wild conjecture that could jeopardise any future conviction.' Her eyes had been roaming across the press pack, but came to rest briefly on Elspeth. 'Please remember that. Thank you.'

Roach picked up her thermos mug and stood, but McIntyre remained seated for a second, studying Elspeth. Terry Hayes lingered behind him until he rose and they followed Roach from the room. Rebecca pushed her way through the reporters filing out to reach Elspeth, but before she could say anything she was silenced by a raised finger.

'Not here,' Elspeth said, and motioned for Rebecca to follow her away from prying ears. Of the many things that a reporter can dread, being scooped is near the top, and Elspeth did not want anyone to listen into her conversation. They may have dismissed her as a daft old bag past her prime, but Rebecca knew better. McIntyre knew it, too, and Rebecca assumed that was what that last appraising look was about. She had something.

In the hallway outside the briefing room, Elspeth looked around her to ensure no one was within earshot. None of the reporters, photographers or camera people filing out of the room paid them the slightest bit of attention. As a couple of uniforms herded the media towards the lift at the far end of the corridor, Lola McLeod shot them a look, wondering why they were hanging back, but Elspeth ignored her as she rested both hands on her walking stick. 'What have you heard about this?' she asked Rebecca.

'Only that it was somehow unusual.'

Elspeth nodded her confirmation. 'If what I've heard is gen up, unusual is the word, right enough. Bloody strange is another way to describe it.'

She did know something, that much was clear. 'So what have you heard?'

With another furtive glance at the police officer, who was now giving them a pointed stare, Elspeth edged in closer. 'Not here. Outside.'

And she was off, her stick clicking on the floor tiles as she headed for the lift, where an impatient-looking constable waited for them. Rebecca was about to follow when Terry Hayes emerged from the briefing room and clattered past her on her high heels, making a beeline for Elspeth. Rebecca picked up her pace. Hayes said something to the uniformed cop, and he nodded and walked away. She reached them just in time to hear the comms chief ask Elspeth what that was all about.

Elspeth's face was the very picture of innocence. 'What was what about, Terry?'

Hayes gave Rebecca a look, as if warning her off, but Elspeth said, 'That's all right. Rebecca and I are working together. She knows everything I know.'

Rebecca knew absolutely nothing but hoped her expression didn't reveal that.

Hayes seemed satisfied and turned back to Elspeth. 'And what is it you know?'

'I know a lot of things, Terry.' Elspeth was clearly enjoying this. 'So unless you want me to talk you through the intricacies of *Grand Theft Auto* or discuss the socio-political nature of the last days of the Roman Empire, maybe you should be more specific. And make it quick because I've not had a fag in almost an hour and my body is crying out for nicotine.'

A smile twitched at the corners of Hayes' mouth. 'Elspeth, don't play silly buggers here. You know what I'm talking about. Those were pretty pointed questions in there. I've known you for years. I know when you know something.'

Elspeth conceded that and dropped the act. 'I know about the clothes.'

'What about the clothes?'

'I know they were straight out of *Outlander*.'

Rebecca digested that, tried not to blink in surprise. *Outlander*? Was the dead man dressed as a Highlander?

Hayes took a moment, too. 'And the weapon?'

'What about the weapon?'

'Elspeth . . .' Exasperation had crept into Hayes' voice. 'Give me a break here, okay? I'm trying to do my job.'

'So am I.'

'The two aren't necessarily incompatible.'

'Oh, Terry – we both know that sometimes that's just not true. Your job is to control the flow of information. Mine is to root it out and let it run free.'

'That's not always in the best interests of justice, Elspeth, and you know it.'

'I do know that. But the police don't always work in the best interests of justice, either.'

'Not in this case. We can't have the information about the clothes getting out there just yet. Similarly, what you know about the weapon. So help me out here and maybe I can help you. What *do* you know about the weapon?'

Elspeth sighed. 'I'm told it was a claymore.'

The thinning of Hayes' lips told Rebecca this was true. A man in Highland dress had been killed with a claymore on Culloden. Sawyer had been right – this was weird. And one hell of a story.

'Who told you?' Hayes asked.

Elspeth smiled. 'You know better than to ask that, Terry. You've been on my side of conversations like this often enough.'

Hayes raised her head slightly. Rebecca usually dealt with communications officers lower down the pay scale, so she'd had limited contact with Terry Hayes, but she knew the woman had been a high-flyer in the tabloids before she had given it all up and taken the Queen's shilling in Police Scotland's corporate comms.

'I have to ask you not to run it,' she said.

'You can always ask.'

'We won't confirm it.'

'You just have, by saying that.'

Hayes sighed. 'If you run it, you'll never get anything more out of my office.'

Elspeth laughed. 'Terry, don't threaten me. If you were me, before you were seduced by the dark side of PR, would that work?'

'I would have considered the wider implications . . .'

'Bollocks! You pulled some strokes back then and didn't think twice. And you were good too, could've taught me a thing or two. But now you're in corporate comms you think your poop don't pong.'

Hayes clenched her jaw. 'We all change, Elspeth. The world changed. Our world changed, you must have noticed it. This is what I do now and, despite what you might think, I do it well. You say I was seduced by the dark side and there was a time when I would have agreed with you. But here I am, trying to do the best I can, just like the people trying to find whoever did this. What we don't need is you running something that really can't be out there right now. I'm asking you, as a colleague – as a friend, for God's sake – don't run this.'

Elspeth stared up at the woman. Rebecca couldn't tell if she was annoyed at the outburst. Then amusement grew in her eyes. 'I really pissed you off with that dark side thing, eh, Terry?'

Despite herself, Hayes also began to smile. 'A little bit.'

Elspeth looked down at the floor. 'You really don't want us to run with this?'

'I really don't. Not yet.'

'But it will be released at some point, right?'

'At some point, probably.'

'I'd say definitely.'

Hayes shrugged, conceding that.

Elspeth's lips pursed as she considered her position. 'If someone else asks about it, you'll give me a heads-up?'

'Yes. Absolutely.'

'And when you do release it, we'll get a heads-up on that, too? Ahead of time?'

'Of course.'

Elspeth looked back at her old friend. 'You know we're still going to root around, don't you? This has got book deal, podcasts, telly docs written all over it.'

'I wouldn't expect anything less. But if you find anything I'd hope you'd bring it to DCI Roach.'

'Find anything like what?'

'Elspeth, I know you. I know you have more contacts than bloody Specsavers. And those contacts have contacts. And lots of them owe you favours. If anyone other than the investigating team is likely to find anything, it's you.'

'Terry, I don't work for Police Scotland.'

'And in return,' Hayes went on, as if it was the continuation of her previous sentence, 'I'll see what I can do towards giving you both some special treatment. Off the record, of course. Can't be seen to be playing favourites.'

Elspeth mulled this over, her cane tapping lightly on the floor tiles. 'Okay, Terry – deal. I'll sit on this, for now. But you tell me at least twenty-four hours before it's made public and also let me know if one of those other buggers stumbles over it. Although most of them can't find their own keyboard without a press release telling them where it is.'

'I told you I would. Thanks, Elspeth. This will make you friends here.'

Elspeth grimaced. 'Aye, that makes me feel all warm and cosy.'

Hayes laughed and, with a nod to Rebecca, walked away in a cloud of perfume probably so expensive that even breathing it in dented her bank balance. Rebecca was about to ask Elspeth a question, but the woman merely shook her head to silence her and flicked her cane towards the lift. They left the building without another word.

Elspeth said nothing as they made their way through the main foyer of the headquarters and exited the glass frontage. She was still silent as they crossed the driveway into the open car park, every space taken. Rebecca spotted Elspeth's battered old Volvo up ahead. Rebecca had been forced to park even further away, outside a bingo hall, so at least they were heading in the right direction. She looked back at the glass-and-brick frontage of the building, at the blue flash of Police Scotland embedded beside the glass door, judged they were well enough away from the building before she said, 'Why me?'

Elspeth stopped at the tailgate of her car, fished her cigarettes out of her coat pocket and fired one up. She took a deep draw, held it for a moment, then ejected smoke from the corner of her mouth to avoid it wafting in Rebecca's face. 'Why you what?'

'Why are you bringing me into this?' Rebecca said. 'You could easily do it yourself. You've done it before.'

Elspeth looked beyond Rebecca to stare at the doors to the police station for a moment and sucked on her cigarette again. 'As Napoleon said after invading Russia, it seemed like a good idea at the time. My gut tells me this is going to be one belter of a story. I told Terry it has book deal all over it and I meant it, but I can't handle it alone.' She waved her cane between them. 'I need someone to do the legwork, someone I can trust. Also, I know you, Rebecca, you're like me. You want the story but you've not lost your human-ity, not yet anyway. And you're good. I saw that when I hired you, or felt it. That stunt you pulled last year, on Stoirm? That showed me you won't stop until you learn everything you can. The fact that you didn't print everything tells me you still care.'

'How do you know I didn't print everything?'

Elspeth gripped the cigarette between her teeth. 'I didn't, until now.'

'So, what's the next step?'

Elspeth fumbled in her bag for her car keys. 'We find out where the clothes and the sword came from.'

'How do we do that?'

The cigarette was fished out from between her teeth. 'That's your first job. Time to work for your keep.'

Elspeth edged to the driver's door and unlocked it. Rebecca mulled the problem over. Then something else occurred to her. 'Didn't Napoleon get a gubbing in Russia?'

A cloud of smoke rose into the chilly spring air to be caught by the watery sun. 'Don't bloody remind me . . .'

16

Rebecca was sipping a coffee and nibbling on an Egg McMuffin as Bill Sawyer pushed through the doors. He was right on time, as usual. She had worried that she might be late but had made it with minutes to spare, which allowed her to order their food. Sawyer was limping but he had shunned the use of a cane, which brought Chaz to mind. The younger man made a hitch in his gait look mysterious; Bill, on the other hand, adopted the look of an otherwise fit older man with a sore leg. Then she thought of Elspeth. What the hell was it with people and limps in her life – some kind of metaphor she was missing?

He dropped into the seat opposite and said, 'You sure know how to show a guy a good time.' He pointed at the brown bag in the centre of the table. 'Mine, I take it?'

She nodded and he opened the bag to peer inside. He disliked the McMuffin and had told her to order him a cheeseburger, which seemed a somewhat unusual choice for eleven in the morning, but hers was not to reason why. Bill squinted at her over the open bag. 'No pickle, I hope.'

Rebecca had forgotten to ask for that. 'You can peel it off.'

He grimaced in distaste. 'I get mustard and sauce all over my fingers.'

'Man up,' she said, smiling.

He made a show of opening his burger to find the green slivers, removing them with his fingertips and dropping them into the bag. 'Don't see the attraction of those things.' He took a bite, chewed, swallowed and waved the bun as he said, 'So, why the big payoff? I didn't give you anything. What do you want, Becks?'

'Can't a girl invite a friend out for a bite of breakfast without there having to be an ulterior motive?'

'Yes, a girl can. But not you. What do you want?'

He knew her too well. She lowered her voice. 'I want to ask you about the Burke family.'

'Ah, fine upstanding pillars of our community. What's your interest?'

She told him about the campaign they were spearheading, then asked, 'You ever have dealings with them when you were on the Job?'

'Tony originally. He's local and been a tearaway since he was a teenager. I lifted him a couple of times myself. Mo is from Glasgow, but you'll know that, right? He met her when he was down there doing some work for the McClymont family, Big Joe and his boy. That was when they were pals.' He took another bite. 'Not so much now.'

'What about Mo?'

He gathered his thoughts while he chewed. 'Her father was a straight arrow, from what I heard, but he dropped out of the marriage when she was about ten, set himself up with another woman and never took any interest in the wee girl. Her mum was a bit wayward, bit of a lass, if you know what I mean, and she had a succession of boyfriends. Mo, though, is nothing like her. She's a one-guy gal. Since she took up with Tony there's never been anyone else. Love being a many splendoured thing.'

Rebecca was tempted to ask him if he thought, or had heard talk, that Mo had been sexually abused, but how would he know? If it had happened, it would have been when she was a young girl in Glasgow. Apart from that, mentioning it seemed like a breach of confidence. She wasn't sure whose, whether it was Mo or Simon. She sighed inwardly. *Life is complicated.*

'What about the boys?' she asked.

'Nolan and Scott? They didn't have a chance from the start, not with parents like that.'

'Even Mo? I thought she came from a decent family?'

'I said her dad was a straight arrow, if a bastard who shirked his responsibilities, but her mum was a randy cow who thought more of a good shag than she did her lassie. And even if Mo was straight, she married Tony and that leads to the whole "lying down with dogs" thing.'

'So have the boys been trouble since they were kids?'

'Not when they were young. No trouble at school. Certainly no trouble at home. Mo wouldn't stand for that. I've got to admit, we never had any shouts to the Burke house for domestics. Some of they type, you're called out because they get drunk or high or just plain pissed off and they start smacking each other around, but not the Burkes. They may be scumbags, but they do seem to care for each other and their kids.'

Rebecca heard her father's voice as Bill spoke. *Villains are people too, Becks. They can love their parents, their kids, their pets. They're people . . . but they're different from you or I.*

'But sooner or later the boys had to revert to type, get into trouble. It's in the genes. It was after they came back from Glasgow that it seemed to kick off.'

She asked, 'Why were they in Glasgow?'

'Tony was doing time for assault, believe it or not, him being such a zen-like soul. Mo had been done for reset. DVD players, as I recall, nicked from a warehouse in Edinburgh. Anyway, the boys were split up to stay with separate relatives of Mo's, including her maw. Scott went to her. She couldn't, maybe wouldn't, take Nolan, so he was palmed off on an auntie. They were away for maybe, what, eighteen months? It was fairly soon after they came back to the happy family home that they went off the rails. Well, Scott did.'

'What happened?'

'The first time I was involved was when there was a claim that he'd tortured a neighbour's cat. I won't go into details but it wasn't pretty. It couldn't be proved, though.'

'Did he do it?'

'Of course he did it. He's a right bad wee bastard. I encountered him a few times after that. His brother, too.'

'What can you tell me about Nolan?'

He laid what was left of his burger down on the greaseproof paper, wiped his mouth on a paper napkin. 'Those two share the same blood but that's about it, as far as I could tell,' Sawyer said. 'Nolan is the oldest by a year, but he is dark, Scott blond, and that seems to be the way of their personalities too. Nolan is quiet, thoughtful; Scott, full of the chat and always smiling. But that smile hides a darker soul. He's unpredictable, is Scott. Nolan has a violent streak too, but it's more focused. It's used strategically, if you like. A means to an end. Scott? He's a bad bastard and he doesn't care who knows it. For him, violence is the end. That's what he lives for. Gets off on it.'

17

There were books on the shelves that lined the walls, books stacked on the floor, books set out on the wide windowsill behind the desk, which was also covered with books, piled on the corners and around the Apple monitor that rose in triumph above them, a metaphor for the perceived supremacy of new technology over old knowledge. Rebecca hazarded a guess that Anna Fowler liked books, which was not a surprise – after all, she headed up the history department at the University of the West Highlands.

If Rebecca ever had a vision of what an historian looked like, it would not have been the woman sitting in front of her: tall and built like someone who worked out, her blonde hair cut short and bobbed around her ears. She wore no make-up and Rebecca imagined her features could be severe if she hadn't such a ready smile. She was dressed in a grey suit and a red shirt, a scream of colour in a room that was a conversation in browns and dust. Behind her was an old-fashioned stand draped with coats, jackets and wet weather gear. Rebecca knew it was always wise to be prepared for whatever Scottish weather has to offer but the jumble of clothing on the stand seemed like overkill.

Rebecca had asked Alan to schedule the chat for around one, which gave her time enough to get back to the office and batter out the story on the press conference, as well as other material. She may not be the best reporter there was, but she could write fast, which was even more of an asset in the industry than it ever had been before. She very seldom took a lunchbreak – a sandwich and some soup from the supermarket at the far end of the retail park eaten at her desk was the norm – but no one could say anything about her leaving the office if she did decide to go out for a break. Thankfully, the university campus was only a ten-minute drive from the office, standing between the Inverness Caledonian Thistle ground and the finger of the Kessock Bridge reaching out across the grey waters of the Moray Firth to the Black Isle.

Barry had been sitting in a vacant seat beside another reporter, leaning back, his legs crossed in front of him, one hand gesturing towards her monitor as he discussed a story point. He gave Rebecca a glance as she stood up from her desk and collected her coat from the rack but said nothing, didn't even break the flow of his own conversation. With an almost imperceptible nod of the head and a tightening of the corners of his mouth, he returned his attention to Yvonne.

Barry knows me too well, Rebecca thought.

Anna Fowler had a very pleasant manner, a warm smile and an easy way of talking that Rebecca guessed would go down well with students. She had welcomed her and offered coffee from a filter machine sitting in the far corner of the room. Rebecca could barely see it behind two stacks of books rising around it. As she poured, Rebecca said, 'I take it you like to read.'

Anna looked back, puzzled at first, then her eyes darted from book pile to book pile. 'I do, but these aren't all mine, I'm afraid. I'm storing them here for a colleague while his office is being decorated. He's a mathematician and that's really not my field. I need a calculator to count my fingers.'

Rebecca laughed as she realised this woman could become a friend. Chaz, Alan and even Bill Sawyer apart, she hadn't made many friends since she had moved to Inverness. And, now that she thought about it, none of them were female. There was Elspeth, of course, but was she a friend? On balance, she'd say yes, but Elspeth wasn't someone she could go out on the piss with, even if Rebecca had enjoyed doing that. She chatted to colleagues at work, but they didn't socialise. Actually, her social life was far from scintillating thanks to her insistence on what she thought was doing her job correctly.

Occasionally, she went out for drinks with the guys, sometimes a film, but more often than not she could be found in her flat, catching up with the work she should have done during the day or watching some old movie. *Thanks, Mum.* She was not by nature solitary; she'd had good friends growing up, close friends with whom she still kept in touch, but they were back in Glasgow. No, this was something she had somehow chosen without knowing.

There had been Simon, of course. She had told him on the phone that she thought of him as a friend, but perhaps he was right, perhaps that wasn't possible. So much water had rushed under that bridge it had damaged the foundations.

Anna brought her the coffee in a mug that said 'Just When You Thought History Was a Thing of the Past', then carried her own around the desk and sat down again. She pushed some books aside so they could see each other better, sipped her coffee and then said, 'So, Alan says you want to know about Culloden?'

Rebecca had taken a mouthful of her own coffee, so she nodded as she swallowed. 'Yes, I do.' She laid her mug down on a clear space on the desk and stooped to find her bag. 'Do you mind if I record this?'

'Not at all,' said Anna. 'As long as you promise not to hold whatever I say against me in a court of law.'

Rebecca fished her recorder out and clicked it on, then set it down on the desk beside her coffee mug. 'I take it you've heard about the body on the moor?'

Anna's eyes, which had sparkled with good humour, shadowed. 'Yes, very sad.'

'It is. But what I need is some background on the battle.'

Interest sparked among the shadows. 'Do you think it's got something to do with the murder?'

Rebecca hesitated. She couldn't mention anything about the costume the dead man was wearing, even though every instinct told her she could trust this woman. 'Well, we don't know. I only thought a bit of background on the historical aspect would be handy. It's an unusual place to dump a body, don't you think?'

Anna sat back in her chair, sipped her coffee, thought about this. 'Perhaps.' Her voice was careful. 'Perhaps not. It is an open stretch of land and not overlooked by any buildings, apart from the visitor centre. It's unlikely anyone would be there after dark and the road isn't overly busy, especially at this time of year. So, unless the person who murdered this man had some special reason to choose the site, it could always be random.'

Rebecca's voice warbled with a slight laugh as she said, 'You've been thinking about this, haven't you?'

Anna smiled. 'Of course I have. Culloden is of special interest to me. If something happens there, I pay attention. So what do you need from me?'

'Well, frankly, I need a kind of pocket guide to the battle. Nothing too in-depth, maybe something for a kind of "Did You Know?" section, to give our readers some historical context.'

Anna set her mug down again. 'How much do you know?'

Rebecca knew very little. 'Treat me as if I'm a complete ignoramus.'

'Ah, I'm used to that.' Anna sat back and stared at the ceiling. As the conversation progressed, Rebecca would come to realise this was something she did when she was gathering her thoughts. 'All right. Let me see. The battle of Culloden, or more accurately Drummossie Moor, took place on the sixteenth of April 1746 and was the final pitched battle of the 1745 Jacobite rising. Most historians will tell you that it was the last battle fought on British soil, but there was a clash in 1820 between a force of Radicals and government troops near Bonnymuir. It wasn't that much of a fight, I suppose, but it's worth remembering. Anyway, Culloden. That was a bloody affair. It lasted a little less than an hour and by its end one and a half thousand clansmen lay dead, but only a hundred government troops. Prince Charles Stuart . . .'

'Bonnie Prince Charlie, right?'

Anna grimaced. 'If you must. He fled the field, even though there is a school of thought that it was his own poor judgement that led to the slaughter of the Highland forces. The cause that had begun so confidently less than a year before, when his standard was raised at Glenfinnan and some of the clans rallied to it, was left hacked to bloody ribbons on that moor.'

'He wanted to regain the throne, didn't he?'

'Yes, he did, for his father. Do you know the history?'

Rebecca felt ashamed. She had paid very little attention to history in school and, like many Scots, knew next to nothing about her own country's past. Her father had taught her a few things, particularly about the Clearances, when landowners had evicted tenants who had lived off the land for centuries to make way for sheep, which were more profitable. Their visit to the battlefield all those years ago had also seeded a few nuggets in her memory.

Anna caught her look of shame and understood. 'Briefly, James the Second – the Seventh of his ilk in Scotland – had to relinquish the British throne in 1688 and William of Orange took over to rule with his wife, Mary, who was James's daughter. Put simply, James was a Roman Catholic but his daughter and her husband were Protestant, and that was far more palatable to the government of the time, not to mention many of the people. Politics and religion were very much synonymous in those days. James died in exile but his son, also James because they didn't have much imagination and tradition had to be observed, was hailed by supporters as the King Over the Water. Those supporters, Jacobites by name, never gave up trying to put what they saw as the rightful king back on the throne. And so, during the eighteenth century there were a number of risings – 1715, 1719 and then 1745.'

'But none after that?'

'No. I think after Culloden and its aftermath, which was savage, there was little appetite for armed rebellion, if I may call it that. But the thing to remember is that, to my mind, the Stuarts were never really that interested in Scotland, not since Mary.'

'Queen of Scots?'

'Yes. She came back with her eyes on the English throne, which she thought was rightfully hers. It's my opinion that she merely wanted to use Scotland as a stepping stone to that. I believe that the Stuart monarchs who followed cared very little for Scotland, unless they needed something. Charles Edward Stuart was the same. He needed an army, the French wouldn't supply one, so he raised one in Scotland. But he was focused on getting his father's backside back on that throne in London. Scotland was merely a means to an end. Not a popular view, but it is my own.'

Rebecca said, 'Isn't that the position that new film is taking? That Bonnie Prince – sorry – Charles Edward Stuart was merely using the Scots?'

'It is, which is why they're using me as an historical advisor. Also, I'm part of a clan battle recreation society which they have found useful in staging the battle itself.'

'That's proved controversial, hasn't it, the production's attitude to Charles, not you being historical advisor?' Rebecca smiled.

'Well, my involvement isn't popular either. Spioraid nan Gàidheal are not my biggest fans, it has to be said. That's reciprocated, though.'

'So, they don't like the film's portrayal of Charles Edward Stuart as – what?'

'Frankly, a drunken, spoiled brat who would perhaps not be so romantic a figure as he is today if he hadn't shown courage and daring while he was escaping Scotland after the slaughter over there on the moor. The film does show that side of him, that his experiences here did have an effect on him and that he did have affection for his Scottish army. But more importantly they don't like the script showing a more human side of the Duke of Cumberland.'

Rebecca dragged one of those nuggets from her memory. 'He commanded the government forces, right? He ordered the slaughter of the wounded.'

'He did, and he also oversaw the quite brutal reprisals that followed. They wanted to dismantle the clan system to ensure that the clans could not rise again. Between that and the Clearances that followed, the traditional Highland way of life was gone for ever. It was a brutal period, certainly, and Cumberland had blood on his hands, but the scriptwriters didn't want to show him just as a monster. He was human, like the rest of us. He was capable of terrible things – most of us are – but we are all still human. So, just as Charles was far from perfect, Cumberland is being shown as far from monstrous. He is, in fact, the conquering hero of the title and I'm told they intend using a piece of music by Handel in the score.'

Rebecca was no classical music buff, but she vaguely remembered reading a story about Handel and his composition celebrating the defeat of the Jacobites at Culloden – maybe that was what the woman was talking about.

'But that's not the only thing Spioraid don't like,' Anna went on, before Rebecca had the chance to ask. 'They don't like an English actor playing Charles – even though he was by birth half Polish and was born on the continent. But, more importantly, they object to the casting of a black actor as one of Charles Stuart's advisors.'

'Was this person black in real life?'

'No. But it's all about diversity, isn't it? It's common – the film a couple of years ago about Mary had a black actor playing the English ambassador. Spioraid can't stomach that and have lashed out publicly and – I think – in secret against the production. They're merely a bunch of bigots in tartan. They may fall short of pulling bedsheets over their heads and burning crosses – an old clan tradition, by the way, usurped by morons – but that doesn't mean they aren't racist arseholes.'

'What do you mean, in secret?'

Anna fell silent for a moment, then sat up again, grasped her mug in both hands and stared at the coffee. 'This can go no further because it's not my place to talk about it. The production company has gone to great lengths not to make these things public.'

Rebecca leaned over towards the desk and thumbed the recorder to OFF. 'Then I'll keep it off the record.'

That seemed to satisfy her. 'Good. There have been – em – incidents on the set and at the production compound. Break-ins. Acts of vandalism. Unexplained fires – nothing major, but still, a fire is a fire. And the actor I mentioned, the black one? He's had to have security with him at all times.'

'He's been threatened?'

'Yes. There is a strong suggestion that Spioraid is responsible. Or their bully boys in New Dawn. I've been threatened, too.'

'In what way?'

'Strange phone calls in the middle of the night. God knows how they found my number. Two letters. Unlike those politicians the other day, no mysterious powder, though. I've alerted the post room here, just in case.'

'Have you told the police?'

'Yes, they know. But what can they do? The production has a very efficient security team now. Donahue Security. But that didn't prevent the most recent incident.'

'Which was?'

Anna paused again and Rebecca could tell she regretted going down this particular path. 'I'm not supposed to know about it. I really shouldn't be talking about it. The police don't even know, because the man in charge doesn't want to risk the publicity. He's the one who insists that news of the vandalism doesn't get out, starving Spioraid of the oxygen of publicity and all that.'

'I promise none of this will be printed, unless at some point it leaks and we have to. All of this is background for now.'

Still Anna hesitated. Then she sighed. 'Ah well, these things do leak out eventually. There was another break-in, a couple of nights ago, at the production compound. It's a bit away from the set. They have built a village for the scenes after the battle and also found a bit of land among the hills to recreate the battle itself. You can't have actors and extras and film crews tramping all over the real site, of course. The compound houses the production offices and also a large warehouse for the costumes, hundreds of them.'

Rebecca felt excitement burn. She knew what was coming next. 'Someone stole a Highlander costume, didn't they?'

Anna's eyes narrowed. 'Yes. How did you know?'

Rebecca regretted blurting out her question. She mentally cursed herself. Elspeth would not have made such a rookie error. 'I'm sorry, I can't tell you.'

The historian scrutinized her from across the desk. 'This has a bearing on the murder, doesn't it?'

Shit, shit, shit. 'I really am sorry, but I can't say anything. I'd appreciate it if you didn't mention . . .'

Anna waved away the suggestion. 'Yes, yes – I won't say a word.'

Rebecca was relieved, although she still berated herself for her stupidity. 'Has this theft been reported to the police?'

'No, I don't think so. John Donahue, the man who owns Donahue Security, is an absolute nut for secrecy. It wouldn't reflect well on him and his company, would it? Security is heightened and yet a bunch of right-wing nutjobs can still get in and steal costumes? Perhaps it should be, though, given our conversation today.'

'But you don't think he will?'

'I doubt it. I can't do it, either. I have signed an agreement with the production company not to talk out of school about anything I see or hear on set. If I broke that, it would reflect badly not just on me but the university.'

'Yet you've spoken to me about the problems.'

'I have indeed.' Her eyes probed. 'Journalists still protect sources, don't they?'

Rebecca understood. Anna could not report the matter herself but she could. The subject of confidentiality regarding journalistic sources was complex, but Rebecca didn't think the police would press for a name.

Then something else occurred to her. 'You said "costumes", plural. So there was more than one taken?'

Anna took a breath. Rebecca waited.

'There was another costume taken that night,' Anna said. 'That of a government soldier.'

18

It is his smell the child remembers most. It is not overpowering and is only apparent when he is close. On those occasions when he doesn't merely return back down the stairs.

It isn't body odour, it is a musk that is perhaps peculiar to him. A mixture of sweat and food and cigarette smoke. And bitterness and rage and all the disappointment of his life. And then he locks the door again and returns to family life below, taking his desires and his musk with him.

The child hears him sometimes, fighting with her. The child seldom sees the woman, can barely remember the name of the man's wife now, thinks of her only as her. *The child hates the man but despises* her.

Because she knows.

The woman knows what is happening on the floor above and she does nothing. When her husband leaves her to head upstairs, is anything said? She has to know what he is going upstairs to do and she does nothing.

Nothing.

Women aren't like that, the child has always believed. Women are sensitive and caring and nurturing.

Not that woman. Not her.

She is as bad as her husband. Maybe worse, because she does nothing.

And then there is the son. The child sees him now and again, passing by the doorway as his father lingers. A thin, sallow-faced boy, his eyes haunted and shadowed with pain. When they speak, at breakfast, at meals, nothing is said of consequence between them. The child wonders if he suffers too, if some-

times the father turns his attentions towards him. Or is the look in those dark eyes something else? Is it guilt? Does the son feel a remorse the father never did?

But the father does feel something, the child knows that, even if he does not know it himself. The day after every visit he brings a new toy. Or a book. Or a video to watch on the little TV in the corner. And he is a different man on those days. He strokes the child's hair and he smiles. Nothing is mentioned of the other visits, the less pleasant ones with the pain and the tears. Sometimes he watches the video with the child, sitting on the little single bed together, the child cradled in the crook of his arm, head against his shoulder, breathing in that warm musky odour and wondering why every day couldn't be like that.

But whatever it is the man feels on those occasion, it is not powerful enough to stop him coming back.

The footsteps on the stairs.

The pause.

The unlocking of the door.

The hesitation.

The breathing.

The smell of him as he draws closer.

There is a lot of guilt in that house. The father. Perhaps the son. And her? Does she feel guilt? Is that why sometimes quiet sobs creep down the hallway in the night to lurk in corners like secrets? Are those tears all that remain of what had once been her compassion?

The child wonders these things, alone in that room, with only the toys and the little TV and the sounds of the rain pattering against the opaque window for company.

19

The hands-free device clipped to the visor wasn't top of the range – at a tenner from a petrol station it was never going to be – but it was good enough for Rebecca's needs. She still had to physically accept calls, which involved that tricky thumb sliding technique on the phone screen that she detested, and terminate them, which was a much simpler punch of a red button, but at least she didn't need to hold the phone to talk. She knew all the restrictions about using phones while driving but it was no worse than chatting to someone in the car. At least, that's how she justified it.

'So, do you think this Fowler woman told you that about the costume purposely? I mean, she knew she was telling you?' Elspeth's voice crackled from the cheap speaker. A light rain dribbled across the windscreen and the wipers scraped across the glass. Rebecca was on the A9, heading back to the office, aware that she was already ten minutes over her allotted hour. Barry would not have bothered unduly about something like that, unless it became a habit, but the project manager was an unknown quantity. He might want to flex his authoritarian muscles.

'Well, I didn't drug her or waterboard her, Elspeth.'

'You know what I mean. She told you for a reason?'

'Yes, I think she wants me to report it to the police. She doesn't want to breach her agreement with the production company by going directly to the law with it.'

'She's breached that already by telling you.'

'Yes, but there are degrees, I suppose. Going to the law is official. Telling me, knowing I won't give up a source, is an indirect way of doing it. So what do you think?'

The line fell silent, or as silent as her cheap kit allowed. The shower had passed and the wipers groaned a little against the glass, so Rebecca flicked them off. 'I think we pass it on,' Elspeth said. 'I said we would and it would show good faith. We can't use the clothes angle yet anyway.'

'So shall I contact them or will you?'

'No, let's give your source a further degree of separation. I'll do it. I'll phone Roach direct.'

In her heart she knew that Elspeth feared she might crumble under police pressure to reveal her source, but she was relieved to be spared talking to DCI Roach. The detective looked shrewd and tough, and Rebecca was not sure herself she wouldn't crack. She hoped she would never be put to the test.

Rebecca asked, 'You think we should check with the production company ourselves?'

'Might be worth a call, just to keep them on their toes. But let's leave it for a day, let the police make their inquiries. That way we further protect your source because, if the cops move on it right away, then the company might think the leak came from them. Let's keep your Professor Fowler on-side. It never hurts to have an expert on our team. And I've a feeling about this story. It's all about the past.'

20

Val Roach knew John Donahue by reputation only. As a former detective chief superintendent in Glasgow his foul temper was legendary. It was said he had the ability to make grown men cry. And these were men who had faced down hardened Glasgow thugs with nothing more than a baton and a few choice phrases. By rights, this trip should have been made by a couple of detective constables, but Edward Moore, the young officer detailed to contact Donahue, who now ran security for the film production company, had been given short shrift. Donahue was too busy, DC Moore had been told. He didn't see why a murder more than seventy miles away had anything to do with him. And then, just to emphasise it, Moore was told once again that Donahue was busy and the phone was put down.

When the information regarding the stolen costumes was passed along, Roach called the man herself, but he didn't answer. She tried three times but no one picked up. That was when she shouted to 'Yul' Bremner that she was taking a field trip, that he should hold the fort, and told young Edward he was behind the wheel.

To be truthful, she was grateful that Donohue had proved to be prickly and uncooperative because she didn't like being stuck in the office. She knew the donkey work should be carried out by other members of the team, but she hated paperwork, hated sitting behind a desk, hated the bureaucratic nuts and bolts of any investigation. She could do them well, and better than most, but what she really enjoyed was being out and talking to people. Donahue had given her the ideal excuse, even though the trip down the

Great Glen from Inverness to Fort William would take up the entire afternoon. However, if the McTaggart woman's tip proved to be genuine, confirming that the clothes had come from the film set could be some sort of breakthrough. After all, they had bugger all else. It had crossed Roach's mind that the Highlander gear might have originated there, but with no report of a theft it didn't seem that vital. Now, though, a visit from a senior officer was just what was needed.

At least, that's how she justified it to herself. Her boss might see it differently, but she'd cross that bridge once she'd burned it.

It had turned out to be a reasonably decent day, for March at any rate. It wasn't raining now, which in Scotland is always a blessing, and the sun was doing its best to break through the slate-coloured cloud cover. Edward Moore wasn't the talkative sort, which she appreciated, so she was able to consider the case as they weaved down the north-western side of Loch Ness. Thinking time, that's what she liked. And there was lots to think about here. An unidentified male, the post-mortem showing he'd been pumped with heroin, although no sign he was a user. A Highland costume. And the sword sticking out of him like it was waiting for King Arthur.

Mysteries, mysteries . . . Too many mysteries.

A day after the inquiry kicked off, she still had no idea who the dead man was. It was too early for any DNA to hit – that's if his genetic material was on the register – and his fingerprints did not appear to be on file.

DS Bremner had attended the PM, which was a relief because she also hated observing the 'dice and slice' side of a murder investigation. It wasn't that she couldn't stand the sight of blood – she had grown used to that – but it was all so clinical. The impeccably clean room itself; the gleaming instruments; the smell of disinfectant; the calm, measured voice of the pathologist as they dissected, removed, weighed, measured and described wounds, contusions, lacerations, organs. It was all so impersonal. She knew such detachment was necessary, she knew to do her job she also had to remain objective, but the post-mortem suite was too much for her.

As her thoughts wondered, it occurred to her that between being desk-bound, doing paperwork, dealing with the press and observing post-mortems, there really wasn't much about policework she liked now. Rank did bring its privileges, but it also had its drawbacks.

She looked through the passenger window at Loch Ness as it flitted past, the faint sunlight stroking the deep waters and winking at her between the trees and bushes like a coy lover. Years ago, she and Joe, her then soon-to-be husband, had camped on the banks of the loch near Urquhart Castle. It was a small, two-person tent and it let in water when it rained. And rain it did, of course. But they were young and they were happy and they laughed as it seeped through the canvas. She smiled as she remembered this. She always smiled when she remembered those years with her husband. At least that version of him.

When she was left alone the year before, she had considered putting in her papers, such was her dissatisfaction with the Job. She had even gone to the length of typing up her resignation. But then she had baulked at actually handing it in. It had suddenly occurred to her that, if she didn't have her job, she would struggle to find something to do with her time.

The truth was, all the negatives apart, she liked being a police officer. She liked bringing the bad guy down. She liked providing victims and their families with a measure of closure. She liked being in a position to help people.

But a change was necessary. Instead of packing it all in, she requested a transfer. The Perth house harboured too many memories. Too many rooms haunted by whispers of the past and echoes of what had once been. She didn't sell – it had been Joe's home, hers and his. She couldn't part with it. So she rented it out to a decent family because she liked the idea of children's laughter bouncing from the walls. They had never had children and that was what the house needed. It needed laughter. It needed life. God knows there had been little of that in the months before she'd moved out.

But she couldn't think of that now. It had been a dark and terrible period in her life, but it was in the past. That was where it had to stay.

DC Moore was a fast but skilful driver and he had them at their destination in under two hours. A makeshift gate had been erected across the small single-track road leading to the site the film production company had chosen for their headquarters. Val had watched a lengthy news report on BBC Scotland about the Hollywood invasion and knew the bulk of the filming was being done in the glen. Culloden itself was an otherwise unremarkable stretch of heathery moor, and the director wanted a more Highland feel for his re-enactment of the battle and that meant mountains. Sure, at the real site, on a clear day, you could see across the Moray Firth to the peaks of Easter Ross, but he wanted the 'true' Highland experience for movie-goers. That was one of the reasons the production was being criticised: that 'true' Highland experience not being true to the real experience of the combatants in 1746. But hey, Mel Gibson didn't want a bridge at the Battle of Stirling Bridge.

Roach had called an old friend in Glasgow about the company's founder. John Donahue had set up the security company after he had retired from the force and swiftly turned it into the go-to firm for the entertainment industry. If you needed guards or bouncers, or close personal protection for your talent, they were the team for you.

They showed their warrant cards to the security guard sporting the company logo, a shield and crossed swords, on the shoulders and left breast of the dark grey uniform top. The guard stepped away and breathed a few words into a radio before he leaned back through the window on DC Moore's side. 'Sorry, Mr Donahue is tied up at the moment and can't see you. He says if you could make an appointment he'd—'

Roach said nothing as she climbed out of the car, moved to the gate and put her hand on the bolt. The guard darted to her side.

'Ma'am, you can't go in there, it's restricted.'

She looked him up and down. 'You an ex cop?'

'No, army.'

'Then you understand chain of command?'

'Yes, ma'am, and that's why I can't—'

'Let me explain something to you.' She kept her voice reasonable. 'You saw my warrant card, you know my rank. Right now, that supersedes anyone else.'

'Mr Donahue—'

'Mr Donahue is a civilian and I'm heading up a major inquiry, which you are currently impeding. Now, we either open this gate or we drive through it.' She jerked a finger over her shoulder to the car. 'That's a company vehicle and fully insured, so it makes no difference to me. Now, which will it be?'

Her tone had not modulated – she might have been ordering a pizza – but her words carried weight. The guard swithered for a few moments, trying to decide if she was bluffing, then reached out and unclasped the bolt to let the gate swing open.

'Wise choice. You'll go far.'

Roach walked back to the car, where Moore was sporting a wide grin. As he nosed the vehicle through the open gate, he said, 'You enjoyed that, didn't you, ma'am?'

She couldn't conceal her own smile. 'Oh yeah,' she said. 'But that was just the opening bout. The main event is coming up.'

The narrow road snaked through some tall pine trees to an open stretch of ground surrounded by hills. They had created quite a complex, even though the buildings were prefabs and the trailers could be towed away at any time. Another fence surrounded the entire area and Roach saw further guards in uniform. These guards were accompanied by powerful dogs and they patrolled the perimeter in a regimented fashion.

'Jeez,' said Moore as they edged along the road to the next gate, 'all it needs is a couple of guard towers and we've got Stalag bloody Thirteen.'

The gate to the complex proper was a more substantial affair and any threat she might make to demolish it with the police-issue vehicle would be an empty one. She had no doubt that the first guard would have been on his radio again as soon as they drove through, and she hoped Donahue would be so outraged by her impertinence that he'd come out to deal with her himself. She felt a twinge of guilt at the position in which she'd placed the guard, but it couldn't be helped.

A tall man with the build of a WWE wrestler wedged into a dark blue suit, white collar and pale blue tie waited for them at the gate. He had his radio clasped in both hands in front of him as if it was a golf club and he was about to swing angry. Roach liked to play a round or two when she could and she knew you should never do that. You might think it gave you an edge, but in reality it handed one to your opponent. The man watched them approach with barely concealed rage. He didn't even wait until they had slowed to a halt before he strode to the passenger side and glared in at her.

'What kind of game are you playing?' He had a harsh voice, one that was used to giving orders and having them obeyed. His hair was like grey iron, his broad face like frozen steel. He was a plain man but his temperament and sense of self-importance made him downright ugly.

'I'm Detective Chief Inspector Valerie Roach,' she said, her voice as smooth as his was rough. 'This is Detective Constable Edward Moore. You are John Donahue, I take it?'

'Yes – and I asked what you think you're playing at?'

'I'm conducting inquiries, Mr Donahue, and you can assist us.'

'Yes, so your lad here said earlier, but I haven't the time right now.'

'I suggest you make the time.'

He stepped back and something like a smile played with his lips. It didn't make him look any more good-humoured. 'Do you, now? Do you really?'

She gave him a full grin in return. 'Yes, I do,' she said. 'Really. I'm conducting a murder inquiry. Now, we can do it here or you can take a wee trip back to Inverness with us. But either way, Mr Donahue, you're going to talk to us.'

He seemed to pull himself erect. She knew what he was going to say before the words left his mouth. 'Listen, dear, do you know who I am?'

She almost laughed. Who he was, or once was, mattered little to her. People like Donahue were all the same. He was a man who had spent his career giving orders and expecting them to be followed, but he was a civilian now and, whether he liked it or not, she gave the orders. 'Yes, I do, sir. But you're still going to talk to me, one way or the other.'

He took out a mobile phone. It looked expensive. Hers was bought in Tesco. 'Who's your boss over there?'

'Superintendent Harry McIntyre,' she said. 'He says hello, by the way.'

Donahue's finger was poised to punch in the number. In his line of business, she presumed, he would have local law on speed dial. 'He knows you're here, then?'

Superintendent McIntyre actually did not know she was there and when he found out he would be far from pleased, but she'd started this particular bluff and, like the one earlier with the car, she had to play it out. The game had changed from golf to poker and she was about to raise the stakes. 'Of course.' She nodded to the phone. 'Go ahead, ask him if you want.'

For a moment she thought she'd fooled him, but he called her bluff and stabbed at the screen with his forefinger, then put the phone to his ear. He watched her closely while he waited for an answer, no doubt hoping to spot a look of concern. Then he said, 'Put me onto Superintendent McIntyre.' His gaze didn't waver as he added, 'This is DCS Donahue. He knows me.' She knew he was waiting for her to say something, to concede her lie, but she was damned if she would give him that satisfaction. She smiled sweetly at him, outwardly calm but inwardly wishing she hadn't overplayed her hand. Any advantage his anger had given her would be moot as soon as he got through to the boss and he would take the pot. But people like him just annoyed her.

Donahue flicked the call to loudspeaker and held the phone out between them so she could hear both sides of the conversation.

'John Donahue!' McIntyre's voice was loud and clear. That was a really good phone. 'Now there's a name from the past.'

'Harry,' said Donahue, 'long time, mate.' His voice was different now. He was talking to another bloke and one of matching stature to himself. All pals together. Brothers in arms. 'Listen, I'll get right to it, if you don't mind. Got a lot going on over here. I've got one of your people here, Roach, a DCI?'

There was a pause on the line. Roach kept her face blank but inwardly she was saying *oh shit, oh shit, oh shit*.

Then McIntyre said, 'That's right. She's heading up a murder inquiry and you can help us out, if you'd be so kind.'

She struggled to keep the relief from reflecting on her face. Glorying in the shock that splashed on Donahue's face, she mentally raked in the chips.

'Harry, I-I . . .' Donahue stammered. Roach would bet her pension it wasn't something he did often. 'Look, mate, I'm really up to my eyes in it. Can't this wait?'

'John, come on. You know the drill. First forty-eight hours and all that? DCI Roach has some questions and you really need to answer them. Okay?' McIntyre paused before he added, 'Mate?' The slight emphasis on the final word suggested to Roach that these men were far from mates. Which might explain why her boss had covered for her. 'Let me have a word with my DCI,' McIntyre said, and a clearly annoyed Donahue handed the phone over.

Roach made sure she took it off loudspeaker before she put it to her ear. 'Sir.'

'DCI Roach, you're lucky I bumped into DS Bremner so I knew you were off on a jolly.'

Roach knew Donahue was watching her closely, so she smiled and said, 'Hardly, sir.'

'Making initial inquiries is not your job, DCI Roach, and you bloody well know that. Your place is in the incident room directing operations, not gallivanting around the countryside.'

'Yes, sir.'

'Had you been here, you would know we have trouble. That BBC reporter, Lola whatsername, has got wind of the clothes.'

Bugger, Roach thought, that didn't take long. She knew it would happen sooner or later but she'd hoped they would keep the lid on a bit longer.

'The ball is up on the slates now,' McIntyre continued, 'and it's only a matter of time before the connection is made to the film people. We've had to let Elspeth McTaggart know, so she'll be feeding it to her clients. That Connolly girl's involvement means the local rag will be running it, too. As you know, I'd love the power to impose a media blackout on any info that doesn't come through official channels, but we live in an imperfect world. You'd better warn Donahue that he can expect an invasion of media people. Wrap it up there soonest and get back here.'

'Yes, sir.'

There was a pause during which all she could hear was her boss's breathing. 'You'd better make this trip count for something.'

'Yes, sir.'

The connection was cut and Roach was left holding a dead phone to her ear. She felt strangely stupid for a moment, then she handed it back to Donahue. *You'd better make this trip count for something,* McIntyre had said. It was time to take control of this interview.

'So, Mr Donahue.'

'You can call me sir,' he snapped.

She ignored him. 'You want to tell me about the missing costumes?'

His look of shock told her that the information was accurate.

21

There was no reason for Rebecca to notice the black Mercedes 4x4 in the car park. There were other businesses in the various offices nearby – it wasn't called a business park for nothing – so the Mercedes could have belonged to anyone. Apart from that, it had been a long day and she was tired. Les had indeed commented on her being back late from lunch, a kind of passive-aggressive, corner-of-the-mouth remark that should have had her reaching for the nearest heavy object, but instead it saw her mumbling a muted apology and heading straight for her desk. She saw Barry shoot her an 'I warned you' look across the room, so she got down to churning out some copy to meet the daily quota. That entailed re-writing press releases and a few calls to make her feel as if she was really in the world of journalism. But inside she felt like a coward. She should be standing her ground, not sneaking about like a guilty schoolgirl.

The two pieces on the murder helped with the story count. The image of the murder victim pinged into her email first. She opened it to see the face, brought to life through CGI, of a man in his late thirties, long fair hair, chin heavily stubbled, some kind of stud in his left ear. The brown eyes were open but even computer trickery could not bring a dead man to life. The details told her that he was five foot eleven inches in height, weighed around twelve stone, was of slim build and had one scar from an appendix removal. And that was it, all that was known about the man distilled into one shot and a few lines of description. Cold, efficient, emotionless. It saddened her and she recalled her father's words from many years before when she'd asked him about investigating murders. He had thought about it for a while and when he spoke it was in a quiet voice, still bearing the wind-blown echoes of his island upbringing.

Murder is always sad, no matter who the victim is. Because it can often mean the end of more than one life. A wife picks up a breadknife and stabs her husband. She faces jail. Their children have to live without parents. A fight in the street turns tragic. A man lies dead, the man who killed him has robbed him of his future and also changed his own life for ever. And his family. And friends. Murder has ripples and they wash over not only everyone involved but also anyone connected with either victim or killer. That one act damages more than just one person.

She had barely completed that story when Elspeth called about the Highland costume line getting out. Terry Hayes had been true to her word and had stalled in order to let Elspeth know, but her old boss was spitting blood.

'Holding that back was our trump card,' she had said on the phone, after she relayed a quote provided by Terry Hayes. 'Gave us all sorts of credit with the police.'

'Who else got it, do you know?' Rebecca asked.

'Aye, that brainless bitch from the Beeb. Although how she stopped looking in the mirror long enough to find out beats the buggery out of me.'

Rebecca stifled a laugh. She knew Lola McLeod was a smart operator and was extremely good at her job. She was a star on the regional channel and it was only a matter of time before she would be poached by the network and whisked away to Salford. Sooner or later she'd be off to Washington or even fronting the breakfast show, exchanging banter with her co-presenter. She had the skills, the looks and the personality. However, for Elspeth, the only journalism that mattered was print. In her mind, TV was just showbiz with soundbites.

'So now we're back at square one with the police. We had a wee opening and we've lost it.'

Rebecca cradled the phone on her shoulder as she typed. She wanted this online right away, especially if the BBC had it. As Elspeth talked, she checked their online news feed but it still wasn't up. She had a window here to get it out first, even before Elspeth's clients. That didn't happen often. She didn't say that, though. The words 'wound' and 'salt' came to mind. 'So what now?'

'Now we bust a gut to keep ahead of the pack.'

Rebecca was under no illusions who the 'we' was in that sentence. It was just as well she had no personal life because until this story was done and dusted she would have very little time to herself.

As she left the office, her body felt as if it had gone a few rounds with Tyson Fury, but she consoled herself with visions of a long hot bath, a glass of wine and then a movie before bed. Something nice and soft and girly, with no blood and no death and everyone living happily ever after. Not like real life at all. There are damn few happy endings in real life.

What she didn't need was Nolan Burke climbing out of a Merc and heading her way.

Her first thought comprised a series of swear words. Her second was whether he was there to pressurise her into not printing any of the interview. She stood beside her car, the key in her hand. She wondered if she could use it as a weapon. But then she saw the flowers in his hand.

Nolan Burke.

With flowers, no less.

'Mr Burke,' she said, trying hard to keep irritation out of her voice but failing miserably. She was too damned tired for this. Flowers. I mean, what the actual . . . ?

His slight smile was different from his brother's. It carried genuine amusement. 'Yeah, I heard about the "Mr" business. Nolan, for God's sake. My maw's no here to impress.'

'What are you doing here?' There was so much edge to her words that she could have cut bread with it.

He raised the flowers towards her, as if he was for some reason ashamed of them. 'Came to see you.' He was trying to be brash but his voice wavered just enough to tell Rebecca he felt out of his depth. The tiny smile was almost boyish.

She glanced up at the office windows. Was anyone watching? Did she need witnesses here? Dear God, Nolan Burke says he's come to see her and he has flowers. She was half expecting him to produce a heart-shaped box of chocolates next.

'Why?' she asked.

He hesitated. 'These are for you,' he said, fully thrusting out the flowers in her direction.

Despite herself, she took them. They were nice flowers. She couldn't say what the blooms were, she was hopeless at that, but they were beautiful and the bouquet was enticing. She wondered where he'd stolen them from.

'I bought them,' he said, as if he'd guessed her thoughts. 'Don't worry, they're no knocked off or nothing.'

'Didn't think they were,' she lied. Convincingly, she thought.

He didn't buy it. 'Aye, I'll bet.' Something of the Nolan Burke she'd heard about, and even seen in court, crept into his voice. Tough, sure of himself, cocky.

'What do you want, Mr Burke?'

He looked around him, but there was no one near. He sighed. 'A bloke brings you flowers, what the hell you think he wants? And it's Nolan, mind.'

Was this his way of asking her out? She supposed it beat a half-brick across the head and being dragged up an alley. 'I don't think it's a good idea, Mr Burke.'

'Nolan.'

'Let's keep it to Mr Burke, eh?'

'Why? We can be friends.'

Earlier she'd been thinking that she needed new friends, but this wasn't quite what she'd had in mind. 'Why me, Mr Burke?'

He smirked. 'Why you? Can you no work that out for yourself?'

She let her eyes roam over the petals in her hand. They were beautiful. She'd only been given flowers once in her life. Simon, of course. Who always did the right thing. She pushed them back in Nolan's direction. 'As I said, not a good idea. Please take these back.'

He stepped away, made a kind of fending-off motion with his hands. 'Naw, what the hell am I going to do with them? And why isn't it a good idea?'

Exhaustion hit her hard again and she let the arm holding the flowers swing to her side. She didn't have the strength for this, she really didn't. 'It just isn't, okay?'

She clicked the unlock button on her fob, hoping he'd take the hint.

'It's because I'm a Burke, right?'

She opened the driver's door. 'No, it's—'

'I know. We're all crooks. The family from hell. Dad's in the jail, Mum's a hard case, brother's a nutjob. We punt drugs and we get into fights and we hurt people that get in our way.'

Okay, she thought, *if you want to do this.* 'And you don't do any of that, right?'

He quickly scanned the area around him again to check they still could not be overheard and stepped closer, his voice low. He had the decency to keep a distance between them, so at least he knew about the concept of boundaries. 'Aye. We do. No point in denying it. We do all that and more. That's the life we lead and we do it really well, you know? But there's more to us, more to me, than dealing smack and sorting out the opposition, you know what I mean? I'm still just a guy, underneath it all.'

'A guy who deals smack and hurts people for a living.'

And reads The Guardian, she thought. *And brings flowers. What's next? Poetry?*

He opened his mouth, a smart reply ready, but he thought better of it. 'Maybe a guy who could change.'

Rebecca thought she detected sincerity in that one simple sentence. She stared at him, trying to find some sign of duplicity in his face, hoping she would see it, but all she saw was raw honesty. Dear God, he really wants to get out. And he's looking for a way to do it. But it sure as hell wasn't her. She turned back to her car. 'Come back when you have changed, Mr Burke. Goodnight.' She leaned in to lay the flowers carefully on the passenger seat and straightened again. 'Thanks for these.'

He merely nodded. 'Fine,' he said, turning away as she climbed into the driver's seat. She was about to close the car door when he stopped and turned back. 'Then maybe this will make a difference. I've got some news for you. You like news, don't you?'

She looked past the open door, her hand on the interior handle. 'What is it, Mr Burke?'

His smile was back. So was his confidence. This was firmer ground for him. 'There's a price.'

'I don't pay for stories.'

'Not money. One drink. You and me. Now.'

'You're extorting a date now?'

'No a date. A drink and a talk. I've got stuff you might be interested in is all it is. You people like your contacts, right? I can be one of them. And a bloody good one. You know that.'

The thing that annoyed her, that really pissed her off, was that he was right. Nolan Burke would be a terrific contact, although she would have to tread carefully. The stories he could steer her way would really be something, but she would always have to be wary that she wasn't being used.

'So what do you say?' he asked, but she could tell he already knew the answer.

'One drink, Mr Burke,' she said. 'One drink and you tell me what you want to tell me, okay?'

His smile expanded. 'No problem. And it's Nolan.'

22

Barney's was the land that hipsters forgot.

By the time they'd found a space and Nolan parked the Mercedes, they had a fair walk back through the Old Town to get to the pub. To Rebecca's mind, streets should allow traffic to move relatively easily in both directions. Along Baron Taylor Street, the narrowest in the Old Town, lorries or vans making deliveries would block its entire width and even pedestrians had to virtually scrape against the wall to squeeze past.

Nolan Burke led her into an alleyway that cut through to the High Street and there was the entrance to Barney's. A slim door, a weathered, faded sign above it saying it was 'a free house' and, high on the wall, a window of frosted glass so opaque there was little reason to have it.

Rebecca had passed the bar's unprepossessing exterior many times with no reason to ever cross the threshold. It was one of those places that you only ever went into if you were a regular. The casual visitor, someone looking for a trendy gin or a designer beer, was very unlikely to be attracted by its drab entranceway; even if they were, one look at the shadowy interior would send them scuttling for the nearest Wetherspoons. There was something depressing about the place, as if it and its customers had nowhere else to go. Here, dying dreams were mourned in hard wooden chairs at scarred tables and any hope for the future saw the last rites delivered at the bottom of a whisky glass. Despite that, part of her was glad that unpretentious places such as Barney's still existed. The other part wondered what the hell she was doing there. It was alien. It was not for her. Was that why she felt so nervous?

It was far from the hottest spot in town, she noted. There seemed nothing remotely threatening at first glance. Three young men dressed in the casual uniform of hoodie, jeans and trainers sat at the bar, their eyes fixed on a TV above the gantry tuned in to some football match or other. A middle-aged couple sat diagonally across from each other at a table in the corner under the narrow window and beside the door. The only other customer was a man in the far corner, facing the entire bar, a newspaper and a mug on the table before him. His black coat was draped over the chair beside him, a brown and white dog lying on its side at his feet, eyes open, watching the room. The man slipped off his glasses to study them as they walked in, then slid them back on and went back to his reading.

Nolan led her to a table under a long mirror that reflected the entire bar and asked her what she wanted. Her first impulse was to ask for something soft – she saw this as a work meeting – but changed her mind and asked for a white wine instead. She would have preferred a gin, her growing tension actually demanded it, but she feared in this place it would have been of the bathtub variety and she didn't want it burning a ring round her stomach. Anyway, a drink might help settle her, for she felt unaccountably on edge. It wasn't every day a known drug dealer invited her out for a drink. Or brought her flowers.

Nolan nodded and moved to the bar, one head jerk being enough to bring the barman to him. He rested both forearms on the bar top as he ordered the drinks and when he spoke one of the young men looked in his direction. Nolan didn't seem to notice. He seemed relaxed in this grotty little bar. She wondered if he came here a lot. She wondered if he brought other women here. She wondered why she wondered.

The butterflies became full-grown birds.

To distract herself, she studied the other customers. The couple near the door did not seem to be speaking to each other. The woman sat at one corner of the table, the man opposite and to her left. Like the young men, his eyes were on the football. The woman stared straight ahead, as if she was studying a piece of art she particularly enjoyed rather than the plaster wall of indeterminate colour. They both had coats on, as if they had just arrived or were just leaving, but the man's pint glass was half full. They had to be together – there were three other empty tables in the cramped space – and yet they neither looked at, nor even spoke to, one another. Married, she decided, probably for years. Was that what happened when you'd been with someone for a long time? Did you reach the point where you had said everything you had to say, leaving you sitting in an anonymous little bar, bound to one another but also separated, the years sitting between them like dead children? She thought about her parents. They hadn't been like that. Or was she guilty of a selective memory, where childhood summers were always filled with sunshine? Had there been dark moments in their relationship? She didn't think so. Her memory was of them talking to each other about everything. And a lot of laughter.

As Nolan walked back to the table with their drinks she saw the young man who had been staring at him swivel round in his bar stool. When his scrutiny switched to her, she felt his eyes reach across the room like a grope. Nolan didn't appear to be aware of the man's gaze as he set her white wine in front of her – a large one, she didn't fail to notice – then sat down himself. His own glass contained something soft, she noted. He was driving, of course – there were any number of police officers who would just love to bust Nolan Burke on a drink-driving charge – but was he also trying to impress her? As she took a mouthful of wine, it hit her that she was also driving. Shit. Ah, well. That's why God invented taxis. Her car would be safe enough overnight outside the office. She took another drink.

'Why here?' she asked. In reply he gave her a quizzical look. 'Why did you bring me here?'

He looked around, as if seeing the place for the first time. 'Not the most salubrious of places, is it?'

Salubrious. No wonder he read *The Guardian*.

'It's quiet, is why,' he said. 'Never much business, not now anyway. It used to be a really popular pub, but things change.'

'Do you come here a lot?'

'Now and then, make an appearance.' He looked about again. 'Could do with a lick of paint, I suppose. I'll need to see about that.'

Rebecca sipped her wine as he spoke. Despite her unwillingness to come along after the day she'd had, it tasted surprisingly good. But she resolved to have only one. 'You'll need to see about that? Mr Burke—'

'Nolan.' He smiled.

She ignored him once more. 'Do you own this place?'

'The family does. Through – eh – intermediaries, I suppose you'd call them.'

She took another swallow, hoping it might drown the nerves. This was a business meeting, a story, that was all. But despite herself she was growing more interested in the Burke family. Of course they would have interests in various businesses. If they were selling drugs they had to launder the cash somehow. And there would necessarily be 'intermediaries' – individuals and shell companies hiding the Burke family's involvement. She wanted to ask more about such arrangements but felt he would not expand on it. Then she saw the young man at the bar was still studying them both.

'You've attracted someone's attention,' she said.

Nolan did not seem surprised. His eyes darted briefly to the mirror above her head. He hadn't chosen this table at random, it seemed. 'Ignore him,' he said, as he settled his attention back on her.

'Gladly,' she said, deciding to get down to business. Colourful though the place was, she didn't want to spend too much time there. Depressing atmospheres could be catching. And she was susceptible. 'So – what's the news? What do you have to tell me?'

He smiled. 'Get right to it, don't you?'

'I told you, Mr Burke . . .'

'Nolan.'

'One drink.' She pointed at her glass, saw that it was almost half empty already. *Jesus, how the hell did that happen? Had it been that bad a day? Why am I so bloody nervous?* The atmosphere was getting to her. She felt out of place, certainly, and she really didn't like the way the bloke at the bar was watching them, but why the fluttery gut? She saw Nolan look at her glass, but if he thought anything of how quickly the wine had vanished he did not show it. *Brazen it out, Rebecca, who cares what he thinks?* 'And you're running out of time.'

He turned his head slightly to the left, towards the man and his dog, as if he was gauging whether he could overhear them, but the guy seemed engrossed in his newspaper. She saw his dark hair was threaded with grey. She recognised the *Chronicle*'s pages and that gave her a tingle of pride. She loved to see people reading a real newspaper, especially her own, but it was not a regular experience now.

She expected Nolan to hunch forward and whisper, but instead he sat back and his tone was normal when he spoke. 'We got word this afternoon. They're going to move that perv into the Ferry tomorrow night.'

'How do you know?'

His look told her that was a question that would remain unanswered. 'We know, that's all. Tomorrow night social work is bringing the bastard in.'

Sources again. Their network rivalled that of Elspeth. As she took this in, she saw the young man lean back in his stool and say something to his friends. Whatever he said, it was enough to divert them from the game, for they too looked in their direction. Heads moved together in conspiratorial discussion. Rebecca began to get a bad feeling about this, which didn't help her nerves.

'We also know who he is,' said Nolan, this time leaning forward slightly.

That brought her attention straight back to him, the young men no longer a concern. 'You've got a name?'

'We've got a name.'

'What is it?'

'Why do you need to know?'

'Because if I have a name that might be enough to stop them trying to rehome him in the Ferry.'

He laid one hand on the table top and sat back again while he thought about this. 'I don't want you to stop it. I want them to try it. We'll stop it.'

'Mr Burke . . .'

'Nolan.'

No way, she thought, *this is all business.* 'Mr Burke, your family has whipped up emotions over this. You know what will happen if the council try to bring him in.'

'I know.'

'And you want that?'

He considered what he wanted. 'A message has to be sent.'

'That's your mother speaking.'

'It's the family speaking. And all the decent people in the Ferry.'

She almost laughed at Nolan Burke talking about 'decent people' but then she saw the young man who found them so interesting sliding off his stool and walking towards them. Nolan kept talking. 'Come down the Ferry tomorrow night, come to the house, bring a photographer. You'll see. You'll get a story, I guarantee it. An exclusive. You folk like that, don't you?'

She did like an exclusive, overused though the word was, but what she didn't like was the rigid way the young man was walking as he closed in, as if he was gearing up for something, nor the grim, determined look on his face. She looked past him to his friends, who had stayed at the bar but were grinning as they watched their pal. What was about to happen was better than the footie.

'Mr Burke . . .' she began.

'I know,' he said. 'Don't worry.'

The young man stopped about two feet away, his legs spaced apart, one slightly behind him, as if he was poised for action. His arms were stiff by his side, his fists balled. Nolan's position did not change, even when the man spoke.

'You're that Nolan Burke, eh?'

Nolan didn't turn round, but Rebecca saw his eyes were fixed on the mirror. The young man stared at his back, as if willing him to face him. Rebecca glanced around the bar. The man's two mates had still not moved; the barman was leaning on the counter, his back more or less to them, watching the football. The middle-aged couple to her left seemed oblivious to what was going on. Only the man to her right noticed. He had eased his glasses from his face to watch them. His dog was alert too, head up, ears pricked.

'I'm talkin' to you,' said the young man. 'You no hear me, eh?'

Nolan still didn't turn. 'Look, mate, I'm just here for a quiet drink, okay?'

'She your burd?'

Nolan's eyes darted down to Rebecca and she saw a smile there that didn't reach his lips. 'She's a friend.'

'So she's no your burd then? I could take her for a wee spin, then, eh?'

Rebecca knew this wasn't really about her, that the guy was merely using her to needle Nolan, but she didn't like being spoken about as if she was a car. She gave the young man a look that hopefully told him he had about as much chance of taking her anywhere as this pub had of winning Nightspot of the Year. 'He just told you. A friend. Now, why don't you just go back to the bar with your pals?'

He held up a hand as if she had physically attacked him. 'Nae offence, darlin'. Just thought, you know, if Nolan here wasnae your boyfriend, if you and him were just pals like he said, we could maybe go oot, you know? Maybe a wee bit of danceen.'

Nolan grew tired of the exchange. He pushed his chair back forcefully, the legs scraping on the floor like a gunshot. He was on his feet and facing the young man with such speed that the latter stepped back so quickly he almost tripped over himself.

'Look, mate. You've got a problem with me, is that it?'

The young man, now face to face with Nolan, was not so sure of himself. However, he screwed up his courage again. 'Aye, maybe I have. Maybe you and me have a problem.'

Nolan took a step closer. The man backed away. Rebecca felt he didn't even know he was doing it. 'Maybe?' Nolan said. 'So you're no sure?'

The guy looked over his shoulder to his mates, who showed no sign of backing him up. The barman, meanwhile, was making a second career out of the art of not noticing. The young man turned to face Nolan again, his Adam's apple bobbing like a spirit level on a bumpy ride. Rebecca sensed he was beginning to regret his bravado, that perhaps things weren't going the way he had planned, if he had planned them at all, which was unlikely. He had recognised Nolan and decided he was tough enough, or drunk enough, or stupid enough, to wind him up. But now that he was actually involved it didn't seem to be such a good idea.

A slight movement made her look at the man with the dog. He had eased his chair back and was swinging his legs out from under the table. She had the feeling he was ready to move if he had to.

'Mate, I'm here for a quiet drink with my friend. We've got things to talk about, okay? You don't want this, no really.' Rebecca realised Nolan's accent had changed. When talking to her he had been well spoken, his accent Scottish but cultured, every letter that needed to be pronounced given the attention it deserved. But when speaking to this young man it had become coarser. The letter 't' was dropped, his voice seemed to come from somewhere at the back of his throat. The word 'to' became 'tae', 'about' became 'aboot'. He took another half step forward. The young man did the same in reverse. 'So, here's your chance, right? You go back to your friends, you watch the game, have a drink on me. But the main thing is, and I need you to listen carefully to me here.' He leaned closer to the young man. 'I mean, *really* carefully, man.' Nolan's face was only a few inches from him now. If anything was going to happen, it would happen soon. Nolan's voice was still conversational, though. 'The main thing is you get the fuck out of my face right now.'

There was silence then, as the young man struggled with the need to take his testosterone for a workout and the obvious desire to back away from the situation that self-same testosterone had got him into. Rebecca could see the turmoil on his face, rippling his chin and quivering his lips, as he attempted to match Nolan's unwavering stare. He tried to maintain a defiant pose but something else had dripped into his muscles. That something else was fear.

Finally, he broke the spell and looked away, taking a full step back as he did so, his need to get out of potential harm's way paramount. He thought about saying something more but realised the moment had passed, so he slumped back to his bar stool.

Nolan watched him go.

'I think we'd better leave,' Rebecca said.

He didn't reply at first – he was still giving the young man's back a hard stare – but then he nodded and he turned to face her. 'I'll set him up with a drink first. You want to wait outside?'

She finished her wine – she could have done with another, but now was not the time and this was not the place – and left. The middle-aged couple still hadn't moved. Maybe they were stuffed and left there to make the place look busy. Perhaps they weren't there at all, were merely visual echoes of past patrons. *Dear God, that wine has affected me more than I thought*, she told herself on her way through the door.

The air in the alley gently slapped her over-heated face with cool fingers and she considered heading straight to the station for a taxi. That would be the wise thing to do. Get a taxi, leave Nolan Burke here. However, something stopped her. She didn't know what. So she leaned against the wall beside the door, letting the sounds of the night keep her company. Footsteps on the High Street. Music from a pub in the other direction. The bell of the High Kirk tolling. Eight o'clock. She hadn't eaten anything since lunchtime. No wonder that glass of wine had hit her so hard.

The door opened behind her and the man from the corner table emerged, his dog at his side without a tether. He paused to pull on his coat, giving her the chance to study him in profile. He was of average height and looked to be in his mid to late fifties. His hair had once been very black but the grey suited him. There were lines around his eyes but the face was still firm enough to tell her that he had probably been a good-looking guy. As he buttoned the dark coat his face turned in her direction.

She turned away quickly, feeling ashamed of having been caught staring at him.

'You work for the paper, right?' His accent was Glasgow, not broad but the cadence still there.

She looked back at him. *Brazen it out, girl.* Blue eyes, she saw. His eyes were very blue. And they missed very little. She'd felt that in the bar. She had known from his poised look that if anything had erupted he would have weighed in. And somebody would have regretted it. 'That's right. How did you know?'

'Saw your photo.'

He'd been reading the *Chronicle*, probably the most recent edition. She had been in a photograph, presenting a cheque to a charity from the paper. It should have been Barry but he was notoriously camera-shy and insisted it was better the reporters' faces were known rather than his. They were in the front line and he was little more than a machine operator, he'd said.

She opened her mouth in a silent *Ah* and turned away again. The sound of traffic hissing on tarmac slick with yet another shower of rain reached her. The damp air had cooled her fevered skin down and she pulled her own coat tighter to ward it off. The man had not moved and she sensed he was still facing her. She willed herself not to turn around. She didn't feel anything threatening in his manner or his scrutiny; it was as if he was building up the courage to say something further.

'He's not for you,' he said, finally.

She faced him once more. 'I'm sorry?'

He jerked his head towards the bar door. 'Your friend, back there. He's not for you.'

'He's not a friend, not really.' She didn't know why she was explaining herself, but there was a sincerity in those blue eyes that had disarmed her.

He pulled the collar of his coat up. 'Keep it that way. Guys like him cause nothing but hurt.'

She should have told him it was none of his business, she should have told him she had no interest in Nolan Burke in that way. But she didn't and again she didn't know why. Instead, she asked, 'Why do you say that?'

His face was blank as he looked at her, but something else crept into his eyes. It was as if he was reliving a memory. A painful one. 'Because I've seen it before.'

And then he was gone, walking past her, the dog at his heels, his coat flapping around his legs as he headed deeper into the Old Town. He did not look back and Rebecca watched as he turned the corner.

Nolan came out of the pub and stood beside her. 'Sorry about that,' he said, jerking his head towards the pub door.

'Does that happen often?'

He adopted a sad little smile. 'Occupational hazard. Always someone who wants to start something he doesn't really want to start. That's why Maw doesn't like us going out alone. You never know who you'll meet up with. Sometimes it's someone who really does want to start something.'

So Mo Burke didn't know her son was with her. That didn't help her nerves any. She was still staring at the corner of the street. 'That man, sitting at the table. The one with the dog. Have you seen him before?'

Nolan tried to place him. 'No, don't think so. Maybe. I don't know. Why?'

'Just curious.'

They stood for a moment in silence. He was hesitating, seemingly debating with himself. Once again she saw something other than what she had seen in court. He blinked a few times, his mouth tightened as if he was trying to keep something in but couldn't. That made two men in the space

130

of ten minutes standing on that same spot steeling themselves to say something to her.

'Walter Lancaster,' he said, eventually.

'Who?'

'The name you wanted. Walter Lancaster. You'll find him in your records or on the internet. He was convicted in Aberdeen, he's in the Sneck now.'

The paedophile. The man they wanted to rehome in the Ferry. 'Why are you telling me?'

He breathed deeply, stared at the night sky. 'I really don't know,' he said, eventually.

23

Rebecca didn't click the light on when she got home but stood in the living room for a few seconds, welcoming the darkness and the silence. Then she stepped to the window and looked out at the street. Nothing moved. No strange cars in the parking areas outside. Her stomach still broiled and she didn't know why – even though the attention of a criminal with a propensity for violence was bound to have unsettled her. That was why all the way home in the taxi she had continually twisted round to search the traffic behind for a glimpse of a black Mercedes.

The problem was that she had warmed to him. He was attractive, there was no doubt about it, and if things had been different she would have been happy to go out with him. She might even have made the first move, just as she had with Simon. She had seen him in court and then, when she'd had to talk to him about a story, up close. She had liked what she saw. He was a nice guy. She'd asked him out.

Don't wait for a man to make the first move because the cows will be home before he does. If you like him, you ask him. This is the twenty-first century. There's no reason to be backward. Her mother's words.

It turned out that her mum had made the approach to her father, which was relatively unusual in the 1990s, despite the rise of feminism. So Rebecca had followed her example and one day she asked Simon. Certainly, it took her two weeks to pluck up the courage, but she did it. Simon seemed unfazed by the overture and said yes. The rest, as they say, was history. And not all of it good.

She clicked on the lamp, fired up her laptop, threw a ready meal in the microwave and poured herself that longed-for drink from the gin bottle. The wine she had drunk so quickly in Barney's was cavorting in her bloodstream. She was careful to take small sips as she waited for the lasagne to ding.

Back in the sitting room, she arranged some cushions on the floor, then sat with her back against the two-seater settee, the computer on her lap. She liked to sit on the floor. It reminded her of home, where she would sit or lie watching TV while her mother worked at the small desk against the back window of their home in Milngavie. Her father seldom brought his work home with him, but her mother was a teacher and there was always marking or paperwork. Her father would often mock whatever Rebecca was watching. *Glee* was a favourite and he had a field day with that, the problems of American teens who suddenly burst into song providing plenty of fodder, even though she suspected he secretly enjoyed it. Occasionally she'd be watching MTV and he would gently poke fun at the music she loved, especially Robbie Williams. That would annoy her until she realised that was the whole point.

She missed her father. She missed just talking about her day. She missed how he would laugh at her when she was being girlie. Sometimes she heard that laugh in her head when she caught herself indulging in diva-like tantrums at work. She'd heard it a couple of times when talking to Barry, as she vaulted onto the highest steed she could find to sally forth to fight the good fight for quality journalism. Hearing her father telling her to calm down more often than not succeeded in pulling her from the saddle and back to earth.

And sometimes, when she was stressed, she would wake to see him sitting in the shadows of her room. It didn't scare her. It comforted her. He was gone but he was still there, in her mind.

No one dies when memories of them live, he used to say. He would live on with her, then. Because she would never forget him or what he'd taught her.

She stared for a moment at the computer screen, blinked away a tear and resolved to phone her mother later. She hadn't spoken to her for over a week. She glanced at the clock. Nine-thirty. Not too late. She would call after she had run these checks.

She sipped her gin, forked a mouthful of beef and cheese into her mouth and punched up Google, then entered *Walter Lancaster+Sex Offender*. A list of choices pinged up, all of them news sites. She clicked on *The Herald*. She subscribed to it, might as well use it.

Walter Lancaster was forty when he was convicted of indecency. Basically he'd been caught exposing himself at the gates of an Aberdeen primary school. His defence that he had been merely relieving himself at the side of a bin shelter carried little weight, even though he'd provided a medical certificate that proved he had a urinary tract infection. What didn't help were the hidden files on his PC, what the courts described as 'material of an obscene nature depicting children'. That convinced the jury that he was not merely a man with an infection who had been caught short but was, in fact, a predator. He was duly sentenced and his name added to the Sex Offender Register.

She studied the photograph that accompanied the report. It was perhaps a bad shot, snatched outside the court room prior to sentencing, but it was not a pretty picture. The word that came to Rebecca's mind was fleshy. Everything about him seemed to be flabby. His body was shapeless, his face full but the skin loose, his eyes burrowing back into his skull as if they wanted to observe without being seen. Even the bald pate fringed by a circle of lank, greying hair seemed slack. Had he not been kept in a prison which was almost wholly comprised of people like him, he would not have had a good time inside.

Although his offence was committed in Aberdeen, he was originally from Inverness. A return to his flat in Aberdeen's Torry district was not possible, primarily because it had been rented to someone else while he was in jail but also because it was not safe for him to do so. His acts had put him in the public eye – a public that viewed him as a sick bastard who should not be allowed anywhere near decent folk. However, the authorities still owed him a duty of care. So, if Nolan's information was correct, it seemed a return to his home town had been called for.

Her computer pinged, telling her she had a Skype call. She accepted and saw Chaz and Alan staring back at her.

'Where you been, girlfriend?' Alan was adopting an American accent. A bad American accent.

She thought about not telling them she had been with Nolan because she knew Alan would make a meal of it, however she knew she had to tell someone. Chaz listened, his face straight, but predictably Alan loved the whole notion.

'Rebecca and Nolan, sitting in a tree,' he chanted as he danced away from the screen.

'Alan, behave,' Chaz warned.

'K-I-S-S-I-N-G.'

'Alan, please,' Rebecca pleaded.

Alan came back into view. 'Oh, for God's sake, why so glum about this? So you had a gentleman caller. You've been asked out before.'

'Yes, but not by someone who can take a power drill to my knees.'

Alan dismissed that thought. 'That was Scott, not Nolan.'

Chaz gave him a surprised look. 'How do you know that?'

'People talk, I listen. Honestly, darling, sometimes I don't think you know me at all.'

Rebecca watched as Chaz shook his head at Alan, mortally offended. 'So, what am I going to do?' she asked.

'What can you do?' Chaz was facing the screen again. 'Just leave it alone. You went out for a drink and made it clear that it was purely business. Hopefully he'll take the hint.'

Rebecca wasn't so sure. 'Hopefully.' Then another thought hit her. 'Oh, hell . . .'

Chaz hunched forward, concern puckering his brow. 'What?'

'All this talk about him asking me out. I feel like I'm starring in *Made in Chelsea.*'

The laugh that erupted from Alan was just what she needed.

24

The desk lamp created a little island of light in the darkness of John Dona-hue's office but he didn't need it to see the photograph on his phone. It glowed with an intensity that seemed to bring the face to life. But it didn't, not really. Nothing could do that now. No amount of expensive technology could do that.

Outside all was silent in the compound, apart from the occasional rustle of a guard walking by on the grass. Donahue's Portakabin was set a little away from the main cluster of temporary buildings. It wasn't much, but he liked the idea of privacy, even if in practice there wasn't much of it. A glass of whisky sat untouched on the desk. His focus was on the image on the screen. One finger traced the curve of her jaw and her blonde hair as it fell over her fore-head, as if he could push it back, just as he'd used to.

Before . . .

She had been so beautiful then. So beautiful and full of promise. Of joy.

Before . . .

He swallowed and fought back the tears he'd thought had dried long ago. He knew now they were always there, waiting to return. Wounds close, they say, but some don't. Some remain forever open, no matter what you do. Time does not heal everything; rather, it makes things worse. Memories pick at whatever scab there is until the welt is left bare again. And blood flows like water.

Like tears.

He wiped his cheek dry with one hand, then reached out, his fingers closing round the whisky glass but not yet raising it. He still stared at the photograph, at a face frozen for eternity. A face not made of flesh and bone but only so many pixels, so many reds, greens and blues, so many bits of digital information, so much metadata. And yet the photograph, and others like it, was more than that to him. For it, and others like it, were all he had left.

And the memories, of course.

And his rage.

25

Nolan arrived home to find his mum and Scott waiting for him in the living room, a laptop lying open on the coffee table. Scott himself lounged on the couch, that little smile of his irritating Nolan immensely. Everything about his brother irritated him these days. Or perhaps it was simply that he irritated himself.

'Where have you been?' his mother demanded.

A welcome scuttling at his feet told him Midge needed attention, so he stooped to rub his ears. The wee dog loved that. Midge was the one thing in this house that made life bearable.

'Out,' he said, unwilling to expand further. 'Why?'

'Out where?'

He straightened and Midge, sensing there would be no more affection, trotted back to his basket. 'I called into Barney's.'

It had been owned by a friend of the family called Barney Maguire. He'd been a cantankerous old bugger, but Nolan had always got on well with him. When he'd retired, Nolan had advocated buying into the place. Mo was always open to any opportunity that could either turn a profit or wash some cash, so they had taken it on. Ostensibly it was Barney's daughter who owned it, she was the licence holder, but real control lay with the Burke family.

Nolan decided that truth was the best policy. Just perhaps not all of it. The barman wouldn't say who he was with, of that he was confident. He was an old friend and he knew the score. Nolan had scoped the place as they entered and there was no one else there he knew who might seep word back to his mother that he had been with Rebecca. Well, fairly certain at least. The young man and his pals were complete strangers, as were the old couple. The other guy, the one with the dog, was a mystery, but he recalled Rebecca asking about him. Why did she do that, he wondered?

'What have I told you about being out alone,' she said. 'Not with McClymont's people sniffing around.'

'They've backed off,' he said, dismissing her concerns with a flick of the wrist.

'Wee Joe McClymont never backs off. He learned that much from his father. All they're doing is licking their wounds.'

Scott sniggered. 'Can you lick your own knees?'

Mo glared at him. 'Don't start me on that, Scotty. You went over the score there. A bloody power drill? You're no Scarface. Understand me? You do anything like that again I'll take a sander to your arse, see how you like me B&Q-ing it.'

Scott's smile didn't waver. 'It was a chainsaw in *Scarface*.'

'Don't back-chat me. You're no too big that you cannae get a slap, okay?'

Scott didn't say anything further. He knew better. Nolan knew his brother, though. He would do something similar again and that worried him. Scott would get himself into serious trouble some day and, by extension, the family. And, despite her stern warnings, he knew their mother would side with his younger brother and let him away with it. Oh, she'd give him a bollocking, but that's as far as it would go. And when that day came Nolan would have to make a choice. They shared the same blood but not the same outlook.

'Well, I'm home, safe and sound, so what's the worry?' Nolan said.

Mo jerked her head in the direction of the laptop. 'You seen the news?'

'No, been busy all day. What's up?'

He moved around the coffee table, lifted the PC to cradle it on his left arm while his right fingered the scroll pad. The screen flashed to life to show

Rebecca's story on the man found at Culloden. He felt something jerk at his mind as he saw her byline, then quickly scanned the story.

As he read, he said, 'Okay, what about it?'

'Look at the photie,' said Mo.

Nolan glanced quickly at his brother, saw the smile still in place, and scrolled down until he found the computer-generated image. He took in the long hair, the lean jaws coated with stubble, the stud. It was a good likeness.

'That's . . .'

'Aye,' said Mo, her voice flat.

26

The child has become adept at hiding the memories, although they are always present, like a shadow on a dull day. The child knew they would never leave, for they were a part of the fabric of existence. To lose them would be like losing a part of itself.

Itself.

It.

The child thought itself sexless even before the term gender neutral was coined. That was what he did to it in that little room with its creature comforts and its terrors. That was what they did to it. Him. Her. The son. They may not have taken part in what happened but they did nothing to stop it. Just as the child could do nothing to stop the memories that fed on its sanity like vampires.

In daylight they hide, as if fearful of the sun. But at night they rise to manifest with such clarity that they shimmer in the dark, whispering in tongues thick with bile and darkness. And the child can name these creatures, for it knows them intimately.

Pain.

Shame.

Rage.

Even killing failed to lay them to rest. They merely lay dormant. Spilled blood does not exorcise them, the child was fully aware of that. Not the first time. Not this time. Even so, the plan was made and executed. As before, at the point of death there came a realisation. The child saw it in his eyes. This is justice, those eyes said. Sins had to be atoned. Death was inevitable.

The child had watched death creep over the man as his blood left him to seep into the land. He had fought it at first, but then had understood that this was necessary, that he deserved this, and the anguish that filled his eyes bled away to be replaced by something else.

Peace.

But his death had failed to satisfy the spectres that tormented the child from the shadows. For a new wraith had joined them and it, too, had a name. And the child knew that to satisfy this fresh presence, further blood would have to be spilled.

For the new persecutor was named Fear.

27

The cathedral always looked to her as if someone had sawn off the tops of the twin spires. They were flat, block-like, and had an incomplete look. Which they were. Rebecca had learned the money ran out before ornate pointed spires could be added. The pink sandstone building sat against the hump of Tomnahurich, the hill of the yews, although she had no idea if the crust of green and yet-to-green trees were yews. The waters of the Ness were grey and rippled by a breeze drifting upstream, its grassy bank speckled with gently waving bright yellow daffodils.

A seagull sat on the railing above the steep drop to the road below and eyed up her lunchtime baguette like a mugger. She gave it a look designed to warn it against any offensive act. It took the hint and flew away.

An American voice made her turn towards the bronze statue of Flora MacDonald sitting in front of the red sandstone castle. A man in a red baseball cap was taking a photograph of his wife at the base of the plinth and telling her, 'Move a bit to the left, honey.' Flora had helped Charles Edward Stuart over the sea to Skye, as the song had it, and the statue depicted her with a dog at her side and one arm raised, as if shielding her eyes from the sun. When Alan had first seen it, he'd quipped that she was checking to see if her deodorant was still working. The statue was a reminder to Rebecca that history was everything to the Highlands, not just in terms of culture and identity but also finance. It lived on in the old buildings and the monuments, it sang out from heather and mountains and forests. There were songs of heroism and loss, celebrations of brave deeds and laments of old wrongs, history and myth melded together to boost the economy. For in the High-lands the past lives on in the present and the present owes allegiance to the past. She had been born in Glasgow, but she had island blood in her, thanks to her father, and she could feel that past keening within her. However, to many, she was still an outsider.

She looked downstream to where the Great Glen opened up. Although the pale sun shone on Inverness from an eggshell-blue sky punctuated with puffy white clouds, misty rain crept in like a thief to rob the hills of their colour and texture. She wondered if it would reach the city and ruin her peaceful lunch. She hoped not.

This was one of the best things about her days on the rota reporting court proceedings in the castle. If it was to be fine, she bought a chicken mayo baguette and a bottle of water and sat on one of the benches that overlooked the river. She knew it was a habit, a ritual, but it was one she enjoyed, although not for long. A new court complex was under construction as she sat there – it had been promised the year before, but still wasn't finished – which would free up the A-listed castle to be used as a tourist attraction. She would miss coming here, though, miss her routine.

The morning session had been predictable, a mixture of assaults, thefts, acts of vandalism, domestic disputes that had turned ugly. She sat in the press box listening to the roll of dishonour and studying the people. Young faces, old faces, faces of those who had aged beyond their years, others who would never grow up and a few who would not celebrate many more birth-days. Private lives were made public in flat monotone statements from lawyers; crimes and misdemeanours, both intentional and accidental, laid bare because justice must be seen to be done. Victim and perpetrator breathed the same air again, the former leaving either satisfied or outraged depending on their view of the outcome. The latter, often young men casually dressed or in ill-fitting suits if they were attempting to curry favour, some still with peach fuzz on smooth skin yet eyes that burned with defiance, accepted sentences with equanimity or displayed flashes of temper. It was all very businesslike, the crisp efficiency of the process making moments of drama almost mundane. The court staff ensured the production line of justice ran smoothly, with only the occasional outburst from an accused or an overly splenetic sheriff to punctuate the routine.

Rebecca's shorthand was, thankfully, impeccable and she was able to follow the proceedings easily, although she would have sight of the court papers later to double check the exact charges proffered against each of the accused. All these sad, even sordid, little tales of human mistakes and failings were grist to the local newspaper mill, but nothing among them cried out as a front-page splash. But then she might already have that in the bag, thanks to Nolan Burke.

In the half-hour before she'd left for the court that morning, Rebecca had placed a call to the council press office, asking them if it was true they were planning to rehouse Walter Lancaster in the Inchferry area. The response was as chilly as a New Year's day dip in the Moray Firth.

We cannot comment on individual cases.

A non-denial denial if ever she'd heard one. And a handy cop-out for local authorities, police and health services across the land. However, Rebecca wasn't letting them off that easily.

She'd pointed out there was a public safety issue at stake.

We cannot comment on individual cases.

They had to be aware that there was a voluble and active resistance to any suggestion that a convicted sex offender be moved into the area.

We cannot comment on individual cases.

And what if I told you that the organisers of the protesters knew about council plans and even had the offender's name?

We cannot comment, etc., etc.

It wasn't much but was enough of a story to punch into the system before she left for court. She would get it out there; that was the main thing.

As she walked from her desk, Barry crooked a finger from the editor's office door. She had been summoned to the sanctum sanctorum. This was never good. She tried to think what she had done wrong lately but came up with nothing that merited being hauled into the room that, since Les's arrival earlier in the week, had been swiftly dubbed 'The Boys' Club' by the women in the office. She felt that was unfair. When Elspeth was editor, had it been called the Ladies' Room? Then she thought, perhaps it was – by the men in the office.

Barry had taken a seat in the corner. Les was behind the editor's desk, staring at the computer screen up against the partition wall to his right, his right hand curled over the mouse like a cat hunched over its prey. He really hadn't lost much time getting his feet under the table and she wondered if she'd ever get used to seeing him there. It had taken months to become accustomed to Barry in that chair instead of Elspeth.

'What's up?' She addressed Barry deliberately. She could reason that it was because he had called her in, but she knew she was simply being thrawn, a fine old Scots word her mother used when Rebecca was being particularly stubborn. Barry nodded towards Les, who turned away from the terminal to face her. He gave her a look that was no doubt intended to show her he was the boss now.

'So, you got a name for the paedo,' he said.

'Yes. I've done some words, you'll find the story—'

'Yeah, got them here.' He jutted his chin towards the screen. 'A few tweaks and it'll go live shortly.'

'What sort of tweaks?'

His youthful face crinkled in an expression that she thought was meant to be reassuring but only came across as patronising. 'Nothing major, no need to worry.'

'I'm not worried, I just wondered what they were.'

'I'll take legal advice about using this guy's name – Lanchester, is it?'

'Lancaster.'

'Yeah, Lancaster.'

Christ, he had the story on the screen in front of him, couldn't he read?

'I think we're fine,' she said. 'He's a convicted felon and it's a matter of public record. We can't really defame him by naming him. And I made it clear it was unconfirmed.'

'Sure, but it doesn't do any harm to have someone with a law degree take a look-see. Anyway . . .' He fiddled with the mouse, clicked with his finger. 'This thing tonight in' – he glanced at the screen – 'Inchferry.'

'The Ferry, yes.'

'Yeah. How reliable is this info of yours, that there will be resistance?'

'Feeling is pretty high,' she said. 'So I'd say pretty reliable. If you heard they were going to move a paedophile into your area, wouldn't you be concerned?'

He didn't answer as he gave the mouse a little push and scrolled down the story she'd just written. 'The council wouldn't confirm they were moving this guy, Lanchester—'

'Lancaster,' she corrected again. How difficult was it to remember that name?

He didn't seem irritated by her correcting him. He seemed distracted. 'Yeah, they wouldn't confirm, right?'

'They wouldn't comment in an individual case.'

He grunted. 'A non-denial denial.'

That's exactly what she'd thought. So he'd seen *All the President's Men.* She wondered if that was supposed to impress her. It didn't. Her university lecturer had brought in all sorts of newspaper-themed films for them to see. If Les quoted a line from *Ace in the Hole* then she might be mildly amazed. Not that she'd recognise it if he did. She'd watched the films, she hadn't memorised them. *Non-denial denial* was the only thing that had stuck.

'Something like that,' she said.

'So your source isn't official?'

Nolan's face flashed in her mind. She saw him pushing his chair back and whirling on that young man the night before. She heard the voice of the stranger outside the pub . . .

He's not for you.

'Hardly,' she said.

'So it may all be utter bollocks?'

She had considered this. Nolan Burke could have been lied to about the plan to move Lancaster in. He could have been given the wrong name. He could be lying to her. He could be trying to impress her. But he didn't strike her that way. Scott, yes. He would say anything that would have an effect, to shock, impress, scare. His older brother, though, was different. At least, that's what she felt. His words had lodged in her mind.

What if a guy could change?

Scott would never think anything like that, let alone say it. He liked the life he led, that much was clear. The two had sprung from the same womb but that was as far as it went.

'I don't think so,' she told Les. 'I think they're going to move someone in there tonight. I'd say the chances are that it's this guy Lancaster. If not, I feel there would have been a flat denial. But if they do, I think there might be trouble.'

Les scanned something on his screen. 'This Burke family. They're bad news, right?'

It was Barry who answered. 'If there's something dodgy going on in Inverness – hell, the west Highlands – you'll find a Burke involved somehow.'

Les looked back at Rebecca. 'What do you think?'

'I think there's a good chance there will be unrest, yes.'

'Because the Burkes are involved?'

'Because I think feeling is high and, even if the paedophile angle is rubbish, all it will take is a few strangers to drive through in a car and all hell will break loose.'

Les pursed his lips as he thought about this. Rebecca wondered what was coming. This was not simply about her story. He scraped the mouse on the desktop again. 'Do the police know?'

'Yes.'

'What did they say?'

'Same as the council.'

Les fell silent. If Barry had been behind the desk, this would have been the point where he would have picked up the dagger-shaped letter opener and twirled it in his hands. But Barry had propped his elbow on a tall, slim table with a plant pot on it, his head resting on his hand. He was watching them with an expression Rebecca could only describe as bored. He was done here. Treading water. Serving his time.

'I've spoken to management down south,' Les said eventually, and Rebecca felt the now familiar sensation of being robbed. Management down south. As far as she knew, none of them had ever put out a newspaper. They were accountants and sales people. They thought in terms of page yield and staff ratios. They didn't understand the necessity of following and breaking a story. Les continued, 'I've done a risk assessment.'

Rebecca felt a sigh building. Risk assessment. What was the company's exposure should anything go wrong? She jumped ahead. 'You don't want me to go, do you?'

'Management doesn't think it's a good idea.'

She gave Barry a pointed look, willing him to weigh in here, but he hadn't moved. He was still watching, still disinterested. If he had been behind the desk, he would have said the same thing, she knew, but she might have been able to talk him round. Les was a company man, through and through. If they sawed him in half, they would find 'NewsMediaplc' etched into his very being.

'They think it is a dangerous situation, given the level of feeling in the area,' he said.

'So we miss the story?'

'We'll get the story, whether you're there or not.'

'No, we'll get a version of the story, an official version. That's not the same as seeing what happens first-hand.'

'You can speak to contacts in the area.'

'That's not the same.'

'You can't go, Rebecca. It's too risky.'

He was covering his own back. He didn't care about her, just the backlash if anything should happen. All company men only cared about themselves. Okay, she thought, if the company didn't want her to cover the story then someone else would. Elspeth would be able to punt anything she got, she was certain.

'It will happen after office hours,' she said. 'I'll go on my own time.'

Les shot a knowing glance at Barry, and Rebecca realised he'd known she would say that. Shit, she hated being predictable. Especially to guys like this.

'I can't stop you,' he said. 'All I can do is point out that if you do, you're not representing the company.'

Suits me, she thought.

'However, I need to remind you that your contract of employment precludes you from working for any other news organisation.'

The conversation seemed to end abruptly. It was as if there was more Les could say but he knew he didn't need to say anything further. Barry was bound to have told him she was friendly with Elspeth, whose agency strung for a number of larger news outfits. She could easily sell an eyewitness account to them. Les and Barry might even know she was working with her – in a way – in regard to the murder. Inverness wasn't that big a place and someone would pass it along. They would have been seen together after the conference. They were probably even spotted talking to Terry Hayes. As long as there were benefits, story-wise, to the company, then that was all fine and dandy. But if she tried to give Elspeth, or anyone else, the lowdown on whatever was to occur that night in the Ferry, they would hit her with the contract of employment. They didn't want to send her out because their risk assessment told them it was too dangerous. But they didn't want her taking any story elsewhere, even if she went on her own time. As far as they were concerned, she was royally screwed and they didn't need to cuddle afterwards.

Now, basking in sunlight that was almost warm, her thoughts turned again to her drink with Nolan Burke the previous night and she felt a fluttering in the pit of her stomach. What was that all about? He had spotted her at the demo, sure, but he had said nothing during her interview with Mo Burke in their home, even though she had sensed his eyes on her almost the entire time. His brother had also been focusing on her, but he hadn't turned up at her door with flowers. God, the notion of Scott Burke paying attention to her was not something she would like to dwell on. And paying attention to her? Where the hell did that phrase come from? Alan had a lot to answer for.

She became aware of a tall figure at her side, and when she looked up Anna Fowler gave her the wide smile she had sported in her university office. 'Fancy meeting you here,' said the historian as she sat down.

Rebecca was surprised but returned the smile. Frankly, she was relieved to see her. Thinking about Les, Barry and Nolan Burke was messing with her head. A chat with a level-headed female was just what was needed.

'I'm working – what's your excuse?'

'Came to see you. Alan told me you were covering court this morning and that it was your habit to sit out here if it was dry and eat your lunch. Your thinking place, he called it.'

Rebecca's laugh barked. 'Ah, well. I don't do much thinking really. It's more a place to decompress.'

Anna squinted down the river. 'It is quite a view. We all need places like this, to think or decompress. Just to let the pressures of the day float off into the atmosphere and hope they don't damage the ozone layer.'

'Do you have a thinking place?'

She nodded. 'Clachnaharry. You know it?'

Rebecca did. It was once a fishing village, now part of the western reaches of Inverness, a couple of narrow streets and terraced cottages where the Caledonian Canal began or ended, depending on which direction you were sailing. A sea lock acted as the gateway into and out of the Beauly Firth.

'I once caused a tailback there – that sharp little hill leading out of the village and onto the main road? With the traffic lights?' Rebecca recalled. 'I kept stalling the car, trying to make that rise and turn left. Then I found myself stuck in a kind of limbo where the sensors on the lights couldn't catch me, so we all sat at red for a long, l-o-n-g time.'

Anna's smile was infectious, and even as Rebecca relived the mixture of rage and shame she had felt, she began to laugh. 'The man behind me kept hammering on his horn and that just made me worse. When the light turned green, I'd move, but then stall again on that damn slope.'

'It's a tough one if you don't hit it right, and we've all been there,' said Anna, 'but you get used to it. It's where I go when I need to get my mind in some kind of order. I sit on a bench on the canal towpath, lose myself in the peace.' She waved a hand at the view around them. 'This is open, but there you have this feeling of – expanse, you know? The water, the sky, the view down to the bridge and across to the Black Isle. For me, after being stuck in the office or the lecture room or even in the town here, it's freedom.'

She stared down the plain, her head cocked to one side as if she was listening to the waters of the firth lapping onto the shore and feeling the wind float in from the North Sea.

Rebecca spoke softly, aware that the court session would begin again soon. 'So what can I do for you, Professor Fowler?'

'Anna, please. Apparently the police visited the compound and spoke to John Donahue about the missing costumes.'

'He doesn't suspect you?'

'No, no. He hasn't spoken to me, but word gets around a set-up like that. It's like a factory or an office – or a university, for that matter. Rumour is like currency. He was furious, apparently. Not a happy bunny.'

Rebecca heard something akin to glee creeping into the historian's voice. It was clear she did not think much of the production company's head of security. However, that didn't seem enough to bring her from the university to the Castle Wynd. 'That's not why you came to see me, though, is it?'

Anna did not answer. She stared down the valley. 'Rain's not far off, I fear.'

Rebecca did not press her – she knew the historian wouldn't have left her book-strewn office just to talk about the weather. She was about to break her agreement with the production company again and it was a big step. Rebecca gave her the space to get to the point. She followed her gaze, saw the curtain of mist and vapour had draped over more of the land. The sky was closing in on itself, the clouds thickening and swallowing the patches of blue. The air had chilled and she felt – or at least she thought she felt – something cold and damp kiss her lightly on the cheek. She hoped Anna got to the point before the weather front hit.

She heard a slight sigh and turned back to face Anna Fowler, who was still staring down river. Her voice was slightly strained as she spoke. 'I saw the photo of the murder victim on your website.'

There was another silence and Rebecca felt she had to fill the void. 'Okay.'

Anna swallowed. 'And I've seen him before, or at least I think I have.'

'Where? Not at the university . . .'

Anna looked directly at Rebecca now, confidence returning to her voice. She had begun this, she would finish it. This was the right thing to do. 'No – at the set, or nearby. I saw him a few times in Fort William. Pubs, in the street, that sort of thing. I think he was working for the production, some kind of construction. The company hired local labour for some of the land clearance and to help put the compound together.'

'Do you know his name?'

'No, I never spoke to him. But John Donahue does, I'm certain of it.'

'How can you be so certain?'

Anna took a deep breath. 'This isn't easy for me, Rebecca. You know I shouldn't rightly be talking to you, the press . . .'

'Of course.'

'I mean, a film is a film, an agreement is an agreement, but a man has lost his life here, right?'

'Right.'

Anna nodded, satisfied, more with her own decision that Rebecca's reassurances. 'I saw him arguing with John Donahue. It was quite heated. Donahue grabbed the man by the front of his shirt and threw him to the ground.'

'What were they arguing about?'

'I don't know. I was quite a bit away and couldn't hear. But I was certain I heard one thing.'

'What was that?'

'John Donahue said that if this man ever came back again, he'd kill him.'

28

Donahue's voice was as irritable as ever, but at least he took DCI Roach's call. That was something. 'Please make it fast, DCI Roach, I'm—'

'Aye, a busy man,' she said, her own voice patient but carrying enough irony to bring the most pompous of arseholes back to earth. 'I have a few more questions, if you don't mind.' The words *even* *if you do mind* were left unsaid.

'I've already told you everything I know. Some bastard, probably someone from that New Dawn bunch of dickheads, nicked the costumes. How one of those costumes ended up on your victim I've no idea.'

'It's the victim I'd like to talk about, Mr Donahue.'

'That's Detective Superintendent Donahue.'

'You're retired.'

'I still deserve the title as a mark of respect.'

My God, he's an insufferable prick, she thought. She was tempted to tell him that respect was earned and not just handed over on a plate because you happened to have a title or had given enough funny handshakes to climb the promotion ladder. But she controlled her instincts. Even so, she wasn't letting him off the hook.

'I'm showing you respect by contacting you myself and not getting a DC to do it,' she said. 'However, if you'd rather, I'll send a car to pick you up and we can talk here in Inverness.'

'You've used that bluff once too often, darling.'

'It's no bluff, *former* Detective Superintendent. And it's DCI Roach, not *darling.* I am nobody's darling.' She thought of Joe. It was a fleeting thought, an impression of his face really. *Jesus, when will this shit end?*

'I can understand that,' said Donahue, and she regretted giving him the feedline. 'So best get on with it. What do you want now?'

'I've received some information that you may be able to help me with.'

She had just put the phone down after speaking to Rebecca Connolly, who had told her that the dead man had been seen arguing with Donohue. She'd refused to reveal her source. Roach had considered threatening the younger woman but decided against it, for now. So far she and her friend Elspeth had been as good as their word. If this tip proved as dependable as their first then this unofficial partnership might be beneficial in the long run. Anyway, she didn't like Donahue. Didn't like his air of male privilege. He was old job and she was new. She wanted the opportunity to noise him up.

'Get on with it then, dar—, I mean DCI Roach,' Donahue snapped. 'I've not got all day.'

'None of us do, *former* Detective Superintendent.' She heard him exhale sharply. She was getting his goat. She shouldn't be doing that but she didn't care. 'Have you seen the image of the murder victim?'

A slight pause greeted her question. There was a lie coming, she knew it. 'I haven't had time to look, I'm—'

'A busy man, yes, that's been established. I'm asking because we've received information that you knew him.'

The line between them fell silent again. Just for a moment. A breath. 'Who told you that?'

'That doesn't concern you at this stage. It seems you were observed arguing with the dead man.'

'That's not true.' The words came quickly. A bit too quickly. Another lie. She was disappointed. She would have expected a former detective superintendent to be a more accomplished liar. Surely, he'd had plenty of practice back in the day, or maybe he was just out of the habit?

'So, you didn't threaten to kill him?'

'I did not.'

'Have you ever threatened to kill anyone?'

'DCI Roach, I'm sure I've threatened to kill at least one person during the course of my career. Haven't you?'

Joe. She threatened to kill her husband once. It had been an argument, a bad one. It had raged back and forth and at one point she had blurted out that she would do him in if he continued. She didn't mean it. She regretted it now.

'We're not talking about me,' she said. 'I mean recently, have you argued with someone recently and threatened bodily harm?'

'No, Detective Chief Inspector, I have not.' His voice had regained its confidence. 'Where are you getting this from?'

Both pieces of information had related to the movie production, so Roach had little doubt that the person worked there. She wasn't about to share that hunch, though. 'Information received.'

'Anonymous?'

'I can't say.'

'I'll bet.' His voice was dry now. He was back on firmer ground.

'So you did not know the victim and did not have an argument with him? You did not throw him to the ground and threaten to kill him?'

'Asked and answered already,' he said. 'Is that all?'

Roach didn't know what she'd expected from him, but she couldn't press the matter further. 'Yes, that's all for now.'

He hung up without saying goodbye. That was hurtful and she might never recover. She stared at the phone for a while, as if it had some answers. Perhaps she should have pressed that reporter for the name. Elspeth McTaggart struck her as an old hand and not easily threatened, but Rebecca Connolly was young and might cave. Whoever it was might be spinning them a yarn, someone who didn't like John Donahue. She felt reasonably certain that was a long list. She had relished the chance of poking the bear

158

but, on the off chance there was something in this report of an altercation between Donahoe and the dead man, she needed to speak to the witness directly. That meant she would have to meet Rebecca Connolly and try somehow to talk her into parting with the name. She had a feeling she would have to come in with guns blazing.

The landline on her desk beeped. 'DCI Roach,' she said.

'Got a call for you, boss.' Yul's voice. What the hell was he doing being a telephonist? 'Came through to the incident room.'

Another mystery solved. 'Okay, who is it?'

There was a slight pause, as if he was embarrassed, before he answered, 'Eh . . . it's your husband.'

29

Rebecca was washing her plate and cup – another pasta ready-meal nuked in minutes – the TV tuned to the BBC news, when the name Walter Lancaster reached into the small kitchen and grabbed her. She stepped into her living room, her hands still wet and dripping soapy bubbles, in time to see that night's *Reporting Scotland* presenter hand over to Lola McLeod, live in Inverness. The reporter was bundled up in a warm coat with the grey waters of the Moray visible in the gathering darkness behind her, the lights of the Kessock Bridge soaring upwards. Rebecca's heart began to hammer as she listened to Lola outline the story. She felt physically sick. It wasn't that they'd got the man's name – they would have picked that up from her online report – it was the fact that they had actually tracked him down to a hostel. She should have done that. She should have found him. She hadn't, but Lola had.

The report cut to daylight on a street in Inverness, and there he was, a plastic grocery bag in one hand, shoulders hunched, eyes studying the ground beneath his feet as if he was counting the cracks in the pavement. He hadn't changed much since the snatched shot Rebecca had seen in the newspaper. His hair was perhaps a bit thinner, still in need of a wash. He'd lost a bit of weight, though. Not much, but a bit. He was still pear-shaped, his legs looking slightly knock-kneed in a pair of wide trousers. He still bore the scars of being beaten by the ugly stick at birth. Some men improve with age, but not Lancaster. Or perhaps it was the ugliness within that shone through.

He didn't speak to Lola when she stepped out to intercept him as he tried to enter the hostel. He seemed surprised to see her, then gave the camera a hunted look. Lola asked him why he wanted to stay in Inverness. He didn't answer, tried to sidestep her, but she smoothly moved with him, not quite blocking his way but not exactly letting him pass easily. She asked him if he thought the people of Inchferry should have a say in whether he was rehomed there. He veered away again, giving the camera another furtive glance, the hand with the plastic bag coming up to try to block its view of his face. Lola let him pass this time but kept asking him questions. Are you still a danger to children, Mr Lancaster? Do you think you're a good neighbour, Mr Lancaster? Do you think you'll be safe, Mr Lancaster?

The last question was posed in a raised voice – Lola was too classy to actually shout – to Lancaster's hunched back as he scuttled into the safety of the hostel. Then it was back to the reporter on the wall near the bridge to sum up in a sentence or two.

So much for Lola McLeod just being lipstick on legs. First she had heard about the clothes and now she had tracked Lancaster down, which was more than Rebecca had done. She had put his face out there, again more than Rebecca had done, as they didn't have the rights to the images she had seen. Lola was fast becoming the main competition in this story. Elspeth and Rebecca would have to work harder to keep up with her if they wanted to stay ahead of the game.

30

The child stares at the face paused on the TV screen. He is a stranger and yet so very familiar. He has never been part of the child's life and yet he has been. Or someone like him.

It's the eyes. Something in the eyes. A look, a light, a glint. A crack in the veneer of normality that shows something else exists within. The child sees that same look in that little room, in the eyes of the man as he stands beside that little bed.

There is regret, yes, in those eyes. There is guilt. But there is something else. As if whatever lives inside him has only been temporarily satisfied. The child knows he will return for more. He might struggle with his desires, he might occasionally overcome them, but whatever creature it is that compels him to come to that little room and that little bed always proves stronger in the end. No matter how friendly, how loving he is as they watch videos together, no matter how gentle his touch as he strokes the child's hair, it knows that something else nestles in his body, within his soul, and merely waits to spring back to life, and that caress will be less loving, less benevolent. Not that night. Perhaps not even the next, or the one after that. But it always comes. And with it, the phantoms.

Pain.

Shame.

They are with the child now as it sits directly in front of the television, up close to the screen. All the better to see those eyes. And the thing that lives within this man, using those eyes as a window. The child can see it there. The child knows it well and recognises it for what it is. And the child sits back, knowing what it must do.

For it has its own creature to feed.

The third phantom.

Rage.

31

If the Burkes hadn't made sure that the word was out on the street about what social services were planning that night – aided, Rebecca had little doubt, by her own online story and Lola's TV report – then the presence of a minibus full of uniformed police officers most certainly did the trick. Of course, there was an attempt at discretion, as much as any vehicle with POLICE SCOTLAND emblazoned on the side can be. It was parked just outside the Ferry boundary, on a side street that led to a stretch of wasteland where a housing company had once planned to build up-market properties but had gone spectacularly bust before a single brick was laid. The little street came to what could be seen as a sad end, never having realised its potential. The tarmac petered out in a ragged line as nature encroached on it. There was no street lighting here – the long grass and scraggy bushes and the occasional fox had no need for illumination – so the officers thought they might rest there undetected.

Rebecca thought they might as well have taken out an advertisement in the paper.

She had spotted them as she drove into the Ferry, Chaz in the passenger seat. He shot a few frames through the car window as they passed but neither of them said anything about it. They may have both been incomers, but they knew the Ferry would already know about the cops lurking on the outskirts. It was that kind of area.

The streets were busier than usual. Rebecca had been to the Ferry many times on stories, but she had never seen so many people walking on the pavements. Men, women, even children and dogs joined a breeze that lifted from the chilly waters of the Beauly Firth and drifted around the streets like it was looking for someone. It was a cold night and normally these people would have been at home, gathered in front of the telly. But not tonight. Something was happening. Some of them knew what it was, but the others merely sensed it. Tonight there was something better to watch than *EastEnders*.

Rebecca sensed it too. She knew the root cause, of course, but there was something more there, something carried on the Firth's cold breath. The atmosphere was charged with expectation, as if someone had pumped a highly volatile gas into the air, and her instincts told her that it would not take much to cause an explosion. There was going to be trouble tonight, she knew it, and there was no way she could miss it, risk assessment or no risk assessment. Chaz had also made the decision to come, confident he could sell the shots on a freelance basis.

She drove directly to the Burkes' home. Nolan had told her to come and she knew that it would be the centre of operations. Sure enough, there were a number of vehicles parked outside, including the black Mercedes SUV the older brother had driven the night before. Butterfly wings fluttered in her stomach, not just because of that feeling of impending violence but because she knew she would have to face him again. She was not looking forward to the awkwardness she would feel.

As before, it was Scott who answered the door. If he was surprised to see her, he hid it well. His smile was still in place and it still creeped her out.

'Smell a story, eh?' he said, then looked past her at Chaz. The smile faltered briefly. Rebecca craned round and saw that Chaz was hanging onto the camera bag draped over his shoulder like it was the last life preserver on the *Titanic*. In his other hand he gripped his stick tightly, ready to wield it as a weapon. He still hadn't grown used to places like the Ferry and tended to believe the fiction that you could be mugged within five minutes of getting out of the car. Scott's eyes fixed on the bag and a frown began to pucker his brow. He obviously didn't like the idea of a camera in their midst.

'Can I speak to your mum?' Rebecca asked, hoping to break the tension.

Scott dragged his attention away from the camera bag and the smile returned. On balance, Rebecca thought the frown less threatening. 'Did the lawyer no speak to you?'

The mention of Simon made Rebecca wonder if he would be here. More awkwardness. 'Yes, and I've agreed to keep what was said out of any story.'

'Nothing was said.' Scott's voice was flat, but there was enough menace in the way he stared at her – that smile – to make his point.

'Well,' she said, 'things were said, whether you like it or not, but it doesn't matter. I'm not going to report them, no need to worry.'

'I'm no worried, eh. Maybe you should be, though.'

There was something implied there, she knew, but she wasn't about to let some little ned threaten her.

Don't let them see fear, her father's advice to new recruits, passed on to her when she was a teenager. *You might be trembling in your size twelves, you might feel as if you're about to soil yourself, but never let them know it. Once they know they have you scared, they know they have you.*

Her voice was momentarily frozen with suppressed anger. 'Mr Burke, I've told you once already and I'm not going to repeat myself. Now, are you going to tell your mother I'm here or not?'

Scott Burke looked her up and down, that same appraising look he'd given her the first time they'd met. 'Why should I?'

She was about to argue the point again when she heard Nolan's voice from the hallway. 'Let the lassie in, Scotty. Don't be an arse.'

Nolan stepped into view, his gaze studiously avoiding Rebecca's. Or perhaps it was her eyes that slid away. Scott stepped aside to let her pass without a word but, as Chaz neared him, he snarled, 'Snapper boy, you keep that camera of yours away from me, eh? You take one shot of me and you'll wear it as a butt plug, you get me?'

'Scotty, stop coming the big man,' warned Nolan. 'Leave the boy alone.'

Rebecca thanked Nolan as she walked by but he didn't acknowledge it. 'You know the way,' he said.

She heard voices coming from the sitting room, so she followed them, checking that Chaz was not being harassed by Scott again. But Scott was giving his brother a quizzical look.

'When the fuck did you get pally with the media?' Scott said in a not too subtle whisper, but Nolan did not respond as he followed Rebecca and Chaz into the sitting room.

Cigarette smoke bit at Rebecca's eyes and lungs as she entered the room, which was considerably less tidy than it had been on her previous visit. People, all locals, Rebecca assumed, stood in groups or sat in every bit of seating available, even the floor. She recognised a few of the faces from the demo outside the council office. She looked for Simon – felt relief when she didn't see him. No Finbar Dalgliesh either, she noted, but then he wouldn't show up here. Standing shoulder-to-shoulder at a public gathering was one thing – he could argue the issue was more important than the players – but to be in the home of alleged drug dealers was quite another. That couldn't be spun quite as easily. Beer cans littered the coffee table, bottles of whisky too, and ashtrays were in evidence, most overflowing. Music was playing, it sounded like a '90s vintage *Now That's What I Call Music*, so Rebecca guessed it was Mo Burke's choice. It seemed like a party, and maybe it was. There was no sign of Midge, the West Highland terrier, and his bed was missing from under the radiator beneath the window. Perhaps the little dog didn't like large groups of people. Perhaps he just made a pest of himself. Or perhaps there were people here who were frightened of dogs. Could happen, even in the Ferry.

Eyes and faces turned to them as they entered, the Ferry residents' well-developed sense of stranger alert ever present. They knew she and Chaz were not locals, of course, but once again she felt she was being judged.

'Maw,' Nolan shouted from behind her, 'the lassie from the paper is back to see you.'

Mo Burke pushed her way through from the kitchen door, a glass of whisky in one hand, a cigarette in the other, her eyes automatically sweeping around the room as if checking no one was doing anything they shouldn't. After all, there were strangers among them. Rebecca knew some of them were partaking of substances proscribed by law. Tobacco fumes were prevalent, but there was also the sweet aroma of wacky baccy.

'Didn't think I'd see you again, love,' said Mo, the words reasonably pleasant but the expression saying she really didn't *want* to see her again.

'I heard about the council's plans for tonight, Mrs Burke,' said Rebecca.

'Aye, saw that on the internet. And on the telly. And the council denied it, which is par for the course with they bastards. Never tell the truth when a lie will do.' She seemed to be addressing her guests rather than Rebecca. She was looking around, waving both arms in an exaggerated fashion. Mo Burke was half-pissed and Rebecca saw her eyes were slightly glazed as they swung back towards her. 'What puzzles me is how you heard about it.'

Nolan had edged around them and picked up a drink he had obviously left on the mantelpiece. He seemed relaxed. He would not want his family knowing he had tipped her off, but if he feared she was going to finger him, he covered it well. She was still puzzled by that tingle in her stomach when she looked at him. *Okay, Becks – what's that all about?*

'You're not the only one with contacts, Mrs Burke,' Rebecca lied.

Mo Burke was unimpressed. 'Oh, aye? So you're back here in the big bad Ferry for the story? Hoping to see some blood spilled, I'll bet.' Mo transferred her attention from Rebecca to Chaz. She looked him up and down like she was measuring him for a suit, her eyes taking in the camera bag. 'You'll no be taking any photies of my family, son.'

'If they're in the street, Mrs Burke, I can do what I want.' Chaz's voice was strong and clear. Rebecca knew he was nervous, but she was proud of him. *Don't show them fear.*

'I've already warned him, Maw,' said Scott from behind them. 'He as much as points that camera at us, he loses it. Simple as.'

There were a few murmurs of agreement and some nodding heads. Rebecca knew she and Chaz were not welcome here. She wished Midge would escape from wherever he had been penned just so she could feel someone was glad to see them. It had been a mistake to come here, even if she had something to say to Mo Burke.

'Mrs Burke, can I have a word in private?'

'We're all pals here,' said Mo. 'Whatever you've got to say to me, you can say to us all, that right?'

More nodding, more murmurs of assent. She heard a female voice say, 'Aye, all pals – which is more than the bloody *Chronicle* ever is.'

Rebecca ignored it. She was used to the ill-feeling people often held for their local newspaper. They had probably run a story about whoever had spoken or a family member, perhaps a court story. Or had got something wrong. It happened.

'Mrs Burke, we saw a vanload of police on the way into Inchferry tonight. They know what you're planning.'

Mo nodded. 'We know they're there. We're no feared of the police, are we?'

The response was very much in agreement with her.

'Anyway,' Mo said, 'it's all going to be very peaceful. We know which flat they've earmarked to put that bastard into and we're going to demonstrate outside it, that's all. No fuss. No trouble.'

'And if they ignore you?'

'They won't.'

Rebecca looked around the people in the room. These were ordinary people in the main, but there were others who were not so ordinary. She saw hard-faced men and harder-faced women. She saw tattoos. She saw scars and muscles. She saw eyes that were bright with booze or drugs. The highly charged vapours touring the streets outside were heightened here. If the spark came, the flint was being sharpened in this room, she knew it.

'You need to call it off, Mrs Burke,' said Rebecca.

Scott laughed behind her. 'Too bloody late for that.'

Mo agreed with her son. 'Scotty's right. They started this with their plan to bring a pervert into our community. We won't let them, right?'

She was still playing to the audience and the roar of agreement was instant and emphatic.

'Look,' said Rebecca, giving it one last try, 'you don't understand. They know about your plans.'

'Thanks to you.'

Rebecca had to concede that, with a slight inclination of her head. 'And so do the police. That being said, the chances are they won't try to bring him in, not tonight. In fact, given the publicity your campaign has had, Mrs Burke, there's every possibility that they won't bring him in ever.'

She was tempted to say that was down to the power of the media, but didn't. She could not try to claim any credit for any perceived victory here.

'Good,' said Mo. 'But just in case they do, we're ready tonight. They don't bring him here tonight, nothing will happen. They don't bring him here ever? Then it all goes away. It all ends. Take him anywhere but here, okay? You put that on your website and your paper. Anywhere but here. What is it they say? NIMBY? Not in my back yard, that right?'

Her friends told her she was right.

'Aye, well, that's us. Not here. Not our streets. We're done being the dumping ground. Decent folk live here, decent folk with families. Oh, I know what you're thinking, love, I see it in your face. Mo Burke and her boys talking about decent folk, what a laugh. But see, I don't care what you think of us – we don't care. Come here, Scotty.'

Scott moved around Rebecca and Chaz to join his mother. She stretched out an arm and pulled Nolan closer. She stood with her arms round both her sons, a family unit, a picture of defiance. She wished Chaz was allowed to capture it. 'We care about this place, these streets. We care even if the bloody council doesn't. This is our home. The Ferry. They do us down, they call us shit, treat us like it too. But every person in this room cares because it's their home too. You folk from the outside don't understand this. You can never understand this. You see us?' She pulled her sons tighter. 'You see them?' She jutted her chin towards her friends. 'This is community. This is family. And the council will learn tonight that you don't cross family.'

It was a fine speech and Mo delivered it well, even half canned. She really had missed her calling; she should be in politics. Rebecca could feel the animosity building with each word, so she decided it was time to leave. She didn't know why she felt it necessary to try to prevent any trouble. She had done what she could. She jerked her head to Chaz and they moved into the hallway. As they headed for the front door, she was aware of Nolan breaking away from the family picture to follow. Laughter and a staccato rattle of applause followed them down the hallway.

At the front door, Rebecca turned to Nolan, checked Scott hadn't also tagged along but still hushed her tone. 'You know there will be trouble tonight, don't you?'

He looked at her properly for the first time and she thought he was going to deny it, to follow the party line spouted by his mother. But all he did was nod.

'You have to try to stop it,' Rebecca said, hoping that whatever made him want to get out of this life he had been born into would come to the fore.

'Can't do that,' he said.

'Why not?

He looked back down the hallway, where the voices had grown louder. Rebecca did the same and saw Scott was now standing in the doorway to the sitting room, watching them. Smiling.

'It's gone too far,' said Nolan, knowing Scott could hear every word. 'And anyway, maybe it's what's needed.'

'So is violence always the answer?'

He faced her again. 'Sometimes violence is the only answer.'

32

The thing that had always annoyed Val Roach about Joe was that he never seemed to look any older. Sure, there were lines around the eyes that hadn't been there when they'd met at university (she was studying sociology, he physics) – but even now, more than twenty years later, he still more or less looked the same. Even his hair hadn't begun to turn grey. Unless of course he was into the Grecian 2000. He had taken to sporting some designer stubble, though, perhaps in a bid to disguise a sagging jawline. There was still something boyish about him, a quality that endeared him to a number of women, including a 25-year-old lab assistant with whom he was now shacked up. It was such a cliché – older man meets younger woman, their eyes meet over a flaming Bunsen burner, or whatever the hell physicists use in the lab. He finds that her youthful spirit reignites things he thought had either died or gone into hibernation in his forty-year-old body. Blah, blah, blah. Etc., etc., etc. But that's the thing about clichés – they only become clichés by being commonplace.

When he had told her about the affair – it had been going on for over a year by that time – Val had wanted him dead. After the divorce she had decided to pull a Jean-Luc Picard and made it so, even if only in her mind. He was, as the saying went, dead to her. She had never taken his name and that helped distance herself. She knew it was a coping mechanism, a means of moving on. She knew he wasn't really in that great physics laboratory in the sky but it helped to think of him as gone and not rutting away in Lolita's bed.

And now, here he was. In Inverness. Standing on the doorstep of her

Culloden semi-detached, giving her that boyish grin. When he had phoned that afternoon, he'd said he wanted to meet up. She wasn't terribly keen but he was insistent, said there was something they needed to talk about and he didn't want to do it on the phone. She could have said no way, she didn't like communicating with the dead, but she'd held her tongue. She was at work anyway and there were things to be done, so she gave him her address and told him to be there by 6.30 p.m. That was fifteen minutes ago. He was always late. The Late Dr Maguire, they used to call him.

There was that smile. She loved that smile. She hated that smile. 'Sorry, got a wee bit lost.'

'Really? It's not that big a place.'

Smile. Love. Hate. 'Well, you know me . . .'

Yes, she did. His complete inability to get anywhere without becoming totally confused by which direction he was travelling had been cute at one time. Now it was just irritating.

She stepped back. 'You'd better come in.'

She had to admit she was curious as to what was so important that he needed to see her. She wondered if things had gone south between him and Lolita. She knew that wasn't the child's name, but it suited her to call her that. She wondered if he was there to tell her it had all been a big mistake and he wanted to come back, wanted things the way they used to be. She was already wondering what her reaction would be, should that be what was said.

She didn't wonder for long because he didn't even sit down or take off his sheepskin coat. He stopped in the living room, had a quick look around, then turned to face her.

'Deborah and I are going to get married.'

He blurted it out, as if the words had been desperate for air.

She was taken aback by the suddenness of it. 'Congratulations,' she said. It was the only thing she could think of at the time.

He had the decency to look ashamed. Somewhat. 'I thought . . . well, I wanted you to know.'

'Kind of you,' she said.

'She, eh . . .' He stopped, swallowed. 'I mean, we, eh, are going to have a baby.'

She felt like she had been slapped. She didn't know why. They had both agreed that children were not on their agenda. Careers. Having the freedom to be happy together. That was what was important to them. Neither of them had ever felt the need to be parents and yet, here he was, over forty now and announcing he was about to become a father.

'And you thought what?' The words came out like a broken bottle. 'To get my blessing? You want me to be godmother?'

'No. I just didn't want you to hear from anyone else, is all.'

They still had mutual friends, acquaintances really. She had left all that behind when she moved away from Perth and their home and all that had occurred. Still, it was always possible someone would get in contact to let her know, or she would see a photograph on Facebook on the few occasions a year she logged on to see what people were eating and where.

'Fine. You've told me.' The jagged edges of her voice slashed defensive strokes in the air. 'Is there anything else?' She didn't want to hear anything more. There couldn't be anything more, could there? 'You want me to sell the Perth house for your child's university fund?'

'No, the house is yours, you know that. There's nothing more. I just wanted to see you to tell you. I thought, *we* thought, you deserved to hear it in person.'

'We?'

'Deborah and me.'

'Ah, Lolita.'

He closed his eyes briefly, as if warding off pain. 'Don't call her that.'

'Why? Does it hurt your feelings?'

It was his turn to bring some steel to his voice. 'It's unfair. What happened wasn't her fault . . .'

'So you forced yourself on her? Should I be taking a statement?'

'It just happened, that's all, Val. We went through all this.'

'Aye, shit happens, right?'

'I never wanted to hurt you.'

'And yet – here we are . . .'

His eyes flashed. 'Jesus, Val – isn't it time you put the cheated wife to one side? It's not as if you were always there for me.'

Her laugh was short and bitter. 'Here we go. I always put my career first . . .'

'Well, you did. There were times when you were on some case or other I hardly saw you. And let's be honest, you're not the most emotionally available person in the world.'

'Emotionally available?' Her laugh this time was more mocking. 'Have you been reading *Cosmo* again?'

'Come on, Val, you know what I mean. When did we ever sit down as man and wife and talk about ourselves? About feelings? You know you didn't like to talk about emotions.'

'It was implicit in our being together. You could tell by the way I didn't shag someone else.'

That really got to him. 'Well, maybe if we had talked a bit more, maybe if you had shown just a bit of human bloody emotion I wouldn't have needed to!'

'Okay, so it's all my fault.'

'It's no one's fault. It just happened, that's all. I met someone. I'm happy with her.'

'And you're going to have a baby.'

'Yes.'

'Which you never wanted with me.'

'Which neither of us wanted.'

'But it's different now.'

'Yes.'

Their voices lost their respective edges. They stared at each other, a gap of three feet and a lifetime between them. There was nothing more to be said, they both knew that. They were both right and both wrong.

'I'd better go,' he said, moving past her. She didn't argue and she didn't follow him into the hallway. He knew where the door was, he didn't need an escort. Not even he could get lost in her home.

Joe stopped in the hallway and turned back. 'I did love you, you know. Back then. Still do, Val. But I moved on.'

'Okay,' she said, her voice hardening again. 'That makes everything all right, then.'

He stared at her for a moment, obviously debating whether to say anything further. Then he sighed, opened the door and was gone. Val moved into the hall and turned the lock. She stood with her back against the door and memories flashed through her mind like lightning bolts. Meeting him at the Student Union. Laughing. The first time they made love. More laughing. Camping at Loch Ness, the rain seeping through the canvas. Laughing again. Their wedding. Holidays. Watching a movie. Always laughing. Happy.

But it hadn't all been laughter. There had been arguments. There had been long periods of silence. They changed. They grew up. And, if she was honest with herself, she had played her part in that. The Job. Her career. The laughter ebbed, the fun times became little more than snapshots in an album. She had grown more attached to the work than her home, and he had – what? On some level she had known he was seeing someone else and his confession only confirmed it. She had ignored what her subconscious had been telling her because she believed he was too decent a man to do that.

She had been wrong and she should have known better. If there was one thing she had learned as a police officer it was that people are capable of anything.

33

Rebecca and Chaz found the street easily. The Ferry wasn't that big and they followed the locals until they came upon a larger group, some with anger tightening their features, others just there to see what was going on, a few for a laugh or because they sensed there was going to be trouble and they wanted a piece of it.

Finbar Dalgliesh was there, of course. He was savvy enough not to associate himself too closely with the Burkes, but Rebecca knew there was no way on this earth that he was going to miss this opportunity. First, he could use it to embarrass not only Highland Council but also the Scottish government. Second, there might be votes in the fact that he was the only politician who deigned to come to the Ferry on this important night.

Rebecca brought the car to a halt a good distance from the crowd. Dalgliesh was easy to spot, his cashmere trench coat keeping the probing breeze out, though it would prove ineffective should it rain again. He stood on the pavement beside the gate of the flats, which looked like terraced houses but were in fact upper and lower apartments. Both flats looked empty and the small garden that led to the wooden fence was slightly overgrown. They couldn't hear what the Spioraid leader was saying, but Rebecca knew he was stirring up the crowd. If there was one thing Dalgliesh was good at, it was whipping up emotion. He could judge the mood of any gathering and tell people what they wanted to hear. Playing to confirmation bias was what he did. And some carefully placed followers would help. A murmur here, a word there, perhaps instigating applause or a cheer. It all helped.

'What do you think?' Chaz asked, as he hauled his camera bag over from the back seat and rummaged inside.

'I think we sit here for a while, see what happens.' She craned round to peer back the way they had come. 'I think if they bring this guy in, they'll come the way we did.'

Chaz produced his camera from his bag. 'You think they will bring him – even after the stories?'

She settled back in her seat. 'Buggered if I know. They would be showing incredible irresponsibility if they did. They know the Burkes and Dalgliesh know about this. They'll know the Ferry will know about it. They should know that, if they do, it will just put a match to the blue touchpaper.'

She watched as he lowered the side window and leaned out, the long telephoto lens of the camera snapping a few shots of the crowd. He pulled himself back in and studied the images on the small screen on the rear of the camera. She sensed his disappointment in the results.

'You need to get closer?'

'Yeah,' he said. 'Bit too dark for this long-range stuff. You think we should risk it?'

She studied the crowd. She wanted to hear what Dalgliesh was saying but, as they had already learned, the press was not welcome in the Ferry. Too many court stories, not enough support. She glanced in the wing mirror, saw the police minibus pull up at the far end of the street, lights off. Their presence in the street was either a precaution or they had been told the situation was growing volatile. But she really wanted to hear Dalgliesh.

Ah, to hell with it. 'Who wants to live for ever?' she said, opening the door.

'Other Queen songs are available,' said Chaz, as he swung open the passenger door.

They began to walk side by side up the street, Chaz scanning the scene ahead, already looking for the best camera angles. 'So, that was Nolan.'

She knew something would be said. She was surprised it had taken him this long.

'Yes, that was Nolan.'

'Bit of a stud muffin.'

'Stop it.'

'If you don't want him, I might ditch Alan and try my luck.'

'I don't think you're his type,' she said, laughing.

'What? He doesn't like photographers?'

They had reached the fringes of the crowd, which stretched across the road and up onto the opposite pavement, blocking any way forward. More people headed towards them from both directions. Dalgliesh's voice reached them easily here.

'. . . would show what they thought of you, the good people of Inchferry. If they carry on with their plan, they would show that they think very little of you and the safety of your children. And I say NO!'

It was very much a copy of what he'd said outside the council office. It had worked then, it would work now. Rebecca looked around her, studied the faces of the people listening to him. He was tapping into rage that went beyond this particular issue. He was kindling years, maybe decades, of prejudice and social inequality. He was making the people of the Ferry believe that they were treated as second-class citizens, as mere fodder for a political elite who cared little for the ordinary Scot. His targets were always whoever was in authority, whether locally or nationally, and he then turned it into a them and us. But tonight he was playing a dangerous game. She could feel it around her, on the wind that plucked at clothes and toyed with hair. It wouldn't take much to set this particular touchpaper aflame.

34

Nolan watched as Maw drained her drink and stubbed out her cigarette in a heaped ashtray on the mantle. It was time to move. He knew it was coming, yet he still dreaded it. He had never been convinced this public display of civic mindedness was wise, given how the family made its way in the world. He strongly felt it would eventually impact on their business and had counselled his mother not to take up the cudgel on behalf of the Ferry. It would have been best if she had allowed him to find someone to act as a front. Maw could still have run the show, but from a distance, just like they did at Barney's. After all, there were many people who would feel as strongly about the issue while also happy to earn some brownie points with the Burke family. But no, she was insistent that she take the lead – backed to the hilt by Scott, naturally.

'Where's Scotty?' Maw asked.

Nolan hadn't seen his brother since Rebecca had left. 'Must've gone up to his room.'

'Go get him. Tell him we're leaving.'

At the top of the stairs, Scott's bedroom door lay open and Nolan heard a woman's voice. He found his brother lying on his belly on his bed, his laptop open before him. He shut the lid down when he became aware of Nolan's presence but Nolan thought he saw the BBC logo and glimpsed a man's face in close-up. As usual, the room was like a jumble sale, with clothes strewn all over the place. The only item that was in any way ordered was the small bookcase under the window, three neat shelves of books, all paperbacks. They were mostly Scottish history – Scotty's passion, apart from finding new ways to hurt people who pissed him off. Nolan had bought a few for him, birthdays and Christmas, back when they actually had something in common other than shared DNA. Even from the doorway Nolan could see the complete set of titles by John Prebble that he had found in the big used book store on Church Street one day, their orange spines faded over the years. Nolan wasn't too bothered about reading books himself – he preferred newspapers – but he did like to wander among the stacks in that place.

'Maw's headed out,' Nolan said, wondering why Scott was up here watching the news. 'You coming?'

Scott rolled over and swung his long legs off the bed. 'Nah, got things to do.'

'Maw won't be pleased to hear that, Scotty.'

'Aye, well – she'll have to live with it.'

If Nolan said he wasn't going, Mo would throw a fit. She wouldn't be happy Scott wasn't there, but he'd get away with it. He always did.

'What sort of things have you got to do?' Nolan asked.

Scott gave him that smile. 'Things. Business.'

Business. Nolan could have pressed the point, dug deeper, but the truth was he didn't really care. For all his desire to see his family flourish, Nolan was conflicted. He had told Rebecca he wanted out and it was true. He had become tired of it all. Scott had seen to that. A power drill, for God's sake. That was over the top and yet, for Scott, somehow expected. His younger brother had become very much a mystery to him in recent years. Nolan couldn't read him, and this latest tendency to seek out violent confrontations was worrying. He was getting more out of hand, more difficult to control.

Nolan had sufficient self-awareness to know that he was also capable of violence; he had used it, even revelled in it, when he was younger. But he had matured and now only saw it as a means to an end, or a defence mechanism. For Scotty, it was a leisure pursuit. This trouble with Wee Joe McClymont had all the hallmarks of a clusterfuck of epic proportions. Nolan had argued for a compromise, but Scotty had taken the opposite view, arguing that if they gave McClymont an inch, the creepy wee bastard would steal a mile. Maw had sided with Scotty, which was no surprise.

Even Scott bringing in his pal Finbar Dalgliesh failed to dent that bond. Scott's connection with that slimeball and Spioraid was a worry. They were a bunch of right-wing cranks, as far as Nolan was concerned, little more than racist thugs led by a man with no real principles other than self-interest. Okay, that didn't make him any worse than most politicians – or crooks, come to that – but Dalgliesh was stirring something almost primal with his divisive rhetoric. Nolan didn't think the man cared if the council placed Lancaster in the Ferry or not. It was just a way to undermine any kind of authority, to promote suspicion. Nolan knew it worried his mother too, but she let it slide, apart from a token warning to Scott to watch himself with those people. So Nolan was on his own. Their father, who might have argued for restraint, was out of the picture. His mother and brother were very much a unit, while he became more and more isolated.

Scott cocked his head to one side. 'So, what was all that about down there, eh?'

Nolan gave him a sideways look. Scott was scrutinising him, his now perpetual smile irritating as usual. He couldn't pinpoint just when Scott started with that bloody smile but one day someone would wipe it off. If he kept going the way he was, it was a coin toss who would do the wiping – McClymont or Nolan.

'What do you mean?'

'The wee huddle with that reporter bint in the hall.'

'I didn't "huddle" . . .'

'Aye, you did, man. At the door. Wee whispers.' Scott made a series of sibilant sounds with his tongue and lips. 'Secrets, man, secrets and whispers.' He made the *psss, psss, psss* sound again.

Nolan stared deep into his brother's eyes, saw the slightly unfocused glaze. He'd been sampling the goods again. That was becoming more common too. Nolan had spoken to him about it in the past and even Maw had pulled him up, but Scott didn't care. Blood and gear. That was Scott's life now.

'Don't know what you're talking about,' he said. He knew Scott wouldn't buy the evasion, but he wasn't going to fill in the details.

'What were you and her whispering about, eh? You making a date or something?'

Nolan felt something quicken in his blood. Did Scott know he'd been with Rebecca the previous night? He had wondered if going to Barney's was a mistake, but there was risk no matter where they went in Inverness. Nolan was a face, and all it would take was for one person – someone who knew him, someone who knew Scott, someone who knew their mother – to clock them and report back. Barney's was dead most nights, apart from Friday and Saturday, and deemed off limits to their immediate circle in order to keep the licence secure, so he'd thought it the safest place to go.

He decided to bluff it out. 'Well, even if I was, can you blame me? She's fine looking.'

Scott pulled the corners of his mouth down. 'Ah, she's no bad. No my style, though.'

Nolan wondered what his brother's style was. Certainly, he'd never known him to have any kind of relationship with a woman beyond a fumble at a party or, at most, for one night. Scott didn't forge long-term friendships. His circle of buddies was fluid and comprised mostly of young men who shared his need for violence. Nolan couldn't fault him for lack of friends, though; he had few himself, and none of them were close. Friendship was a luxury he couldn't afford, not with the life his family led.

That was another reason to get out.

He wanted to have a normal life. Maybe get a job – although doing God knows what. Have a family of his own. Not have to worry about a tap on the shoulder from the law or a rival. Not have to keep changing his phone and his number. Not have to take circuitous routes in order to ensure there was no one at his back. Not have to sit in a corner table with a full view of the room or, as he had done the night before because that stranger had taken the best table, with his eye on the mirror. He wanted to be able to take a woman out for a drink and not be hassled by arseholes.

He wanted all of that, but in his most honest moments he knew he would never have them.

Scott must have sensed something. He scrutinized his brother, then said, 'What is it with you these days, bro?'

'How do you mean?'

'You've no been yourself, you know? You've been quiet and kinda strange. As if your heart's no in this any more.'

Nolan knew his question related to the family business, but he decided to evade it.

'Scotty,' he said, his right hand flicking to the doorway behind him and, by extension, downstairs, 'my heart's never been in all of this. You know that. This business tonight is just asking for shit to happen.'

Scott smirked. 'I'm no talking about the night, bro, and you know it. I'm talking about our business in general. There's something no right about you these days and I cannae quite put my finger on it. But I will, bro, I will.' He stood up. 'I've always got your back, bro. Don't forget that.'

Nolan knew that on the face of it his brother was showing him filial love, but he knew Scotty better than that. It wasn't a show of family loyalty. It was a warning.

35

A movement overhead caught Rebecca's eye.

Dalgliesh was spouting his usual vitriol in a tone that was casual, cultured and cultivated but using it to enflame the crowd. She had to admit he was smooth and accomplished at making outrageous ideas sound reasonable.

She looked up and saw the white underbelly of a gull floating like a ghost. It made no sound as it glided over the heads of the gathering, its feathers glowing white as they caught the light from below. It drifted against the dark sky, its wings barely moving, assisted by the breeze. And then it was gone, a silent visitor that had observed and found the scene below not to its taste.

As Rebecca lowered her eyes to Dalgliesh again, she knew how that gull felt. He had paused to take breath, to come up with some new lie or mangled half-truth, and was looking towards the edge of the crowd. Rebecca followed his gaze and saw Chaz as he wandered the periphery, very like the gull overhead, his cane under his arm as he snapped off some shots. Then the Spioraid leader's eyes found Rebecca standing at the very back under a streetlight and she knew he had a new subject to broach.

'Friends,' he said, 'and then we have the media and the way they blindly follow the dictates of the ruling elite. They do you no favours with their coverage. They spout lies on screens and print lies in the pages of their news-papers – not that anyone reads those now.'

There was laughter and Rebecca saw some of the crowd begin to take note of Chaz and his camera. No one had looked at her. Yet.

'We have to be very clear about this. The media is not your ally, not in this issue or any other. Its sole intention is to spread the agenda of the liberal elite. The middle classes who sit in their detached homes in their detached communities and defend the rights of the immigrants and the sexual deviants who they see as the underdogs in our society. And they chatter about it at dinner parties and bemoan how terrible life must be for the poor migrant who comes here to find a better life. They promote sexual perversions as somehow the norm. And they influence their fellow liberals in the media to present such perversions as a valid way to live and to ensure that they show different races on our screens. Diversity, they call it. Who here hasn't watched a drama in which homosexual couples have been presented as a normal family unit? Where black actors have been given roles that should have gone to white people, even to the point of manipulating historical fact?'

He stopped to look around. 'Now, there are people who say I am racist. There may even be some here.' He nodded towards a few people who had shuffled their feet when he took this particular tack. 'Let me assure you, I'm not.'

He's going to say 'Some of my best friends are black or gay', Rebecca thought. But he didn't.

'Although I can understand why people may believe it. I have nothing against anyone, no matter what their race, colour, gender, sexual predilection or religion, as long as they obey our laws, pay their taxes and don't try to inflict their beliefs or morals on the people of this country. I don't wish to see anyone harmed in any way. I do not condone violence.'

Yeah, right, Rebecca thought, *but you have people at your back who do. And you give them a voice.*

She studied the crowd closely, looking for anyone who might be a Spioraid plant, but despite the street lighting it was too dark and the problem was she didn't really know what she was looking for. These people looked just like everyone else.

'But what I ask is this – what about people like you? While the migrant and the immigrant, the homosexual and the transsexual are all given priority, are all given a voice, what about you? While the black experience and the gay life is dramatised and analysed and normalised, what about your experience? Why isn't the media talking about you, the ordinary, hard-working, hard-pressed Scottish men and women? Do you think the council would even consider placing this deviant in the midst of a community that is predominantly black or Asian? No, they wouldn't. And why? Because there would be an uproar. They would be accused of prejudice. But it's all right to dump him here, among you good people. And why? Because you are expected to take everything that they throw at you. And the media backs them all the way.'

Rebecca was growing increasingly uneasy and beginning to regret coming to the Ferry. Maybe Les had been right, with his risk assessment and his corporate responsibility. The focus of the demonstration was changing, Dalgliesh was seeing to that. He was savvy enough to have realised that the council plan to relocate Lancaster to the street – if they ever had intended to do so – had been abandoned. That meant he needed a new target. These people had come here in a common cause but, with time passing, that was being snatched away. With nothing tangible on which to focus their anger and hatred, he needed something else to bind them. And he had found it. Rebecca stared at Chaz as he snapped away, willing him to pay attention to what was being said and not what he saw through his lens.

Dalgliesh's smooth, cultured voice, with just enough smoker's grit to give it what Alan called *graveltas*, continued.

'Now, I won't go as far as to say that they are the enemy of the people. That would be wrong. But let me ask you this: when was the last time anyone in the media cared what happened here in the Ferry?'

When was the last time you cared, arsehole, Rebecca thought, *other than now, when there's something in it for you?*

She listened to Dalgliesh, she couldn't help it, but she began to move around the fringes of the crowd, her focus on her friend, who was too intent on his craft to notice that he was attracting far too much attention. One man in particular – muscular, shaved head, tattoos crawling up the back of his neck like rising damp – was staring at him intently. Rebecca didn't like the look of that stare.

'Oh, they'll report on how this place is like hell on earth. They'll drag your names, or your children's names, or your neighbours' names, through their pages and online when they are unfortunate enough to end up in court. But they will fail to recognise that most of you are honest, law-abiding Scots. To them, you're nothing but fodder for the legal industry – and a means of filling space so they can sell advertising or suck in your licence money.'

More faces had noted Chaz, still oblivious as he edged nearer to Dalgliesh in his search for that perfectly framed shot.

Damn it, Chaz, look the hell around!

As she moved, Rebecca caught a few glances in her direction too. She thought – perhaps imagined – recognition flashing in a few faces. Perhaps people who read the paper had seen her photograph, like the stranger in the bar the night before. Perhaps someone had seen her in court. That last thought hit her hard. Shit! Was there some truth in what Dalgliesh was saying? Would that notion even have entered her head if she was in one of the better areas of Inverness, like the Crown? This wasn't the place for soul-searching, though. She was still willing Chaz to give her as much as a fleeting look so she could somehow signal that it was time to go. To hell with the story. To hell with the Ferry. It was time to get out.

Rebecca saw Dalgliesh nod towards the walking muscle that had been eyeing Chaz. It was barely imperceptible – no one else would have noticed. Rebecca only spotted it because she was on the alert. But it confirmed to her that the guy was a Spioraid plant. She didn't have time to pat herself on the back because the man shifted slightly towards Chaz, who was still unaware of the attention being paid to him. Rebecca cried out his name and began to run, but she was hindered by too many bodies in her way and Chaz seemed deaf to her, his eye seemingly glued to his Nikon's viewfinder.

Rebecca inched her way between a man and woman cheering Dalgliesh on, bumping against them slightly. She apologised. They stopped cheering and stared at her. This time there was most definitely recognition. She heard the *Chronicle* being mentioned. This was not good. This was not good at all.

Chaz finally became aware that someone was at his elbow. He turned, the camera in his hands lowering slightly. He frowned, said something as if in answer to a query.

Rebecca only had a few feet to go. She shouted, 'Chaz!'

This time he looked towards her. The man swivelled too, just briefly, enough to take her in, then he reached out for the camera. Chaz caught his movement and stepped back, stumbled back really, one hand snatching his Nikon away, the other manoeuvring his cane from under his arm. It was instinct, but in the long run it was a bad move because the man also saw it and his hand snapped out to catch Chaz's wrist and jerked it and the cane higher, as if he was preventing a downward blow.

'Haw, take it easy, son,' he shouted, his Glasgow accent strong, then glanced around as faces turned. 'Bastard photographer was takin' my picture without permission.'

'I didn't,' Chaz shouted, struggling against the grip.

'Then when I asked him to quit it, he tried to brain me with his stick.'

Rebecca was beside them by this time. She reached out to Chaz to show support, to communicate calm. She stared at the man oozing self-righteous anger at his privacy being invaded. It was so obviously fake and yet she feared the people now clustering round them would buy it. Passions were high. Steam was building. It needed to blow.

'Let's just all relax here,' she said.

'Relax? I didn't come here for the media to use me to help boost their profits.' He looked at the circle of faces now clustered around them. 'He's one of they press photographers, like Finbar said. They're only interested in us when it suits them. When there's money in it.'

'Aye,' said a woman, nodding. 'That's right. The only time they pay a blind bit of notice to the Ferry is if it's crime or whatever.'

Rebecca heard agreement from all sides. The man and woman she had nudged closed in behind her.

'Bloody right,' said the man, still holding Chaz. 'And when I stand up for myself, for my rights, this bastard tries to pan my head in!'

'I didn't . . .' Chaz began, but he was shouted down.

'I saw ye, ya bastard!' said another voice, male. Rebecca sought out the source, found another burly individual whose broad face was lined with belligerence and whose forehead went all the way to the nape of his neck. He could have been the first man's twin. She suspected he was another Spioraid stooge.

'They think we're scum,' said the woman, and Rebecca wondered if she was part of it too.

Dalgliesh had stopped speaking and was pushing his way through the crowd towards the disturbance. So that was it, Rebecca realised: start a commotion, defuse it, become a hero.

'What's the trouble here?' Dalgliesh said, a flick of his eye telling his man to relinquish his grip of Chaz's arm.

'This guy was taking my picture. I asked him not to. He tried to take my head off with his cane.'

'Aye, and I saw him,' said the second stooge.

'Thinks we're scum,' the woman chimed in.

'This true, friend?' Dalgliesh oozed oily charm. 'Were you taking this man's photograph?' He touched the man's arm lightly. 'I'm sorry. What's your name?'

'Andy,' said the man. *Yeah, and I'm Meghan Markle*, Rebecca thought.

'Thank you,' Dalgliesh tilted his head in Chaz's direction again. 'So, were you taking Andy's photograph?'

'I was taking general shots of the demonstration,' said Chaz. 'We're in a public street and I'm legally entitled to—'

'Did you take Andy's photograph?' Dalgliesh brushed the legalities off and stuck to the main point.

'Not him specifically, but—'

'When he objected, did you try to strike him?' Dalgliesh kept going. When selling a lie, don't let the facts muddy the waters. Retain control of the narrative.

'No . . .'

'Lying bastard, I saw you,' shouted the second man, the one who claimed to have witnessed Chaz raise his cane. He jutted forward but was stopped by Dalgliesh's raised hand. Rebecca could tell this powerful personality act was playing well with the crowd.

'Thinks we're scum!' The woman was now addressing everyone around her. And everyone around her agreed.

Rebecca pulled Chaz away, but found her backward path blocked.

'Okay,' she said, more to Dalgliesh than anyone else, 'the point has been made. No one was hurt and there's a difference of opinion.'

'Oh, a difference of opinion, was it?' Andy's voice was heavy with sarcasm. He'd adopted a mock English accent. She didn't know why – Chaz spoke with a Scottish accent. 'This little bastard invades my personal privacy—'

'I did not!' Chaz interrupted, but Rebecca silenced him with a tug of the arm.

'And I'm supposed to just let him off with trying to brain me? That's no right . . .'

'Now, now, Andy.' Dalgliesh was all slick conciliation. The man in charge. The man of the moment. Cometh the hour, cometh the man. 'Let's just take it easy. As the young lady said . . .' Rebecca bristled – at the tag and the way it was said – but felt this was not the time or the place to give him a lesson in gender politics. 'There's no harm done. Let them get on their way.' He looked from Rebecca back to Chaz. 'I'm sure if Andy is in any of the photographs, you will have the decency not to use them.'

'Decency?' said the woman. 'They know bugger all about decency. They think we're scum. They're the scum! Muckraking bastards, the lot of them.'

Rebecca felt the heat rising around them, despite the freshness of the

191

breeze. She looked from face to face, seeking a friendly expression, but in the main found only hard lines and tight mouths made even more severe by the deep contrasts thrown by the LED streetlights. She finally landed on Dalgliesh, saw his half smile, the one that told her he knew he had the upper hand. She wished she could wipe that smile from his face somehow. She wished she could say something that would turn this entire situation around, but fear had frozen her tongue. She should never have come out here, not tonight. She could have reported on it from the safety of a telephone line. She should have listened to Les. She should have talked Chaz out of coming. She should have . . .

Rebecca didn't know who cried out next, such was the cluster of bodies around them, but it was the next three words that really kicked things off.

'It's the BBC!'

Heads turned, eyes swivelled, even Dalgliesh craned upwards to see over the throng. Rebecca peered through breaks in the bodies crowding around them to see a blue Land Rover pull up and Lola McLeod climb out, still wearing the thick jacket she'd worn for her report earlier, while her bearded cameraman moved round to the rear to collect his gear.

The BBC. They had produced a half-hour documentary on Dalgliesh and Spioraid that had been far from complimentary. Dalgliesh had dismissed it as an amateurish hatchet job on social media. He was none too fond of the *Chronicle*, but he really hated the corporation.

He jerked his head towards Andy, who instantly pushed his way through the crowd to where Lola was fixing her hair before she did a piece to camera. 'You're no wanted here, hen,' he said, loudly enough for everyone to hear. After all, there's no point in putting on a show if the audience can't catch every word.

Lola was taken by surprise and seemed momentarily speechless. She glanced at the cameraman, who was hefting a digital camera onto his shoulder. Quickly, she regained her composure, but her smile was more like a nervous twitch.

'We're here to report what's—'

'You're here to gloat, like you always do, is that no right?' Andy interrupted, looking around at the crowd, playing to a gallery that had turned away from Rebecca and Chaz to focus on the TV people. Dalgliesh kept well back. Intervening to 'save' two members of the print media was one thing, but being caught on camera, his every word recorded while purporting to do the same, meant risking being misconstrued. Or even correctly construed.

'Fuck off out of here,' said Andy. 'We don't want you reporting back to your bosses in the government about us here. This is our business, nobody else's.'

Lola felt the need to defend her employer. 'We are independent of government, as I'm sure you—'

'Aye, right! They bastards in Westminster control you like they control all the media, like they control Holyrood and the council. So get the fuck out of here!'

Lola attempted to salvage the situation by seemingly placing herself on the man's side.

'I'm sorry, sir, but if you'd just like to tell us what has made you so angry, maybe we can help. I take it you're against the council placing Walter Lancaster in your area?'

In any other situation it might have worked. Rebecca had done it herself many times. But this man had an agenda. He wasn't from the Ferry, of that Rebecca was certain, and he didn't care about Walter Lancaster. He was here to back up Dalgliesh and cause trouble.

She looked to where the Spioraid leader had been standing, saw he was gone. He had done enough to make it look as if he had defused the situation. Now he could claim his minders had spirited him away when they saw trouble brewing. Whatever happened would be spun in such a way that made it look as if the media was to blame, that they had shown up where they weren't wanted, had refused to leave. His followers would believe it because they wanted to. That was the secret of modern-day politics. Tell people what they want to hear, even if it's a lie. Then repeat it, again and again. The lies become truth, the truth becomes irrelevant. Only the message matters, not the substance.

The cameraman made the mistake of putting an eye to the eyepiece. Andy saw this and reached out with one hand to clamp his meaty fingers over the lens.

'Don't you film me, ya bastard. I've already had my photie taken without my permission and I'm no havin' you bastards filmin' me too!'

The cameraman tried to ease Andy's hand from his expensive kit. Bad move, Rebecca thought, as Andy pushed the cameraman back, yelling something about him going for him. Rebecca didn't know how many Spioraid people were present – so far she had counted two more: Andy's twin and the woman whose favourite word was scum – and she was certain they would back up their friend's version of events. Eyewitness accounts are subjective and can be manipulated. People come to believe they saw something other than what they actually did see.

The cameraman stumbled backwards, lost his footing, went down and his kit flew from his hand to crash onto the hard concrete. Lola moved forward to help him up but had to push Andy out of her path. That was also a bad idea, Rebecca thought. Andy spun, reached out to her, his face contorted with rage and hatred.

'Right – that's enough.'

The voice was loud and carried the weight of authority. Andy froze, his fingers barely clutching the fabric of Lola's jacket. He watched as a man shouldered his way through the onlookers. Rebecca heard people say the name Tom. He was a small man, his head shaven like Andy's, and he looked as if he could give him a good twenty years, but there was power and confidence in the way he stood that made Andy eye him warily.

'I don't know who you are, pal,' the newcomer said, 'but I've been watching you and I think you're at it.'

Andy looked around for support from his Spioraid buddies.

'Maybe you should keep out of this, mate,' said the woman.

'Darling, I've kept out of it up till now, but I'm no havin' you folk cause trouble in my streets, okay?' Tom jerked his thumb in Andy's direction. 'Does anybody know this guy? Or him? Or her?' He gestured to the second man and the woman. 'Cos I've never seen any of them before.'

There was muted mumbling all around and Rebecca heard people agree they'd never seen them before. They weren't from the Ferry. 'You're right, Tom,' one woman shouted. 'Who are they?'

Andy's face was a study in ferocity. 'What's it to you, pal?'

Tom was unfazed. 'Well – Andy, is it? I'll tell you. I saw that boy there taking his photos and he never once turned it in your direction. He was pointing it at your man Dalgliesh. And this fella?' He stooped to offer the cameraman a helping hand back to his feet. *Your man Dalgliesh*, Rebecca noted. This Tom, whoever he was, had it all sussed. 'He was defending himself, far as I could see.'

'Now, wait . . .' Andy began, but Tom was having none of it.

'Naw, son – you wait. You're trying to stir the shit here and I'm no havin' it.' He looked back at the crowd, his neighbours. Many obviously knew him and were beginning to wonder who Andy really was.

Andy really should have walked away. But he didn't. He decided to brazen it out. 'I cannae believe this.' He turned to his friends, his arms out as if he was being crucified. 'Can you believe this?'

His two cohorts were less enthusiastic about prolonging this any further. Tom had brought a new and, to them, unwelcome dynamic to the proceedings. Rebecca saw them dart anxious glances at the people now surrounding them. They gave each other a quick look and began to quietly back away, but the ranks closed behind them. A big hand descended on the man's shoulder and a head shook, a clear sign that he should stick around.

Andy saw this, swallowed, really should have sensed the wind was in his face now, but he opted for another approach, one the desperate and the stupid everywhere take when things don't go their way. He went on the attack. 'You know what I think?' He faced Tom, his eyes narrowing. 'I think you're someone sent here to disrupt this peaceful demonstration, this display of the will of the people.'

That's right, Rebecca thought, *when in trouble just shout 'WILL OF THE PEOPLE'. That's not overused at all.*

Andy squared off in front of Tom. 'You been paid by the council, or maybe Westminster, to come here and—'

Tom grinned and shook his head; it was enough to stop Andy in his tracks. There was a smattering of laughter from the crowd. Someone said they'd known Tom all their life.

'Son,' said Tom, 'I came here to listen to your man Dalgliesh tonight and you're right, I came with a mind to speak up if I had to. But not to disrupt and not to defend the council or Holyrood or Westminster. The folk here know that's just no me. He talked about outsiders and folks no understanding the Ferry. But see, he doesn't understand the Ferry. Aye, we're no happy with the idea of this Lancaster bloke maybe coming here . . .'

He looked around and acknowledged those who nodded their agreement. Some didn't, though. He was one of them but not everyone agreed with him. Rebecca heard some muffled insults. *Arsehole. Dickhead. Interfering old bastard.* If Tom heard the comments, he paid them no heed.

'But you want to know something about us, son? And it's maybe the one thing your man got right. We are decent. We're just ordinary folk. We work, we have a wee drink now and then, we look after our families. This is home to us, you know? Sure, there's bad apples, there's bad apples everywhere. Sure, there's problems, and maybe we are ignored because we're no one of they special interest groups or whatever. But this is still our home and we'll fight to protect it and we won't let people like you, or your man, wherever the hell he's gone, bring us down with your hate.'

Judging by the nods and the small cheer, Tom had most of the crowd on his side. Rebecca wondered who he was. He spoke well and he seemed to command respect. His next words answered her unspoken query.

'I've been a trade unionist all my life, you all know that.' He was address-ing the crowd more, as if he'd forgotten about Andy, who stood behind him like a petulant schoolboy being dressed down by a headmaster. 'You all know that I went down south, worked the pits. When I came back I was a coun-cillor here for many years.'

'Aye, and a bloody good one, Tom!' shouted someone. 'We need you back!'

'Bastardin' communist, that's what he was,' muttered a man behind Rebecca.

Tom waved the suggestion away. 'I've done my bit. I'm retired, and it's all different now. But my old grandfather, God rest him, he was in the International Brigade and he shouldered a rifle in the Spanish Civil War and then he volunteered to go to France in 1939. He was one of the first from the Sneck to sign up. But you know what he said was the greatest evil threatening the working man? It wasn't the bosses. It wasn't politicians or police or their own kind on the make. He said the greatest evil the working man faced was his own prejudices. He said that men like Franco and Hitler and Mussolini fed on the fears and the prejudices of ordinary folk and then vomited them up like bile. They were his words. Vomited them up like bile.'

He paused to let that sink in. He circled Andy, no longer looking at him. He had taken command of the situation.

'I came here tonight to support my neighbours. I don't want that guy Lancaster in the Ferry. I don't want my grandchildren to be in any danger from a wee shite like that. I don't want my daughter to worry about her kids being out in the street with him around. But I listened to that fella Dalgliesh.' He swivelled to face Andy again. 'Your pal. And as I listened I heard my old grandad's voice, talking about hatred and prejudice and bile. I heard lies and half truths and – what do they call it? – spin. So, aye – protest. Demonstrate. Exercise your democratic prerogative to say no. But don't let folk like this' – he jerked his thumb over his shoulder – 'hijack your rights, your feelings. Tell that fella Dalgliesh and his flunkeys here to get the f—' He hesitated briefly, thinking better about swearing, his passion taking over his tongue. 'To just get away from here. Leave us alone. We can take care of our own problems. Because we are the Ferry!'

That brought a loud cheer and Rebecca realised that what she had seen in many faces earlier was not anger because they agreed with Dalgliesh's rhetoric but quite the opposite. She had been totally wrong about these people. And Tom, whoever he was – and she resolved to get an interview with him, if he was agreeable – was now their spokesperson. She wondered how Mo Burke would react to that.

It all became too much for Andy. He had come here for trouble, that was his function. He glared at the people around him, his jaw set so tight it was in danger of locking, his eyes darting arrows through narrow slits. He had been shamed. He had been found out. He had been deserted by his boss. He was isolated and he was angry and he did what the isolated and the angry all do. He lashed out.

He waited till Tom turned to face him again, then threw the punch. It was a powerful swing and it came up from his gut to his shoulder to his fist. It was designed to land with the force of a piledriver.

But Tom moved faster than his years suggested. Perhaps he had been expecting it, even been planning on it. He leaned back to allow the fist to curve harmlessly a few millimetres from his face.

His own punch was measured and swift and hit the mark. It was the blow of a man who had done this sort of thing before. Andy rocked back, but didn't go down. He had taken punches in the past and could shake most off, it seemed. He crouched, his eyes flashing as the crowd roared their anger.

He really should have taken a telling. He should have sensed the mood in the air and tried to get away, but once again he didn't. He made things worse. He reached into his back pocket and came out with a small cosh. Rebecca had never seen a real cosh before and this one looked home-made, a leather bag filled with coins or nuts and bolts. He lunged, the weapon swinging in an upwards arc, aiming for Tom's face. Tom may have been older but he was nimble. He stepped aside and grabbed the arm, yanking it behind Andy's back, then jabbed at the man's kidneys with his left hand. Andy grimaced but kept his footing. He jerked his neck backwards, smashing the back of his head into Tom's nose, sending him reeling.

This was the signal for his friends to move. The man shook the hand from his shoulder and drove his elbow deep into the stomach of its owner. The woman whirled in a roundhouse and punched the man behind square on the jaw.

And that was when all hell broke loose.

36

Walter Lancaster had been told to stay in his room at the hostel, but after all that time in jail he couldn't face four walls closing in on him. He had to get out. He had to walk in the fresh air. He had to be outside, with the sky wide and free above him, even if it was cold and damp and dark. So he pulled on his coat, an old parka he'd bought in a charity shop, and set out in the hope he could walk off the anger and disappointment that had made him pace his shoebox room.

That telly reporter had ambushed him, the bitch. He had wanted to scream at her to leave him alone. He'd wanted to rage at the old bloke with the beard behind the camera to get it out of his face. Couldn't even walk down the street without them peering at him, poking at him, pressuring him. Couldn't they see all he wanted was peace? All he wanted was to be left alone.

He should have been starting that new life in his own place but instead he was stuck in that poxy room in that poxy hostel, being gawped at by junkies and prossies and the homeless. He shouldn't be homeless. He had a place in Aberdeen, had decorated it himself, all nice and clean. Spotless, it was. But they took it away from him, rented it out to someone else while he was away. They couldn't keep it as pristine as he had, he knew that. He would have taken that flat in the Ferry and fixed it up, he was good with his hands, always had been. He could do a bit of joinery, plumbing, even electrical work. He would have turned it into a home. His room in that hostel was clean enough, but it wasn't home. All he wanted was a home, even if it was in the Ferry.

But they had snatched it away from him. All they bastards. The demonstrators. The press. The social workers. *For your own safety*, they said. Aye, right. They didn't give a bugger about his safety; they were only thinking of themselves, of their jobs. So he was stuck in that poxy wee room until they could find somewhere else. Might not be Inverness, they said, and that pissed him off no end. He had wanted to come home. But now that looked doubtful, thanks to all they bastards.

Did they not understand that he wasn't a danger to no one? Could they not get that? He wasn't a threat to no one. He just wanted to get on with his life, that was all. Just live and let live. He'd done his time. He'd been punished. Society had sliced their pound of flesh out of him.

And for what?

For taking a piss. That was all. Taking a piss. They were taking the piss, so they were, saying he was a sex offender. He had never touched a kiddie in his life, not in that way. Yes, he had pictures and videos on his computer, but looking wasn't touching. Who was harmed by just looking? But they slapped the sex offender label on him and they put him away. He lost his home and his job. Just for taking a piss near a playground he couldn't even see and for looking at stuff in the privacy of his own home. And now he was living out of a poxy wee room in a poxy wee hostel in a town that he once thought of as home but didn't want him any more. And that bitch on the telly plasters his face all over screens again and the social workers and the police tell him not to go outside. Did they not know he was going crazy in there? After months and years inside, he needed to be able to come and go as he pleased. He had his freedom, now let him be free.

He walked aimlessly into the Old Town, turning onto Church Street, passing by skinny trees sticking out of raised slabs that seemed to burst from the ground like rocky outcrops. They were meant to represent perseverance, insight and open-heartedness. Aye, right. Inverness was showing open-heartedness all right. Not much insight into his needs either. Perseverance, aye. They were doing their best to persevere him the hell away from there.

He gave the sculpture a disdainful look from under the hood of his parka as he walked past. It wasn't raining, but the hood hid his face. He didn't want any more hassle, not tonight. He didn't want someone to recognise him and give him grief. He'd had enough of that in his life, thank you very much. Nobody was giving him a second look, though, so that was something at least. People were just passing him by without a glance. Young people, old people, all heading home or out for the night. Looking for somewhere to eat. Looking for something to do.

The paving stones were still slick from the rain earlier and everything smelled fresh and clean. He didn't mind if it rained again, though, because he liked to walk in the midst of a downpour. He liked the cool, clear feel of the drops on his face. Also, it kept most others off the streets and he liked that. It made him feel as if he was the only man left on earth and that the world was his and his alone. He was uncomfortable among other people, especially now. He was only happy alone. People scared him, they always had. His time in the jail, even though much of that was spent alone, had terrified him. The court had terrified him. The hostel terrified him. He found it difficult to relate to others. He couldn't talk to men, much less women, had never had a sexual relationship in his life. He didn't tell people that, though. He was forty-two and had never touched a woman. Or a man. He wasn't that way inclined. That was why he watched those things on his computer, those kids. He would never touch in real life, but on the screen it was different. He felt safe. He felt secure. He found images of children unthreatening but he would never, ever approach a real child. That was why he wasn't a danger. Why couldn't they get that and for Christ's sake leave him alone?

A figure brushed past, dunting his shoulder. He had been lost in his own thoughts and hadn't heard the footsteps behind him. The person, who neither apologised nor looked round, was clad in a long, loose waterproof, like a poncho really, and the hood was up, waterproof leggings underneath. All camouflaged. Despite his anger and disappointment, Lancaster felt a

202

smile twitch as he watched the person stride on ahead. Camo gear. In the middle of Inverness. Frightened the seagulls will see you, mate? Lancaster permitted himself a slight laugh and it made him feel better.

He rubbed his shoulder where a dull ache persisted. The guy must've hit him harder than he thought. He glared at the figure striding ahead.

He kept walking, heading away from the bustle of the Old Town grid, not that there was much of a bustle that night. Fewer people were walking the pavements on this part of the street, not at this time, with the shops closed and most of the pubs behind him. Even the pancake place on the other side of the road was quiet, no one going in or coming out, no one having a smoke in the elaborate archway. He looked ahead again. The bloke in the camo gear had vanished.

Lancaster was passing Church Lane when he began to feel strange. His vision began to swim, the edges of the green signs of the second-hand book-shop up ahead and, beyond it, the stark grey architecture of the BT building growing indistinct, as if someone had smeared Vaseline across them. He squinted to try to clear his sight, stopped, swallowed hard, rubbed his eyes, but his arms felt so heavy.

There was a small stone bench near the opening of the lane and he managed to reach it before his legs gave way. He didn't feel well at all. He wondered if he had eaten something, or was it merely the stress of the past few days catching up? Hell, the past few years. His heart thudded in his chest and he began to panic. Was he having a heart attack?

He hunched on the bench, his chin down, and threw up. It happened so suddenly he couldn't even bend over properly, so the vomit shot from his mouth to spatter across his chest. He didn't care. This wasn't right, not right at all. He tried to raise his head, to even move it, in the hope that someone might be passing, but he couldn't even do that. He couldn't move at all now. His arms were useless at his side, palms up, knuckles resting on the damp bench. Not that he could tell it was damp because he felt nothing at all, apart from his heart setting blood roaring in his ears. He opened his mouth to cry out, to perhaps attract someone's attention, perhaps someone living above the shops, but all that came out was a hoarse croak and more puke.

And then someone stepped into view. Waterproof boots, waterproof leggings, the bottom of a waterproof poncho. Camouflaged. The person who had brushed past him so rudely earlier. But Lancaster was glad to see him. He tried to speak, to explain he wasn't feeling well, but couldn't. Surely the guy would see the vomit all down his front and put two and two together? He felt hands grip him under his armpits and hoist him to his feet. Good, he was being taken somewhere to get help. He'd be fine. He'd get some treatment and he'd be fine.

Everything was going to be okay after all.

But when he looked up, trying to say thanks, his gratitude evaporated. He wanted to scream but his throat was as paralysed as his limbs. All he could manage was a strangled but terrified groan.

For the person who was helping him had no face.

37

Swearing.

Fists.

Bodies surging around her.

That was what Rebecca was aware of after the first punch was thrown. She didn't know how many Spioraid people had infiltrated the crowd; there couldn't have been that many, but perhaps old enmities had been aroused. Tom had his supporters certainly, but not everyone agreed with him. She had heard that in muttered comments and seen it in faces. Some people bought the Dalgliesh version and they were taking the opportunity to express their views with fist and foot.

It grew worse when the youths piled in. Rebecca didn't really see where they came from, merely heard them shouting and saw a bunch of them running up the street, some with sticks, others wielding home-made weapons.

She had to assume they had been lurking somewhere, waiting – hoping – for trouble to kick off. They hit the crowd like a wave, sticks rising, falling, connecting.

Glass smashed.

Screaming.

Yelling.

Rebecca and Chaz were pushed together for a moment, then she was snatched away as waves of bodies surged to and fro, people either joining in or trying to get away. Chaz vanished in the swell and she cried out his name once, pushing people out of the way to try to clear her path, before someone shoved her from behind with such force it knocked the wind from her lungs and she pitched forward. She managed to get her hands out to break the fall but she still hit the road hard, the shock of it travelling up her arms and jarring her shoulders. She was on her hands and knees in the centre of a perfect storm of anger and panic and she realised this was not a good position to be in.

She sucked in a jagged breath, her lungs still recovering from the force of the blow, and tried to edge her feet under her, but someone slammed into her and threw her onto her side on the unyielding road. This was worse, a lot worse. She felt something thud into her back and she realised with horror and panic that someone was kicking her, actually kicking her. She tried to roll away, but the forest of legs in her way, each jostling for position or escape, meant she couldn't get far.

She managed to evade whoever was putting the boot in and heard someone call her name. Chaz, she thought, and she cried out in reply, but her voice was muffled by the very vocal fury and fear around her. She tried to get up but was knocked back again. Shit, she thought as she attempted to catch her breath, she could be trampled to death here.

She saw something white drift across the sky, a languid movement at odds with the frantic activity below, and for a fleeting moment it was as if everything froze, all movement stopped, all sound died, as if she was in the eye of a storm. The gull's flight seemed so relaxed, so peaceful, as if it was in a completely different world. It floated out of her eyeline and the roar around her erupted in full voice again and she knew she had to move.

A slight lull in the pushing and shoving around her meant there was space for her to pull herself up. Agony took shape in voices. Anger formed in words. Hatred manifested in actions. There were calls for it all to stop, but they went unheeded. She saw dark uniforms now among the civilians, the police wading in, pulling combatants apart, the occasional baton being flicked open. She searched the heaving mass of struggling bodies for Chaz, saw him briefly, then lost him again as she was jerked to the side once more.

A man stepped in front of her, his hands on her shoulders, his face drenched in rage and hatred. He swore at her, called her a media cow, might have said more but she wasn't in the mood, so she rammed her knee deep between his legs. His hands slid away and he doubled over. He might have called her something unpleasant but she couldn't hear. Okay, maybe she shouldn't have done that, but she'd been insulted, pushed, kicked and damn near trampled. She wasn't going to be a victim, not tonight.

She felt another set of hands grab her and she whirled to fend off what she thought was an attack, but it was Nolan. He let her go, held his hands up in a placating gesture. 'It's me,' he shouted. 'Take it easy, slugger.'

She had never been so glad to see anyone in her life. Not that she would ever tell him that. The man she had felled was trying to stand up again, but one look from Nolan made him slink away, still slightly doubled over.

Nolan pulled her tightly to him and began to shoulder his way clear of the fray. Her back hurt and she was still slightly winded but she managed to gasp one word: 'Chaz.'

He looked down and turned her left hand over. The skin had been scraped off when she fell and blood seeped through. 'You okay?' he asked. He seemed genuinely concerned.

She pulled her hand away. 'Chaz,' she said again, still unable to form more words.

His mouth compressed. 'Let's get you clear, then I'll find him.'

'Now,' she said. She wasn't going without him. Nolan sighed, pushed someone out of the way and stretched to see over the heads around him. Rebecca did the same, the dull ache in her back sharpening, but she could not see much.

'He's clear,' said Nolan, pulling her away again. She didn't know whether to believe him, so she tried to stand her ground, but once again was pushed from behind. Nolan thrust this person away with one hand and faced her. 'Look, he's safe, believe me. Now, come on . . .'

Without waiting for an answer he grabbed her hand and dragged her the few feet to where people merely stood and watched the drama in front of them. Some had their phones up, videoing for posterity and the possibility of a few quid from the hated media. She saw police officers dragging people away. Behind her, the riot was losing steam. It had only lasted a matter of minutes.

'Where's your car?' Nolan asked, and she nodded down the street.

And then he was gone, skirting around the main body of what trouble there was, to find Chaz. She waited for a moment, her lungs still protesting, her hands stinging and muscles growling at their mistreatment, then wondered why she was waiting. She was about to turn away when she saw what was now a familiar face finishing off a conversation with a police sergeant.

'Mister . . .' She stopped, realised she didn't know his surname. 'Tom!'

He looked in her direction, saw the traces of blood on her hands. 'You're hurt, hen.'

She looked at the blood. It wasn't too bad. Some Savlon and a couple of plasters would set it right. She'd cut herself worse shaving her legs. 'I'm fine,' she said. 'Took a tumble. My name's Rebecca Connolly, I work for the *Chronicle*.'

'I'm sorry to hear that,' he said, but he smiled.

'I'd like to talk to you, if you have time.'

He looked back at the crowd, where the police had finally brought some semblance of order. 'Not tonight, darling.'

She reached into the pocket of her coat and produced a card. It was crumpled and tattered because it had been in there for some time. She'd had them printed up herself because the company had decided reporters didn't need them. 'Please take this. I really would like to talk to you about all this. That's my personal mobile number, so call me if you change your mind.'

He took the card but barely looked at it before he thrust it into the pocket of his jeans. Then he nodded at something behind her. 'Your boyfriend's here – and he has your snapper.'

She craned round to see Nolan and Chaz heading their way. Nolan had

Chaz by the arm, as if he was under arrest. She guessed that he had not come along willingly. 'He's not my boyfriend, he's . . .' she began, but when she turned back Tom was gone.

'Let's go,' said Nolan, 'unless you want to be hoovered up by the law.'

She led him down the street to the car, Nolan still gripping Chaz by the arm, the occasional grunt and curse following them from pockets of violence. Chaz tried to protest but Nolan told him he had enough shots for one night. When Rebecca took his side, Chaz finally relented and came along quietly. Reluctantly, though, and he kept casting eyes back for photo opportunities.

Once behind the wheel, Chaz safely ensconced in the passenger seat, Rebecca lowered the driver's side window. 'Thank you, Mr Burke,' she said.

'What do I have to do to get you to call me Nolan?' When she didn't answer, he leaned in closer, his face serious, as if he was looking for a kiss. She was about to say something when he said, 'Listen, that guy, the one they found on Culloden?'

'Yes?'

He paused, looked around, moved in even closer. She edged back a touch but he didn't comment on it. 'I've got a name for you. Jake Goodman.'

'You know him?'

His head bobbed slightly from side to side. 'Kind of. I've seen him kicking around with Scotty.'

'He's a friend of your brother's?'

He shrugged. 'As much as Scotty has pals, aye.'

'Is he local?'

'No, came up from Edinburgh a couple of years ago. He works – worked – as an odd-job man kinda thing. Last I heard he was doing some bits and pieces for that film company over by Glen Nevis. But here's the thing. This guy, Goodman? He was a member of Spioraid, far as I could tell anyway. I heard him and Scotty talking one night. They mentioned Spioraid and Dalgliesh. And I heard this guy say something about New Dawn.'

He paused to let this sink in and Rebecca's mind began to move in many directions at once. The dead man was known to Scott Burke. Scott had links to Finbar Dalgliesh. Did this Jake Goodman? She already knew he was working on the film set, but now he may have been a member of the very group that had not only protested over the content matter but had also been responsible for a number of thefts and acts of vandalism on set. And he had talked about New Dawn. She needed to talk to Finbar Dalgliesh and she needed to talk to that security chief and she needed to talk to them really soon. Dalgliesh should be relatively easy, but she had tried to reach Donahue by phone and he had blanked every call. She'd have to drive over there. That thought did not fill her with pleasure – not the drive, but the inevitable hassle with Les Morgan. She could phone in sick, of course, she'd done that before, but . . .

She realised she had drifted away into her own thoughts and looked back to Nolan Burke, still leaning into the window. 'This is all off the record, of course,' he said.

'Of course,' she replied. 'Mr Burke.'

'Nolan.'

'Mr Burke, why are you telling me this?'

He gave her a look that told her to work that out herself and stepped away. She knew she wasn't going to get anything more from him and turned the ignition.

As she pulled away, she saw Mo Burke had been watching them from the pavement on the other side of the road.

38

Rebecca leaned against the ticket machine outside the railway station, her eyes on the door to the hotel where Dalgliesh stayed when he was in Inverness. She could have waited in the comfortable lobby area, with its soft furnishings and dark polished tables, but she liked the place and didn't want to sully the atmosphere with what might prove to be an unpleasant encounter. She planned to ambush the Spioraid leader, to burn him, and she didn't know how he would react. Sometimes he was all charm and bonhomie, eager to get his face and name in front of his public, but other times he could prove less welcoming.

A squad of taxi drivers chatted at the rank in the centre of the square and parked cars lined the spaces on either side. She would have preferred to have waited in her car, but she hadn't been lucky enough to find a free space this time. Hotel guests had to be quick to nab one of the few dedicated spaces here, otherwise it meant paying for public parking.

It was another grey Inverness morning. Commuters and travellers filtered in and out the glass doors of the station. Voices. Languages. Tannoy announcements on the concourse. Laughter from one of the taxi drivers. The sound of luggage on wheels rasping against the concrete. Life, doing what life does, going on.

And here she was to talk about a dead man.

She shifted her position and arched her back a little to try to ease the stiffness in her shoulders. Aftershocks of being knocked to the ground and kicked the night before still reverberated through her body. Her hands were already beginning to heal – they were little more than surface scrapes – but she had positioned herself in front of the full-length mirror in her bedroom earlier in order to study her back and could see bruising where she had been pushed. *Bloody hell,* she thought, *someone had really meant business.* She wondered who was responsible. Was it a random thing, or did someone recognise her, have something against the paper? A Spioraid member, perhaps?

She hadn't yet found out exactly how many arrests had been made, but an early morning call to the communication office at Inshes told her that there had been damage done to cars and windows, while nine people had been treated at Raigmore Hospital's A&E for contusions and lacerations. Others had declined medical assistance. That made them tough in the Ferry.

She was beginning to wonder if she was on a fool's errand when Dalgliesh stepped through the hotel doors and down the steps, flanked by his two minders, each carrying two suitcases. The only thing Dalgliesh carried was an air of superiority. He saw her immediately, of course, because he was not the kind of man to miss anything. To his credit he made straight for her, his politician's grin slipping easily into place. Today was a charming day, it seemed.

'Miss Connolly,' he said. They had never been introduced, but he had obviously made it his business to find out her name. 'Glad to see you are unscathed.'

She thought about her bruises, but she wasn't going to tell him about them. 'Do you have anything to say about last night, Mr Dalgliesh?'

The grin was replaced by something more sober which, like the smile, was as sincere as a scorpion promising not to sting. Dalgliesh was feigning concern, but it simply was not in his nature. 'I am deeply troubled by what occurred.'

'Even though it was supporters of Spioraid who started it?'

'You have proof of that?'

She didn't and he knew it.

'No, I didn't think so,' he said, a look of triumph briefly moving from eyes to tone. 'From what I understand, passions ran high and spilled over.'

'Passions you enflamed.'

The grin again. 'Who can say what caused it? I was not the only one talking last night, as it turned out. And the trouble only began when your photographer invaded a gentleman's privacy.'

'Allegedly. And that's not really when it began, was it? It was when your members were called out for what they were.'

His grin was still in place, as if it had somehow been pasted there. 'If you can prove they were members of my movement then I'd be happy to condemn them. Now, if you'll excuse me, I have a train to catch.'

He began to move past her and she let him. It wasn't likely she could prove anything of the sort. It occurred to Rebecca that Andy and the others might not even be members but merely hired, a Rent-a-Mob, like movie extras. That thought brought her back to why she was really there.

'Jake Goodman,' she said, and that made him stop and turn again. But not before she perceived a slight bracing of the shoulders.

'I'm sorry?'

'Does the name mean anything to you, Mr Dalgliesh?'

He moved closer to her again. 'Should it?'

'I understand he is a member of your – movement, is it? Or rather, he *was* a member.'

'Miss Connolly, it may surprise you to know that Spioraid has over five thousand members and many, many more supporters. Am I expected to know every one of them by name?'

'He's dead, Mr Dalgliesh.' If the news surprised him, it was not apparent, although the paste on his smile had melted. 'He was murdered.'

'That's very sad and I shall, of course, make immediate enquiries. If this poor man – what was his name again?'

'Goodman, Jake Goodman.'

'If this poor Mr Goodman was indeed a member of the movement then I shall ensure that we reach out to his family and offer our support. You say he was murdered?'

'His body was found on Culloden Moor. Perhaps you read about it.'

She watched him closely for any sign that he already knew that, but saw nothing more than a studied look of sympathy from a politician who was about to send his thoughts and prayers to a bereaved family and make sure everyone knew about it.

'The *Outlander* Murder,' he said. The headline-friendly phrase had been coined by a London-based red top. Rebecca hated it – it cheapened the loss of life and turned real tragedy into little more than a label. Even if Goodman was a Spioraid member, he deserved some respect in death. 'I didn't think he'd been formally identified.'

'Not formally.'

'And yet you have his name?'

'I have sources.'

'Ah, a reporter and her sources. Well, that is very sad, very sad indeed. But as I said, let me make some enquiries and if your – ah – sources prove correct, a statement will be issued directly.'

He turned away again and Rebecca stepped forward, only to be blocked by one of the minders who loomed over her like a dentist's appointment.

'He may also have been connected to New Dawn,' she said, raising her voice and peering over the minder's shoulder. She had no idea if Goodman was – all she had was Nolan Burke's claim that he'd heard the man mention them. She was very much shooting in the dark, but sometimes even then you hit something.

He stopped again, turned, his eyes flicking to his minders, and she wondered if they were hired hands or actually part of New Dawn. 'Sources again, Miss Connolly?'

'What would we do without them? Do you condemn the actions of New Dawn, Mr Dalgliesh?' She took time to check out the faces of the minders, but they remained blank. She pressed on. 'They have reportedly committed acts of violence, a bit like last night. They have sent bomb threats and hoax packages. They firebombed a mosque the other night. And it wasn't the first time.'

Dalgliesh waved all this away as if it was a vaguely troublesome fly. 'New Dawn is not affiliated with my movement in any way.'

'Not officially.'

The politician's smile was long dead now. In its place was the stony glare of the lawyer. 'Sources are one thing, facts are another. I would be very careful in what you print. Unless you can prove that this poor man is indeed a member of my movement and have concrete evidence that he was also connected to this . . .' He feigned a vague recollection of the group's name. 'New Dawn, then it would be unwise to publish anything that might suggest such a link.'

Dalgliesh didn't look back again as he vanished into the station. She inched forward to follow, but the minder in her way gave her a look that told her she should not push her luck. She decided to take the warning to heart. He gave her a nod and followed his boss inside.

Rebecca thought about the exchange. What had she learned? Nothing concrete, although it had made her feel good to scrape that smile away. However, she had the feeling that Dalgliesh had been shaken by the news that the dead man was connected to Spioraid, not to mention New Dawn. What did that mean?

She didn't have a clue.

She looked across the square to the statue, the tribute to men who had fought in a campaign in Egypt, complete with miniature Sphinx. A seagull stood on the head of the kilted soldier and she wondered if it was the same one that had floated high above the seething humanity the night before. Unfortunately, they all looked alike. *Very inconsiderate,* she thought.

Her phone rang and she fumbled in her coat pocket. It was Bill Sawyer. 'Where are you?' he asked.

'Outside the station.'

'Taking a trip?'

'No. On a story.'

'Get yourself to the High Kirk then,' he said. 'They've found a body.'

39

At first glance, the tree was still gripped in the small death of winter, the skeletal fingers of its branches reaching out towards the red-hued brickwork of the church made drab by the anaemic sun. And yet, there were traces of life. Sprigs of green sprouting from the bough and, if Roach looked hard enough, she would see buds forming on the twigs. New life. New beginnings.

None of that mattered to Walter Lancaster, though. The rebirth of nature after the cold season was something he would never witness again. He was spread-eagled across a flat headstone, a raised stone slab really, its inscription worn thin by the generations of rain, snow and wind that had raged over this exposed mound above the River Ness. It was a typical Scottish kirkyard with no uniformity to the graves. The memorials were of differing heights, widths, shapes and materials. They were littered around the church itself, as if they had been simply thrown there like seeds, and an unruly crop had sprouted from the uneven ground. Each stone represented a life, a history. A death. Men and women who had lived through events both momentous and mundane, their existence only marked by yellowing documents in an archive, their passing only remembered now by fading letters etched in these stones. What had once been flesh and bone now mouldering beneath the damp earth.

Roach didn't know whose memorial Lancaster had been left on, but she suspected that if there was anything to the old saw of turning in the grave then they would be whirling like a dervish on speed. Deceased he may be, and in its way it was sad, but he was not a good man and the dear departed would be somewhat disconcerted that their final resting place had been so defiled. His arms were outstretched as if he had been crucified, his eyes open and staring towards the slate-grey heavens as if it was somewhere he longed to be. Lancaster wouldn't get to paradise, though. Roach knew that, if there was an afterlife, he was somewhere else.

She knew who he was, of course. She had never dealt with him, but she had been privy to the plan to rehome him and had even been involved in a couple of the meetings to discuss it. So, now he would be rehomed in Inverness after all. Or at least his ashes would be stored somewhere, she supposed.

She stood on the gravel footpath running alongside the walls of the old kirk, keeping her distance as the experts did what the experts did, but she could see the blood that had burst from his ruptured throat glistening dark against the grey stone and draining down to the grass below. The duty pathologist was on her knees, studying the wound. As with the as-yet unidentified man at Culloden, there was no question of cause of death here, but formalities had to be observed.

'Yul,' Bremner stepped to her side and surveyed the scene. 'Well, at least we know where that other uniform is.'

She didn't answer. Her eyes flicked over the heavy red material and the pantaloons, at the leather strap across his chest and then back to the wound gaping black and still slightly wet at his throat. She felt queasy, but it was nothing to do with the dark blood and open flesh. Her encounter with Joe the previous night had left her drained, for some reason. She had opened a bottle of wine after he left and had it tanked within an hour and a half. Then she had opened another and managed to dispose of almost half. She was no drinker, and it meant she had slept that strange half-sleep of the drunk, that curious feeling of being awake and yet not, while all around her the room spun as fast as her thoughts.

She didn't know why his news had hit her so powerfully. After all, they had been divorced for some time now. But it had. She no longer loved him, of that she was certain. The affair had seen to that. And his point was correct – even before he'd told her about Lolita, things between them had not been perfect. He had his career, she had hers, and they had become more interested in the work than each other. They were little more than house-mates, although she had not realised it at the time. It was just something that had happened. What she'd thought was happiness was merely habit. They each had become accustomed to the other's face. Except he had become interested in something other than his work and his marriage. He had humped some little postgrad assistant. Then he had divorced Val to marry her. And now they were having a child.

Was that what was bothering her?

The idea of children had never been part of Roach's vision for the future. Marriage, yes. A partner, yes. A home, a life, a future. But no children. She was not the motherly type, she knew that. When babies were brought into. the station, she did not coo over them. She did not jostle for the chance to hold them and remark on how lovely they were. Joe had been of similar mind, or at least he had said he was. And yet, here he was, facing impending fatherhood. He would be in his late fifties when the child was at its most troublesome teenage years. Good luck to him with that, she thought.

She looked beyond the body and the personnel clad in coveralls moving around it and the police officers weaving between the gravestones in search of anything that might assist the inquiry. The ground dipped away beyond them to slope quite sharply towards the river. From where she stood she could see the arches of the footbridge and the roofs of buildings, spires on the far side, and the dull featureless sky extending to wooded hills beyond. Her eyes scanned upwards to the church tower and its patchwork of ornate but rough-edged brickwork. There would be quite a view from up there, she thought, but she knew they didn't allow visitors to climb the stairs now. Health and safety was paramount.

'Any CCTV cameras?' she asked Bremner.

'Community Safety cameras in the street might have picked something up.'

'Door to door?'

'Underway, but the only thing anyone saw was a guy who seemed drunk being helped by his mate along the road.'

'Descriptions?'

'Sketchy as hell, but the drunk guy could have been Lancaster.'

'And the friend?'

'Tall. Waterproof gear. Hood up.'

'Got a time?'

'Witness couldn't say. The Curfew Bell hadn't rung, so it was before eight.'

'The Curfew Bell?'

Bremner raised one finger to the tower. 'The bell rings every night at 8 p.m.'

'Why?'

He shrugged. 'Tradition.'

She exhaled sharply. 'Another mystery.'

She hated mysteries.

Roach gave the crime scene a long final look. Bremner and the team had this covered and there was little for her to do. It was cold, and she was tired and wanted to feel as if she was doing something other than just standing there being cold and tired. And irritable. Apart from that, she needed a coffee. Her bad night meant she had overslept and hadn't been able to brew up her thermos of French roast.

'I need you to keep on top of things here,' she told Bremner.

'Where you off to?'

'I need caffeine.'

'I can send a uniform.'

She shuddered with mock horror. 'God knows what kind of sheep dip they'd come back with. I'll find somewhere with a decent brew and I'll take it back to the ranch. I've got paperwork that has to be done.'

'Ah,' Bremner said with a sage nod. 'Time, tide and paperwork await no man.'

'Or woman,' she added.

'Yes, ma'am,' he agreed.

'Get it up you,' she said as she headed to the iron gates that led out to where the circus was in full swing. The street was like a used-car sales forecourt of official vehicles. A cadre of uniformed officers guarded a picket of crime-scene tape strung between a line of traffic cones. The makeshift barrier corralled a crowd of people outside the shops on the opposite pavement.

Roach had stopped for a moment, wondering where she might find a decent coffee, when she caught sight of two familiar faces.

40

Nolan heard the shower going as he walked past Scott's room, so he nipped in, leaving the door slightly ajar to allow him to hear the water being turned off. The bed was unmade, clothes littered the floor and a plate with the residue of jam and toast crumbs lay by the small table. Maw would have a fit when she saw it, Nolan thought, but she'd tidy it all up. She always did. Nolan's room was as neat and clean as a five-star hotel. His bed made, his dirty clothes in a laundry basket, other clothes all squared away. He wasn't here to snoop into Scott's housekeeping, though. He had other things in mind.

His brother's laptop sat on top of a chest of drawers and he opened the lid, waited for the screen to spring to life, listening to the sound of the water thundering in the shower. Scott was messy, but he was scrupulously clean, he'd give him that. His showers were sometimes so long Maw threatened to have his meals delivered.

The screen was live and Nolan expertly clicked on Google Chrome, manoeuvred the arrow to the three vertical dots on the top right-hand corner and then down to History. He wanted to find out what Scott had been watching the previous night. The furtive way his brother had closed the laptop over had made him suspicious.

The most recent item, above a number of entries for a free porn site, was a BBC news report – 'CONVICTED SEX OFFENDER TO BE REHOMED'. The video showed that guy Lancaster walking on the street and being fronted by a good-looking, dark-haired reporter. So, what was

Scotty so squirrelly about? Nolan had had the distinct impression he hadn't wanted him to see what he was looking at. Why shouldn't he be looking at an online news report about the guy they were protesting against? Didn't make a lot of sense. Unless he'd been looking at something else and had deleted the entry. Nolan tried to remember what he'd glimpsed just before Scott had closed the laptop. It had been a close-up of someone's face, a man. Lancaster? Someone else? Could've been either because he really didn't get much of a look.

He closed the laptop, returned it to where he'd found it, listened to the shower again. His eyes rested on the pile of clothes at his feet, recognised them as those Scott had worn the previous night. Something on the collar of the polo shirt made him stoop to study it further. He tugged the garment free from the tangle and unfurled it completely. Stains on the collar, more on the sleeve and on the chest.

Blood.

Nolan stood in the kitchen, his back against the Formica surface beside the sink as he sipped a glass of orange juice and waited for the bread in the toaster to brown. His mother was at the small table, a cigarette smouldering in an ashtray in front of her, a mug of tea beside it. She was watching Scott shaking sugary breakfast cereal into a bowl. Her face was expressionless, but she moved in a stiff way, as if she was fighting anger. Nolan knew she was unhappy that Scott had blown off the demonstration the night before, even angrier over what had happened, and he sensed she was going to say something to him about it. Nolan didn't want to miss this. Scott so seldom was pulled up for anything.

Scott poured the milk into his bowl and dug his spoon into the heap of cereal to shovel up a huge mouthful. Nolan was no health nut, but he really couldn't see the attraction of eating a whole bowl of that shit.

The silence was broken only by the sound of Scott's crunching and the clink of his spoon against the bowl. Maw raised her mug to her lips, still staring at Scott. Then she laid the cup down, sat back in her chair and tapped away the excess ash from her cigarette.

'So,' she said, 'what was that all about last night?'

Nolan waited for Scott to reply, then realised she was looking at him.

'What?' he said, thinking the bastard was getting away with it again. He couldn't believe it.

'You and that reporter lassie. Rebecca whatsername.'

'Connolly,' said Scott, his mouth full.

'Aye. So, what was that all about?'

Nolan stared at the back of his brother's head. This was unbelievable. He slopes away when he's needed to God knows where, and still bugger-all is said to him. He knew Maw was waiting for a reply, but he would be damned if he would make it easy for her. 'What's what all about?'

'I saw you, pulling her out of there, then helping that photographer bloke. And walking them to their car like a bloody bodyguard! What's going on, then?'

When Nolan didn't reply instantly, Scott waded in again. 'Aye, Maw, I saw them thegether out in the hall too. Dead cosy, they was. Practically kissing.'

Nolan gave Scott's head another glare, then said, 'The demo was supposed to be peaceful. It went pear-shaped, thanks to Scotty's mate Dalgliesh. The lassie was there doing her job and I helped her get out the way. So what?'

Maw took a draw on her cigarette, narrowed her eyes against the smoke drifting upwards. 'How'd she find Lancaster's name?'

'How am I supposed to know? She's a reporter. They find things out.' It was time to go on the attack. 'And where was Scotty last night, eh? He should've been there with us, family solidarity and all that.'

Scott didn't even pause in his eating. 'I told you, I was out on business.'

'Never you mind where your brother was. I want to know what the hell you're playing at with that lassie. She's media, Nolan. We cannae trust that lot, you know that.'

'I'm not playing at anything, Maw. She was in trouble, thanks to Scotty's pals, and I helped her. That's all. What? We want innocent people getting hurt now, that it? That looks really good on us, doesn't it?'

'Last night was nothing,' Maw said.

'It wasn't what you wanted. You said that you didn't want trouble or any violence. Christ – that Lancaster guy didn't even show up. Good going, Maw. You started all this stuff up, not me. I was against it. But you and eejit features here ran with it. Community spirit or some such shite. Well, look what happened. The press got hassle, Dalgliesh spouted his shite and the Ferry is once again seen as a shithole. And us? The family? We're right in the middle of it and drawing attention when we should really be getting on with business. And I don't mean whatever Scott was up to. I mean the real business. Dad's business.'

He heard the toaster click behind him, but he wasn't hungry now. He tossed the remains of his orange juice into the sink, slammed the glass down on the working surface and walked out. He knew he should have kept his head, but his patience with his mother and Scott was at an end. He should have somehow forced her to focus on where Scott had been and what he had been doing. Business, he said. Aye right.

As he slammed the front door shut, he wondered if he should have told Maw about finding blood on Scotty's polo shirt. Not a lot, just some smears, as if he'd wiped his hand on it. Nolan would bet his life that blood wasn't Scott's. So, whose was it?

41

Rebecca had decided it would be quicker to walk – or rather run – from the station to the kirkyard. She had cut through the Victorian Market, dodging between tourists gawping at the small shops packed with tartan memorabilia, her phone to her ear as she called first the office to tell them where she was, cutting the line before Les could come to the phone, then Elspeth, but there was no answer. Typical, she thought. She considered nipping into her office on the way but decided against it. She would have answered if she was there. She knew Chaz was covering a ministerial visit to a fish farm on the Dornoch Firth, so she didn't try him.

As soon as she hit Church Street, she saw the blue lights dancing ahead and wondered how close she would be able to get to the actual scene. With Chaz unavailable and no staff photographer, she knew she would have to grab a shot with her phone, a risky proposition at the best of times, given her variable skills, but a useless one if she couldn't get close enough.

She was breathless by the time she reached the crowd knotted behind the makeshift barrier, where she found Elspeth leaning on her cane. Of course she was here. Nothing happened in Inverness, the entire north-west, without her hearing about it. In fact, Bill had probably called her first.

Her old boss gave her a mocking look. 'You took your time.'

'I forgot to pack my running shoes,' Rebecca panted. 'What's the story, Balamory?'

Elspeth jerked her head across the road to the black gates of the kirkyard.

'They found a man dead in there this morning.' She lowered her voice. 'I'm told it might be Walter Lancaster.'

'Bloody hell,' said Rebecca. How long had he been dead? The night before? Was that why he and his social work minders were a no show in the Ferry? She raised her phone to take a landscape shot of the scene, making sure she got the nearest police vehicle in the frame with the black iron gates of the kirkyard in the background. As she lowered the phone, she saw DCI Roach.

The detective's gaze fell on her and Elspeth and was followed by a nod of recognition, and she began to walk across the road directly towards them. She was wearing a long, black woollen coat, unbuttoned, but her hands were in her pockets, hugging it closer as if to ward off the chilly morning.

Rebecca gave her a little wave. She really didn't know why.

Roach stopped at the tape and gave them another nod. Elspeth gave her one in return. Rebecca half expected one of them to say 'Whassup?'

'I'm going for a coffee,' said Roach. 'Where's good?'

'There's a little place just up the road a bit I like,' said Elspeth. 'Do you want company?'

Roach considered this, then said, 'Sure, why not?'

Roach ran a practised eye over the varieties of coffee available and selected an Americano. No milk. She also ordered something sweet and sticky. Rebecca, a confirmed spoonful in a cup gal with little time for the current obsession with coffee, had learned to ask for a flat white. Elspeth eased her knee at a table looking out onto the street and Rebecca placed in front of her a large cup and saucer containing tea, then sat down in the seat opposite Roach, who was peeling off her coat to reveal a dark pinstripe suit and white shirt.

The detective looked tired. She had what Rebecca's mother would call 'a pinched look'. She poured a sachet of sugar into her coffee and stirred it with one of those thin strips of wood that did very little to circulate the sugar through the liquid. Rebecca tipped three sachets in and stirred like it was a workout.

'So,' said Elspeth after taking a mouthful of tea, 'is that Walter Lancaster lying dead back there?'

Roach smiled. It did very little to disguise the dark circles and the colourless cheeks. 'Are you ever off duty?'

'Are you, DCI Roach?'

Roach's head twitched to the side as she conceded that. 'This is an off-the-record chat, so call me Val.'

'Okay, Val,' said Elspeth. 'Is that Walter Lancaster lying dead back there?'

Roach laughed and took a long drink of her coffee, then sat back and seemed to revel in the taste. 'That's good. I've been desperate for that.' She gave it another stir all the same. 'I've heard you can be like a dog with a rat, Elspeth, when it comes to stories.'

Elspeth waited for an answer to her two questions. Or rather her single question asked twice.

'I'll tell you what,' Roach went on. 'Ask again, and if you're wrong I'll tell you.'

'Is that Walter Lancaster lying dead back there?'

Roach kept stirring her coffee. Elspeth gave Rebecca a knowing nod, then asked, 'Will the name be announced soon?'

Stir.

'Then we haven't much time.' Elspeth pulled herself to her feet and hooked her cane from where it rested against the window.

'Don't you want to know if it's connected to the Culloden murder?'

Elspeth stopped, leaned on her cane. 'Is it?'

'Is what?'

'Is Walter Lancaster's death connected to the Culloden murder?'

Roach raised her cup again, her eyes meeting Rebecca's over the rim. Elspeth lowered herself back down again.

'What's the connection?'

'That's not how this works.'

'You've already told us it's Lancaster and it's connected, so . . .'

'I haven't told you anything. You've asked questions I have not answered.'

Both reporters knew this was Roach's way of giving them information while keeping her integrity in some way intact. It was a stretch, but it seemed to work for her, and Rebecca wondered if she'd done this before. Then she wondered why Roach was doing it now.

Elspeth still had her hand on the curve of her cane and she tapped the bottom against the floor as she wondered how to ask the next question. Rebecca tried to think how the death of a pervert in a kirkyard had anything to do with the death of Goodman at Culloden. Was the body outside or in the church? It had probably happened overnight, so she guessed outside. She had been in the graveyard once. It was old. Something nibbled at the edge of her memory. Something about the graves.

'They're both historical sites,' Rebecca said, dimly recalling something connected to the '45. She would call Anna later. Roach dipped her eyes. Rebecca felt there was more, though. What else would make Roach link the two deaths? What else . . . Two historical sites. One victim found in period clothes, but two costumes stolen from the film set.

Rebecca had a flash of inspiration. 'Was Lancaster dressed in the stolen uniform?'

Roach laid her cup down on the table and sat back. She said nothing. She didn't need to.

'Okay,' said Elspeth, rising again. 'Thanks, DCI – Val. It's heartening to see that Police Scotland keeps its word.'

'Again, I don't know what you mean. We've shared a coffee and you've made some wild statements which I have neither confirmed or denied.'

'Understood,' Elspeth said, smiling. Rebecca smiled too. This was the first time she had ever encountered an information exchange like this and it was exciting. 'We have to go,' said Elspeth to Rebecca.

Roach's voice made Rebecca stop halfway to her feet. 'There is one thing you can help me with, Rebecca.' Rebecca sat back down. Elspeth remained standing, eager to get away and file copy, but Rebecca knew she would stand by like a minder. Roach twirled the big cup in its saucer. 'I need the name of the person who told you about the theft of the costumes.'

'I can't do that,' said Rebecca.

'It's important that I speak to this person.'

'I understand that, but I gave my word.'

'We have two murders here, Miss Connolly.'

Miss Connolly. Maybe they weren't pals any more.

'I'm aware of that, DCI Roach.' *Two can play at that game*, she thought. 'But I promised I would not tell anyone my source's name. There's little enough confidence in the media these days without the likes of me breaching trust.'

Roach thought about this as she stared at her coffee. Rebecca could not tell if she was angry already or on her way there.

'You're out of order asking that, Val,' said Elspeth. 'You know Becks can't give you that name.'

Roach's eyes lifted from the tabletop to Rebecca. 'I could have you charged.'

Her voice was low and flat and devoid of any heat, but that made it all the more intense. Rebecca felt fear rise in her throat like bile.

'That's bollocks and you know it,' said Elspeth. 'Have you heard of the European Convention of Human Rights, Article Ten?'

'I have, but I also know that if I make a strong argument that I need that name in the public interest – and catching a killer is very much in the public interest – then a court may well support my position.'

Elspeth laughed, but there was no humour in it. 'You're bluffing.'

'Am I? What do you think, Rebecca?'

A tremble in Rebecca's voice betrayed her. 'I have to take that chance.'

'So you'd risk jail to protect this person?'

'It wouldn't come to that,' said Elspeth. 'You're just trying to scare the lassie. And we were getting on so well, too.'

Roach stared at Rebecca. It was a long stare, one that said she meant what she said. Rebecca felt her knees weaken and she wished her father was around to give her advice. But he was gone, at least physically. She wondered if she should just walk away, get back to the office, talk to Les and Barry. They were journalists. Surely they would support her on this. Or maybe not. She thought about Simon, giving him a call, taking legal counsel. Would he talk to her? Would he help? She stared back at Roach, trying to see a hint that this was a scare tactic to make her give up the name. Taking a journalist to court to reveal a source was a risky move that could so easily backfire. Police Scotland had had its fingers burned a few years back when it had intercepted a journalist's communications during an anti-corruption probe.

'DCI Roach – Val,' said Elspeth, her voice losing some of its harshness in an attempt to calm things down. Rebecca knew her, though, and knew she would be wondering if she could get away with using her stick in a manner for which it was never intended. 'We, Becks and I, have been nothing but cooperative so far. We have provided you with information ahead of time when we could quite easily have let you read about it over your Rice Krispies.'

'Only because it suited you.'

'It suited everyone, including the interest of the public you mentioned. So why, suddenly, do you get all Gestapo on us? Becks can't give you that name, you know it. And maybe you could have her jailed, although the chances are you couldn't, but what would that get you? Bad publicity, enemies in the press and, more importantly, still no name.'

'I have a counter offer,' said Rebecca. She'd had another idea. Both Roach and Elspeth looked her away again. 'Another name.'

'What other name?'

'The name of the first victim.'

42

The bastard had been darting glances at Scott for bloody ages and it was beginning to piss him off. He didn't sense any form of threat from him, but the way he kept looking in his direction was getting his goat. Scott had come into Barney's with Deke and Andy, a couple of mates, just for a visit. Not really to drink anything because it was mid-morning and, anyway, Scott wasn't a great drinker. He had other ways to get a lift. They had been jawing with the barman for a while, the bloke at the end shifting his focus from the telly, some shitty property show, to Scott and his pals. He'd tried to ignore it at first; Scott was used to people being uncomfortable around him and, if truth be told, he liked it that way. He liked being the guy they feared. It made some things easier, some things harder, but he often liked to do things the hard way. It was more fun.

So for a time they talked to Jack, the manager, who was also barman that day. Business was shite, he said, as usual, but that was fine. It was supposed to be. All the while, that bloke's head was swivelling like he was at bloody Wimbledon, telly to Scott, to the telly, to Scott. It was really aggravating and Scott wondered if the bloke was steeling himself to noise him up. He'd seen it before: boy wants to be the big man, ends up with a sore one. Thing was, they usually had a girl around they wanted to impress, or at least some mates. This boy was on his tod. So what was that all about? *A shirt-lifter who's taken a fancy to me*, Scott wondered. *Aye, I'll smack that notion right off of his coupon, sharpish.*

Still, all he was doing was the back and forward thing with his head, so no harm done, even though it was irritating. Scott didn't want to start any trouble, not in Barney's, and not after the talking-to Maw had given him about that business with the drill the other night. *That was fun*, he thought, *who knew a kneecap would bleed so much?* But he had to keep his head down, and landing one on some stranger was the exact opposite of that. He'd have to keep his nose clean, as far as Maw was concerned, for a wee while at any rate.

The boy didn't make any move towards him until they were leaving. He'd been looking for the balls to say something, Scott reckoned, and this was his last chance. He sidled their way, caught Scott's eye, which wasn't hard, as he'd been keeping one on him all the time they were in there. Deke saw him come closer and stepped in the way.

'You got a problem, son?' Scott said.

A nervous smile flickered on the boy's face, but he kept his eyes on the floor. 'Naw, eh, Mr Burke, just wanted . . . well . . . eh . . . a wee word, if that's okay?'

Bastard wants some work, Scott thought. Or buying, not knowing that Scott was a supplier not a seller. 'What kind of wee word?'

Another nervous smile, a glance at Jack, then at Scott's mates, then finally to Scott himself. 'An apology, eh?'

'For what?' Scott was puzzled. He'd never seen this boy before, far as he could remember, so what was he apologising for?

The eyes dropped again, then bounced up like they were on bungees. 'Well, really it's for your brother.'

'Nolan? You know him, like?'

'Well, naw, no really. It's just, well, eh . . . I had a wee run-in with him the other night and I was out of order, eh?'

'How?'

The boy looked ashamed. Or scared. Or both. 'Nothin' really. Just me being stupid, eh? Actin' the big man. You know how it is, too much to drink.'

Scott didn't know how it was. Not with drink anyway. 'He give you a kickin'? I don't see any bruises or nothin'.'

'Naw, never laid a hand on me, but he still sorted me out.'

Aye, that was Nolan. Talk himself out of it somehow, wouldn't soil his hands. Scott, on the other hand, would have given this balloon a sore face and then discussed the situation after.

'The thing is, Mr Burke, I was out of order, you know? Well out of order. And I just wanted to say sorry. I wondered if you would pass that along to your brother. I mean, he was just in here for a quiet drink with his burd and that . . .'

Scott had grown bored with the conversation, was thinking what did it matter to him if Nolan'd had a set-to with this dickhead. Then his interest piqued. 'What burd?' he asked, suddenly curious.

'No a bad-lookin' lassie. I mean, no what you usually get in here, you know? Longish hair, reddish.'

That reporter, Scott thought. He was out with that reporter, Rebecca whatsername. Scott walked away from the boy. He was still talking, but a look from one of Scott's mates stopped him in his tracks.

In the lane outside he gave himself a minute to process this information. He'd been winding Nolan up the night before about the way they'd been talking at the door. At least, he thought he'd been winding him up. Now he wondered if he really had spotted something. And Maw said Nolan had pulled a big hero act at the demo.

Nolan, son, what you doing with that lassie? he thought, shaking his head.

234

43

Roach had intended to go straight to the incident room with the information provided by Rebecca Connolly when she got back to Inshes. Bugger the paperwork. However, a call from McIntyre's secretary as she walked across the car park informed her that the divisional commander wanted to see her right away.

She was ushered into his office immediately. McIntyre stood at the window, his eyes cast downwards, his hands clasped behind his back. As usual, he looked as if he had been ironed recently. Roach had seen him at the end of a bad day and he still looked crisp, clean and fresh out of the packet.

The man lounging on the couch in the sitting area of the large office was more like an unmade bed. Where McIntyre was trim and fit, he was stocky and looked fit to drop. His blond hair was wispy and too long, his chin stubbled with fine hairs, his skin pallid, and he was hunched into a sheepskin car coat that had seen better days, even when the sheep was wearing it.

'You wanted to see me, sir,' she said, wondering who the stranger was.

McIntyre turned and she saw his face was stiff with something that might have been fury. When he spoke, his voice was little more than a growl. Something had pissed him off and it didn't take a detective of Roach's ability to work out that the man now blowing his nose into what looked like a very damp tissue was in some way the cause.

'You're just back from the locus?' McIntyre asked.

'Yes, sir.'

'And this man Lancaster was in full costume?'

She glanced quickly towards the man trying to find a dry patch on his tissue.

'Speak freely, DCI Roach.' McIntyre was eyeing the soiled tissue in the man's hands as if it was carrying Ebola. Roach fought the smile that struggled to reach her lips. Her boss's fear of germs was a joke around the division that was not to be sneezed at. He continued, 'This is DCS Lonsdale. DCS Lonsdale here is up from Glasgow.'

'Sir,' she said, bobbing her head towards the visiting detective, and he reciprocated. She made no move to shake his hand. She didn't share her boss's pathological aversion, but she didn't want to run the risk of coming down with something. She looked back to McIntyre. 'Yes, sir, the victim wore the stolen soldier's costume.' She wondered why the mucus-filled officer was in Inverness but knew all would soon be revealed. Anyway, she had other news to pass on. 'And I have a name for the first victim, sir. Apparently he's a Jake Goodman and he's in some way connected to—'

'That's what we want to talk to you about, DCI Roach. But I'll let DCS Lonsdale here fill you in.' McIntyre's lip almost curled. He seemed to relish saying the man's name in a way that conveyed it was something deeply unpleasant a cat had recently disgorged onto a Persian rug. 'DCS Lonsdale is with Specialist Crimes.'

Lonsdale sneezed. McIntyre physically recoiled. He was probably thinking about reaching into his drawer for the anti-bacterial spray Roach knew he kept there. He took a few steps further away from any possible contamination.

'Sorry, got a serious viral infection, been laid up for days. The worst has passed, though,' said Lonsdale, the hard tones of his native Yorkshire Moors made nasal by his blocked passages. He blew his nose again. Viral. Infection. Roach would bet her boss was only one more sneeze away from calling for a hazmat suit. She gave the Specialist Crimes unit officer her full attention while he put the tissue away and produced a packet of lozenges. He popped one from the blister pack and slipped it into his mouth. Specialist Crimes covered a multitude of sins and she wondered if the investigation was being taken away from her.

Lonsdale seemed satisfied he had cleared his nasal passages sufficiently to speak further. 'Your victim out on that battlefield.' He paused to suck the lozenge. She waited. 'He was one of ours.'

She blinked. 'As in . . . ?'

'As in, he was a counter-terrorism officer working undercover.'

Spooks, she thought, *now we have spooks. Wonderful.* She looked at McIntyre, his face still shadowed with rage.

'Jake Goodman was his cover name,' said Lonsdale.

'And what was his real name?' Roach asked.

'Detective Sergeant Brian Roberts.'

'And he was working on what, exactly?'

Lonsdale's face contorted as if he was about to sneeze but the moment passed. 'That's above your pay grade.'

Roach faced McIntyre. 'Do you know, sir?'

McIntyre gave Lonsdale a stare that was hard enough to scare any germs daring enough to waft his way. 'It has become quite clear that I don't get paid enough either. This operation was kept from me, for some reason.'

'It was nothing personal. We had our reasons.' Lonsdale gave a slight shrug. 'Sorry,' he added. He didn't sound in the least bit sorry. That was the problem with spooks, Roach thought. They told you bugger all unless they wanted you to know, and even then it was likely to be a lie.

McIntyre cleared his throat, or growled, Roach couldn't tell which.

Lonsdale kept talking. 'The chief constable approved the operation and the need to keep it under the official radar. If you wish to make a formal complaint then be my guest, take it to him. In the meantime . . .'

'What took you so long to come forward?' Roach asked. 'It's been three days. Surely our fingerprint and DNA search pinged somewhere along the line?'

All police officers had their biometric data stored so they could be identified should there be any inadvertent contamination of a crime scene.

Lonsdale's face was deadpan. 'There were operational reasons for this. DS Roberts' data was sealed and I've been sick. I did not become aware of this until last night and I drove straight up from Glasgow.'

'So who did DS Roberts report to locally?'

'No one. This operation was based out of Glasgow.'

Roach and McIntyre exchanged glances, both knowing immediately what that meant. No involvement in Inshes meant they didn't trust the local law. But then Roach had learned that spooks didn't trust anyone. As for the operational reasons for the delay, DNA profiling would take some time but the fingerprint hit should have raised an alert immediately. Roach was fairly certain the dead man's police service record was safely under some digital lock and key, lest the bad guys use a friendly copper to access it and check up on him. It was conceivable that a glitch in the procedure had caused the delay – even what used to be called Special Branch was not infallible – but heads would roll.

The way McIntyre glared at the visiting officer made it plain he was more than happy to start the lopping. 'I think, under the circumstances, you had better explain what you and your department are up to. In my division. Without my knowledge.'

Lonsdale didn't say anything at first. He shivered and pulled the thick sheepskin closer to his body. 'I don't think we can.'

'I think we can, and I think we will,' said McIntyre. 'Speak up, man – we're all friends here. No one is listening in. I have one dead police officer and another corpse that seems to be connected somehow. So, what the hell was your man into on my patch? And don't give me that "need to know" bollocks. I now need to know, as does my DCI here.'

Lonsdale gave it some thought as he blew his nose. Then he sighed. 'What I say goes no further than this room. Clear?'

'Get on with it, man,' said McIntyre, his voice suggesting he was an inch away from wheeling out a portable guillotine.

Lonsdale hesitated again, the lozenge clattering around in his mouth like a key in a washing machine. Roach felt he had intended on telling them all along, that this was just for show. Then he said, 'DS Roberts was investigating Spioraid nan Gàidheal and its connection with New Dawn. As you know, the alt-right has become more mainstream than alt in recent years and the likes of New Dawn pose a very real threat to security.'

'Not to mention the public,' said Roach.

Lonsdale conceded with a decline of his head. 'This has been a two-year operation, beginning in Edinburgh, then moving here, where DS Roberts had managed to get himself deeply entrenched with individuals close to Dalgliesh and by extension New Dawn.'

'As what?' asked Roach.

'Low-level drug dealer working for a local family.'

'The Burkes?'

'That's right. Seems one of the sons, Scott Burke, is a member of Spioraid, or at least closely connected with it. Roberts, using his alias—'

'Jake Goodman.' Roach was a touch peeved that her big reveal had been upstaged.

Lonsdale nodded. 'Jake Goodman. Using that alias – small-time dealer – he inserted himself in the organisation. The main target was Dalgliesh and his connections with New Dawn. Scott Burke was merely the gateway.'

McIntyre interjected, his voice still heavy with anger. 'And did he actually sell drugs for the Burkes?'

'Yes.'

McIntyre's fury could now barely be held under control. Roach feared he would burst something. 'And why was I not informed of this operation?'

Lonsdale's face remained impassive as he took his time before answering. Clearly, the divisional commander's ire was not something that worried him.

'I'm sorry, but we could not be sure that your division had not been infiltrated.'

That was it for McIntyre. 'You what?' The words exploded out of his mouth. He took a step towards Lonsdale, then thought better of it. Roach didn't think it was his fear of germs that held him back this time; rather it was the fear that he couldn't control himself. He breathed heavily and forced himself to sit down in his chair. His voice remained strained, as if the gas that had heated it was merely turned down and not off. 'Detective Chief Superintendent Lonsdale, you'd better explain yourself. And make it good.'

Lonsdale's voice remained calm. 'I can name at least three of your officers who have attended Spioraid meetings. One of them at chief inspector level. Just because they pull on the uniform, it doesn't mean they leave their political views in the locker. We couldn't take the risk that my man would be exposed.'

'Yet he's still lying in the mortuary,' said Roach.

Lonsdale gave her a fleeting look, but she saw the pain in his eyes. 'Yes,' he said. There was a moment's silence between them.

'You know something, Detective Chief Superintendent,' McIntyre said, 'this has been a cock-up of the first order. You place a man undercover in my division and you don't even tell me about it. You accuse my people of being in league with right-wing extremists. You take three days to give us your man's identity after he is found dead. You know what? I think I *will* get in touch with the chief constable about all this.'

Lonsdale shrugged, dug his packet of paper tissues from his pocket and peeled off a fresh one. 'Feel free.'

McIntyre gave him a long hard stare. 'I don't need your bloody permission,' he said.

44

When she finally returned to the office, Rebecca received the usual disappointed look from Barry, but he didn't ask for an explanation for her absence, even though she had a good reason. No sign of Les, so that was something. She seated herself at her terminal and set about crafting the words to go with her amateurish shot of the police activity on Church Street. She had discussed it with Elspeth and they had decided to go with the line that the victim in the kirkyard was named locally as Walter Lancaster. They had also agreed that they would mention the uniform too, their experience of holding back with the Highlander gear having taught them a lesson. Lola McLeod would sure as hell be sniffing around this soon if she wasn't already, and she had proved her sources were as good as Elspeth's. Roach was too experienced a cop not to know what she was doing when she effectively confirmed it all and they were pretty sure she was not steering them wrong, even though the conversation had taken a heavy turn pretty damn quickly. Rebecca could still feel her heart hammering slightly, and it was nothing to do with her run back to her car and then a madcap drive to the office. Roach had rattled her. Rebecca had no fear of the police, not with her father having been a detective in Glasgow, but Roach had a quiet determination that was unnerving. Rebecca knew it was highly unlikely she'd get anywhere with her threat but, at the same time, her gut told her that the detective would most certainly do her best to follow through on it. And Rebecca was unsure how much support she'd get from her employers.

She called the communications department at Inshes and spoke to her favourite press officer, a young man who, like her, was an incomer to Inverness. He gave her the official line on the murder, something bland and hugely uninformative, but at least it was a quote. She attached the photographs she'd uploaded from her phone but before she hit SEND she stopped and thought for a moment. Lancaster had been wearing the stolen uniform and that connected his death somehow to Jake Goodman – another story she was about to break, again using the 'named locally as' line. Goodman had been found at Culloden, a site of historical significance, Lancaster at the High Kirk. It was an old church, certainly, but she wondered what was so significant about it. Something was still whispering in her mind, but she couldn't quite hear it.

She picked up her mobile phone, found Anna Fowler's number, hoped she wasn't lecturing. It rang and rang. Shit, Rebecca thought, listening to the ringtone droning as she pulled up Google and typed in the name of the church. She would have preferred to speak to an expert than rely on the internet, but that was—

'Anna Fowler.' The history professor's voice cut through her thoughts.

'Anna,' said Rebecca, her relief evident. 'Listen, I need to pick your brain.'

'If you pick it, it won't get any better,' said Anna.

Her father used to say that all the time, but Rebecca dutifully laughed. 'The Old High Kirk, on Church Street?' There was that inflection again. Anna would know where it was, for God's sake. 'What's the history and what connection does it have to Culloden?'

'It's the oldest church site in Inverness – St Columba is said to have preached there, to King Brude – although the church building itself only dates back to the early eighteenth century. Government prisoners were held in the tower by Charles Edward Stuart's forces until Culloden, when the tables were turned and Jacobite soldiers were held there, among other places – the old Gaelic church round the corner, where the used bookstore is, was another. Cumberland had them executed at the door to the tower. They say the pits in the stonework were left by musket balls. Others, the wounded who could not stand to meet their fate, were propped up against a headstone in the yard and a government trooper used a V-shaped notch in another to steady his weapon in order to execute them. You can still see those headstones, although there's a large memorial of more recent vintage now between them.'

Rebecca scribbled all this down. Her story didn't officially link the two murders but by mentioning the uniform and adding a sidebar, ostensibly to illustrate the significance of the location of the body, she would at least be satisfying herself that she had done so.

'Has something happened there?' Anna had launched immediately into her thumbnail lecture. Now, she was clearly curious as to why Rebecca was asking.

'A man's body was found there this morning. Walter Lancaster. You may have seen him on the news.'

'I tend not to watch the news now,' said Anna. 'Too depressing. Too much Trump, Brexit and death. Who is he? Or was he?'

'A sex offender who was due to be rehomed in the Ferry. The locals have been actively working against it.'

'And he was found in the kirkyard?'

'Yes.'

'How did he die?'

They hadn't asked Roach that. It was doubtful she would have confirmed anything about the manner of death anyway. 'He was murdered,' she said.

'And judging by your question about the church's history, you think his death is linked to that man found at Culloden?'

'Yes.'

The line went silent for a moment. When Anna spoke, her voice had changed slightly, was distant somehow. 'Was he dressed in the missing uniform?'

'That's right. Em, I'm sorry, Anna, I have to go.' Rebecca was eager to get the information fed into the system and online. 'I'm under the gun here.'

A little laugh breathed over the phone. It was a sad little noise. 'Given the kirkyard's history, that's very appropriate. I have a class anyway. Please, keep me informed of developments, will you? I feel as if I have a vested interest in all this. One thing, though, before we go, and I'm sure it's one that's already occurred to you. These sites aren't random. Culloden and the High Kirk are both linked by blood. Whoever did this chose them for a reason.'

45

The child sees the men walking to their deaths for the past is present and the present is past. They are ragged and weary, their wounds rudely tended to, blood seeping through dirty linen. For why give medical care to those who are about to die? They sit in the tower, hearing the gunfire outside and the impact of musket ball on stone. And flesh. They hear their comrades, their friends, their brothers scream and groan and fall. Then the door is opened again and another one is taken away.

It is a production line of death, the child knows. One by one, or in groups, they are taken from the cramped prison and into the cold daylight. A shouted order. A musket report. A man dies. Another takes his place.

And then they come for the weak and the wounded. They are hauled outside, dragged across the grass and thrown against the headstone. The earth beneath is cold and wet, the stone at their back rough hewn. And there, a few feet away, is another stone, the V-shaped notch now home to the barrel of a musket, the soldier behind it a mere red-coated mound. And then the shot, smoke puffing from the musket and perhaps brief, fresh pain before merciful oblivion. The soldier's comrades watch, some horrified at the slaughter. Others grin. Some men are blank-faced – this is merely a duty, an order to be carried out with no question. They are oppressors, those who slaughter with workman-like precision. They are the victors and history belongs to them.

The child sees them now, oppressor and victim alike, as Lancaster dies. They stand among the graves, even though none of these markers are for them. The *mortal remains of the Highlanders moulder beneath the path leading to the door of the kirk. The soldiers – both English and Scots – lie under the sod on some foreign field perhaps, or in their home towns or villages. And yet something of them lingers here, little more than outlines in the night, shades of darkness within shades of darkness. They watch as the body is first clothed in red and then bathed in it as the neck is opened and life bursts forth in a jet.*

He jerks on the slab, like a beast left to bleed out by the butcher. The ragged Highlanders understand, the child thinks, but the soldiers, English and Scots, are perplexed. The child feels their question floating on the night air.

Why?

Why? The child replies in words that take shape only in the mind. Because he exists and he does not deserve life.

The question comes again.

Why?

Because he is of your flesh. Because he is one who preys on the weak and the fearful. Because he must answer for his crimes. Just as the one they called Goodman did. Just as the man in the little room at the top of the stairs did, all those years before.

46

The incident room was almost empty, apart from DC Edward Moore and another young officer, a blonde woman on secondment from uniform whose name she could not remember. Roach offered Lonsdale a cup of coffee, was even willing to supply it from her personal stash, but he preferred tea. She had never been one to delegate such tasks to junior officers, so while she made the beverages he stood by the white board and studied what they had. She handed him a mug, apologising that it wasn't a Yorkshire blend, and stood beside him but not too close. As if to underline her point, Lonsdale wiped his nose with a fresh tissue.

His eyes scanned the information on the board.

'We're on the same side, you know.'

She sipped her coffee. The earlier one in the old town was good. Hers was better. 'All evidence to the contrary.'

They smiled at each other. Neither smile was terribly sincere.

'So, do you think Spioraid found out your man was working undercover?' Roach asked, her smile dropping.

'You tell me,' said Lonsdale, his attention back to the board.

'As we've just discovered this link, there's nothing we can tell you,' said Roach. 'Maybe if we had known . . .' She left the thought dangling like a hanged man and thought once again that she saw something like regret cross his face. Or perhaps his lozenge had disagreed with him. You never could tell with these people.

'How is the investigation progressing?' he asked.

'Still early days.'

Lonsdale sniffed. 'So, no leads, then?'

'A few.'

'You willing to share?'

'Were you?'

'I am now.'

'Are you?' she asked, her head cocked to one side. 'Are you really?'

His face was suddenly very serious. 'Look – DCI Roach, was it?' She nodded. 'Look, I've got a man dead. He was my guy. I was his boss and his handler. I put him in place here, so I feel responsible. So yes, I am willing to share.'

'To an extent, though, right?'

He looked at her, as if he was sizing her up. 'You know the score.'

'Yes, I do,' she said. 'You people don't like sharing, unless you can help it.'

'Sometimes we simply can't.'

They fell silent again, as Lonsdale took in what little they had, lingering only slightly over the printout of the image of the dead man's face before moving on again.

'We'll need a formal ID,' said Roach.

'His wife is on her way.'

'He has a wife?'

'And two kids.'

Roach could not imagine what kind of life that woman had, her husband on long-term undercover work, living another life under another name. Now dead in a city that was probably alien to her.

'But I can make the ID,' Lonsdale continued. 'Save her that at least.'

He seemed to have focused on one name on the board, written up in Bremner's fair hand, she noted. 'This John Donahue,' he said. 'You spoken to him?'

'In person and on the phone. He's a positive delight.'

'Brian told me about him. We managed to finagle him a job on the set of that film they're making.'

'*Conquering Hero.*'

'Yeah.' He sipped his tea. 'Ah, that's good stuff. Anyway, he had managed to infiltrate Spioraid up here, thanks to him getting chummy with that Scott Burke.'

'And selling drugs for him.'

'Lesser evils, DCI Roach, lesser evils.'

'Really? Tell that to the families drugs destroy.'

He ignored her. 'Anyway, we managed to finagle that job on the film set, odd jobs, toting that barge, lifting that bale sort of thing. That brought him into contact with Mr Donahue.'

'I've been told they had an altercation.'

Lonsdale's eyebrows lifted. 'Where did you hear that?'

'I'm only willing to share to an extent too.'

She thought she saw a smile kindle in his eyes. 'Fair enough. Yeah, they did have a row.'

'Was your man selling drugs to the crew?'

'Of course, but that wasn't what it was about. Donahue and Brian had a history.'

'They worked together?'

'No, Donahue was Strathclyde, Brian Lothian and Borders. This was before we became one big happy family under Police Scotland.'

'Okay. So what happened?'

Lonsdale held his mug away and the hand holding the tissue darted to his nose to catch a sneeze. 'Sorry,' he said. 'This virus is a bastard.'

'Should you even be up and about?'

'I told you, Brian was my guy. It's bad enough I missed seeing his face on the news. I need to be here, whether it kills me or not.'

Roach understood. She would feel the same. 'Just don't die in my incident room. I've got enough paperwork.'

He smiled. 'I'll do my best.'

Maybe they were bonding, she thought. Then she remembered he was a spook, and they only bond when their first name is James. 'So, Donahue and Brian. History.'

He put the mug down on the corner of the nearest desk and blew his nose. Then he said, 'About ten years ago Donahue's daughter was sexually assaulted during the Edinburgh Festival. It was pretty bad, by all accounts. Brian was the investigating officer.'

'Did they get the guy?'

'Guys. Plural. Posh blokes at the festival for a jolly. One was the son of a government minister.'

'What happened?'

'Guess,' he said, but Roach didn't need to. Convictions for sexual assaults were maddeningly low. Often the only witness was the victim and they were often in no fit state to give proper evidence. Unless there was cast-iron DNA, good lawyers could cast enough shadows and doubts to blot out the sun. And if the accused was well-connected, their legal team was normally the best money could buy.

'So they got off?'

'Yup. And Donahue blamed Brian, said he didn't work hard enough. Had a go at the advocate-depute handling the case too, publicly dressed her down outside the High Court. Bit of a meltdown, by all accounts. Donahue was encouraged to retire soon after.'

'So he saw your man, recognised him?'

'That's about it. Started to lay into him about it being all his fault. That he was a disgrace to the profession.'

'In front of witnesses.' Roach wasn't asking a question. Whoever Rebecca's source was had seen it.

'Brian said no, but obviously he was wrong. So if there were any Spioraid, or New Dawn, people around . . .'

'New Dawn haven't killed anyone before, have they?'

'Not to my knowledge. There have been a couple of beatings that we know of and a device was planted in a Glasgow mosque just after the Brexit referendum. It was discovered in time and dealt with. That same mosque was firebombed this week. So, no – they've not actually killed anyone. But there's always a first time.'

Roach thought about this. If New Dawn had graduated to murder, then yes, the killing could be viewed as a message to anyone else to mind their own business. The costume, the weapon, the location – all linked to Scottish history. New Dawn, or Spioraid, or whatever bunch of cranks and halfwits they were, could have been making a statement. But what the hell did a recently released sex offender have to do with it all?

Whatever the solution to that particular conundrum, she knew what her next step was. She turned away from the board and raised her voice. 'DC Moore, I want you to give John Donahue a bell. Tell him he is wanted here at Inshes. This is not an invitation and you will not accept an "I'm too busy" or "I'm washing my hair" as an answer. Donahue has some questions to face and he will do it in an interview room before this day is out. Should he body swerve you or give you any kind of grief, then you have my permission to go down the glen and drag him here in handcuffs. Clear?'

Moore grinned and reached for the phone.

Then another thought struck her. 'And tell him to bring a list of anyone employed at the compound and on the set itself. Any snash about that, put him on to me.'

She still wanted to know who the Connolly girl's source was. It had to be someone employed by the production company in some capacity and perhaps a list would help. Certainly wouldn't hurt.

Lonsdale was studying the board, no doubt judging them on what little they actually had. Well, perhaps if the Branch had been more open about their operation, they would have had more. She tapped Donahue's name on the board. 'So what happened to Donahue's daughter?'

Lonsdale blew his nose again and then answered matter-of-factly, 'She hung herself soon after the trial.'

47

Rebecca had been trying for days to reach John Donahue, with no luck. The man simply refused to take any of her calls. She really wanted to talk to him about what Anna had told her, especially now she had a name. She considered crashing the production company's centre of operations, but it was a long journey to Glen Nevis, maybe two hours each way, and for what? To be turned away at the gate? She couldn't think of any plausible reason to present to Les that would cover taking herself out of circulation for an afternoon. She couldn't even justify it to herself.

Her stomach had been telling her for a while that it was well past lunchtime, but she had ignored it in order to pile in copy. She finally finished, tried Donahue one more time, predictably failed to reach him, and decided to head over to the supermarket for soup and a sandwich. One of the benefits of the office being in the retail park was the proximity of a large supermarket for shopping and lunch.

She saw the black four-wheel drive as soon as she stepped out. Nolan Burke. Was the bugger stalking her? She felt that flutter in the pit of her stomach. She didn't like it.

He must have been watching for her because he climbed out and made his way across the car park. She glanced up at the windows of the office, but no one was looking out that she could see. The first time had been after hours; this was broad daylight. If someone did peer out, what would they think if they saw her talking to one of the notorious Burkes? Would they put it down to a story and leave it that? Or would they suspect something else? Yet there was no something else for them to suspect. Nolan Burke was only a source and/or a story to her.

Wasn't he?

'Mr Burke,' she said. 'What brings you here?'

'I came to see you were all right after last night,' he said. 'And it's Nolan, remember?'

She did remember, but she still would not go down that road. 'I'm fine,' she said. 'A bit sore but my hands aren't too bad.'

She let him see the palms of her hands, where there were only a few red welts visible. He reached out as if to touch, then thought better of it. She snatched her hands away anyway and they stood awkwardly for a moment, neither saying anything. She felt like she was back at school, the first time a boy had asked her out. He had been pretty ham-fisted about it too, but she hadn't helped by playing hard to get, even though she'd really wanted to go out with him. Not that this situation was the same, of course.

'Anyway, I'm just heading over the road for something to eat, so unless . . .'

'I'll keep you company,' he said, even though she did not recall issuing an invitation. At least, she didn't think she had. No matter, she was stuck with him now, unless she could think of a way to wriggle out of it.

'I'm only going for soup and a sandwich,' she said. 'I need to take it back to the office.'

'That's okay,' he said. 'I'll just make sure no one annoys you on the way.'

'I don't think that's likely, do you?' she said, her voice dry. 'Although you might manage it.'

He smiled. He had a nice smile for a drug-dealing gangster, she thought, then instantly chided herself. *He's a source, no more than that.*

'I see that Lancaster bloke was found dead, in the Old Town,' he said as they trudged across the vast space.

'Yes.'

'Was he really murdered?'

'It would seem so.'

253

He was silent for a moment. 'How was he killed?'

'I don't know.'

'Do you know if they have any suspects?'

'Why are you so interested?'

His pace slowed for a moment. 'Because this was the guy we were protesting about and he ends up dead. You know my family, you know our reputation. The law will be looking at us.'

She stopped and faced him. 'Did your family have him killed?'

'No.'

She believed him. 'Then you have nothing to worry about, do you?'

He laughed, but it was brittle and humourless. 'Aye, right. I thought you knew the score, Rebecca. Innocence is no defence. If they want to make it look like we're responsible, they will.'

He was talking about a fit-up. Her father had told her that strokes were often pulled in the force and there had been incidences of serious wrongdoing. 'They don't do that sort of thing any more,' she said.

Another laugh, same as the first. 'Aye, you keep on believing that.'

She held his gaze steadily, trying to gauge if there was any real guilt there. She saw nothing. But she detected something else. He was worried. Was he really concerned the police would stitch him or his family up? Or was there something else? Did the family actually have something to do with Lancaster's death and, by extension, the murder of Jake Goodman?

'Is there something for you to worry about?'

The way he avoided her gaze confirmed it. He stared across the car park, as if looking for something but not finding it. 'Mr Burke . . .' she said.

'Nolan,' he said automatically.

'Is there something in all this for you to worry about?'

He still did not look at her. 'Let's just drop it, okay?'

'I can't just drop it, you know that.' She took a deep breath before she asked the next question. 'Your mother.' She took another breath. 'I need to ask – was she abused as a child?'

254

A muscle worked in his cheek as he considered not replying. 'When she was a wee girl. Her father.'

So, not such a decent guy after all, her father. She was going to ask him if Scott knew about it too, when he made a show of looking at his watch.

'Listen,' he said, his voice hurried. 'I've just remembered, I need to be some place.'

Just remembered, she thought. He comes all the way to the retail park, camps outside the office until she comes out, then when the conversation seems to turn difficult he remembers a previous appointment.

He checked the horizon again, still found nothing, but he studied it anyway. Then he shook his head, turned and walked away.

She watched him, knowing she was both none the wiser but better informed. Nolan Burke had information, maybe merely a suspicion, but he wasn't going to share. She had suspected there was a story in the family, in him – was that what the fluttering was all about? – but now she knew.

48

John Donahue's temper was on default setting, which meant it was barely under control. He was sitting in the interview room, his posture so taut Roach expected he could shit diamonds. Apparently he had not come quietly.

She gave him a brief smile. 'Thank you very much for attending this interview, Mr Donahue.'

He grimaced. 'It was made clear to me that refusal was not an option. Your young officer was insistent to the point of being threatening.'

Roach kept a fresh – and sincere – smile from breaking out. So, young Moore had asserted himself. She must remember to give him an attaboy. 'I'm so sorry, Mr Donahue,' she lied, 'the officer will, of course, be reprimanded. However, it is important that we have a wee chat.'

Donahue twisted round when Lonsdale, standing at the door, blew his nose. 'Who's this?' he barked.

Lonsdale completed his nasal ablutions before he said, 'Detective Chief Superintendent Lonsdale, Mr Donahue. Specialist Crimes.'

Donahue grunted and faced Roach again, unimpressed by Lonsdale's credentials. 'DCS Lonsdale has a bad cold, so he has opted to keep his distance,' Roach explained. 'He's merely observing this interview.'

Donahue flicked a thumb at the tape recorder on the table against the wall and then at the various cameras around the room. 'We're not recording this?'

'Do you want us to record it?'

'Not particularly. So this is not an interview under caution?'

'Do you want this to be an interview under caution?'

He leaned forward, clasped his hands on the tabletop. 'Look, love, let's just stop the games. I've played them all my life and I probably invented a few of them. I'm a busy man, so can we just cut to it and get this over with? You want to know about me and Brian Roberts, right?'

'That's right.'

'Brian Roberts was a shit police officer. He screwed up the investigation into my daughter's assault. He didn't deserve to be in the Job, if you ask me.'

'Did you threaten him?'

Donahue shifted in his chair. 'Aye, heat of the moment. I saw him on the set, recognised him right off. I'd been told he was selling dope to the crew.'

Lonsdale spoke up. 'You could have blown his cover.'

Blown his cover, Roach thought. *They do like to talk like they're in a bad crime show.*

Donahue swivelled to face him again. 'I didn't know he was still Job. I thought he'd finally found his calling. And before fingers are pointed, who was it who placed him undercover without knowing I was on site?'

'But you did threaten him,' insisted Roach, wishing to keep any finger-pointing within her control.

'I said I did. I didn't mean it. We all say things when we're angry.'

'A death threat is pretty extreme.'

'I already told you, heat of the moment. No way would I follow it through.'

'And yet you said you didn't know who he was when I asked.'

'I hadn't seen the photograph at that time.'

Roach paused, aware she had heard the first lie. 'Who else was around when you had your outburst?'

Donahue considered. 'I don't know, some of the crew. A couple of my guys. Why?'

'Because one of them may have overheard and passed it on to Spioraid nan Gàidheal,' said Lonsdale, forcing Donahue to turn in his direction again. 'And perhaps New Dawn.'

Donahue shook his head. 'No, not possible.'

'Really?' Roach scanned the printout of the crew list Moore had handed to her before they began. 'Lot of people on this list, how can you possibly vouch for each one of them?'

'You've had issues with Spioraid,' said Lonsdale. 'Vandalism, thefts, threats. Costumes have been taken, one of which was found on Brian Roberts' body. You're an experienced copper, Mr Donahue, you must have suspected it could be an inside job.'

'I investigated each incident myself,' Donahue said. 'I was satisfied no one working on the crew was responsible. Each time it was a breach of security. We identified where they came in and went out.'

'Or it was made to look like that,' said Roach, still looking at the names.

'You can't be certain,' said Lonsdale.

'Anyone could be a Spioraid member,' said Roach.

'Or related to one,' said Lonsdale.

'Or just sympathise with the cause.' Roach's eye fell on one name on the list. Interesting, she thought, then looked up at the former detective opposite her. He had stopped flailing between them, either because he was tired or because he had sussed out their little ploy. The old stress interview technique. One person directly in front, another behind. Keeps the subject on edge. Frankly, she was surprised he had fallen for it. Then she saw the glint of amusement in Donahue's eye. He hadn't fallen for it.

'So you don't think I killed him, then?'

She laid the printed list of names on the table. 'I keep an open mind,' she said. 'So, just for the record, where were you on Sunday night and Monday morning?'

'I was in the office on the compound until about midnight, then in my flat in Fort William.'

'Can anyone verify that?'

'People saw me in the office – security guards are on duty all night.'

'But no one after that.'

'There's a cat lives in the flat next door and I gave it a pat on my way in. I doubt he'll speak to you, though.'

'Do you keep your phone on overnight?'

'Yes, I like to be on call.'

'Did you use it that night?'

'I called my wife. She doesn't sleep well and I always speak to her before turning in.'

'May I see your phone?'

'Do you have a warrant?'

'Do I really need one?'

There was a pause then, as they each held the other's gaze in a battle of wills. Roach sensed the man had nothing to hide, but she wanted to confirm it. She could tell his desire to get this over with was at odds with his need to be as awkward as possible. Finally, he reached into the inside pocket of his jacket and slid the fancy mobile to her. She nodded her thanks and thumbed through his call list. There was a call to a Glasgow number at 12.45 a.m. on Monday morning. It had lasted ten minutes. She scribbled the number down, more for show than anything else because she knew it would be his home phone. They would check the GPS for his number but she had already satisfied herself that he was in Fort William around the time of the murder.

She pushed the phone back to him. 'Do you know a Walter Lancaster?'

'I know *of* a Walter Lancaster,' he said, returning the phone to his pocket. 'I've never laid eyes on the man.'

'He was found dead this morning in the graveyard of the High Kirk in Inverness. He was wearing the soldier's uniform stolen from your film set.'

He took this in. 'So what connection does he have with Roberts?'

'We wondered if you could tell us.'

'How the hell would I know?'

'There is CCTV coverage on Church Street, Mr Donahue. There are lots of pubs dotted around there, so it's needed for community safety. We have footage of the person who killed Lancaster. A big individual. Powerful-looking.'

'But not his face?'

'No, not the face. It's obscured with something, balaclava maybe. But you're, what? Six-four, six-five?'

'Six-three.'

'You work out, Mr Donahue?'

'I keep trim.' Donahue's voice was terse. His fleeting amusement was dead, his patience had finally deserted him. Roach was surprised it had taken so long. 'So let me just sum all this up, in the interests of saving time. Whoever you've got on that video isn't me. I don't know this Walter Lancaster. I had no reason to kill him. I was not in Church Street last night, this morning, or ever, as far as I know. No, I can't prove it – again I was working late and then I went home. I did not kill Brian Roberts. My threat was made in anger and I had no intention of harming him. I regret my outburst. I admit it is possible that someone overheard my remark and accept the possibility that someone on the crew could be in some way connected to Spioraid.' He stood up. 'But now, unless you wish to caution me, at which point I will require the presence of a lawyer, I'm leaving.'

Roach looked up at him as he glared down at her. 'Thank you, Mr Donahue, you've been most helpful. I'll arrange for you to be driven back to Fort William.'

'Save the resources,' he said. 'I'll make my own arrangements.'

He walked to the door, pausing beside Lonsdale. 'I take it he was your man?'

Lonsdale nodded.

'I'm sorry you lost your officer. I can only imagine how you feel. But I'm not going to mourn him. I thought he was a disgrace to the Job and I'm not going to change my mind just because he's dead. But I didn't kill him, no matter what I said in anger. Killing him wouldn't bring my girl back. It wouldn't make things right. It wouldn't give my wife enough peace of mind to let her sleep at night. I caught killers, thieves, dealers, ponces, pimps and perverts for a living. I didn't kill them. I didn't kill him.'

Donahue didn't wait for an answer. He jerked the door open and walked out, his shoulders straight, his head high. Lonsdale blew his nose again as he took the chair Donahue had recently vacated.

'I don't think he did it,' he said.

'Neither do I,' said Roach. 'But I did enjoy noising him up. And I got this.' She picked up the list of names once more.

'And that helps how?'

She let her eyes run down the list again, stopping at the one she recognised. 'Because I think I've just found who has been assisting Her Majesty's Press.'

49

Scott tried to ignore Nolan as they both arrived home at the same time. Nolan touched his arm, made him turn to face him. 'We need to talk,' he said.

That little smile as he began to head to the door again. 'We really don't, bro.'

'I need to know where you were last night.'

Scott stopped, faced him, his back to the house. 'None of your business, is it?'

'If you were on family business, like you said, it is my business too. *Bro.*'

Scott held Nolan's gaze. Nolan really wanted to slap that smile away like it was an annoying insect. 'Tell you what,' said Scott, 'I'll tell you what I was doing if you tell me what you're up to with that reporter.'

'I'm not up to anything with her.'

'Not the way I see it.'

'I don't care what way you see it.'

'You were with her in Barney's the other night.'

Shit. Nolan felt something stab at him – guilt? Regret at his own stupidity? His mind raced through his options. He could deny it, but what good would that do? He could ignore it, but Scott was unlikely to let it go. Or he could tell something like the truth in the hope that it prompted his younger brother to come clean about his actions the night before.

'I'm keeping her on side. She could be useful. It doesn't do any harm to have a pet reporter.'

'A pet reporter?' This seemed to amuse Scott even further. 'You sure you're not just petting that reporter?'

'I'm certain,' said Nolan, and he wasn't lying. He had told himself he started up with her in order to keep tabs on her, but deep down he knew that wasn't true. He'd seen her around the court and then outside the council HQ the other morning. He found her attractive, but he was aware she was uncomfortable with that, although now and then he swore he'd caught her giving him a look. Or was that just wishful thinking? His dad called people like her straight arrows and he said they didn't want anything to do with the likes of the Burkes. So he kept it professional, steered her info. Though that had almost got her hurt when the demo went pear-shaped. It had suddenly hit him when he saw the grazes on her hand and the way she walked awkwardly, as if there was pain from a wound he couldn't see. He had fled then, because of that, and because he feared Scott had done something more than just a bit of business the night before.

'Your turn,' he said. 'Where were you last night?'

Scott's smile didn't waver. 'Fuck off.'

'Scotty, it's important you tell me.'

'It was important you told me about your girlfriend but all you gave me was shit.'

'There's nothing to tell.'

'Aye, right.' Scott turned again.

'What happened last night?'

'Nothing happened last night,' Scott said over his shoulder.

'I saw blood on your shirt.'

That stopped him. He turned, his eyes widening slightly. 'You been snooping, bro?'

Nolan ignored the question. 'Whose blood was it?'

'No mine, if that's what you're worried about.'

'Then whose?'

'Told you, none of your business.'

Nolan breathed heavily down his nose. He had to keep calm. 'That guy Lancaster was murdered last night, did you hear?'

'No loss.'

Nolan gave it a beat, his eyes holding his brother's steadily. 'Scott, did you kill him?'

The little smile seemed to twitch a little. 'And if I did, so what? Kiddie fiddlin' bastard deserved it, if you ask me.'

'Did you?'

There was a long pause as they stared at each other, Nolan itching to grip his brother by the shoulders and shake him until the smile slid off.

Finally, Scott spoke. 'Bro, the thing is, I don't need to tell you anything. And I don't want to tell you anything, because I don't trust you any more. I've been watching you this past while. You're not the Nolan Burke I used to know, the Nolan Burke Maw and Dad used to know. There's something different about you that I can't quite put my finger on. This thing with that reporter lassie makes my arse itch, you know what I'm saying? I don't know what's causing it but I can't scratch it away. I don't trust you, bro. Simple as. And if I find out you're betraying us, betraying the family in any way, you and me will be having a conversation and it won't be polite like this one and it won't be where Maw can see us. And that conversation won't end well for one of us.'

He opened the front door and stepped into the house, leaving Nolan on the doorstep.

50

Jane Roberts was so thin she almost wasn't there; in fact, she was so small that the Inshes conference room seemed like a cavern around her. She sat in a chair facing Rebecca and Elspeth. Roach was at her side, Terry Hayes standing just behind her, exuding a meld of switched-on media manager and Royal Marine gym instructor. They were like bodyguards. When the invitation had come for Rebecca and Elspeth to talk to the wife of the dead man, Hayes had said they were being given the exclusive as a thanks for their cooperation so far.

Elspeth knew the real reason. 'They want to avoid a feeding frenzy,' she had said to Rebecca as they waited in the foyer to be taken into the conference room. 'They know the media will want to talk to her. This way they can prevent her from being hassled and also control the flow of information.'

Roach had made her views clear from the start. She told them she was against this but had been countermanded by McIntyre. She didn't ask about Rebecca's source again, much to Rebecca's relief.

There was another man present, obviously a police officer, but not one the reporters had seen before. He was loitering by the door as if he needed a quick getaway. His blue suit was crumpled and a size too small for him, his skin was waxy and his stringy fair hair needed to be introduced to a pair of scissors. He held a packet of Kleenex in one hand, a single tissue in the other, into which he kept blowing his nose in what he probably hoped was an unobtrusive manner. Rebecca had clocked Elspeth studying him as she settled herself into a chair but no introductions were made.

That would only make Elspeth more curious. Rebecca too, come to that. So much for him being unobtrusive.

Then the woman was introduced to them by Terry Hayes. Jane Roberts. The Culloden victim's wife.

Brian Roberts.

Detective Sergeant Brian Roberts, no less.

Rebecca was just growing used to the name Jake Goodman; now, it seemed that was a fiction. She could guess why. In a very swift statement, Terry Hayes had informed them that the deceased had now been formally identified as a serving police officer on operational duties. She stilled the questions as to what those operational duties were by stating that they could not expand any further. But that hadn't been good enough for Elspeth.

'Is it true to say that DS Roberts was not based in the Highland and Islands?' Elspeth asked.

'As I said, we can't say anything at all regarding the reasons DS Roberts was deployed here,' Terry replied.

'But can we assume he was working undercover?'

'You can assume what you like, Elspeth.'

'I will, thanks. And if we accept that assumption – and, given that DS Roberts' identity was unknown until recently, we can – can we also assume that senior officers here at Inshes did not know about it?'

Hayes' voice hardened. 'Elspeth, what part of "we can't talk about it" do you not understand?' Then, as if to move swiftly on, she laid a hand on the woman's shoulder. 'Mrs Roberts here has very kindly agreed to talk to you in the hope that her privacy will be respected from here on. This will be a very difficult time for her, as I'm sure you will understand, and after this briefing there will be no further comment from her. I would expect you to share copy with your colleagues, if requested. Is that understood?'

Jane Roberts sat quietly throughout the exchange, very erect in the wooden chair, as if she was holding herself in check. She did not cry but she had done, and recently, judging by the puffy skin around her eyes.

She was in her late thirties, her cheek bones high and sharp, her nose thin and straight, her shoulder-length fair hair held away from her face with a clasp in the shape of a blue butterfly. One hand kept fluttering to it, as if she was straightening it, but Rebecca felt there was something more to it. Perhaps it had been given to her by her husband.

Her husband.

Her dead husband.

Elspeth's voice softened. 'Mrs Roberts, first, we are very sorry for your loss. It must have been a terrible shock to hear what happened.'

Jane Roberts inclined her head slightly as her hand darted to the clasp. Rebecca was convinced it was an involuntary movement and she was not even aware she was doing it.

'What can you tell us about him?'

The woman looked puzzled. 'In what way?'

'In any way. Just tell us about him, please.'

Jane Roberts looked over her shoulder at Hayes, as if for guidance, but Elspeth jumped in before the communications chief could speak. 'Mrs Roberts, just talk to us. We're not here to trip you up, we're not here to sensationalise. Just tell us about your husband, about Brian. When did you meet, how long have you been married, about your family. Anything.'

Rebecca knew what Elspeth was doing. It was something she'd taught her early on. Get people talking about themselves, let them settle into an interview. Being questioned by a reporter is alien to most people and it is best to let them relax.

Eventually, haltingly, Jane Roberts began to talk. There was no structure to it, no real order, and they let her words flow without interruption.

They had met at a party when they were in their twenties, fell for each other almost immediately, married within the year. They weren't blessed with children at first and had almost given up trying when the twins came along, girls, Chrissie and Carrie. That was ten years ago. They were happy together, most of the time. Brian was a good father, a good husband. Most

267

of the time. He worked hard in Lothian and Borders, as it was then, got out of uniform and into CID, got his promotion. He was good at his job. But then he moved department . . .

'Which department?' Elspeth asked, and Rebecca was aware that hankie guy at the door had straightened slightly. She knew Elspeth would have spotted the change in his stature. Elspeth spotted everything. She had probably hoped she would get an answer before they realised. She was sympathetic, but she had a job to do.

'That is not something we wish to talk about,' Hayes said, her hand on Jane's shoulder again. Elspeth and Rebecca exchanged looks. It was most certainly something they wished to talk about but knew they wouldn't get anything, so Elspeth let it pass.

'Okay, go on, Mrs Roberts. You're doing fine.'

He was away a lot with his new job, she said. It took its toll on family life. He phoned in when he could, of course, he always did that, but his children were growing up without him. Things became strained, words were said.

'Eventually, I told him that, as he was away all the time, we might as well make it permanent,' she said, and her hand fidgeted with the butterfly fastener again. 'So we separated. I think maybe he was relieved. The job was always important to him. When he was in CID he had regular hours, more or less, unless there was a major inquiry or something. But this new job. Well, it changed him. When he wasn't away, when he was at home, he just wasn't the same Brian. He was always on edge, paranoid even. His temper was short, with me, with the girls. And he got bored very easily, as if just sitting at home with us, watching telly or whatever, just wasn't enough for him.'

Her fingers caressed the clasp. Roach said nothing. Her face was impassive but something in her eyes told Rebecca that the woman's words resonated. Hayes shifted behind her, and she shot a look at the man at the door, who was clearly unhappy with the direction this was taking.

'So we had a huge row, the first really big one we'd ever had, and I said I'd had enough. If the job was so important to him, more important than his family, then he should just do it full time. He promised he would change, that he would put in for a transfer back to CID, but he never did. At least, I don't think he did. Finally, after a series of barneys, big ones again, I told him I wanted him away from us. I couldn't take his moods any more. He never raised a hand to us in all that time but I felt that maybe he had it in him, you know? I mean, what with his father and all . . .'

'His father?' Elspeth leaned forward.

'Okay, that's enough,' said the man at the door. Yorkshire accent, thick with mucus, but carrying an authoritative edge that was unmistakeable. He stepped forward. 'I'm stopping this right now.'

'And you are . . . ?' Elspeth asked.

'Someone who is calling a halt to this interview right now.'

Elspeth looked at Hayes. 'Can he?'

'He can, and he is,' said the man, before Hayes could answer.

Jane Roberts, though, was made of sterner stuff than they all thought. 'No,' she said. It wasn't loud but it was forceful enough to stop him in his tracks. He stared at the back of her head.

'Mrs Roberts,' he began.

'No,' she said again. 'You people asked me to do this. I'm doing it.' She twisted in the chair and gave him a look that told him she meant business. 'I lost my Brian years ago. Someone killed him, but you took him away from me first. You did. You can shut this down now if you like, but I'll contact these people later and I'll tell them it all. Your choice.'

The man's jaws worked as he listened to her. 'Mrs Roberts, what happened to Brian's father has no bearing on this whatsoever.'

'Then it won't matter if I tell them, will it?'

He looked to Roach for support. She gave him a cool gaze and said, 'I'd like to hear what Mrs Roberts has to say.'

He looked around at the women facing him and realised he was outnum-

269

bered. He exhaled harshly, turned and left. Rebecca thought he would have slammed the door but the bracket device fitted to the top prevented such a dramatic gesture.

Jane Roberts watched him go, then turned back to face Elspeth and Rebecca. She looked slightly deflated now, as if defying the man in the suit had taken every last bit of her strength. She was silent for a few moments before she spoke again.

'Brian's father was a police officer too. Well respected in Edinburgh.'

She stopped speaking abruptly. Rebecca hoped she wasn't having second thoughts now. She leaned forwards and spoke for the first time. 'My father was a police officer. Glasgow.' She hoped providing this common ground would help. Jane looked at her, nodded, gave her something like a sad, nervous, fleeting smile.

'What happened to Brian's father?' Elspeth asked.

Hand to the hair clip again. Touching. Stroking. Caressing. She studied the floor between them. There was a silence in the room that was thick enough to blot out any noise from outside. They waited.

'He was murdered,' the woman said, her voice so quiet and yet so loud. 'When Brian was a teenager, around thirteen.' Her eyes came up from staring at the carpet to hold Elspeth in a steady gaze. 'By his sister . . .'

51

The child did not wake up that morning with the intent to kill. It would just happen.

The man has not been to the child's room for a month, which is not uncommon. One year he left the child alone for six entire months. That was the happiest spring and summer of the child's life, with memories of long, warm days and blissful, pain-free nights. There was laughter then, throughout the house and in the garden. Laughter and perhaps even love. Even she, the woman, seemed more relaxed, content even. The boy was less introverted, less troubled, less detached.

But the summer ended, as it always must. The air chilled. The blooms wilted and shrivelled and died. The nights grew darker and longer and colder. The yellow days turned to brown and then grey.

But long before the first frost misted the milky glass of the bedroom window, the man returned. And with it the pain and the shame and the rage.

The child had a birthday during that month reprieve and there were presents, of course. There were always presents — afterwards. But birthdays and Christmas were special. Perhaps outsiders looking in, not seeing the full picture, thought of the child as spoiled. Certainly, there were many toys and books and videos and clothes and cake. Everything a child could wish for. Except the feeling of security, of experiencing real love, the kind glimpsed during that summer. The presents were still piled in the corner of the room. One very special present propped up against the wall and towering over the others. The child had asked *for it and had received it. The request had been innocent, for the child had no intention of using it in any way other than that for which it was designed.*

The child does not know what prompts the man to visit, cannot say whether it is events in his life that force him to somehow relieve the pressure in this little room. But the child hears his footsteps and cowers beneath the bedclothes, eyes on the door, hoping that those steps will not hesitate outside, will pass by. It has been a month. Please let it be longer.

The steps climb the stairs.

Please don't linger . . .

They stop outside the door.

Please don't open it . . .

The door opens.

Please don't come in . . .

The man comes in. Closes the door. Turns to the bed.

Moves closer.

Afterwards, the child lies and listens to his breathing. He is sleeping, which is unusual. It is more normal for him to get up and leave, his own shame forcing him out of this little room and away from his victim. And then, later, the present.

But this time he stays, lies back and is soon asleep. His breathing is even, a slight roughness as he inhales, but the child knows he is deep into whatever dreams he has.

The child does not intend to kill.

Easing off the bed, the child creeps slowly towards the presents in the corner. A slight cough from behind causes alarm, but he has merely moved slightly. His breathing remains regular, his eyes closed, a slight flutter indicates a dream in progress.

What does he dream of, the child wonders. Are they pleasant dreams? Or, like the child's, are they filled with darkness and shadows and creatures that emerge from the gloom to touch and stroke and penetrate?

It is not a large room but it seems vast now that the child has to cross it unnoticed and without a sound. Step after step, short ones, lungs in stasis, easy movements, fearful of a creaking board, of a scuffing noise, of the child's own breathing waking him, rousing him, warning him, until – finally – the short distance is covered and the presents are in reach. The one present on which the child's eyes are fixed, the one requested in all innocence.

For the child has never intended to kill. Even in the midst of the pain and the rage and the shame, it has never entered its mind.

The baseball bat is heavy but it can be swung, that had been proven during a game in the garden. The child is growing big and strong, many people have said that. Big and strong. On the outside. They did not know that the child was still an infant inside. An infant scared of the dark and what might lie within it. And what comes through the door of that little room.

Back across the room now, swifter than before, for what must be done must be done quickly. Beside the bed, bat raised, both hands.

Hesitation.

This is wrong.

This is oh so very wrong.

Lower the bat, put it away, lock it away, for this is wrong.

But the child does not lower the bat. The child merely stares at the man sleeping, his eyes still twitching as he exists in two worlds, this one and the dream state of his mind. He is smiling. He is happy wherever he is.

Happy.

The child has only known happiness fleetingly. The child and happiness are merely casual acquaintances. A moment here, a summer there. And sooner than later, inevitably, it is back to this little room and the footsteps on the stair. And that, the child knows, has to end. The pain and the rage and the shame have to end.

And yet, the hesitation remains. The bat still poised overhead, the need to bring it down still present, but the deliberation to do so is less pressing.

This is wrong. You should not do this. You must not do this.

And then his eyes flip open and he sees the child standing over him, the bat raised. And he knows the mistake he has made.

He begins to move. He begins to cry – no, bellow – as he reaches for the child, for the bat . . .

The child did not intend to kill that day.

It just happened.

52

They were back in the kitchen, in the same positions as before, as if none of them had left but had been frozen there in some kind of family tableau. This was not a happy family picture, however. There was rage in this room and it flowed from Mo Burke. Her face was a reservoir of fury and for once it wasn't soaking Nolan. She had a lit cigarette in one hand, while with the other she tapped the gold lighter Nolan's father had given her for their tenth wedding anniversary on the Formica table, then twirled it between her fingers before tapping it again. From where he stood leaning against the sink, Nolan could see the name *S.T. Dupont* etched in script. Over two hundred quid, it had cost him, he once told Nolan, but it was worth maybe three times that. Fell off the back of a lorry and he was there to catch it.

Scott sat opposite her, his head low, but in the way he spun the large star-shaped heavy glass ashtray with his finger in front of him displaying more attitude than she would have wanted to see. At least he wasn't smiling.

There had been shouting and a considerable amount of swearing. Mo seldom swore, she thought it showed a lack of education. But when she did curse, she showed considerable skill and inventiveness. There was a point when Nolan thought she was going to give his brother a hiding. It would have been long overdue, but Maw hadn't raised a hand to either of them for years. The worst of the swearing and the threat of impending violence had subsided now, but the anger was still there. The only sound was the tap of the lighter on the tabletop, the only movement her fingers.

Tap.

Twirl.

Tap

Twirl.

'He was polis,' she said, eventually. She'd said it a few times already, but it was obvious she was not going to tire of saying it anytime soon.

Scott had heard it enough, though. 'Aye, Maw, okay, you've made your point.'

'A fuckin' cop, Scott!' Scott, not Scotty. She was really pissed at him. And with good reason.

'I know, Maw, awright!'

'Aye, you know now that it's all over the bloody paper.' She flicked the hand holding her cigarette at the screen in front of her, trailing ash across the keyboard. She swept the flakes away with her other hand, her mouth narrowing into an irritable line. 'Gie us that ashtray.'

Scott slid it to her side of the table and she tipped what was left of the ash into it, then she stubbed the cigarette out, grinding it into the cut glass with considerable force. When she was finished, she glared at her son again. 'How much did he know about the business?'

'No much.'

'How much, Scott?'

He shifted slightly in his chair. 'He sold a bit of gear, is all. To the folk on that film set.'

'Sold a bit of gear. Gear we supplied to him?'

'Aye.'

Mo leaned forward. 'Gear you supplied to him?'

Scott raised his head. 'You think I'm a complete dildo, Maw?'

'Naw, a dildo is useful. You didnae give him the gear to punt, did you?'

'Naw! I'm no stupid.'

Mo's expression suggested the jury was still out on that.

'He was supplied through one of the boys,' Scott said. 'I wasn't part of it. I know the score, Maw.'

She sat back again, apparently mollified, but Nolan wasn't buying it.

Tap.

Twirl.

Tap.

Twirl.

Maintaining degrees of separation was Tony Burke's first rule. Never let the product get anywhere near you.

Tap.

Twirl.

'So, you met this Jake Goodman through Dalgliesh's bunch of chancers, right?'

'No, met him through this boy I know.'

'What boy?'

'Just a boy I know. He's nobody, Maw. Anyway, he introduced us and as I got to know him turned out he was of the same opinion as me about stuff.'

'Stuff? This Spioraid shite?'

Scott bristled slightly at the description, but Nolan knew he would not rise to it, not with Maw. 'Aye. We shared the same political views.' He ignored Maw's snort and carried on. 'I took him along to a meeting. That was months ago. Maybe a year.'

Nolan wanted to say that he had warned them both about being in any way connected with that crowd, but he held his tongue. He knew if he waded in there was every chance Maw's ire would turn on him. He wasn't particularly enjoying seeing his brother being lacerated by her tongue, but he did know it wasn't before time. He thought about the blood on the shirt. He thought about Scott's not-so-veiled threat earlier. He thought about them but remained silent.

Mo fished a fresh cigarette from the packet lying open beside her, her eyes never leaving her son as she fired it up with the lighter, dragged in the smoke, then vented it from the corner of her mouth. Her fingers set the lighter back on its little dance once more.

Tap.

Twirl.

Tap.

Twirl.

She shifted her attention to Nolan. 'You got nothing to say?'

'Nothing much I can say, Maw.'

'No even I told you so?'

'About what?'

'This Dalgliesh bastard and his group – what's it called?'

'Spioraid nan Gàidheal,' said Nolan, and Scott gave him a glance that seemed to say he had no right talking about it. He was not a believer.

'Aye,' Mo said, sucking in more smoke.

Tap.

Twirl.

'You said we should keep well away from them,' Mo said. So, she remembered, he thought. That's something. 'I should have listened to you.'

He affected an air of nonchalance, as if it was all water under the bridge, but inside he felt elation.

'So, what do you think about this cop then?'

He had been giving it some thought while she had been ripping Scott a new one and believed he had reasoned it all out. 'Obviously he was undercover.'

'No any more,' said Scott, that smile beginning to creep back, but it was chased away once more by a single look from Mo. Scott's head sank again and she stared at his hair for a while.

Tap.

Twirl.

Then she faced Nolan again, his cue to speak once more. 'The fact that they're not banging on our door right now could mean we weren't his target. It has to have been Spioraid and Dalgliesh.'

'They're just a bunch of cranks,' Mo said.

'Maybe, but they're affiliated with a group called New Dawn.'

'That's bollocks!' Scott said.

'And who the hell are they?' Mo never watched the news, didn't read newspapers, unless something was pointed out to her.

'Terrorists, Maw,' said Nolan. 'Or would-be terrorists. They've sent fake packages to politicians, said there was anthrax in them. They've made a few threats, smashed some windows and the like, firebombed a mosque.'

'So, dickheads then?'

'Aye, but dangerous dickheads. It's only a short step from sending snide parcels to real ones. And planting bombs. I reckon this bloke Goodman, or Roberts, was after them.'

'And used Scott here to do it.'

Scott looked up again. 'I didnae know, Maw. These guys, they're convincing, you know? I just got friendly with him, that's all. And when he said he thought he could punt some gear to the film people, I saw a business opportunity.'

'Aye, maybe. But you being part of that Spioraid carry-on has put the family business in danger.'

Tap.

Twirl.

'Cut off all ties, Scott,' Mo said. He looked about to argue the toss but she cut him dead. 'It's no a suggestion. Keep away frae they bastards. I mean it.'

Scott pushed his chair back and turned away without a word. His face told Nolan that he should hide the toolbox.

53

Roach had declined the offer of coffee. She had very little time and wanted to get right down to business. She did give herself a minute or two to take in the office around her, and it reaffirmed her belief that she was not a fan of clutter. How could the woman work amidst this mess? she asked herself. Then she noticed a heavily laden coat stand in the corner behind the desk. *Why would she need so many jackets, coats and scarves in the office?*

Professor Fowler sat down in her large leather chair behind the desk and looked over at Roach. 'Please do accept my apologies for the books. I'm helping a friend by storing his library at the moment.'

That explains the books on calculus and algorithms and Cartesian coordinates, thought Roach. Her own reading tastes ran to non-fiction – she never had much time for fiction, literary stuff bored her, and SF and fantasy were beyond her. Any suggestion she should read something from the crime genre would have her heading for the hills. To spend what little spare time she had reading about made-up crimes, where the author invariably got something wrong about police procedure, was anathema to her. Which was ironic, considering she was here in this dull, book-strewn office in the university and not back in the incident room. As McIntyre had said, her job was to oversee investigations, not carry them out herself. This, though, verged on the personal. She really wanted to see if she was right about this professor.

The window on the far side of the desk looked out onto the Moray Firth and in the corner Roach could see the far end of the Kessock Bridge as it touched land on the Black Isle. The drab sky was smudged with dark patches that hinted the short dry spell might not last. The overhead light was on, but it didn't help much with the gloom.

'So how can I help you?' Anna Fowler's voice was cultured but still carried a hint of an accent. East coast. Fife, maybe. She was a tall woman, Roach noted, and obviously worked out. Roach felt she knew her from somewhere. Did they go to the same gym, maybe?

'First, thank you for seeing me on such short notice.'

'It's my pleasure.'

Roach dipped her head in acknowledgment that the pleasantries were over. 'I'd like to talk to you about the set of *Conquering Hero*, if I may.'

There might have been a slight frown as Fowler replied, 'In what connection?'

Roach kept her voice light. 'Just routine. I'm investigating a murder, well, two . . .'

'The man found on Culloden and the one in the kirkyard.'

It was a statement, not a question, but there was no reason why she shouldn't make that leap, given the media coverage. Roach pressed on. 'There may be a connection to the film unit.'

'In what way?'

'I'm not at liberty to expand further, I'm afraid. But you're the historical adviser, correct?'

'One of them.'

'And you visit the set regularly?'

'Only when I'm invited. Mostly it's a phone call or an email, a quick question about some detail or other.' Fowler leaned forward. 'However, I have to be careful. I've signed an agreement with the production company not to discuss anything about the content or any of the details regarding filming.'

You should have thought about that before you started talking to the press, Roach thought, still trying to figure out why she looked so familiar. Something about the eyes. 'I understand that and I'm not interested in the film itself. Do you know Mr Donahue? John Donahue?'

Fowler's smile was slightly rueful. 'I think knowing him would be something of a stretch. Let's just say I've met him.'

Roach had the impression the experience had not been not pleasant. They shared common ground there, at least. She studied the professor without seeming too intense. 'Do you know anything about the thefts of costumes and props from the set?'

'I heard about it. I've learned a film set is very much like a small village. Everyone gets to know everything fairly quickly.'

The answer was smooth and easy. Roach sensed no evasion. 'What's the feeling among the crew about it?'

Fowler hesitated. She was either trying to formulate her answer or wondering if she should be talking about this. Roach couldn't tell which. 'Well, originally the general belief was that it was Spioraid who had done it.'

'And now?'

'I don't know. I've not been out there for a couple of weeks.'

'You've had no contact?'

'No.'

'Phone? Email?'

'None.'

'But you were there a couple of weeks ago?'

'Yes, they had routine queries. The use of the targe, things like that.'

'The targe?'

'The small, round shield the Highlanders used.'

'And that's something an historian would know about?'

Fowler laughed. 'You mean a female historian?'

'Not at all,' said Roach.

'Well, I'm also adept with the use of Highland weapons. I'm a member of a re-enactment society.'

'Theoretical and practical knowledge, then.'

'Very much so.'

Roach pursed her lips. 'So, two weeks ago . . .'

'Or thereabouts.'

'Or thereabouts. Did you happen to hear Mr Donahue argue with a member of the crew?'

'I did not.'

Roach tried to decide whether the answer had come too quickly, but Fowler seemed relaxed, showing no signs of stress. But what about her was so familiar? It was something fleeting, a will o' the wisp sensation that Roach couldn't quite pin down.

'Does the name Brian Roberts mean anything to you? Detective Sergeant Brian Roberts?'

'Of course. Isn't he the man found dead on Culloden?'

Okay, thought Roach, she reads newspapers. 'You'll have seen the photo issued this week? Did you recognise him?'

A shake of the head. 'Can't say I did. Should I have?'

'He was part of the crew.'

'About two hundred people work on that set at various times. It's a village, but I don't know everyone.'

'So you didn't see Mr Donahue and the dead man arguing?'

'I've already told you, no.'

'Have you ever had any contact with a reporter called Rebecca Connolly?'

A pause. Slight. Ever so slight. But there all the same. Roach knew from experience to look for such pauses, little beats, tiny fragments of dead air when someone was about to lie but thought better of it. In those few seconds the mind races as it goes through the permutations of truth or falsehood and which is better.

'Yes, she contacted me with some questions about the historical aspect of Culloden.'

It was, on the face of it, the correct answer because Professor Fowler's name appeared on the historical sidebar that accompanied Connolly's stories. That was what had pinged in Roach's memory when she saw the woman's name on the list provided by Donahue. Coincidences happen, but Roach mistrusted them and every instinct told her that in this instance she was on the right trail. That tiny hesitation, that little abyss between truth and lie, had told her everything she needed to know. Professor Anna Fowler was Rebecca's mole.

'Someone from the film set has been feeding this reporter information, Professor Fowler,' said Roach. 'They told her about the theft of the costumes, they gave her a name for the dead man and they told her he had been seen arguing with Mr Donahue. Now, you'll understand that I really need to speak to that person. I need to find out why this person is speaking to the press and not to me.'

'I can understand that, but I only spoke to Ms Connolly about the history of the '45.'

'Professor Fowler, I'm investigating two murders. This is important. If you have any information, you have to tell the police and not the press.'

'I understand that. And if I had anything that would help you, I would. Has Ms Connolly said she's been speaking to me about anything other than the history?'

'Yes, she has.' She knew the woman would believe her — after all, why would she lie about that? She watched for any reaction but was disappointed. That one small lapse apart, Anna Fowler was very good at hiding herself. Yet, the more she looked at her . . .

'Well, I don't understand why,' said Fowler, 'because it's simply not true.'

Roach had heard enough. She knew who the informant was but there was little she could do about it. At least now she may have sealed that off and hopefully the woman would see sense and come to her in future. As she stood up, her eye fell on a pool of water under the coat stand and she saw the lower hem of a waterproof garment directly above it. 'You need to wipe that up. It's not good for the wooden floor.'

Anna Fowler had also stood and she glanced over her shoulder at the damp patch. She plucked some tissues from a box and threw it on top of the puddle, then flicked a coat across to hide the waterproof. As Roach caught a glimpse of it, something in her mind clicked and sent a shudder of excitement through her.

She kept her voice calm as she asked, 'So, you're not local to Inverness?'

'How do you know?'

'I detect the vestige of an accent, not local. Fife?'

Another beat. 'That's right, Falkland originally.'

Another lie. The faint shadow of an accent she had caught was east coast but not Fife. It was further south. And in that moment she knew what she had seen across her eyes. Roach headed for the door, knowing she had to get back to the office so her mind could click the pieces together like a jigsaw puzzle. The waterproof. The fleeting familiarity. The—

She didn't reach the door. She didn't even hear Anna Fowler step up swiftly behind her. But she felt something heavy and hard crash into the back of her head and the sharp pain as her temple cracked into the doorframe. She tried to turn to face the woman but another powerful blow to the back of her head caused her nose to smack into the wood and she felt something give. Lights flashed behind her eyes and the wall she was pressed against began to tilt and fade. She lurched around, saw Fowler raising something again – what was that? A book? What the f—?

And then there was another shard of agony as the heavy object slammed across the side of her head, snapped her to the side, and the dark, threadbare carpet rushed up to meet her. But she didn't feel the impact. Instead she found herself falling, falling, falling into a dark whirlpool where books and waterproof coats and Highland costumes swirled and eddied around her. And all the while she could hear the drip, drip, drip of water that had turned to blood.

54

It was just the two of them, Les and Rebecca, in the editor's office. Outside, on the editorial floor, phones rang and keyboards clattered. Indistinct voices. A laugh. Someone happy in their work. Someone who didn't get the memo.

There wasn't a lot of happiness in this room, not on Rebecca's part anyway. Les seemed relaxed, confident, but she didn't know him well enough to tell if it was an act. She wondered how many times he had done this before. She wondered if he liked it, hated it, couldn't care less. She suspected the latter. Whatever the case, she felt she was heading for a big decision.

He had just told her that he didn't think she was fully committed to the company.

'I don't know what you mean,' she said, knowing full well what he meant but taking some delight in making him explain himself.

'Just that, Rebecca,' he said. 'I've been watching you and I get the feeling you're not happy with the way things are now. The way they're going to be if we are to move forward.'

Rebecca couldn't help herself. 'Your way, you mean?'

Irritation flashed on his face briefly. 'Not my way. This is company policy.'

'What if I think it's wrong?'

The irritation was replaced by something more like smugness. 'And there we have the root of our problem.'

'Do you have an issue with my work?'

'No, your work is impressive.'

'Then what?'

'Your attitude.'

'My attitude?'

'Yes. Frankly, you seem to think you know better than everyone.'

'Maybe I do.' She regretted saying that as soon as the words were out of her mouth. She didn't know better, she knew that. She just felt things should be done differently.

'That is growing more apparent by the day. Also, your absences from the office.'

'Doing my job.'

'Your job is here, unless I tell you to go elsewhere.'

'Elsewhere is what we are here to report on.'

'There's this thing they've invented, Rebecca, perhaps you've heard of it. It's called a phone. You pick it up, you punch in a number and as if by magic you speak to someone. There's no need to go off gallivanting around Inverness—'

'Gallivanting? I've—'

Les ignored her, kept talking. 'In order to get stories you—'

Rebecca refused to be silenced and they were now talking over each other. 'Brought in good stories—'

'Can easily get over the phone.'

Rebecca yelled, 'Exclusives!'

They both fell silent, each entrenched in their positions. She'd had similar conversations with Barry in the past, but this time it was different. The tone, the subtext, was more serious.

Rebecca knew her job was on the line.

'You have to realise one thing, Rebecca, if you're to stay here.'

'If I'm to stay here?'

He ignored her. 'Things have changed. Barry was too lax with you, for whatever reason. He let you away with murder, frankly, and that is going to stop. Right now. You've been given free rein but I'm pulling you in.'

287

'I'm not a horse.' She was trying to keep her temper but his entire manner was getting to her.

'I know you're not. I'm speaking figuratively.'

She was tempted to raise her middle finger and see if he could figure that out, but she didn't. She could be hot-headed but was not foolhardy.

'So here's the way we move forward,' he said. 'As I say, your work is impeccable, if a bit wayward.'

Wayward? she thought, but willed herself to keep silent.

'So, from now on, you check with me before you head out on a story. If I say no, then that's it. No arguing the toss, no appeal, no going off on your own. If this place is to work, then the editor has to be God, you understand?'

'Project manager,' she said. 'We don't need editors, remember?'

He was silent for a moment, his eyes boring into her. When he spoke, the calm, businesslike tone was replaced by something harsher. 'Let me lay this on the line for you. From now on, you do as I say, when I say it. No ifs, no buts, no arguments. You want to keep working here, those are the rules. You have to decide what you want to do.'

Rebecca sat very still but did not reply. Angry, hot tears stung behind her eyes. *You want to keep working here*, he'd said.

That was the question.

'Okay,' she said, her voice a little choked. She knew she had to bring this to a close because this mixture of rage and fear was not something she could keep in check much longer. She just wanted away from this cramped room, away from his smooth tones and his patronising manner.

'Okay, what?' he pressed.

What did he want? To be called Sir? A salute? She should be diplomatic here, say something, anything, that bought her some time to think, to plan, to make some sort of rational decision. That's what she should do. The problem was, she couldn't think of anything remotely like that.

'Okay,' she said, her voice stronger now, the burning in her eyes gone. 'I'll have to think about that, won't I? Are we done here? Because, you know, I've got work to do.'

He gave her that look again, a kind of passive-aggressive stare, then simply nodded and turned away. She was dismissed. She resisted the impulse to click her heels as she left.

At her desk, her phone was ringing, so she answered it, heard Alan say, 'Christ, Becks, I've been trying to get you.'

She glanced at her mobile, which she'd left beside her keyboard when she was summoned to Les's office, saw she had missed two calls from Alan. Her anger and apprehension over the meeting was replaced by one of concern. 'What's up? Chaz okay?'

'Of course he is,' said Alan, then his voice dropped as he added, 'Shouldn't he be?'

'No, of course, it was just you seemed so, em, flustered.' The interrogatory rise in inflection had returned, but this time because she wasn't sure flustered was the right word.

'No, it's Anna Fowler,' said Alan. 'What the hell have you done to her?'

It was Rebecca's turn to be flustered. 'Anna? Me? Nothing.'

'Well, you've done something. She stopped me in the corridor about half an hour ago, tore a strip off me for introducing you to her.'

'What?' Rebecca's mind flicked through what she might have done to upset the woman, came back with nothing. 'Alan, I don't know . . .'

'She said you named her to the police.'

'I didn't!'

'Well, apparently that's not what the police told her. A detective was here, a woman. She left Anna with the distinct impression that you ratted her out over something. What have you done, Becks?'

Roach, it had to be. She was desperate to find out who had been leaking material from the set. Rebecca was confident she had not even inadvertently identified Anna. Elspeth didn't know, Barry and Les didn't know, not even

Chaz and Alan knew that she had been her source regarding some aspects of the story. And she told them everything.

'Alan, I don't know what's happened, but I didn't tell the police anything of the sort. I'll call her, sort this out.'

'She's left for the day. She was very upset. Said she had to go and sort her head out, or something. Fix this, Becks. Anna is a nice woman and I don't like seeing her hurt, especially by a friend of mine.'

'Alan, believe me, I did not give her name to the police. You know me better than that.'

'Fix it, Becks.'

'Leave it with me.'

She was already selecting Anna's number from her mobile's contact list as she hung up on Alan. It rang out, then jumped to voicemail. Shit! She heard Anna's voice dictating a stilted message, then a tone.

'Anna, it's Rebecca. Listen, I don't know what DCI Roach told you, but it's not true. We need to talk.'

She terminated the call and stared at the blank face of her phone for a time. She felt guilty for no reason. The woman had been doing what she thought was the right thing. Rebecca had protected her. But now she was being manipulated by a police officer. Bloody Roach! Rebecca liked Anna, she felt they could be friends. She didn't like the idea of her being angry or, perhaps worse, disappointed in her. She had to see her, talk this out, convince her she had not let her down. She looked at the clock. Half three. She couldn't just leave the office, not after the conversation she'd just had with Les. On the other hand, she couldn't let someone she liked believe she had been let down.

A few minutes before, she had known she was heading towards a decision, but she didn't think it would happen this soon.

She stared at the clock, at the second hand jerking oh so slowly, time passing in increments, one second, another, another. Her mind ticked along with it.

Go.

Stay.

Go.

Stay . . .

55

Nolan remained deadpan as he contemplated the young man on the opposite side of the table, for he knew that would only unnerve the boy even further. He had called him up, told him to meet him at Barney's, warned him to say nothing to Scott. There was always the chance that the boy would tell his brother anyway, but Nolan gambled that his fear of him was greater than his loyalty to Scott, whose power over the lads was based on flash and bang. Nolan was much more subtle. They all knew that when it came down to it he was the one to watch because you didn't know what he was thinking. Scott would be away mouthing off, smiling, acting the big man, but Nolan was quieter, on the fringes, calculating. The boys knew where they were with Scott, there was a predictability to his unpredictability, but they were out of their depth when it came to Nolan. In many ways he was at his most expressive when he was inexpressive. It scared the shit out of boys like Deke.

'So where was my brother the other night?'

The boy's name was Derek but he preferred Deke. 'What other night you talking about?'

'Couple nights ago, when that guy was killed in the graveyard.'

'The perv?'

'Aye. Were you with Scott that night?'

Deke preened. 'I'm wi' Scotty most nights. Him and me, we're pals.'

Nolan let that pass. Scott didn't have bosom buddies. It was a failing they shared. 'Of course. So where were you?'

Deke's expression turned decidedly shifty. 'How you want to know, eh?'

Nolan kept his face stony. 'All you need to know is that I want to know.'

Deke tried to maintain an aura of stoic manliness but Nolan's cold gaze had its effect. His tongue darted out to dampen his lips. 'So . . . where did Scotty say he was?'

'Never mind what Scotty said. I want you to tell me.'

Deke worked this over in his mind. Nolan knew how much effort that would take, which was why he'd asked Deke and not the other balloon who palled around with his brother. There was more chance he would talk without thinking. When the boy reached towards the phone on the table, Nolan wondered if he'd underestimated him. 'Maybe I should check with Scotty, you know?'

Nolan pulled the phone towards him. 'Maybe you should just answer my question, Deke, and maybe you shouldn't piss me off. I don't like being pissed off. It pisses me off.'

Deke watched his mobile being dragged away from him and swallowed hard. He looked around the bar, as if searching for backup, but the place was empty. The telly wasn't even on and Jack wasn't about, Nolan had seen to that. He watched Deke work out the odds. He could lie, but he wasn't too good at that. He could refuse to tell Nolan what he wanted to know, but that might not end up too good for him. According to legend, there were bloodstains in the cellar of the bar that couldn't be washed out. Nolan knew there weren't, but it was a handy rumour to cultivate. Deke's final option was to talk, but Scott would be none too pleased if he found out. The boy was in a quandary. Nolan felt bad putting him in it but he needed to know.

He decided to raise the ante. He rose slowly to his feet. 'Come on, son, let's take a wee trip through the back . . .'

'We were down the shore by South Ferry,' Deke blurted.

Nolan sank back into his seat again. 'Doing what?'

'Sorting out this boy that was skimming gear. Scott said he had to teach him a lesson.'

Nolan knew this was the truth. Deke was too scared to lie. 'Sorting out how?'

Deke fidgeted. Doing it was one thing, talking about it another. 'Well, you know, sorted him out. Give him a slap or two.'

Nolan thought about the blood on Scott's shirt. 'How much of a slap?'

Deke was uncomfortable. 'Well, Scotty was really annoyed by it, you know? He worked the guy over really bad. We tried to stop him, we really did, Nolan, you've got to believe me, but it was like he was out his head, you know?'

Nolan knew. 'Had my brother been using?'

'Aye, we all had, but see what happened? That was out of order. We tried telling him but Scotty was away on one, you know? I mean, giving a boy a slap is one thing, but beating him up and then sticking a gun in his mouth . . .'

Nolan felt something crawling up his back. 'A gun? Scotty had a gun?'

'Aye. We didn't know he had it. He was battering the boy about, and then he had him down on the ground, lying in the rocks and seaweed, and he pulls out this gun and rams it in the boy's mouth. Seriously, man, I was shitting myself. I really thought he was going to pull the trigger.'

'He didn't, did he?'

'No, he just yelled at the boy, then yanked it out. I think he broke a couple of his teeth.'

'And this boy, where is he?'

'My sister's. We didn't want him going to a doctor or nothing. She's a nurse. She's taking care of him for now.'

A gun. Scotty had a gun. The one thing that Maw – and Dad – never wanted, because once you bring guns into the equation, things change. The drill was bad enough, but a gun was something else.

The question was, where the hell was Scott now? 'Have you seen my brother today?'

'Aye, a wee while ago. He wasn't in the best of moods, you know? He said he had something to deal with. I was gonnae tag along, but he said it was personal. Family stuff . . .'

Scott hadn't taken his eyes off the doors to the newspaper office.

He drummed the steering wheel with his fingers, as if he was following a music beat, but he had none playing. He had done a few lines of coke while he waited, to take the edge off his jitters, but he was still hyped. Nolan would have said that the gear would not help, but his brother was a sanctimonious bastard who didn't know how to enjoy himself. Except maybe with that reporter lassie. Scott would bet his stash he had shagged her. If not, what the actual fuck was he doing with her? That's all lassies were good for, wasn't it? Looking good and getting horsed.

He didn't know why he was here, hadn't really thought it through. He had stormed out of the house, got in his car and drove around for a while, hoping his anger would evaporate, but it didn't. Maw had no right to tell him to cut off all ties with Spioraid, no right at all. She couldn't see what he saw, how their way of life was threatened by all this liberal political correctness. When it came down to it, Scott had nothing against foreigners or queers. They bought his product like everyone else. But they had to know their place. Moslems, though, were a different matter. He didn't trust them one bit. They were all terrorists, if you asked him. Potential terrorists at least and that was just as bad. They had to be watched and they had to be sorted. They had to know that Scotland was for white people. He'd never darkened the door of a church but in his mind he knew this was a Christian country and Moslems and Jews and whatever had to understand that. Go and worship whatever you want, but don't try to take over, mate, because you know what? We'll fight back. And we will win. You want your fucking Sharia law, go back to where you came from. We'll wave you off. Bye fuckity bye.

Perverts, though. Perverts were a different matter. They needed to be wiped off the face of the earth. The gays were one thing, as long as they stuck to their own, but the pervs went after the kiddies. Cut their bollocks off, stuff them in their mouths and string them up, that's what Scott would do.

Maw didn't see it his way, though. The perverts, aye, but not the others. She didn't know the danger their way of life was in. Finbar did, and the folk in Spioraid too. Patriots is what they were. Scottish patriots. Cut ourselves off from they bastards in Westminster and keep the rest of the world at arm's length. Trade, aye, but fuck your European Union – there's a whole world out there — and fuck your open door policy to immigrants. We've got enough of them now, we don't need any more. And them that are here he'd happily wave bye fuckity bye to and all.

Nolan, though. He should understand. He's seen the way they bastards look at everyone else, like this was their country, like white people weren't welcome. Scott had invited him to join Spioraid but he'd laughed at him. Actually laughed at him. Said they were a bunch of cranks. None so blind. Scott knew Nolan was a weak link, had known it for ages, man, and he'd been whispering in Maw's ear, poisoning her against him. Now, with this reporter lassie in the picture, it was time for something to be done.

And Scott was just the boy to do it.

56

The sun had finally broken through the clouds, as if in a final show of defiance to a day that had been resolutely dull and damp. No rain had fallen, but it was in the atmosphere like a premonition. Yet, there was the sun, reminding the world that it still existed, bursting through in a brilliant flash, striping the sky with colours and bathing the serrated surface of the water in a golden spotlight. However, the daylight was dying and would soon breathe its last behind the low hills beyond the Beauly Firth.

In the east, the grey light was already diffusing the edges of the Kessock Bridge, its lights glittering on the drab waters not washed by the golden glow in the west. The beams of the vehicles blinking as they moved over the water like little glowing insects. The hump of the Black Isle grew even darker, and the houses that lined the shore and the wooded hill were already indistinct and only identified by the pinpoint glow of bulbs as they were switched on in living rooms and kitchens and porches.

The late sun cast shadows across the grass, on which Rebecca had parked. A dog walker nodded to her as they passed each other on the towpath, his Labrador snuffling at the edge of the Caledonian Canal as it sliced its way to the firth. She wondered if it had ever jumped in. The water was black in this light and it looked deep, the bank itself steep. But the thought was washed away as she saw who she was looking for on the far bank, sitting alone on a bench, staring out at the bridge and the Moray Firth beyond. With the dog walker gone, the stretch of canal at Clachnaharry was left solely to Anna and Rebecca.

The waist-high lighting that lined the path cast a faint glow as Rebecca headed towards the canal authority building, its white walls catching the sun in its death throes. There were two narrow retractable bridges framing the sea lock that allowed boats to manoeuvre the differing levels of water. The offices had closed at 4 p.m. and no boats waited for the morning. Rebecca's footsteps on the bridge seemed very loud in the still air and she thought Anna would have heard her approach, but she didn't. The woman was hunched into her coat, her hands thrust deep into her pockets, and she didn't move even as Rebecca sat beside her on the bench. They sat in silence, each looking across the water but perhaps neither really seeing it. Now that she was here, Rebecca tried to think of what to say. When she shot a glance at Anna, she saw her eyes had a strange, unfocused look, as if only her body was there while her spirit, her consciousness, was elsewhere. Lost. Wandering.

Rebecca took a deep breath. 'Anna, I didn't tell DCI Roach about you.'

Anna didn't seem to hear. She didn't move. Her eyes were still lost in the water, so leaden, so cold, its surface chopped by the breeze stiffening from the Firth. Rebecca didn't know what else to say. To repeat herself would seem like begging forgiveness for something she didn't do. So she let her words float there between them in the hope that Anna would respond.

It was a full two minutes before she did. Not long in the scheme of things, but sitting there on that chilly promontory as the light eased slowly away behind the low hills to the west, its dying rays catching the wispy clouds floating like smoke against the denser cover, it seemed like an eternity. An eternity in which Anna seemed lost.

Finally, softly, she spoke. 'It doesn't matter now.'

'It does matter,' said Rebecca, glad Anna was at least speaking, even if her voice did have a faraway quality to it. Once again, she had the sensation that the historian wasn't really with her. Had DCI Roach's lie really upset her that much?

Another long silence. Then Anna mumbled something. It sounded like *all too late now*. Rebecca couldn't be certain. 'Too late for what?'

Anna seemed to withdraw even further into her coat. She was a powerful woman but she seemed to be shrinking before Rebecca's eyes. This wasn't about DCI Roach's lie. Something else had happened and Rebecca felt concern growing. 'Anna, what's wrong?'

Nothing. Movement stilled, apart from the breeze ruffling her short blonde hair. She didn't even seem to be breathing.

'Anna? Tell me what's wrong. Whatever it is can be fixed.'

Anna's eyes moved then and Rebecca saw fully the pain that lived in them. 'It can't be fixed. Not now.'

And then she removed her hands from her pocket, as if in slow motion, and Rebecca saw the blood caked on her fingers, her knuckles, the palms. She reached out and grasped Anna's hands, turned them over, looking for wounds, flakes of blood scraping off with her fingers, but found nothing. 'Anna, are you hurt?'

Anna retracted her hands. Pushed them back in her pockets, slouched again. The sound of Robbie Williams floated from Rebecca's bag. Her phone. She ignored it. The call jumped to voicemail.

'Whose blood is that, Anna?' Rebecca asked, trying to keep the urgency from her voice. She needed to speak calmly to the woman. She needed to draw her out. Because something was very, very wrong here. 'Anna? Tell me – whose blood is that?'

It was Alan who found her.

He had sat in his office for an hour, completing paperwork automatically, but his mind on Anna Fowler and her face as she had spoken to him. He felt guilty, because for an instant he had believed Rebecca had told the police about the history professor, but the more he thought about it, the more he was certain she would never do that. He had failed to assure Professor Fowler of that and felt he really needed to.

University corridors can be lonely places when the students are in class or away for the day, as they were now. It was not a large campus – the university had other sites across the west Highlands – but the corridors did seem long when you didn't meet another living soul. Sensors picked up his movement as he turned corners or pushed through doors, flickering lights on and off. Conserve energy. Stop the charge of the Light Brigade. His footsteps squeaked on the polished floors as he passed door after door. Lecture rooms, offices, toilets. Occasionally he glimpsed someone through the narrow glass panels that ran lengthwise down the door, but more often than not the rooms were empty, dull, chairs vacant, desks bare, computers dark.

The door to Professor Fowler's office was locked. Alan cupped his hands at the glass panel and peered in, but the room beyond was in darkness, the blinds drawn to block out what daylight was left. He could just make out her desk and the piles of books. He had left it too long. He should have come by sooner instead of sitting at his own desk ticking digital boxes. He gave the handle another jiggle, he didn't know why. The door held, as he knew it would. He sighed, turned. He'd speak to her tomorrow. He didn't know if Rebecca had spoken to her but even if she had he would make sure the professor knew Rebecca was one of the good guys.

He was about to walk away when he heard the groan from inside.

Chaz glanced at the read-out on his mobile before he answered it. Number withheld. He contemplated not answering it, but sometimes a newspaper withheld its number, so it could be work.

'Chaz, it's Nolan Burke.'

For an instant Chaz felt concern grip him. Why the hell was Nolan Burke phoning him? And how the hell had he got his number? But he took a deep breath and said, 'Hi.' Then he added, 'How you doing?'

Hi. How you doing? Like it was an everyday thing for a known drug dealer to call out of the blue. Two mates, having a natter, arranging to go out for a drink.

Nolan's voice was urgent. 'Where's Rebecca?'

Shit, Chaz thought, he's going to use me somehow to get to her. 'No idea, Mr Burke.'

'Nolan.' The response seemed automatic now. 'I need to find her.'

'Have you tried calling her?'

'I don't have her number.'

Well, you're not getting it from me, mate. He didn't say that, though. 'What's up? Maybe I can give her a message when I see her?'

A pause then. Nolan was thinking. 'Chaz,' he said. 'Is it okay to call you that?'

'Of course.' What the hell else was he supposed to say?

'Listen, I need to find her. Believe me when I say it's urgent.'

Chaz's phone beeped another call. Alan. 'Okay, let me try to reach her and I'll call you back.' As he rang off, he realised he couldn't call the man back as his number was withheld. He picked up Alan's call. 'You'll never guess who I just—'

'Chaz, have you heard from Rebecca?' Alan's voice sounded as urgent as Nolan Burke's. Something was wrong.

'No, I've just had—'

'I've been trying to call her but she's not picking up. She's not at the office, she left early. We need to find her.'

Chaz's phone beeped again. He hoped it was Rebecca, but it was 'Number Withheld' again. Nolan Burke. He ignored it for now. 'What's going on, Alan? I've got Nolan Burke looking for her too.'

'Nolan Burke? Why would . . . ? Never mind that now. Get round to her flat, see if she's there.'

'Alan, will you stop a minute and tell me what the hell is going on?'

'I haven't got time to explain, Chaz. Just get round to her flat now. Call me back.'

Alan hung up, leaving Chaz with the phone still to his ear.

Chaz glanced out the window and saw their car parked outside. Alan car-pooled with a workmate and it was her turn to drive, which meant Chaz had wheels. He looked at the keys in a bowl beside the front door, took a deep breath, felt a phantom pain gnaw at his leg as he realised he would have to get behind the wheel.

As he stepped outside, the first splashes of rain began to fall.

57

Anna did not speak for a minute or two, but it seemed longer. Rebecca's phone rang again but she let the call go because whoever it was would wait. Probably the office, wanting to know where she was. She could not be distracted. She must not be distracted.

'I had built this new life,' Anna said, her voice low, her head slumped. 'I thought I was a different person. New name, new life, new me.'

Rebecca wasn't sure what she was talking about but she feared if she asked for clarification the woman would stop. She had to let her talk.

'But the past is always with us, isn't it? Wherever we go, it follows, and there is no escaping it. I'm Anna Fowler, an adult, an academic, and yet I will always be that child, that poor, tormented child. I left that room so many years ago, but in many ways I'm still in it. Still in that bed, staring at the door, listening to the footsteps on the stairs. But this time when the door opened, it wasn't him, it was the boy I saw. And the boy had become him. It was his face I saw, and everything I had carefully created just fell apart. He was using a different name, but then so was I. But he was still Brian and I was still Yvonne. I would always be Yvonne. I would always be the child.'

Rebecca felt the first raindrops brush her cheek like tears.

Scott had parked beside the reporter's car on the patch of ground facing the canal and then watched her move along the towpath towards the bridges. A man with a mutt had walked by, peered through the windscreen at him.

Scott wanted to give the bastard the stare, but he purposely kept his face angled away. No need to draw attention. He was just a guy out for a wee twilight drive. Nothing to see here. The dog walker kept moving.

The lassie had crossed the bridge and headed towards a bench where a woman was already sitting. He'd hoped they would have the place to themselves. He wasn't completely sure what he was going to say to her, but he knew for certain he didn't want anybody eyeballing them. The lassie had sat down on the bench and Scott drummed the fingers of his right hand on the steering wheel again while he thought what to do next.

Unconsciously, his left rested on the passenger seat, cupping the gun.

'Some people die when they take a life, but not the child. For the child, the taking of a life was the beginning of life.'

Rebecca still had not said a word, recognising Anna's need to talk, to vocalise thoughts she had been harbouring for so long. Somewhere along the line she had begun to talk about herself in the third person. She had become the child and yet not. Even her voice had changed, the timbre slightly higher. Rebecca felt her body shiver and not because of the chill or the weak rain that draped itself over them. Fear was at the root of the trembling, but not because she felt at risk. This fear had reached out from Anna like a cold hand and was stroking her flesh with fingers of ice. She was not fearful of the woman but fearful for her. And the child she had become.

'He was the child's father but he was a monster. The child loved him and hated him and feared him. And when the child killed him, it felt that love and hate and fear go. And after that, it was numb. Nothing left within. Nothing.'

She mumbled something incoherent which Rebecca strained to catch but it was washed away by the rain. Then the voice grew stronger again, not much, but enough. 'It became an adult. A new name. A new life. A new person. A life carefully constructed. But still, nothing within. All dead. All dead. All dead.'

Chaz's phone rang again just as he reached Rebecca's flat. Nolan Burke. 'Any news?'

The drive, short though it was, had been difficult. The pain in his side had niggled and tormented him. He knew it was imaginary, but it felt real. The rain had sprayed across the windshield, making the pain worse. It had been raining that night on the island. The pain, the stress, the imaginings had taken a toll on his patience, so his reply to Nolan Burke's query was curt.

'Look, what the hell is going on here? I've got you in one ear and Alan in the other, all wondering where Rebecca is. And I'm dashing around like a blue-arsed fly with no real clue why. So what's wrong? Is Rebecca in trouble?'

He knew he shouldn't have talked to Nolan in such a way, but he'd had enough. There was silence on the line; Chaz feared he'd stepped over a line and that Nolan had hung up. But then he heard heavy breathing. 'She could be, Chaz. That's why I need to find her.'

'What kind of trouble?'

Another silence. 'If I'm right, the worst,' he said. 'Please don't press me, just believe me. We need to find her. I need to find her. And you need to help me. She's not at her office.'

'I know. She's not at home either. And she's not answering her phone.'

'So where could she be?'

Chaz couldn't answer. He stared at Rebecca's windows as if he was hoping she would appear. Nolan sounded worried. Alan had been worried. Chaz was battling his fear of driving with his concern for his friend. He tried to think where she could have gone.

'Text me your number,' he said. 'I've got a couple of calls I can make . . .'

'He didn't recognise the child in the adult, even if he noticed it at all. It had changed, grown into a woman. Even when it bought that poison from him on the set, he didn't recognise it. But it was still yet the child. That poor, frightened child he did nothing to protect. It wasn't until it pumped him full of that poison that he realised. It was very easy. So very easy. Follow him, wait until no one was around, brush past him in the street and then wait until it took effect. So very easy. That part at least.'

Anna stopped again, as if reliving what she had done, her words becoming stronger, more lucid. The icy fear that had stiffened Rebecca's flesh was beginning to thaw once more. Anna posed no threat to her, of that she was certain. She had no idea whose blood was on Anna's hands but she needed to find out, for someone might be in need of medical attention. And yet she was loath to ask even a single question, for she feared she might break the flow of words. The woman needed to get this out now, to purge herself, and all Rebecca could do was listen.

'They say killing gets easier. It doesn't. The child knows that now. The father was the first. The son the second. It knew it was wrong. Even as it planned it, it knew what it was doing was wrong. But it had to. That man, the father, and that boy, now grown up, had stolen its childhood. Its innocence. Its love, its trust, its self-respect. It could not let them take what was left of its life.'

Rebecca's phone rang for what seemed like the tenth time and she mentally cursed it, regretted having Robbie Williams as a ring tone, his voice bouncing out an upbeat number out of place on this spit of land draped in a sheen of rain and caressed by a chill wind while a woman talked of murder. Moving very slowly, Rebecca reached into her pocket and eased the mobile out, glanced at the screen. Chaz. He would have to wait.

'Sorry,' she said, her voice sounding alien after being silent for so long.

Anna didn't seem to notice she had spoken. 'He lay there on the heather, staring at the child above him. He couldn't move, not much anyway. The child sensed he knew what was happening, knew why this had to be. Because he knew the child now, you see. Had seen the child *that was* in the woman *that is*. And in him the child saw some kind of acceptance as it raised the claymore and brought it down. And watched him die. It wasn't like the father. That had been violent, swift even. This death floated into the night as his breath slowed and stilled. And then he was gone, and what he was became vapour in the mist.'

Rebecca's phone rang again. Chaz. She had to answer it this time, if only to tell him to stop calling.

She didn't get the chance to say anything before Chaz said, 'Where are you?'

'Clachnaharry, but listen . . .'

'What the hell you doing there?'

'I'm . . . with someone. I'll explain later.'

'Who are you with?'

She shot a glance at the woman beside her, but she was lost in the past again. Distant or recent, Rebecca could not tell. Even so, she turned away slightly and lowered her voice. 'Anna Fowler, but . . .'

'Stay there. Don't move. We're coming to get you.'

'Don't . . .'

Chaz had already cut the connection.

Rebecca gave the phone a puzzled look, as if it knew what the hell was going on, then turned the phone off completely and put it away. She had more pressing matters to attend to. And perhaps Chaz coming wasn't such a bad idea. Calling the police had crossed her mind more than once. This way she could get him to do it while she kept Anna company. And talking. Because Rebecca wanted to know it all now.

Nolan was still in Barney's, waiting for Chaz to call back. He paced the back room, a tiny office and storeroom, absently flicking the business card he had lifted from Chaz's bag during the trouble in the Ferry against his thumb. He felt so helpless. He knew Scott was out there somewhere and he had a gun. He had no way of knowing if he had gone after Rebecca, not for certain, but his gut told him that was the case. He thought about calling Maw but decided against it. She couldn't do anything. He tried Scott but it went straight to voicemail. No surprise there.

His phone rang and he recognised Chaz's number. He thumbed the button to green and heard him say, 'Clachnaharry.'

58

The rain was soft but persistent. It wafted across the lights that marked the towpath like a fine mist. Darkness had claimed the sky now. On the other side of the canal, at the makeshift car park in front of the low terraced houses, a car's headlights beamed into the night. A dog walker, probably. Rebecca turned back to Anna, her white face and short blonde hair catching the low light. The historian hadn't spoken for a few minutes. She sat very still, her bloodied hands still deep in the pockets of her coat, staring into the darkness, the water slapping softly against the land, like a clock marking time. For Anna, it was ticking backwards, taking her to times past, both recent and more distant. Rebecca had realised the woman was no longer here. Her body was there, but her mind was lost in the ripples of her life, adrift in the eddies of memory and regret.

Rebecca risked a question. 'Tell me about Lancaster?'

At first she didn't think Anna had heard her, and Rebecca wondered if she had been swept away by the tides. Eventually, though, she replied, her voice coming from far away.

'He was like him, the father. A predator. He deserved to die. The child had to protect itself.'

'How was Lancaster a threat?'

'He wasn't, not directly. But he deserved to be punished. No one would mourn him.'

Anna's narrative was fragmentary again, slices of information, but Rebecca was able to forge a narrative. After she murdered her father, after she had served whatever time a child can be sentenced to, she had forged a new identity through the courts, with the help of social services. She had created a new persona and a new life for herself. That was threatened when her brother turned up, even though he didn't recognise her. She couldn't be certain that would last, though, so she first bought drugs from him, or had them bought, and then killed him. Anna's plan had been to muddy the waters as much as she could. The theft of the costumes, the choice of locations and, by luck, even the victims' links to Spioraid. Anna couldn't have known Goodman, or Roberts, was investigating them, but she would have known from Rebecca's own stories that Lancaster was in Dalgliesh's sights for political purposes. Even her attempt at implicating Donahue was a diversion.

Rebecca felt anger stir, because she had been used by this woman to do it. She thought the historian had been motivated by genuine concern over events but in reality she was only trying to control the situation, pointing fingers all around. Rebecca could not tell if her anger was directed at Anna or at herself for being so gullible. But anger was not what was needed here. There was something else she needed to know.

'Anna, the blood on your hands – whose is it?'

Alan was on the sidelines, watching as the paramedics treated the woman he had found in Professor Fowler's office. He knew who she was now, of course. DCI Roach. Rebecca had mentioned her. When he heard the groan, he had rushed off to find someone with a key, finally came upon a janitor. They found her on the floor, groggy, bleeding and incoherent, apart from mumbling that she was a police officer. He had no idea why Anna Fowler had attacked this woman with a book on world history that proved to be both heavy in weight and content. It still lay on the floor where it had been dropped, its pages both literally and figuratively covered in blood.

There had been blood that night too. On Stoirm. All over the seat of the Land Rover.

A paramedic gently probed the bloody welt on the back of DCI Roach's head with latex fingers, having already tended to another gash on her temple. The police officer was more compos mentis now and was talking to the bald detective who had been first to arrive after Alan dialled 999. A uniformed officer had poked through the coat stand and held up a large, camouflaged waterproof and a dark woollen ski mask.

There had been paramedics too, that night. And police. And Chaz, bleeding . . . he thought dying.

Alan had been told not to move and that was exactly what he had done, apart from trying to contact Rebecca, then reaching Chaz. His phone was in his hand, his palm sweating, and he checked the screen every minute or so, as if he wouldn't know if it was ringing. He'd tried Chaz again a few minutes before, but he had not picked up. He tried Rebecca once more, but this time it didn't even ring, it just switched immediately to voicemail.

Rain stroked the window frame, just as it had done that night.

And Chaz was out there, somewhere. Alone.

Chaz had been here before. Behind the wheel. Rain. Lights in the rear-view. But this time a voice. The one in his head. *It could happen again.*

His fingers gripped the steering wheel so tightly it seemed to bite into his palms. His windscreen wipers swept at the rain as it spackled the glass, the slight scraping noise a metronome keeping a beat, reminding him that time was passing. He was still unclear about what kind of danger Rebecca faced – Alan hadn't said and Nolan Burke had been decidedly mysterious – but he knew he had to get to his friend quickly. He had to ignore the anxiety screaming in his mind.

It could happen again.

He had to ignore the stabbing sensation in his side and leg.

Remember this? Remember the rain and the wind and the lights?

He had to ignore the beams from behind as they burst against his rear-view mirror or blazed from the opposite carriageway.

Always the lights.

And the pain.

He knew there was no pain, he told himself there was no pain, and yet there it was, biting, surging, burning.

Stop now.

Pull over.

Traffic was heavy, as workers flooded from the centre of Inverness to their homes. He swore each time he was brought to a halt at traffic lights or roundabouts. He cursed drivers who were too slow or who lingered too long at a turn. Lights flared, glinted.

Just as they did on the island.

He willed the voices to leave his head. He forced the pain to ebb.

He kept going. He had to.

Anna's words became jumbled and even more incoherent, but Rebecca managed to piece together what had happened. DCI Roach had spotted something in her office – a raincoat, was it? Then Anna had seen something in her expression that made her believe she had been recognised.

She couldn't let her go, she said. *Couldn't let her go.*

So she stopped her. Left her. Came here, where the air is clear and fresh and she could think. And remember. The breeze rippling her memories as it floated over the water.

Whether DCI Roach was alive or dead, Rebecca couldn't tell. Anna herself didn't even know. But the blood caked on her hands spoke volumes. It was time to make the call.

Rebecca took out her phone again and pressed the switch at the side. It was an old phone and would take a few minutes to power up. She should not have switched it off, but it had seemed like a good idea at the time. Napoleon's apocryphal words again.

'I'm going to call someone now,' she told Anna, keeping her voice even and soothing. She still did not feel in any jeopardy, but it didn't do any harm to keep everything calm. This woman had already killed three people, maybe

312

four, and Rebecca had no burning desire to become number five. Anna didn't respond. She didn't move. She was done.

The bars flared up to tell her she was connected to the network and Rebecca began to poke out the three nines. She managed two before she heard a man's voice from behind her.

'I wouldn't do that, darling.'

She looked over her shoulder to see Scott Burke standing three feet away. It was dark, but she could see him well enough in the glow of the lighting across the canal. She could see his blond hair and his camouflaged jacket and his nasty little smile.

And she could see a gun in his hand.

59

She couldn't expect any help from Anna, for she didn't seem to notice that Scott Burke was there. She didn't move when he spoke, didn't as much as glance in his direction. All she did was stare into the dark, her mind finally lost somewhere in the deep water. Rebecca rose slowly, her eyes on the barrel of the gun, her earlier fear as she'd realised Anna was a killer now nothing compared to the sheer blind panic with which she was gripped. She wanted to run but her legs would not respond. They were like lead, cold and useless. The lapping of the water faded; she no longer felt the rain wash over her. All she saw was the little hole in that barrel and the smile behind it. She opened her mouth to speak but words wouldn't come. The hand holding the phone dangled at her side, all thought of getting help flooding from her mind.

The barrel.

The smile.

Scott Burke.

'You're a wee bitch, you know that?' His words were slightly slurred, she noticed that. Drunk? Drugged? Or was it just pure unadulterated rage? If so, why? She wanted to ask, but she still couldn't speak. The icy terror had travelled from her legs and had clamped its frozen fingers round her throat. *For God's sake, Rebecca, say something . . .*

The smile morphed into a snarl as he answered her unspoken question anyway. 'Getting into my family business. My maw. My brother. Messing shit up. We were fine until you showed up, turning Nolan's head so much that I cannae trust him any more. You did that, bitch. So . . .' He twitched the gun slightly, as if in explanation.

Say something, Rebecca. Anything.

Scott looked as if he was about to speak further, then thought better of it. His mouth opened, closed. The smile, that smile, that nasty little smile, crept back.

Make him talk, Rebecca, Chaz is coming. He'll be able to call for help.

She found her voice. It was strangled, as the glacial fingers retained their grip, but she forced it out. 'Mr Burke, I don't know what you're talking about.'

'No? So you've no been shagging my brother, filling his head with shite?'

'Did he tell you that?'

'No, but that doesn't mean it's no true.'

Despite her paralysing terror, she felt relieved. She didn't want Nolan Burke to be discussing her in such a way. 'It's not true.'

'Aye – sure.'

'It's not. You have to believe me.'

He leaned closer. She wanted to move away, but she couldn't. 'I don't have to believe anything, darling. I'm the one with the gun.'

She could see his eyes now. They were dancing, like he was on something. *Christ, the guy is out of his head*: a thought that did not comfort her. She darted a quick look at Anna, who was still sitting on the bench like some kind of sculpture, except now she was muttering to herself. Scott heard her, flicked the gun briefly in her direction. 'What's she saying?'

'She's sick. She needs help.'

'That right? Maybe when I've helped you out of the way, I'll put the cow out her misery.'

Rebecca forced her legs to take her away from the bench. She needed to do something, to get the blood flowing again. She wasn't trying to flee because putting distance between them wouldn't help her. You can't outrun a bullet. Not that she had any experience of bullets. She thought he might tell her to stand still, but he didn't. She edged round Anna and onto the path. He moved with her until his back was to the bench, that gun in his hand – he was left-handed, she noticed, for no reason at all – always pointed at her. She'd never seen a gun before. She didn't know how easy it would be to fire one. She didn't know if he had ever done it before. Was she the first? Were there others?

She moved slowly, but her mind galloped and got nowhere. Her legs were weak, sluggish, her mouth dry, her palms damp. Her breath was a sharp jab and acid smouldered in her stomach. Talk, she decided. Keep him talking. After all, what else could she do?

'Mr Burke . . .'

He smirked. 'Still polite, eh?'

'This is a mistake, you have to see that. You can't do this. People know I'm here, I've got friends heading here now. This woman is very ill, she needs help. She killed Jake Goodman.'

That surprised him, and he half turned to look at Anna in a fresh way. If this had been a movie, Rebecca would have rushed him then, taken the gun from him. It crossed her mind, briefly. But this wasn't a movie. Rebecca wasn't a Hollywood actor. If she got it wrong, there was no take two.

'She killed Lancaster,' she went on. 'She might have killed a police officer today too.'

That broadened his smile. 'Yeah? Maybe I'll take her out to dinner, then. Could do with someone like her working for the family.'

His words were really slurred now. He was totally gone, she realised. Nothing she could say, nothing she could do, would penetrate. Whatever he was on, he was as lost as Anna, sitting there in her own little world. Rebecca opened her mouth, closed it again. She had run out of words. *Think of something.*

Scott faced her again. 'Anyway,' he said.

Say something more.

He raised the gun slightly.

Anything.

He cocked his head. 'Bored now.'

Rebecca's mind froze and the hole in the gun seemed so very big as it now levelled. Maybe she could throw herself out of the way just as he fired. Maybe he would miss. Maybe she could leap into the canal, hide under the water. Maybe . . .

'Scotty!' It was as if the voice had stepped between them, even though it came from behind her. Scott's head jerked in the direction it had come from, the gun thankfully dipping again. Rebecca half turned to see Nolan sprinting along the towpath on the far side, his face turned towards them. The lights of a car swung into view from the village, came to a sudden halt and Chaz leaped out, began to run towards them too.

Rebecca had never thought she'd be so glad to see Nolan Burke in her life. He was almost at the footbridge now, Chaz halfway along the path, his limp preventing him from getting up too much speed. The only thing that had been keeping her upright was tension; now, relief sapped what little strength she had and she felt her knees begin to give. She might have gone down, too, if Scott hadn't lunged and grabbed her round the shoulders to wedge her in front of him like a shield. She struggled against him, but his grip was firm, though she could feel his body trembling, as if he was cold. The hand with the gun hung loosely at his side, but it wouldn't take much to bring it up, place it against her temple. A little bit of pressure on the trigger and she'd be gone. She felt sick. She felt weariness wash over her. But she had to calm herself, to think, to wait for a chance. Anything.

Don't be a victim, Becks.

I won't be, Dad. Not tonight. Not ever.

'Stay the fuck out of this, Nolan!' Scott yelled. Nolan skidded to a halt on the bridge, recognising what Rebecca had already worked out. She was in a worse position now than before. 'One more step, bro. One more step and I do her, I mean it.'

And that was when the gun was raised to her head.

Nolan rested one hand on the railing, raised the other in a placating gesture. 'Easy, Scotty, just chill, eh?'

Scott laughed. It was a brittle sound and there was no humour in it. 'I am chilled, man. Mr Freeze, that's me. You need to chill, though, lookin' a wee bit flustered there.'

Chaz had come to a halt on the far side. Nolan sidled across the bridge. 'Listen to me, Scotty, this is nuts, okay? Put that thing away and let's talk.'

'Get tae fuck, man! What good's talkin'? Eh? You're no right in the head, no since this bitch came onto the scene.'

'That's nothing to do with Rebecca.'

'No? What is it, then?'

Nolan stepped off the bridge now. Every movement measured, his hands held in front of him, his voice even. 'You're right, I'm no the same. I'm tired, Scotty, that's all. Tired of what we do, of our life. The business. I need something more.'

Scott pulled Rebecca tighter against him. 'And is she something more? You've been feeding her stuff, just 'cos you want to get into her knickers . . .'

Nolan didn't deny it. 'I told you, nothing to do with her, mate. You've got to believe me, bro.'

That laugh again, like something shattering. 'Believe you? Believe *you*? Why should I? You're a fuckin' traitor, man, nothin' but a fuckin' traitor.'

Nolan was close now, and Scott seemed to notice for the first time. He jerked her body slightly to the right and the gun swung away from her towards Nolan. 'I told you to fuckin' stay the fuck where you were.'

Rebecca knew this was her chance. Her only chance. Her Hollywood moment. She'd had enough of being threatened and thrown about.

Don't be a victim . . .

Scott Nolan was a nutjob out of his head on drugs and she'd had enough. Her father's voice was loud inside her mind, advice he'd given her about defending herself.

If you can, go for the soft tissue. Gouge eyes, kick them in the testicles . . .

But she couldn't reach his eyes and she wasn't in the right position for his groin.

But if that's not possible, go for the joints.

She raised her right leg as high as she could and rammed the sole of her foot hard into his knee. She heard him swear as he automatically listed to one side, but she wasn't done. She ran the heel of her shoe down his leg and jabbed it forcefully onto the bridge of his foot. She was wearing a sturdy pair of shoes and he was in trainers. She knew it would hurt, but was it enough?

It was – just enough to make him relax his grip – and she jerked free as he roared. What followed was like a slow-motion dance.

Her, whirling away from him.

Nolan, moving again.

Scott, his face contorted with pain and rage.

The gun, swinging back towards her.

Her, realising she had nowhere to go now.

Nolan, too far away.

Chaz, feet clanging on the bridge.

Scott, bringing the gun level again, ready to fire.

Clang.

Her, bracing herself, wondering how it would feel, to be shot, to die.

Clang.

And then . . .

Clang.

Anna, rising like a wraith behind Scott and wrapping her arms around him, one hand clamping over his wrist, twisting him to the side.

Chaz, on the path.

The gun, a shot, going wild.

Scott, hauled over the bench and tumbling down the bank with Anna, over and over, struggling to break free but she was too strong, she was too powerful. All his power lay in weapons and having men at his back. The gun flying . . .

And then a cry from behind her. Rebecca's name. She turned away from Anna slamming Scott's head against a rock. Someone on the ground. Blood, dark and wet.

60

Rebecca knelt on the rain-slick path, not noticing the dampness seeping through the knees of her jeans as she took in the blood oozing from his chest and heard him cough softly, flecks of something dark bubbling on his lips. The immediate danger had passed, but she was still numb and didn't know what to do as her hands hovered over the wound. Ambulance, she thought, call an ambulance.

'Don't worry,' she said. 'I'll get help.'

Her phone was still in her hand so she punched in the final nine, waited, told the operator she needed an ambulance. And police. An afterthought. His hand came up and she gripped it as she talked, squeezing it, reassuring him. She plastered a smile on her lips. It'll be fine, that smile said. You'll be fine. She wondered if he saw the terror she felt burning in her eyes.

He coughed again, blood spattering on his chin and cheeks. Rain caught them, diluted them, washed them away. Not completely, though.

Chaz was there now. 'Jesus,' he said, as he looked down at her beside Nolan, holding his hand, talking to the operator. His face was ashen and he clearly did not know what to do. *Join the club*, she thought.

She held the phone to her chest for a brief moment. 'Check on Anna,' she told him, surprised at how calm her voice seemed, even though her heart hammered and her mind reeled, then she placed the phone to her ear again. Chaz hesitated, his eyes fixed on Nolan at his feet, then moved across the grass to where Anna had dragged Scott towards the water.

Nolan's fingers tightened and his body trembled as a spasm ripped through him. The operator told her to stay on the line, so she clicked it to loudspeaker and set it down on the path. The rain wouldn't do it any good, but she didn't care.

Nolan pulled her closer to him. 'Scotty,' he said, his voice thready.

'Chaz is checking on him,' she said. Frankly, she didn't really care what had happened to Scott. She was more concerned about Anna. And Nolan.

There was an almost imperceptible nod. 'You okay?'

'I'm fine. I'm not hurt.'

That nod again. Just a small one. 'Good,' he said.

Chaz limped back. 'Scott's out for the count. Still breathing.'

'What about Anna?'

'No sign of her.'

She was going to question him further, but she felt Nolan's fingers relax in hers. She looked back down to him, saw his eyes flutter and then close. His body sagged, seemed to deflate.

The rain wept.

The breeze sighed.

'Nolan?' she said. 'Nolan?'

He never heard her call him by his first name.

61

The child swims.

Out. Far out. As far as it can go. Far out in the cold water, arms straining, legs kicking. Slow, easy. Have to keep going. Not escape, though. There is no escape, not from the past, for it follows. It lives in the air and exists in every breath. It waits, it lurks, it repeats. It bides its time. For most people, time is just a measure, but for the child it is a sentence.

For a time it had been almost happy. At least, what passes for happiness. But it was merely marking time. Doing time. And time had caught up with her.

And so, she had to bring it to an end.

The child swims and the adult swims with her, guiding, encouraging, even though the cold seeps into bones and freezes muscles.

Have to keep going, *says the adult.* Until it's time to stop

When will that be?

You'll know.

When the time comes.

And they swim together into the west.

62

Rain thundered outside Elspeth's office. It rattled against the window like a visitor demanding entry. And it was cold, despite the heat radiating from the glowing electric fire oscillating in the corner. Rebecca was still enveloped in the thick woollen coat she'd pulled on that morning without thinking, the collar up, her hands wrapped round the mug of coffee Elspeth had made. But she could not seem to keep the heat in her. She hadn't felt warm since the previous afternoon. Ordinarily she would have feared she was coming down with something, but she knew that not to be the case. She was chilled, but not by a bug.

She hadn't gone to work that morning. Her phone had rung three times, the office number flashing on the screen, but she had ignored it. She knew she was in for a bollocking after walking out the day before, but she didn't care. Not today. Perhaps not ever. Elspeth had said nothing about it, but Rebecca knew her old boss understood.

'So,' said Elspeth slowly.

Rebecca sipped her coffee but tasted nothing. It was hot, that was all that mattered, and perhaps it would thaw the cold knot in her guts. 'So,' she said. 'You okay?'

It was what people asked, wasn't it? Are you okay, hon? Twitter, Facebook, whenever someone wants to draw attention to themselves. Sadfishing, it was called apparently. A comment – *I'm so fed up* – and the responses – *You okay, hon?* Rebecca was not okay. She had listened to a woman she liked, who might have become a friend, outline how she had killed three people. She had been threatened with a gun. She had watched a man die on the wet ground, his blood merging with the rainwater and creeping away to sink into the earth. It could easily have been her, or Chaz. But it had been Nolan, who had once asked her out in an awkward fashion. Brought her flowers. And read *The Guardian*. And was a drug dealer and a violent man, and had died helping her. And the cold had soaked its way into her body and into her soul, and she didn't know how she felt about his death or whether she would ever be okay again.

'I'm fine,' she said.

Elspeth gave her a look that told her she believed she was fine as much as she believed aliens built the pyramids. 'Have you heard how DCI Roach is?'

'She'll live,' said Rebecca. The police officer had lied to Anna about Rebecca. That was something she wouldn't forgive.

'Was she really put out of action by a book?'

'Yes.'

Elspeth puffed her cheeks. 'Words really can hurt.'

She was trying to be cheerful for Rebecca's sake. The phrase whistling past the graveyard came to mind.

Elspeth asked, 'And Anna Fowler?'

'No sign of her. She'll wash up, they say, somewhere. Sometime. Or maybe not.'

Anna. Everything she had done had been haphazard, not properly thought through. She had reacted. Or the child within her had reacted. The child Rebecca had heard speaking towards the end. She killed her brother, using her own sword, for goodness sake. Of course, they only knew that now, thanks to her home being searched and a photograph found of her holding it. It would have emerged sooner or later, though. Then she had killed Lancaster but didn't dispose of the waterproof clothing with the dead man's DNA all over it. It was as if she had wanted to be caught.

'What about Scott Burke?'

'He'll live too. Serious concussion, but he'll stand trial.'

Mo Burke had lost both her sons. Rebecca visualised her sitting in her pristine home in the Inchferry, the dog on her lap, a cigarette burning, the house silent. Her husband in jail. Her youngest son facing it. Her eldest lying on a slab in the mortuary. Was the family business worth that? Was anything worth that?

'And what about you?'

Rebecca had been staring at the coffee in her mug. She looked across the desk to Elspeth. 'What about me?'

'What now?'

Rebecca didn't know. The job was all but over. She had stared death in the face, a little round hole and a creepy smile behind it, and she had held a man's hand as he slipped away, a cough, a sigh and he was gone. Life was loss. Her father. Nolan. Her unborn child. She felt these thoughts hollow her out. Was this grief? Was this the way it was to be for her? Loss, always loss? Was it to be a lonely future?

She felt tears smoulder in her eyes but she fought them back. No, she decided. This was self pity and that would not be her way. Yes, she mourned, but she would not allow it to rule her. Her father had once said that life will be what life will be – challenges, opportunities, trials – and all we can do is make the best of it. Rise to the challenges, seize the opportunities, endure the trials. That's what she would do.

Elspeth waited a few moments before she said, 'I have a proposition.' Rebecca waited. Elspeth fired up a cigarette. 'I've got not a bad wee business here, but it only pays for one person. The thing is, I don't need the cash. I've got savings, I've got a pension kicking in and Julie's shop is doing well. The main thing, though, is that I'm too old for all this running around. This place needs someone younger, who can drop everything when needed and head off into the wilds to follow a story. Someone who knows what a bloody story is in the first place.' Elspeth sucked on her filter tip and gave Rebecca a long look, then said with heavy emphasis, 'Someone I trust.'

Rebecca squinted at Elspeth as she took this in. 'Wait a minute – are you offering to give me the agency?'

'Hell no, get over yourself. I'm offering you a job. I'll still own the place. Any profit I'll trouser faster than you can say hold the front page. I can offer you the same as you get at the *Chronicle*, maybe a bit more. But the good thing will be this – you'll more or less be your own boss. I'll be around, if you need help, advice, guidance, a kick up the arse. But apart from that, you'd be on your own.' Another puff of smoke. 'What do you say?'

Rebecca was so shocked she forgot to be cold. This was not what she had expected when she had called into Elspeth's office that morning. She had come here to get away from everything that had happened. Now she had a job offer. However, she didn't know what to say. Too much had happened in the past few days for her to think clearly.

'Tell you what,' said Elspeth, 'you think about it. The offer's there, if you want it. If not, no problem.'

Rebecca was still trying to formulate a response when her mobile rang. She thought it was the office again, but she didn't recognise the number. She thought about ignoring it but then decided to risk it. If it was a cold caller asking her about an accident in which she had been involved but wasn't her fault, she might blow off some steam giving them a few choice words.

But it wasn't a cold caller. 'Ms Connolly? It's Tom Muir . . .' She didn't recognise the name. 'We met the other night, in Inchferry?'

The man who had spoken so passionately against Dalgliesh's people. The trade unionist to whom she had given her card. 'Ah, yes, Mr Muir. What can I do for you?'

He exhaled hard. 'Well, love, I'm not one to trust the press as a rule. I think I said that. I've got my issues with the *Chronicle* but to be honest I think it's time I spoke to someone about this. You're the only reporter I know and I read your account of the demo the other night. It was accurate and fair. I liked that. I've also read some of the material on the murders. You seem to have a grasp of how these events affect people.'

You don't know the half it, she thought. 'What is it you want to talk about, Mr Muir?'

'You know anything about the Kirkbrig murder?'

She shook her head, even though he couldn't see it. 'I'm afraid not.'

'Aye, maybe before your time, love. Ten years ago. Young lad sent away for killing a lawyer up from Glasgow in Kirkbrig. It's a wee village down the west coast there. I've been working with his family to clear his name . . .'

Rebecca listened as Tom Muir filled in some of the details of the case. And as he talked she felt the cold that had permeated every cell of her body dissipate. Her mind sharpened, her instincts sat up and took notice.

'I'm very interested in this, Mr Muir,' she said. 'But I should tell you that I'm leaving the *Chronicle.*'

'Oh,' he said, his voice suddenly guarded. 'Well, maybe someone else . . .'

'I'm not moving away, though.' Rebecca met Elspeth's gaze across the desk and gave her a tiny nod. 'I've got a new job here – and I think I can help you with more than just the *Chronicle.*'

As Rebecca explained, she watched Elspeth sit back, her cigarette still clamped between her lips, smoke curling towards the blackened ceiling, and smile.

Rebecca smiled back.

ACKNOWLEDGEMENTS

The *Highland Chronicle* does not exist. It and the parent company are fictitious, although the challenges they face are very real. Inchferry also doesn't exist. I made it up. Don't look for it.

This has been a tough year and the book a tough one to write, so there are many people I need to thank. I am bound to forget someone so apologies in advance.

Professors Lorna Dawson and James Grieve answered queries expertly, as did Laura Thomson, Advocate. Any errors are mine, of course. David Kerr also helped me with some Inverness colour. I have, however, taken a few liberties with actual police procedure.

Crime writer pals helped keep me keep on track with this one – thanks must go to Neil Broadfoot, Gordon Brown, Mark Leggatt, Michael J. Malone, Denzil Meyrick, Caro Ramsay and Theresa Talbot. If I have flown off the rails, it's no fault of theirs.

To those friends who rallied round during a difficult time, my heartfelt thanks. There are too many to mention but a special nod must go to Gary McLaughlin for looking after the boys (Mickey the dog and Tom the cat), allowing me to attend events.

As ever, my gratitude is extended to all the bloggers, reviewers and booksellers who supported Rebecca's first venture and who, I hope, will do the same this time around.

My editor Debs Warner did a wonderful job of turning this into a finished product and I also thank Hugh Andrew, Alison Rae, the entire team at Polygon and my agent Lina Langlee for everything they have done.